…g him to advance.

The Troyian sprang to his feet and dashed around the corner, blaster in hand. La Forge tracked his progress with the tricorder.

In a matter of seconds, Velex had reached the next point of limited cover, just a few meters shy of the entrance to the control center. La Forge put away his tricorder, crawled forward to the corner, and peeked around it. From across the empty stretch of gravel road, Velex beckoned him to move up.

His heart racing, La Forge got to his feet and sprinted away from the factory, toward Velex. He was halfway there when something unseen slammed into his face, and something else swept his legs out from under him.

The engineer landed on his back, dazed and blinded with pain. He reached reflexively for his nose, which throbbed with deep pain and coated his hand with fresh blood. Blinking to clear the red haze from his vision, he saw Velex break cover and move toward him.

Then several humanoid shapes shimmered into view between them . . .

STAR TREK
THE NEXT GENERATION®
COLD EQUATIONS

BOOK I
THE PERSISTENCE OF MEMORY

DAVID MACK

Based on
Star Trek and
Star Trek: The Next Generation
Created by Gene Roddenberry

POCKET BOOKS
New York London Toronto Sydney New Delhi Mangala

Pocket Books
A Division of Simon & Schuster, Inc.
1230 Avenue of the Americas
New York, NY 10020

This book is published by Pocket Books, a division of Simon & Schuster, Inc., under exclusive license from CBS Studios Inc.

First Pocket Books paperback edition November 2012

Manufactured in the United States of America

10 9 8 7 6 5 4 3 2 1

ISBN 978-1-4516-5072-3
ISBN 978-1-4516-5075-4 (ebook)

For Glenn, my personal High Epopt of Slack

HISTORIAN'S NOTE

The events in Parts One and Three of this story take place in January 2384, approximately four years and two months after the events of the movie *Star Trek Nemesis*. The events of Part Two transpire over a span of seventeen years, from 2367 to 2384.

For I will go down into the grave unto my son mourning.

—Genesis 37:35

PART ONE
ENTERPRISE

2384

1

With a sonorous hum and a luminous flare, the transporter beam faded and Commander Geordi La Forge found himself alone in the dark, staring down the barrel of a phaser rifle. The hard-eyed Tellarite security officer behind the weapon lurched forward, tensed for confrontation as he challenged La Forge in a harsh voice. "Identify yourself!"

Hands raised and palms open, the veteran Starfleet engineer recoiled, only to freeze in place as he noticed on the edges of his vision more rifles being brought to bear against him. "La Forge, *Enterprise*. What's going on?"

The Tellarite glared down his snout at La Forge, his bearing laced with suspicion and hostility. "We'll ask the questions." He nodded at someone behind La Forge. "Search him."

Singsong tones from a tricorder broke the eerie silence as La Forge was scanned, then rough hands patted him down, stripped his field tricorder from his hip pocket, and plucked the padd from his left hand. A burly Denobulan with sinister-looking ocular ridges stepped into his line of sight and showed the confiscated devices to the Tellarite. "These are all he had on him, sir." Somewhere in the distance, sirens wailed in the night, their cries faint but drawing closer.

Despite his subordinate's assurances, the Tellarite lieutenant commander kept his rifle aimed squarely at La Forge's face. "What are you doing here?"

"I was invited," La Forge said. "I'm a guest of Captain Bruce Maddox. He contacted me via subspace two days ago and asked me to come here in person. He said it was urgent."

A Trill woman with a crew cut that matched her severe features edged into view on La Forge's left. "Sir, I just confirmed the *Enterprise* is in orbit. He is who he says he is."

The news seemed to disappoint the Tellarite, who scowled as he lowered his weapon. "All right, stand down." He stepped forward and offered his three-fingered hand to La Forge. "Lieutenant Commander Teg. No hard feelings, Commander."

"We'll see about that." La Forge stepped around Teg and got his first good look at the exterior of the Starfleet Annex of the Daystrom Institute. It had been nearly a decade since the *Enterprise*'s last visit to the facility; not much seemed to have changed. The five-story building was bland and utilitarian, and its surrounding lawn, which sloped gently downhill to a dense sprawl of old-growth forest, was impeccably manicured. He looked back at the dour Tellarite, who continued to watch him with wary, flat-black eyes. "Where's Captain Maddox?"

Teg beckoned La Forge with a tilt of his head. "Follow me." Rifle slung at his side, he led La Forge inside the Annex through its open main entrance.

Stealing looks around the wide-open ground floor, La Forge noted that the facility's interior was far more spartan than he had remembered. If not for the armed Starfleet security personnel milling about, he might have thought the Annex deserted. Force field-partitioned work spaces that once had been crowded with fabrication equipment and computers now stood empty. What had been an office was now a stack of crates. It looked more like an academic laboratory than an active research environment at one of the Federation's preeminent scientific institutions.

At the far end of the floor, Teg ushered him inside an elevator and pressed the button for the recently added sublevel, where Captain Maddox's new lab was situated. Ten years earlier, Maddox had conducted his studies in the spacious main laboratory on the ground floor. With its state-of-the-art accoutrements and commanding view of the Annex's wooded environs, it had seemed like an ideal working environment—until its overall exposure had left it vulnerable to a devastating sneak attack that had nearly cost Maddox his life. Since then, Maddox had erred on the side of safety, eschewing the luxuries of sunlight and scenery for the practical benefits of privacy and security.

The elevator doors parted, and bitter smoke rolled in over La Forge's head. Teg led him out into the sublevel and down the hallway toward Maddox's lab. Walking slowly, La Forge squinted through the smoke at the numerous scorch marks dotting the corridor. Then he saw that the airlock-style double doors to the lab were open, and through the doorway flowed a steady haze tinged with the acrid stench of burnt metal and melted circuitry. He dodged a departing firefighter as they both stepped through the doorway. Once inside, La Forge's worst fears were confirmed: the high-tech cybernetics lab had been demolished.

Standing in the middle of the wreckage was Bruce Maddox, one of the Federation's leading experts on cybernetics and artificial intelligence. He was in his mid-sixties but still retained the trim physique of his youth; only his salt-and-pepper hair betrayed his years. Dark circles of fatigue ringed his eyes, and his disheveled uniform suggested to La Forge that the man had been involved in whatever crisis had just unfolded.

Maddox's first brush with the *Enterprise* crew, nearly twenty-five years earlier, had been adversarial; he had tried to have Data declared the property of Starfleet so he could disassemble the android to further his own research. That legal battle had been decided in Data's favor, setting the first precedent that eventually led the Federation to recognize the legal personhood of artificially sentient beings—an argument that Maddox himself had made before the Federation's highest civilian court, in defense of Data's older brother, B-4. In the fifteen years between those two legal milestones, Maddox and Data had developed a mutual if guarded professional respect. It still amazed La Forge that Data had never borne a grudge against Maddox, not even after he'd acquired his emotion chip. Inspired by Data's example, La Forge had put aside his own anger at Maddox long ago and since then had come to respect and admire the man's work. If pressed, La Forge would have had to admit that Maddox was likely the only person alive who knew more than he did about Soong-type androids.

They met in the middle of the lab and clasped hands. Maddox looked exhausted and desperate. "Geordi! Thank God you're here. Please tell me the *Enterprise* is with you."

"Yes, it is." He put a hand to Maddox's shoulder in reassurance. "Bruce, calm down. Tell me what happened."

Maddox pressed his dirty palms over his eyes, then pulled down, stretching his face into something that looked like it belonged in a funhouse mirror. "It happened so fast. One minute I was upstairs in my office, preparing for our meeting. The next, alarms started going off. I raced down here, and when I stepped out of the elevator, they started shooting."

"Who did?"

"I don't know who they were. I couldn't get a good look at them." He turned and pointed at a wall console that had been blasted to pieces, leaving only an ugly scorch from floor to ceiling. "They knocked out the security system, including the scattering field. Then they beamed out—I heard the sound of the transporter from the end of the hall. I ran toward the lab, and that's when something exploded."

Teg stepped between La Forge and Maddox. "Five somethings exploded, actually." He grunted and shook his head. "Hell of a way to cover an escape."

La Forge surveyed the damage inflicted by the explosives. "That wasn't part of their exit strategy. If that's all it was, they'd only have needed one—but they brought five, one for each of the lab's computer banks. This was about terminating Captain Maddox's research." He turned toward Maddox. "Bruce, what have you been working on?"

The cyberneticist looked flummoxed. "Nothing except helping B-4." Recoiling from La Forge's incredulous glare, he insisted, "I'm serious, Geordi. I haven't done any new work in years—not since that fiasco with the Exo III androids."

"Then what was this break-in about?"

Maddox flung his arms wide in frustration. "I don't know!"

"Start by telling me what secret project was so urgent that you needed to have the *Enterprise* pulled off-mission to race here at maximum warp."

The scientist took a deep breath and regained some of his calm. "It wasn't a secret project so much as a personal emergency. It's about B-4."

"What about him?"

"It's complicated." Maddox walked toward an empty corner of the lab and gestured for La Forge to follow him. "I'll have to show you."

The mention of the prototype android's name had filled La Forge with worry. An early creation of the late Doctor Noonien Soong, B-4 had been a relative simpleton compared with his younger kin, such as Data, Lore, and the replicant of Juliana Tainer. B-4's positronic brain was far less advanced than the others' were, though much of his physical body was comparable to those of his twins. What now made B-4 of keen personal interest to La Forge—as well as the rest of the *Enterprise* crew, to say nothing of Maddox—was that Data, less than a day before embarking on a suicide mission to save Captain Picard and destroy the planet-killing weapon of the usurper Praetor Shinzon, had uploaded a complete copy of his memory engrams into B-4 for safekeeping. Because of limitations in B-4's hardware and software, he had never been able to consciously access those memories, but knowing they resided within him, as if he were a living memorial to his lamented sibling, had meant a great deal to those who'd known Data.

Maddox stopped in the corner of the room and opened a panel to reveal the lab's environmental controls. He activated the interface with a single tap of his finger. "A few months ago, I noticed that B-4's response time to stimuli was slowing down." He turned toward La Forge. "At first, I thought it was a simple biomechanical problem. But then I ran a full diagnostic. Something was going wrong in B-4's positronic matrix. It was breaking down, and it was because of Data's memory engrams. There must have been traces of operational code mixed in with his memories, and when B-4's operating software tried to incorporate the new subroutines, it started a slow-motion cascade failure."

"You mean like what happened to Data's daughter, Lal?"

A grimace and a nod. "Exactly." He turned and started entering commands into the environmental panel. "B-4's mind simply wasn't made to harbor software that advanced. Once the cascade failure began, I did all I could to reverse it, but I failed. I've managed to slow it down, but unless we find a way to halt the degradation of his matrix, he'll suffer a complete cascade failure in less than a week." He finished keying in commands, and with a soft hiss, a large section of the wall began to creep open. "The only solution I've come up with so far has been to purge all of Data's memories from B-4's brain."

The mere suggestion horrified La Forge. "Bruce, you can't . . ."

"I don't want to, Geordi. But if B-4's mind fails, it'll purge Data's memory engrams as part of the final cascade error. If we're doomed to lose him either way, I'd prefer to save B-4."

The towering, floor-to-ceiling secret door opened wide enough for Maddox to slip past it, into the alcove hidden behind it. He stopped abruptly just a few steps inside, and La Forge nearly stumbled into him. "Bruce, what's—" His question trailed off, forgotten, as he realized that he and Maddox were in a room with sarcophagus-shaped alcoves for six Soong-type androids. The three on the left side of the room were labeled for Soong's first three unnamed prototypes. The three on the right were labeled for B-4, Lore, and Lal.

All six alcoves were empty.

Maddox faltered, and La Forge put a hand to his back to steady him. Slackjawed with grief and shock, the cyberneticist muttered, "Gone. . . . They're all gone."

"I think it's safe to say we know what the intruders were after." La Forge stepped away and tapped his combadge. "La Forge to *Enterprise*."

He was answered by the gruff baritone of Commander Worf. "Enterprise. *Go ahead."*

"Captain Maddox's lab has been attacked, and all six of the Soong-type androids in his care are missing and presumed stolen. We need to lock down this whole planet right now."

"Understood. Stay there. I'll join you shortly. Enterprise *out."*

La Forge returned to Maddox's side and clasped his shoulder in consolation. "Don't worry, Bruce, we'll find them."

"Who? The thieves? Or the androids?"

He regarded the empty alcoves with cold fury. "Both."

Every word that issued from the mouth of Governor Eloch, the head of the civilian government on Galor IV, seemed calculated to annoy Worf, who stood outside the main entrance of the Starfleet Annex of the Daystrom Institute and listened to the freakishly tall, pot-bellied Kobliad politico's whining. "A class-one planetary security alert. Do you have even the slightest idea what such a protocol entails, Commander?"

"Yes." Worf hoped the simplicity of his answer would obviate Eloch's impulse to continue. But as he expected, he was disappointed.

"I don't think you do, Commander. All nonessential, nonemergency communications have been suspended. The planet's transporter network is locked down, beyond even my authority to reinstate. Every aircraft, spacecraft, and starship on the planet's been grounded; every publicly accessible computer system has been shut down; and every law enforcement and defense agency on my planet is at a state of high alert, awaiting instructions from your vessel." The governor crossed his arms and radiated contempt. "A class-one planetary security alert is a very rare thing, Commander. There hasn't been one on Galor IV in ten years. Would you care to guess what that incident and this one have in common?"

"No, I would not."

"Your ship, that's what! An officer from the *Enterprise* plunged this world into a state of panic ten years ago, for reasons that were never explained. Now, here we are again, seized in a state of global paralysis on the whims of another *Enterprise* officer. Trouble seems to follow your ship, Commander. Has it occurred to Starfleet that perhaps the *Enterprise* is the problem?"

"I do not think it has." Tiring of the one-sided conversation, Worf looked around the grounds for any small objects he might use to commit ritual suicide.

The governor gesticulated clumsily at the assorted armed Starfleet security personnel moving about outside the Annex. "Are we even going to get an explanation for what's gone wrong this time? Or are we supposed to sit by while Starfleet places us under martial law?"

"With all respect, Governor, your planet has *not* been placed under martial law. We are enforcing a temporary state of heightened security in response to a direct threat. These measures are as much to ensure your people's safety as they are to aid our investigation."

Eloch appeared unconvinced. "Does that mean the perpetrators of whatever crime has been committed here will face justice in our civilian courts under Federation law?"

"It does not." Worf hadn't planned to elaborate, but the sudden reddening of Eloch's visage made it seem a prudent course of action. "The Daystrom Institute is a civilian research entity, but the Annex remains under Starfleet's jurisdiction. As such, the offenses that transpired here will be dealt with by a military tribunal."

The middle-aged Kobliad was the very portrait of frustration. "Can you even tell me when the lockdown might end? There's an entire planet full of people out there waiting to get back to their lives and businesses."

"I cannot. We have just begun our investigation. There is no way to know how long it will take to reach its conclusion."

Eloch crossed his arms and raised his chin at a haughty angle. "I want to talk to your commanding officer."

"I will inform him of your desire."

Narrowed eyes conveyed Eloch's suspicion. "He told you to stonewall me."

"It might be some time before Captain Picard is able to speak with you." Worf motioned for the governor to depart. "Perhaps you would be more comfortable waiting in your own home."

The governor bristled at the suggestion. "You think you can get rid of me that easily?"

It took all of Worf's willpower not to respond, *Actually, I hope you will leave me no choice but to use deadly force.* Instead, he marshaled an insincere smile and exorcised any trace of hostility from his voice. "I merely suggest, Governor, that it might be some time before the investigation yields results. Until then, the demands of operational security strictly limit the intelligence I can share with you or the planet's civilian law-enforcement agencies. Rather than ask you to suffer further inconvenience by waiting here for our next report, I thought you might prefer to return to your residence or office."

"A most politic suggestion, Mister Worf. Well played." Eloch started to walk away, then stopped and looked back over his shoulder. "I still want to talk to your captain."

"I am sure he will look forward to it, Governor. Good night." Worf delivered the last two words with sufficient gravity that Eloch had no choice but to infer the conversation was over. He stood and watched the governor depart; it was nearly half a minute before the Kobliad stooped through the hatchway of his executive shuttle and passed from Worf's sight. Several seconds later the small craft made a near-silent vertical ascent until it was well above the highest local buildings, then it accelerated away toward the capital, three hundred kilometers to the north.

As the ship vanished into a bank of low atmospheric haze and the hum of its engines faded, Captain Jean-Luc Picard exited the Annex and stopped at Worf's side. "You handled that well, Mister Worf."

"Thank you, sir." The Klingon turned a curious eye toward his captain. "Why did you not wish to speak with him?"

Picard drew a deep breath and adopted a pensive mien. "I've been a starship captain for nearly half a century. In that time, I've had countless conversations exactly like the one you just had with Governor Eloch. Learning to placate the egos and tempers of those in power is a skill every starship commander needs to cultivate, sooner or later."

Worf was both flattered and discomfited by the implication of Picard's explanation. "I was not aware that such a career path remained available to me."

"Why? Because of your actions on Soukara?" The captain spoke as if it was a minor infraction, but Worf's record had been blemished by a formal reprimand after he scuttled a vital mission during the Dominion War in order to save his wife, Jadzia Dax. It had been a grave offense during wartime, but now Picard verbally waved it off. "That was *ten years* ago."

"Captain Sisko was certain it would bar me from ever attaining my own command."

Captain Picard remained upbeat. "That was before you served as the Federation's ambassador to Qo'noS. I know you hold Captain Sisko in high esteem, but he was wrong, Worf. If Starfleet didn't think you were ready for command, they wouldn't have let me appoint you my first officer. Your job isn't merely about being my Number One; it's about acquiring the necessary experience to command a ship of your own."

The topic of conversation made Worf distinctly uncomfortable. "That may be so. However, I think it is premature to speak of my promotion."

Picard's mood turned quite earnest. "Far from it. You've been my first officer for more than four years, and during that time your service has been exemplary. I have no doubt that you're more than ready to take on greater responsibilities."

Ever since Worf was a child, he had never liked being pushed into decisions. Now, as ever, he could not help but push back, even if only obliquely. "If memory serves, you allowed Captain Riker to serve as your executive officer for fifteen years."

"Well, in my defense, he was a slow learner." With a rakishly arched brow, Picard added, "Look how long it took him to marry Counselor Troi."

Worf conceded the debate with a frown. "Good point."

"No decisions need to be made in haste," Picard assured him. "Just give it some thought."

He looked his captain in the eye. "I shall."

A soft chirp warbled from Worf's combadge, followed by the mellow, feminine voice of the *Enterprise*'s chief of security. *"Choudhury to Worf."*

"This is Worf. Go ahead."

"We've finished our sweep of Captain Maddox's lab—and I think you and the captain need to see this immediately."

Picard hurried back inside the Annex, and Worf followed him. "We're on our way."

After more than a decade in Starfleet, Lieutenant Jasminder Choudhury had seen her share of crime scenes, and in all that time not one had ever struck her as being the site of a "perfect crime"—but she had to admit, Commander Maddox's ransacked lab came closer than most.

The criminal investigation team, a half-dozen experts in various scientific disciplines, had retreated to the room's periphery to pack up their test kits and doff their blue disposable field suits, which both protected the investigators from airborne and contact pathogens and minimized the risk of contaminating the scene with their uniform fibers or traces of their genetic material. Choudhury stood at the door of the lab, waiting for the all-clear signal that would mean she was free to enter and begin her own walk-through of the lab. Pending that clearance, she reviewed the investigators' preliminary findings on her padd and was dismayed by what she read.

Her sensitive ears picked up the low thrumming of the elevator arriving at the end of the hallway. Its doors parted, and Captain Picard was the first person to emerge, followed by Worf. Focusing her thoughts, Choudhury maintained a mask of professional reserve as her ship's two most senior officers approached. As much as she wanted to smile whenever she saw Worf, she knew it would be improper to let their intimate relationship color their behavior toward one another while on duty, either aboard the ship or on away missions. It wasn't that their romance was the least bit secret; most of the ship's senior officers were well aware of it, and as long as they didn't let it interfere with their performance as officers, they had the captain's tacit blessing.

She stepped forward and met her CO with a polite nod. "Captain."

"What have you found, Lieutenant?"

She handed him the padd. "This was a professional job. According to Captain Maddox's statement, there were three intruders. They were well-equipped and knew their way around the Annex." She walked to a door along the main corridor. "At 2315, they remotely disabled and hacked a subset of the Annex's sensors—just enough to mask their entrance, path to target, and actions inside the building. To the Institute's main security center, nothing seemed to be wrong. They didn't notice when their visual feeds on these areas switched over to looped recordings."

She pushed open the door to reveal stairs leading up. "One minute later, the intruders breached the building's only entrance by sabotaging the retinal scanner and magnetic locks with a parasitic plasma charge, and they crossed the first floor to this emergency stairwell."

Worf asked, "Why didn't they beam directly into the building?"

"Because the Annex's scattering field was still active. It was hard-wired so that it could be controlled only from a panel inside Maddox's lab. It would have prevented them from using sensors or transporters within ten meters of the Annex."

The captain motioned for her to continue. "What happened next?"

"Once inside, they reached this sublevel in less than thirty seconds." She closed the door and led Worf and Picard back to the lab's open doorway. "They gained access to the secured laboratory by force, cutting through the doors' locks with high-intensity plasma torches. With the fire sensors offline, they were able to set the torches to maximum power. I believe they breached these doors in under a minute."

They followed her inside the lab and stayed close behind her as she walked them through the crime scene. "Based on footprint patterns, we think that one of them placed the explosive charges on the computer banks while the other two broke into the androids' hidden alcove. They appear to have finessed their way through this door's security systems, because Maddox noticed no sign of damage when he opened it for Commander La Forge an hour ago." The trio stopped amid the six empty sarcophagi. "I suspect they placed transport pattern enhancers on all six androids, then exited the chamber. According to Elfiki's review of the Institute's security office computers, a Trojan horse program was uploaded from this lab at 2320. It initiated a series of system failures in the Annex's scattering field generators. To the main security office, these would have registered as simple mechanical malfunctions. That's when the alarm sounded."

Picard looked up from the padd, his attention keenly focused. "What alarm?"

"The Institute's general security alert." Choudhury pointed at several scorched blocks of sensor hardware mounted high on the walls around the lab. "These auxiliary sensors started flashing and wailing—and transmitting signals back to the security center. The guards on duty saw only a few seconds of vid before the intruders shot the backup sensors, but it was enough to make the sentries summon reinforcements from the nearby Starfleet barracks."

Worf stepped back out into the hallway and cast an inquisitive eye at the blaster damage on the walls. "At what time did Captain Maddox reach the sublevel?"

"By his own reckoning, roughly 2321. That's when the intruders opened fire at him. About ten seconds later, they beamed out—and took the androids with them."

The captain tapped the padd's interactive screen, looked around the lab, then faced Choudhury. "Captain Maddox said the charges on the computer banks exploded almost immediately after the intruders beamed out. Were they remotely detonated?"

"No, sir. We found traces of molecular timers. That suggests the intruders had a rigidly planned exit strategy that included blowing up the computers regardless of whether they'd been detected. If the general alert hadn't been sounded and hadn't tripped the auxiliary sensors, the explosion and subsequent fire might have gone undetected long enough to reduce the entire lab to slag. It could've been days before we confirmed the androids were stolen."

Picard furrowed his brow as he reached the end of the notes on the padd. "Do we have any leads to the intruders' whereabouts?"

Choudhury shook her head. "Not yet, sir. We know they didn't use the planet's public transporter network to beam out of the lab, and they didn't beam to a ship in orbit, because we would have detected that on the

Enterprise. That suggests they beamed to a smaller vessel made for atmospheric flight, such as a shuttle or a small transport. Given the limitations of transporters as a line-of-sight technology, and the fact that they can beam through only a limited depth of a magnetically active planet's surface, we think the escape vessel is still somewhere on the planet." Sensing that Worf was about to tell her to do what she'd already done, she added, "I have Šmrhová collating all of the planet's air-traffic data from the past hour to see if we can narrow down the list of targets. With the *Enterprise*'s computer, it should take under an hour."

Worf looked concerned. "What if the escape vessel was cloaked? A small starship could operate cloaked inside an atmosphere."

"Not without kicking up a storm of neutrinos. If there was a cloaked ship in the atmosphere, we'd have detected it the minute we made orbit."

The first officer seemed irked at being corrected. "A ship with a phasing cloak would give off no such emissions."

Having neither the time nor the inclination for a debate, Choudhury mustered her most politic tone of voice. "Phasing cloaks require a tremendous amount of power to operate, sir. Any vessel large enough to deploy one would be unable to navigate safely inside an atmosphere, and it would be unable to beam up the intruders without disabling the cloak—and revealing itself in a very dramatic fashion. With all respect, I think we can rule out cloaked ships as an element of the crime—especially since there's a far more pressing question we need to answer."

The captain traded a bemused look with Worf, then asked, "What question is that?"

"Who triggered the Institute's general alert?"

"I presumed the intruders triggered the alarm when they uploaded the Trojan horse."

She shook her head. "No, sir. It went undetected."

Worf nodded at the environmental controls. "Perhaps when they opened the alcove."

"Again, no. All primary sensors in the lab had been shut down and spoofed, and the auxiliary sensors weren't active yet."

The mystery sparked a heightened level of interest from Worf. "Could the guards in the security center have tripped it?"

"No, I checked. And it wasn't Captain Maddox. He was upstairs, getting ready to meet with Geordi, when he heard the alarm. There's no record of where the alert originated, but I suspect it was triggered remotely, just like the intruders' hack of the sensors."

Picard's focus on the question grew more intense by the moment. "Could it have been part of their plan to be detected?"

"I don't see any way in which being detected would have benefited them," she said.

"Maybe they were betrayed by an accomplice who had second thoughts," Worf said.

Choudhury acknowledged the possibility with a measure of doubt. "Perhaps."

"One thing is for certain," Picard said with conviction. "Whoever triggered that alert knows more about this situation than we do. Lieutenant, continue the search for the intruders. Number One, do whatever it takes to track down our good Samaritan."

2

Asking favors of Starfleet Command was never something Jean-Luc Picard enjoyed, but he suspected that his supervising officer, Admiral Alynna Nechayev, disliked granting him those favors even more. The stern cast of the silver-haired admiral's angular features, which had become more pronounced in the years since the Borg invasion and the rise of the Typhon Pact that followed it, were larger than life on the wall-mounted screen inside Captain Maddox's private office. *"Captain, if I let the* Enterprise *take over the investigation of the Annex heist, Admiral Andell will never let me hear the end of it."*

"I understand his objections, Admiral. But the *Enterprise* is better equipped for this task than his security garrison. We have greater manpower, more sophisticated resources, and a superior vantage point, all of which enable us to respond more quickly to leads."

Deep creases lined Nechayev's brow. *"I could place your ship and crew at Andell's disposal. He does outrank you."*

The proposition did not sit well with Picard. Despite his best efforts, he knew his displeasure was likely evident to Nechayev. "I think that would be a mistake,

Admiral. While I have the utmost regard for Admiral Andell, he's never commanded a starship. I don't think he's prepared to exercise the full capabilities of the *Enterprise* or her crew."

Maddox, who had been standing a short distance behind Picard, stepped forward and interjected, "For what it's worth, Admiral, I think we need to remember that it was Admiral Andell's garrison that allowed this break-in to happen. As the director of the Annex, I'd prefer a fresh perspective on the investigation—and frankly, I'd like the *Enterprise* to lead it."

His declaration seemed to rob Nechayev of her will to argue. *"Very well. But just so you know, when Admiral Andell screams bloody murder, I'll be laying the blame at your doorstep."*

"That's fine. He already hates me, anyway."

"So I've heard." She sharpened her gaze at Maddox. *"Since you've been good enough to join the conversation, Captain, maybe you could take this opportunity to tell us what you've been working on that someone would go to this much trouble to steal."*

"As I've already told Captain Picard and his crew, I haven't been working on anything new—not since the Rhea McAdams incident ten years ago."

"Why not?"

Maddox momentarily averted his eyes from Nechayev's accusatory stare. "After helping Emil Vaslovik invent the holotronic brain, and then losing all that data after the computers were wiped, I just didn't think I could ever duplicate that achievement. I didn't even want to try. And once I understood the full scope of our encounter with the Fellowship of Artificial Intelligence, I began to doubt we were ready as a society to continue this research."

Nechayev appeared confused. *"You mentioned Pro-*

fessor Vaslovik, but didn't Admiral Haftel and Commander Barclay also work on the holotronic android?"

"Yes, but their contributions—and mine—were minor, at best. Vaslovik was the real visionary on that project. I think the fact that neither Admiral Haftel nor Commander Barclay have made any progress in their efforts at developing new AIs should serve as proof of that."

His answer apparently troubled Nechayev. *"Captain, what have you been doing at the Annex for the last ten years?"*

To Picard as much as to the admiral, Maddox explained, "I spent the first six years after the McAdams incident reviewing my research into Soong-style positronic matrixes—when I wasn't teaching classes on the ethics of cybernetics and biomechanics at the local branch of Daystrom University, that is. I'm sure you remember where I was in 2380, when I petitioned the Judiciary Committee on behalf of B-4. Well, after the decision affirming B-4's personhood, he joined me here and let me study him, non-invasively, as part of my continuing effort to document the work of Noonien Soong. He also brought with him the bodies of his fellow Soong androids, which were bequeathed to his care after Data died."

His curiosity aroused, Picard looked askance at Maddox and asked, "How much progress had you made in your study of Doctor Soong's work?"

"Quite a bit, actually. Some of my civilian colleagues at the Daystrom Institute developed new scanning technologies that let us study the inner workings of the androids without taking them apart. We still couldn't replicate Soong's method of incepting new positronic brains, but we were closer than ever before to understanding how an active matrix works."

The more Maddox spoke, the graver Nechayev's countenance became. *"If your research fell into the wrong hands, could it be used to create new Soong-type androids?"*

The scientist seemed doubtful. "Not unless they knew how Soong made the positronic brain in the first place, or had access to far more advanced cybernetic technology than we do."

"But if they did . . . ?"

"Then hypothetically, yes. It's possible."

Picard recognized the expression on Nechayev's face: it was the look that comes from realizing a situation has turned out to be far worse than one ever expected. The admiral breathed a low sigh, then fixed her weary gaze on Maddox. *"Captain, the* Enterprise *crew will need you to help guide their investigation. Can I count on you to provide that aid?"*

"Absolutely, Admiral. No one wants to bring B-4 home safely more than I do."

She nodded. *"Excellent. Jean-Luc, I'll inform Admiral Andell that he's to place his forces at your disposal. For both our sakes, please use them judiciously."*

"I will. You have my word, Admiral."

"Then good hunting, Captains. Keep me apprised of your progress. Nechayev out."

Nechayev closed the comm link, and the wall screen switched briefly to the Federation emblem before it faded to its standby mode. Picard tapped his combadge. "Picard to Worf."

The reply came almost immediately: *"Worf here."*

"I'm returning to the *Enterprise* with Captain Maddox. Join us in the observation lounge in twenty minutes, and bring Commander La Forge and Lieutenant Choudhury."

"Aye, sir. Worf out."

Picard faced Maddox. "Captain, let's go find your missing androids."

"We need to narrow the list of suspects," Choudhury said. She alone of the five officers in the curved lounge was up and pacing between the table and the master systems display set into the bulkhead. "How many entities do we know of that are capable of an operation like this?"

"Too many," Worf grumbled. He sat with his back to the windows, whose view was dominated by the northern hemisphere of Galor IV. "All of the Typhon Pact powers. The Grigari, the Talarians. Even a well-prepared band of Ferengi could have done this."

Across from him, La Forge turned his chair away from the table and faced Choudhury as he struck a more positive note. "Okay, but how many do we know of that can also make use of Soong-type cybernetic technology?" He shot questioning looks down the table at Maddox and then Picard. "Not many, in my opinion: the Romulans, maybe the Breen. Before the Dominion War, I might have said the Cardassians, but these days I think that'd be a long shot."

"Agreed," Picard said. Seated at the head of the table with Maddox on his right, he reclined slightly and regarded the evidence posted on the companel. "Lieutenant, can we make any deductions based on the equipment the intruders used?"

Choudhury called up the latest scans and enlarged the data on the main display screen for everyone to see. "Unfortunately, no. Several different species and nations use variations on the plasma parasites that disabled the retinal scanner and magnetic locks at the entrance. The trace evidence we found at the scene was pretty generic. It could be Tholian-made, or it might be of Klingon design." She switched to another screen of reports. "The plasma torches are a common industrial tool on worlds throughout the Federation, Klingon Empire, and Typhon Pact. Based on the residues left on the lab's doors, we believe these were acquired locally, on Galor IV." With a tap on the MSD's control panel, she put a chemical analysis on the screen. "The explosives that fragged the computers were Nausicaan-made, as were the timers. They're both fairly common on the black market right now. And the intruders' sidearms were Orion-made disruptors. Also a black market staple."

Captain Maddox massaged his forehead with his fingertips. "I don't suppose there were any witnesses? Or security vids the intruders overlooked? Or trace DNA at the scene?"

"Sorry."

Picard leaned forward. "Be that as it may, in the absence of other clear suspects, let's suppose for now that our burglars were either Romulan, Breen, or perhaps both working in unison." He pressed a finger thoughtfully to his upper lip for a moment. "Lieutenant, you said the plasma parasites might have been of Tholian design. Assume that's true; that would suggest this might have been a coordinated effort by several powers of the Typhon Pact."

It sounded like a reasonable hypothesis to Choudhury. "I could see that."

The captain nodded. "All right. Mister Worf, if you were planning an operation such as this, how would you have begun?"

"With reconnaissance of the target," the first officer said.

La Forge seemed possessed by a sudden insight. "Except the Annex is shielded from external scans. You'd need people on the ground, someone who could get close enough to the facility to compromise its security without being recognized as an enemy operative."

Choudhury followed La Forge's thinking. "Like a Romulan passing for a Vulcan—or an unmasked Breen humanoid, a member of one of their species we haven't identified yet."

The engineer pointed at her. "Exactly."

"Good," Picard said. "Worf, what would be the next step?"

The Klingon thought for a moment. "Selecting, equipping, and deploying a team."

Maddox was growing impatient. "I think we know what happens after that. The big question is: How did they plan to get away?"

Picard stood. "Lieutenant, call up the time line of the robbery." He joined Choudhury beside the master systems display as she posted the crime's sequence of events. "They didn't expect the general alert to call attention to them. They'd planned to be long gone before their crime was detected. . . . They might have made a run for it even *after* being detected, but at the time of the heist, we'd already arrived in orbit. That may have foiled their chance for a clean escape." He cast a hopeful look at Choudhury. "Did Galor IV's air-traffic data yield any leads?"

"More than we could follow." Choudhury changed the display to show a cluttered graphic detailing the positions and flight paths of innumerable small craft. "There were six hundred fifty-eight possible targets, and we've had time to track down only a few dozen of them. By now, the thieves could've transferred the androids to a hiding place or a new spacecraft."

La Forge's metallic cybernetic eyes were fixed on the massive block of data. "Were any of the targeted ships warp-capable?"

She applied a filtering parameter to the data. "No."

The chief engineer gestured at the display. "If they were using a short-range shuttle to avoid drawing attention while on the planet, how did they plan to get away with the androids?"

Worf met La Forge's keen stare. "They had another ship."

"Or planned to rendezvous with one."

"Either way," Choudhury cut in, "they must still be here, because no warp-capable ships have left Galor IV since we arrived."

Picard's mood brightened a bit. "That's the first good news we've had since this started. How long will it take to identify and search every warp-capable ship on the planet's surface?"

Choudhury made an educated guess. "A couple of days."

"Then we'd best get started. Mister Worf, contact Admiral Andell and let him know we'll need his garrison's help impounding all warp-equipped vessels on the surface."

"Aye, sir."

"And let's do all we can to expedite this process. The unchecked proliferation of Doctor Soong's technology, especially by a power such as the Typhon Pact, could have dire—"

The whooping Red Alert klaxon cut him off, and it was followed moments later by the voice of the ship's operations officer, Glinn Ravel Dygan. *"Bridge to Captain Picard."*

"Picard here."

The young Cardassian exchange officer spoke quickly. *"Sir, we've received a priority alert from the planet's security forces. They say they've sighted B-4."*

The captain was already on the move, with the others close behind him. "On my way."

The bridge of the *Enterprise* was abuzz with activity as Picard moved at a quick step to the center seat. Worf settled quickly into his own chair on Picard's right, and Maddox perched on the edge of the guest chair to Picard's left. Glinn Dygan resumed his normal post at the forward ops console beside senior flight controller Lieutenant Joanna Faur, while La Forge and Choudhury took their posts opposite each other, at the engineering and tactical consoles. Several junior bridge officers manned the secondary stations, and tactical officer Lieutenant Aneta Šmrhová and contact specialist Lieutenant T'Ryssa Chen jointly manned the aft master systems display.

Picard checked the command console by his chair for updates. "Glinn Dygan, report."

Dygan began superimposing inset vids and graphics on the left quarter of the main viewscreen. "Two minutes ago, civilian law-enforcement personnel on the surface reported an alert from automated facial-recognition scanners in the planet's capital." He highlighted one of the inset vids, then froze the image. "This individual registered as a ninety-nine percent match for the missing androids B-4 and Lore. Because Lore remained decommissioned as of Captain Maddox's last report, we are proceeding on the assumption that this is B-4."

Worf looked suspicious. "Magnify and enhance."

The young Cardassian did as instructed, and the freeze-frame resolved into a portrait of what appeared to be a human man whose features were a perfect match for those of Soong's self-styled androids—but this subject's hair was a long, wild mane of unkempt white locks, and a scraggly grayish-white beard contrasted with his natural-looking complexion. Picard cast a curious look at Maddox. "Captain, have you made any cosmetic changes to B-4?"

"None." Maddox seemed as perplexed as Picard by the image on the screen. "I don't know who or what that is." He leaned forward. "Glinn, has that person been scanned?"

The ops officer checked his console. "Yes, sir. Street-level sensors indicate he's human, likely between twenty and thirty years of age. He appears to be unarmed."

La Forge stared in amazement at the man's image. "Could he be *related* to Doctor Soong? And if he is, what's he doing here now?"

"Let's not get ahead of ourselves," Picard cautioned. "The android copy of Data's 'mother,' Juliana Tainer, also registered as human—right down to her age-related illnesses. This might be another of Doctor Soong's creations—one made to fool sensors, as Juliana was."

Worf leaned forward to look past Picard at Maddox. "Is B-4 capable of masking his true nature? Could he, too, appear human to sensors?"

"He wasn't as of a few hours ago, but it wouldn't be a difficult modification to make. Anyone with college-level training in cybernetics could probably do it in under an hour."

Choudhury considered that for a moment. "To what end? What would someone gain by modifying B-4? And why would they let him walk the streets of the capital by himself?"

"It could be a distraction," Worf said. "Perhaps the thieves have released him to draw our attention away from them."

Picard was skeptical. "If he's a lure, why disguise him?" He decided he'd heard enough. "Whether this is B-4, another android, or a human who bears an uncanny resemblance to Doctor Soong and his creations, I refuse to believe his presence is merely a coincidence. Glinn Dygan, instruct the planetary authorities to set up a cordon in a one-kilometer radius around the subject, and to keep us apprised of his location at all times. Number One, beam down with an away team and take this person into custody. Lieutenant Choudhury, you'll serve as the coordinator for the away team, the civilian authorities, and Admiral Andell's garrison on the surface." He pointed at the man's image. "Whoever or whatever that is, I want to have a word with him."

3

Misting rain shimmered in a glow of searing neon light as Worf materialized inside the protective cocoon of a transporter beam. He and his away team stood on a city street crowded with angry civilians penned in by Starfleet's security cordons. The wide boulevard was flanked by dizzying architectural marvels of steel and glass whose façades were awash in blindingly bright advertisement vids—some two-dimensional, some holographic, all of them garish. A low-lying fog turned figures in the distance into apparitions. The cold, damp air was thick with aromas both sweet and savory, courtesy of a number of food carts at nearby intersections.

Rumbles of discontent susurrated through the sea of bystanders as word spread of the away team's presence. Tensions were high, and Worf sensed that the sooner this situation was resolved, the better. He tapped his combadge. "Worf to *Enterprise*."

Choudhury replied, *"This is* Enterprise. *Be advised, this is an open channel."*

"My team and I are in position." He looked around, trying to pierce the colorful chaos of shifting bodies so he could see the other Starfleet personnel who were supposed to be occupying strategic locations around the square. "What is the status of the other away teams?"

"All ground units are in place, and the perimeter is secure. The runabout Roanoke *is touching down above you right now."*

Worf looked up, and through the fog he saw the running lights of the *Roanoke* as it landed on the rooftop of the tallest building inside the cordon. A team of the *Enterprise*'s best sharpshooters were no doubt already deploying from the vessel to act as high-ground lookouts. *Right on schedule.* "Let me know as soon as the spotters are ready."

"You're good to go. They're sweeping the crowd now."

The rest of Worf's away team, which consisted entirely of security personnel, looked to him for instructions. He nodded for them to follow as he gently shouldered his way into the wall of people ahead of them. "We are proceeding into the crowd. Have the other units move in."

A man's voice issued from his combadge. *"Braddock to Worf."*

"Go ahead."

"I've got eyes on your subject. Eighteen-point-four meters ahead of you, on your ten."

"Paint the target," Worf said. "*Enterprise,* prepare to lock transporters." He drew his phaser and leaned his shoulder forward, cutting a path through the knot of bodies. Paying no mind to the scowls of reproach or the mumbled epithets cast in his direction, he kept his eyes focused straight ahead, on infrequent glimpses of the subject's bone-white hair.

The crowd parted for a moment, and Worf saw him—and he looked back at Worf. Without thinking, Worf said, "B-4?" But even as he said it, he knew the person looking back at him couldn't be Soong's simpleton android. This man's stare burned with a keen intellect, a profound affect of knowingness. It felt to Worf as if the man stared straight through him.

Then, in a blur, he was gone. A nervous murmur went up from the crowd. Braddock cried out over the comm, *"He's on the run! Moving eastbound, heading for Merchant Street!"*

Determined not to let the quarry slip away, Worf shoved his way forward as he roared, "All teams, move in! Lieutenant Davila, stand by to—" A phaser blast split the night, and hundreds of people started screaming as if they'd never been in the middle of a potentially deadly crossfire before. Running bodies surged toward Worf, who checked them roughly aside, clearing a path for himself and his team. When they reached the intersection that led to Merchant Street, they found Lieutenant Peter Davila and his security team unconscious, and a wall of panicked civilians receding down the shop-lined thoroughfare.

Lieutenant Kirsten Cruzen knelt between the fallen Davila and one of his comrades. The slightly built but steely-eyed human woman checked Davila's pulse with her fingertips, then she touched the Bolian ensign's jugular. She looked up at Worf. "Stunned but alive."

"Go forward," Worf said. "Worf to *Enterprise.* Bravo Team needs a medic."

"Braddock to Worf. Subject took the first left, down that alley. Lost him after that."

Choudhury's voice snapped over the open channel. "Enterprise *to Echo Team. Divert left down Foundry, then right into the alley. Cut off the subject's escape route."*

Worf picked up the pace. "Double time!" He rounded the turn into the alley at a full run, his phaser leading the way. Unlike the streets of the capital's main square, which were ablaze in primary colors, the windowless alley was steeped in shadows, a yawning canyon of darkness that reeked of garbage and excrement. Keeping his phaser steady in his left hand, he pulled a palm beacon from his belt with his right, thumbed it on, and pointed its harsh blue-white beam ahead of him. Behind him and ahead of him, the other Starfleet personnel surging into the narrow passageway between two commercial high-rises did the same, and several beams crisscrossed as Alpha Team, led by Worf, converged with Echo Team.

Both squads met in the middle of the alley. Worf stared expectantly at Echo Team's leader, Lieutenant Randolph Giudice, a tall, broad-shouldered, bearded hulk of a man, a human whose stature would impress even a Klingon. All the dark-haired man could offer Worf in return was a gaze of blank confusion. Shining his palm beacon on the alley's walls, Worf shouted, "Look for a door! A hatch! Any way out of this alley!"

Seconds passed in frantic fits until a member of Worf's team called out, "Sir! Here!"

He ran back to see Ensign Mlawr shining his palm beacon beneath a bulky metal trash bin on struts, illuminating an open sewer grate. The white-furred Caitian looked up at Worf. "It's the only thing we've found, but we can't imagine how anyone could—"

Worf lunged and threw himself against the end of the bin. Its weight was prodigious, and the effort required to shift it even a meter to expose the grate left him howling with exertion and agony. Funneling all his rage and frustration into one crazed push, he displaced the bin. The friction of metal on pavement filled the alleyway with an ear-splitting screech.

As soon as the grate was exposed, Worf leapt at the opening and poked his head down through it. He saw pipes, larger pipes—and an underground catacomb of maintenance passages. With a growl of annoyance, he pushed himself back to his feet.

"Worf to *Enterprise*. Suspect has moved underground, into the maintenance tunnels."

"Acknowledged," Choudhury replied on the open channel. *"Delta Team, you're up."*

The subterranean labyrinth of maintenance tunnels was immaculate and well lit, but that was no comfort to Lieutenant Aneta Šmrhová as she led Delta Team in a leap-frogging advance toward a confrontation with a subject who had already outrun two other teams and evaded one of the *Enterprise*'s best sharpshooters. The underground passageways were stiflingly hot and arid, the result of thermal radiation leaking from massive steam mains.

She reached the front of the squad and held up a fist, halting the rest of her team while she listened and checked the corners. There was no sign of activity. A glance at the tactical display mounted on top of her phaser rifle indicated that the point at which the subject had breached the maintenance network lay ahead twenty-nine meters to her right. There were no life signs on her weapon's sensors, but minute changes in air pressure lit up the motion tracker. Something man-sized was on the move, and it was close. The dark-haired tactical officer looked back at her team and with silent hand signals deployed them forward in a covering formation.

Stealing forward, she glimpsed the markings on various conduits and bundles that were packed along the concrete walls. Delta Team was surrounded by countless junctions and relays that governed the capital city's water, power, and communications.

Two soft snaps of her fingers drew her team's attention, and she ordered in quick gestures that all weapons be reduced to light stun. *Can't risk any collateral damage down here,* she realized. *All it would take is one stray shot to knock out the city's whole—*

Pitch-black darkness fell without warning, followed by the dwindling hum of generators and other key municipal systems losing power. With a short, sharp whistle, Šmrhová directed her people to fire up the targeting beacons mounted atop their rifles. Shafts of pure white light sliced through the sepulchral gloom. Šmrhová whispered and hoped her combadge was able to pick up her voice clearly. "Šmrhová to *Enterprise.* We just lost power down here."

"Acknowledged," came the reply, much louder than Šmrhová's discreet sotto voce. *"The whole block just went dark. Be advised, Romeo Team is converging on your position from bearing two-seven-one."*

"Copy that." With quick gestures she sent her team around a corner to the right, in a bid to trap the subject between her squad and Romeo Team. Her motion tracker confirmed the target was only one passage away and about to run headlong into a whole lot of heavily armed—

Shrieks of phaser fire and howls of pain echoed wildly in the claustrophobic maintenance passages, directly ahead of Šmrhová and her team. A flurry of motion overwhelmed the readout of her tracking device. She ran forward. "Move up!" The clamor of battle and the cries of the wounded escalated, and then just as suddenly fell silent. Heedless of the danger, she sprinted around the final corner—then she tripped over a body and nearly fell on her face.

Catching her balance with a lunging step, she swept her beacon over the fallen. All she saw were people in Starfleet uniforms. Then she heard the rising whine of something building up to detonation. As her team logjammed in the passageway behind her, she looked over her shoulder and pointed at her ear. "You all hear that?" Nods of affirmation. "Fall back!"

A mad scramble of retreat was obstructed by a clumsy series of collisions. Šmrhová and her team had just ducked back under cover when something ahead of them detonated with a low thump—but little else. No flash, no fire, no great sonic effect. Only when she opened her eyes did Šmrhová realize her rifle's targeting beacon and tracking device had gone dead.

She tapped her combadge. "Šmrhová to *Enterprise*!" There was no response, not even the mournful chirp of a dysfunctional combadge. *Subspace pulse,* she realized. *Damn it!*

The Czech-born tactical officer led her team forward, desperate to stay in the hunt despite having been left behind in the dark. "Move out!" They sprinted past the fallen members of Romeo Team, through an open doorway—and then Šmrhová slammed to a halt. Her team piled up at her back with a clatter of colliding rifles and stumbling footsteps. Ahead of them lay a wide-open section of the penumbrous underground maze. Despite all her efforts to discern fresh sounds from the reverberations of the space, she couldn't hear any footfalls from their escaping subject, and her eyes were unable to pierce the dark curtain that surrounded them.

Mumbling curses under her breath, Šmrhová turned back to face her team. "We need to find the closest route to the surface. Tell me the second any of you gets a comm signal."

She knew she would catch hell for losing the subject when she returned to the *Enterprise*. All she could do now was hope no one died for her mistake.

There was nothing to see through the rifle scope but a colorful flurry of fear-driven motion and patches of impenetrable white fog, but Lieutenant Austin Braddock kept on looking, hoping to catch sight of the unknown subject, or "unsub," if he made the mistake of returning to the main street. Pivoting his telescopic sight from one intersection to the next, Braddock heard security chief Choudhury's urgent query over the comm: *"Does anyone have eyes on the target?"*

"Braddock, negative," he said, kicking off a round robin of bad news from the other sniper-spotters on the rooftop. When the collective check-in was done, he asked, "Any updates from Delta Team?" Seconds passed as he scoped another row of faces and came up empty.

Choudhury replied, *"No contact with Delta Team. They don't answer hails."* That was bad news. Braddock knew it; everyone did. Seconds later, his fears were confirmed by the security chief's next round of orders. *"Oscar and Sierra teams, redeploy into the tunnels and meet up with Delta Team. Tango and Victor teams, start a grid sweep. All other units, widen the cordon to two kilometers. Spotters, fall back to position two."*

As soon as the order came down, Braddock heard the *Roanoke* fire up its engines. He broke down the duopod support for his rifle and shouldered the weapon for the short jog to the runabout. Ignoring the painful crick in his lower back, he pushed himself to his feet and turned toward the ship.

The next thing he noticed was his fellow sharpshooters, all sprawled in various awkward poses on the roof, either stunned or dead, their weapons at their sides. Braddock's imagination reeled. He'd heard no shots or sounds of conflict, felt no inkling of a sonic attack, smelled no toxins in the air. He waved to the pilot to power down the engines and get on the comm—and that's when he saw the unsub through the runabout's cockpit windshield, his youthful face framed by wild white hair, his eyes gleaming with excitement and mischief.

A whine and a roar kicked up a swirl of dust from the rooftop, and the *Roanoke* began its vertical ascent with a subtle pivoting of its nose.

Braddock hefted his rifle for a snap shot at the runabout.

The compact ship fired its phasers. An excruciating screech rent the air and forced Braddock to drop his weapon to cover his ears. Something off to his left exploded, peppering him with debris and scalding him with steam as a prodigious cloud billowed across the roof, slammed into him, and knocked him flat on his back.

It took a few seconds for him to regain his wits and hack out between rasping coughs, "*Enterprise*! This is Braddock! Do you copy?"

"This is Enterprise. *Go ahead."*

"Target has hijacked the *Roanoke*."

Picard listened with mounting concern as the manhunt went increasingly awry. To his left, Choudhury pivoted nimbly between three separate consoles in a desperate bid to track all the data coming in from the pursuit on the planet's surface and coordinate an effective response.

"Stand by on phasers," Choudhury said. "If I can take control of the runabout remotely, we won't need to . . ." Her sentence trailed off as new information appeared on her console. The svelte, no-nonsense security chief was visibly chagrined. "The subject disabled the runabout's transponder. Now we have to shoot it down. Dygan, lock phasers on the runabout. One-quarter power. We just want to knock it down, not blow it up."

"Target's accelerating," the Cardassian said. "Moving out of phaser range."

At the helm, Faur reacted ahead of the order. "Increasing orbital velocity," she said. "We'll recover line of sight for targeting in eight seconds."

Lieutenant T'Ryssa Chen spun around from the master systems display. "Power surges on the planet's surface! Someone's charging an ion cannon!"

"It's Admiral Andell's garrison," Picard said, bolting from his chair and hurrying back to join Chen at the MSD. "Hail him! Tell him to stand down before—"

"Too late," Chen said, pointing at a screen packed with ominous sensor readings. "They've fired on the runabout." Checking the latest intel, she added, "Direct hit."

Dreading what he'd see next, Picard returned to his chair and faced the main viewer. "On-screen, Lieutenant."

A high-orbit vantage of the smoldering runabout appeared on the forward display, flanked by flight telemetry relayed from several ground-control stations. The badly damaged small starship corkscrewed at a shallow angle through the lower atmosphere, leaving a thick twist of black smoke in its erratic wake. Moments later it cut a fiery scar across the landscape as it crashed in an unpopulated marsh several dozen kilometers shy of the seacoast.

Picard shot a disapproving glance at Choudhury, who seemed to need no reminding that this was not the outcome they had hoped for. She worked quickly at her console. "Locking in the coordinates of the crash site." A tap of her finger opened an intraship channel. "Fire and rescue teams, beam down and secure the site. Signal when it's ready for evidence recovery." Another tap switched her outgoing channel to the teams on the surface. "Alpha and Delta teams, stand by to beam to the runabout's crash site as soon as we get the fire under control."

"Acknowledged," Worf answered. *"Standing by."*

The *Enterprise* team had followed the rules of engagement to the letter, Picard knew, and he didn't blame Choudhury for the operation's outcome. Someone else would have to take the blame for this. He got up and walked toward his ready room with a steady bearing. It had been a while since he had been in a position to dress down a superior officer. He planned to enjoy it.

The hum and glow of the transporter beam faded away, leaving Worf to squint into the searing glare of portable searchlights and wrinkle his nose at the fetid stench of the marshlands across which the *Roanoke* had gouged a kilometer-long wound.

A firefighting team in soot-stained full-body gear trudged away from the mangled wreck, most of them toting heavy equipment over their shoulders. Within ten meters of the downed craft, the temperature was so extreme that Worf couldn't move any closer. All he could do was stare at the pillar of jet-black smoke climbing into the sky from the ship's broken-open midsection. *At least the heat and smoke mask the stench of this forsaken place.*

He waved over the chief of the firefighting team. The brawny noncom joined him and removed his headgear, revealing a face made for going to blazes: splotchy skin, thinning hair, crooked teeth, and eyes ringed by dark circles of fatigue. He sounded tired. "Yes, sir?"

"The pilot." Worf nodded at the runabout. "He's dead?"

Raising one grayed eyebrow, the chief petty officer shook his head. "There is no pilot. That thing was empty when it went down."

Šmrhová stepped up beside Worf and asked the chief, "Could the pilot have beamed off the ship before it was shot down?"

"Anything's possible," the chief said. "As soon as we cut the flight recorder out of the slag, you'll know as much as we do. Till then . . . I need a drink. Excuse me, sirs." The chief waved good-bye and departed with a stiff gait, despite not having been formally dismissed.

The XO masked his anger with solemn intensity and tapped his combadge to deliver the bad news. "Worf to *Enterprise*. Our subject has escaped."

4

As soon as the door of the *Enterprise*'s observation lounge closed behind Captain Picard, his senior officers started talking.

"Whoever that was," Worf said, circling the table to his chair, "it was *not* B-4."

Choudhury took a seat opposite Worf. "He was a step ahead of us all the way."

"More like two steps ahead," Šmrhová concurred as she sat beside Choudhury. Doctor Beverly Crusher circled the end of the table to sit beside Worf.

Picard claimed the chair at the table's head. "How did he gain the upper hand?"

The driven young tactical officer wore a look of concentration. "If I had to guess," she said with a mild Slavic accent, "I'd say he tapped into our comm frequencies. He knew to run just before we called for the transporter lock; he waited until the spotters lost sight of him before he went underground; and he successfully ambushed two different security teams."

The security chief seemed doubtful. "None of the vids show him with a combadge, or anything else he might have used to tap our comms."

Worf scowled. "If he was an android, he might have such a system built into his brain."

That speculation roused Picard's concern. "Do you think he's an android?"

"Yes, sir." The Klingon picked up a padd and used it to call up an orbital view of the alleyway between Merchant and Foundry streets. "He eluded pursuit here by slipping through a grate into the maintenance passageways under the streets. This grate was covered by a fully loaded metal trash bin that I found extremely difficult to move. When I did move it, it caused a great deal of noise as it dragged over the pavement. But the subject made no such sound during his escape, which suggests he lifted its end, held it up as he opened the grate, and lowered it on top of the open grate as he made his descent—all without making a sound. To do so would require a tremendous amount of strength."

The implications of Worf's account troubled Picard. He reclined and considered the facts for a moment. "Such a feat would be within the capabilities of most Soong-type androids. Are we absolutely certain this wasn't B-4?"

"Yes," Worf said. "I looked into his eyes. It was not him."

Šmrhová appeared confused. "How could you tell? If they all look alike, I mean."

The first officer searched for the right words. "If you had ever met B-4, you would understand. He was . . . simple. Guile was not in his nature. The person I saw in the square . . . the man who looked back at me . . . was no stranger to deception."

Choudhury threw a question out to the group. "Could it have been a Changeling? They could easily mimic a Soong android, and they'd have no trouble lifting that bin."

Crusher shook her head. "If it was a Changeling, alarms would be going off all over the planet. Sensor networks in most major cities and starports throughout the Federation now have detection protocols for Changeling life signs."

"Assume for the moment that we're dealing with an android," Picard said. "If, as Worf says, it's not B-4 . . . what is it?"

Tapping a slender, swarthy index finger on the tabletop, Choudhury projected a pensive demeanor. "Is there any chance this might be Lore?"

Worf's stern features grew even more tense. "I do not see how. His positronic brain was destroyed when the *Enterprise*-D's saucer crashed on Veridian III nearly thirteen years ago."

The assembled officers seemed stymied. Picard broke the silence. "Then it stands to reason that we're dealing with a previously unknown Soong-type android—one whose identity, allegiance, capabilities, and motivations are all currently unknown to us."

"Not entirely unknown," Šmrhová said. "We've confirmed that this android has great strength and agility, can mimic human life-readings, and might have a native ability to eavesdrop on subspace comm frequencies. If his other senses are also enhanced, it stands to reason that we might be up against a very formidable opponent."

Picard nodded. "Excellent points, Lieutenant."

Casting a confused look at Worf and Picard, Choudhury said, "Sirs, I thought all the Soong-type androids had been accounted for."

"We've thought so many times," Picard said with a self-deprecating smile. "Before we met Lore. And Juliana Tainer. And B-4." He breathed a sigh of resignation. "I often marvel at how prolific Doctor Soong really was."

Heads turned as the lounge's starboard door swished open, and La Forge strode in, holding high a padd. "We've finished analyzing the data from the runabout's flight recorder—what was left of it, anyway." He stepped in front of the master systems display and called up the engineering report on the main screen. "Our hijacker fired a phaser directly into the recording unit about sixteen seconds into his flight, just before the runabout slipped out of our view"—he highlighted a segment of the recorder's data—"and just after the pilot powered up the emergency transporter. But before you ask, we couldn't recover any coordinates. He put those in after he shot the recorder. So I can deduce that he beamed out, but I can't say to where."

Leaning forward, Šmrhová narrowed her eyes as she studied the data. "He clearly knew he couldn't outrun us if he tried to break orbit. And it looks like he chose the only course out of the city that would make sure the runabout ditched in an unpopulated area."

"This might be a good time to point out something else," Choudhury cut in. "Our subject never once resorted to anything like lethal force during his escape. Most of the personnel he neutralized were incapacitated by stun shots, minimal-impact strikes on pressure points, and, in a few cases, by use of Vulcan nerve-pinch techniques. Whatever else we might say about this subject, he acts with great precision and minimal violence."

Picard was willing to take good news where he found it. "Let's count ourselves lucky for that—and hope our good fortune holds." He stood and looked at Worf. "In the meantime, continue the search and update me on any developments." To the group he added, "Dismissed."

Worf, La Forge, and Choudhury huddled around a windowside table in the Happy Bottom Riding Club, the *En-*

terprise's crew lounge. Named by the ship's former first officer, William T. Riker, before he left to captain the *U.S.S. Titan,* the sprawling compartment at the front of the saucer section had been decorated by its civilian barkeep, Jordan, in a motif of classic aviation memorabilia from the middle of Earth's twentieth century. In addition to photos of Pancho Barnes, the founder of the club's Terran namesake, the accoutrements included such touches as a horseshoe, replicas of the commissioning plaques from several starships named *Enterprise,* a *d'k tahg* donated by Captain Picard, and several other pieces of assorted bric-a-brac.

Naturally, there was a story behind each item, and Jordan knew them all—as Worf had learned to his annoyance when he'd made the error of asking about the facsimile of the original Riding Club's liquor license, which was posted prominently behind the bar. This night, however, was not a time for reminiscence; there was work to be done.

"We need a plan of action," the Klingon said, careful to keep his voice down so their conversation could remain private despite the setting. "I doubt the thieves are sitting idly."

La Forge suppressed a glimmer of amusement. "Actually, I suspect that's exactly what they're doing, Worf. It's not as if there's much else they can do."

"Geordi's right," Choudhury said. "Until we lift the ban on incoming and outgoing flights, they really don't have any way off this rock." She raised her hand and caught the attention of a passing server. "An iced chai, a prune juice, and . . ." She pointed at La Forge.

The chief engineer said to the waiter, "French roast, black." As soon as the young man hurried away to fill the drink order, La Forge leaned back into the conversation. Fatigue seemed to be taking hold of him. "The ban on traffic helps, but not much. A planet's still a really big thing to search—especially when you don't know exactly who you're looking for, or when the one target you know of can fool sensors into thinking he's something he's not."

"Let's think about what we know versus what we don't know." Choudhury lifted one finger at a time as she counted off items. "One: Three intruders broke into the Starfleet Annex and facilitated the theft of six Soong-type androids, one functional, five not. Two: Even though they did everything right, someone sounded the Annex's general alarm, botching their exit strategy. Three: We have no idea who sounded that alarm—but within hours of the heist, we spot an unknown Soong-type android in the planet's capital city. Four: We have no idea if the android was a conspirator in the heist or the good Samaritan who tipped us off, but either way he had no intention of being taken into custody, which suggests that his interests and ours aren't the same."

Worf's patience waned. "This is not helping. We must find out who we were chasing, so we can learn what he wants. Only then will we know his part in this."

The waiter returned and set down their drinks: iced chai for Choudhury, prune juice for Worf, and La Forge's piping-hot black coffee. He stepped away without fuss or comment, leaving the senior officers to continue their low-key but palpably intense conversation.

La Forge sipped his coffee, winced at the temperature, then smiled at the flavor. After a second sip, he set down the mug. "Maybe it's time to roll the dice on this one."

The security chief sounded mildly suspicious. "Meaning . . . ?"

"We could spend months or more trying to search every square meter of this planet for our suspect or those missing androids, but I think that'll be a waste of time."

After palming a residue of prune juice from his lower lip, Worf said, "Explain."

"The only reason that Soong android tripped our sensors is that he resembles Soong himself, like most of the doctor's androids. But there's no reason he has to keep that face. He could remake himself into almost any humanoid of similar size he wanted, and probably spoof the life signs to match. If we keep the pressure on, he's almost certain to change his appearance, and then we'll have no idea who we're looking for." He made his next point to Choudhury. "Do me a favor, Jas. Imagine you're one of the three thieves. You're in hiding with the stolen androids, watching us dragnet the planet, wondering when our search will find you. If we start to get close, and you don't see a way off the planet with the androids, what do you do?"

Choudhury's angular features registered her understanding of the ugly truth. "I'd cut my losses and melt down the androids—then lay low until it was safe to leave the planet."

The engineer nodded. "Precisely. If we don't ease up on this search, we might be condemning B-4 to death—and Doctor Soong's legacy to oblivion."

Worf clenched his prune juice and reminded himself not to crush the glass in his fist. He exhaled and calmed himself, then looked at La Forge. "What options do we have?"

"We let them go." La Forge lifted a hand to forestall Worf's and Choudhury's protests. "But not until we take a few steps to turn that to our advantage."

The security chief cracked a sly smile. "This ought to be good."

La Forge felt his mood improve as he spelled out his idea. "I've been thinking about the cloaked-ship theory we ruled out a few hours ago. It occurs to me that even though a cloaked ship couldn't have breached the atmosphere without causing a ruckus, that doesn't mean there isn't one somewhere in this system, acting as a support ship for the operation."

Choudhury's smile widened. "Waiting to recover the heist team, or at least take possession of the androids." La Forge's nod of confirmation set off a chain reaction of thoughts inside the slim, athletic woman's head; Worf knew that distracted gaze well. "If the thieves are of Breen or Romulan origin, as we thought, they might be able to move freely on the surface without drawing attention, but they still would have needed a cloaked ship to get them into Federation space undetected. And since their target is bulky, easily identifiable, and highly valuable, they'd probably want to use a cloaked ship to smuggle it out."

"A reasonable theory," Worf said. "If it is correct, our next step is to identify where in this system a cloaked vessel might hide while awaiting its rendezvous. Then we lift the ban, withdraw to an ambush position, initiate surveillance of those coordinates . . . and wait."

The chief engineer picked up his padd, tapped in a few commands, then handed it to Worf. "We have a full complement of Class V recon probes. I could upgrade them with sensor countermeasures in less than an hour. Launch ten or twelve of those at low impulse, and we could have eyes on every blind spot in the system by 2100."

"Then," Choudhury added, "if a ship drops its cloak for a clandestine meeting, we'll be able to get a clear reading on their energy signature. If we're lucky, we might get enough data to test the new cloak-penetrating sensor protocols the R-and-D office cooked up." She checked some information on her own padd. "I can have a list of target sites for the probes in an hour."

Worf nodded, gratified to be taking action rather than merely waiting for something new to happen. He downed the rest of his prune juice in one decadent gulp, then stood. "I will speak to the captain and have him ask the planet's government to cancel the alert and lift the ban." He gave La Forge a fraternal slap on the shoulder. "Notify me as soon as the probes are ready." Walking toward the Riding Club's exit, he wore a broad smile of dark satisfaction.

The hunt continues.

Deprived of the undercurrent of low-frequency engine hum and the often barely audible white noise of the ventilation system, Picard was unusually aware of his breathing and heartbeat. He sat in his command chair, the side of his fist pressed against his mouth as if to stifle any sound that might try to escape into the hush of the bridge. The normal ambience of the *Enterprise* was absent, leaving only an eerie quiet broken at long, odd intervals by the soft chirp of a computer feedback tone from one of the few bridge consoles that were still active.

On his right, Worf sat with his arms crossed, his eyes unblinking and focused on the forward viewscreen, which had been subdivided into a dozen panels, each tracking the signals from one of the concealed reconnaissance probes the *Enterprise* crew had dispatched to various sites throughout the Galor system. The selection process had been swift but logical, targeting those locations that would be most likely to offer potent natural camouflage for a cloaked ship lurking in low-power mode—just as the *Enterprise* was currently doing.

The command consoles beside Picard's and Worf's

chairs were dark, as were the helm and most of the secondary mission stations around the bridge. Only the operations and tactical consoles remained active. Glinn Dygan manned ops, collecting the data from the recon probes, enhancing it through various filters, and forwarding it to Choudhury at tactical.

Persuading Captain Maddox to return to his shambles of a lab on Galor IV had been difficult. The man clearly harbored a profound sense of obligation to B-4, whose positronic matrix, he'd explained, was rapidly failing. Only after La Forge had assured Maddox that he would do everything possible to help B-4 and return him safely to Galor IV had they been able to get the cyberneticist onto a transporter pad and beam him back to the planet. In contrast, it had taken very little effort for Picard to convince Governor Eloch to cancel the alert and let Galor IV return to "business as usual." The only difficult part of that brief conversation had been finding a polite way to refuse the governor's demand for an official apology.

Picard was just beginning to indulge himself with a flight of fancy, imagining all the scathing retorts with which he might have rebuffed the governor, when Choudhury looked up from her station, her eyes and voice bright with anticipation. "I think we have something." She selected one of the recon signals and expanded it to fill half the main viewscreen. On the other half she patched in a standard interplanetary traffic control feed. "A medium-sized civilian yacht has deviated from its filed flight plan and is on a course toward one of our blind spots."

"Identify that ship," Picard said, leaning forward.

Glinn Dygan worked at his controls. "The *S.S. Velatida,* a *Manta*-class luxury vessel, Risan registry. Standard crew complement of six, up to twelve passengers."

"Risan registry," Worf said under his breath. "Convenient."

As one of dozens of planets entirely obliterated during the Borg invasion three years earlier, Risa was now frequently listed as the port of registry for vessels with fraudulent identification, simply because it was very difficult to prove such a registration hadn't existed before its alleged world of authentication had been vaporized.

On the viewscreen, the broad, flat yacht cruised past the hidden recon probe. "It's slowing to one-tenth impulse," Choudhury said. "Now they're answering all stop."

Dygan chimed in, "Neutrino pulse detected!"

No one needed to narrate what happened next. The wide expanse of deep space beyond the yacht rippled and then was obscured by the sudden appearance of a massive military vessel. In less than a few seconds, it went from being spectral to solid.

"That is a Breen ship," Worf said through his teeth.

Choudhury remained cool and calm as she keyed in commands on her panel. "Logging its energy signature and running it against known vessels in the database."

Echoing the security chief's sanguine manner, Dygan added, "Standing by to log the interference pattern in its cloaking field."

Everyone watched with muted fascination as a broad pair of doors opened on the underside of the Breen warship, revealing a spacious docking bay. Then, like a predator engulfing its prey, it descended and swallowed up the yacht. As soon as the luxury ship was fully inside the docking bay, the Breen ship's ventral doors crept shut.

"It would appear that someone's arrival was expected," Picard noted dryly.

Worf nodded. "Indeed."

The Breen ship began to cloak. Dygan and Choudhury worked quickly, trying to lock in the data that would, hypothetically, enable the *Enterprise* to track the Typhon Pact vessel even while it was cloaked. If their ploy was successful, it would represent a significant step forward in Starfleet's ongoing arms race with the Federation's rivals.

Several seconds after the cruiser vanished from sight, Picard grew anxious awaiting a report. "Lieutenant Choudhury. Do we have a fix on the Breen vessel?"

"Not exactly." She continued to key in commands on her console. "We're getting intermittent readings, enough to approximate a course, but if they make any sudden changes, or move even slightly out of optimal sensor range, we'll lose our lock."

Dygan turned from ops to face Picard and Worf. "I might be able to clean up our signal and improve our range and accuracy, but it will take several hours."

"We don't have several hours," Picard snapped. "They're leaving now."

"Yes, sir," Dygan said, duly chastised as he turned away and returned to his work.

"All systems to full," Picard said. In a second, the bridge surged back to full operating mode, and all the familiar sounds of the ship thrummed back to life. "We need options, quickly."

Lieutenant Šmrhová turned from the master systems display behind Picard and Worf. "Sirs, I'm reading another ship moving on what appears to be a pursuit course for the Breen cruiser." Picard and Worf got up and joined her at the MSD. Choudhury was right behind them. Šmrhová continued. "There was a small starship hiding in the asteroid belt between the fourth and fifth planets, not far from the yacht's rendezvous with the Breen." She pointed out its transponder ID and other details on the screen. "It's a private transport capable of high warp speeds. Flight logs show it left Galor IV a few minutes behind the yacht—and followed it."

Worf asked, "Why didn't we detect it earlier?"

"Because it kept its distance and used the same trick we did: it ran silent and used the natural kelbonite and fistrium content of the asteroids to mask its sensor profile. I didn't see it until it started maneuvering clear of the field." She traced its trajectory and extrapolated its likely course. "It appears to be tailing the Breen cruiser." She added a cautionary note. "Of course, I can't be certain of that, since we can't verify the cruiser's position or heading."

Choudhury threw a questioning glance at her superior officers. "Is it possible the pilot of that ship has a better means of tracking the cloaked ship than we do?"

"Scan the transport," Worf said. "Are there any life signs on board?"

Šmrhová ran the scan, then shook her head. "No life signs, sir."

"So," Picard said. "Either that vessel has a strangely prescient autopilot program, or it has a pilot who doesn't register on our sensors and seems once again to know more than we do about this increasingly worrisome situation."

From ops, Dygan added, "The Breen ship has jumped to warp." Seconds later, he added, "The transport ship has also gone to warp, maintaining its pursuit course."

Worf asked, "Do we have a clear sensor lock on the transport?"

The Cardassian checked, then replied, "Aye, sir."

Picard noted Worf's keen stare; it was decision time. He strode to the center of the bridge, knowing without a doubt that his first officer was at his back, both literally and figuratively. Then he stood tall and infused his voice with the rich tenor of authority.

"Helm, follow that ship."

5

Lying in bed beside Jasminder Choudhury, Worf listened to her postcoital breathing and noticed that the rhythm of her respiration was in sync with his own. All he wanted was to clear his mind of its nonstop activity, its fixation on details both grand and mundane, but his senses drank in every detail. Hunter-green bedcovers and a silver-gray comforter lay crumpled on the deck at the foot of his bed, kicked aside an hour earlier in his and Choudhury's initial flurry of passion. Pieces of their uniforms lay on the deck, strewn like a breadcrumb trail leading back to the door from the corridor. Lulled by the deep thrumming of the ship's warp engines, he relaxed, drew a slow, deep breath, and savored the musky perfume of their commingled sweat, which lingered like a pleasant memory and coaxed him into letting slip a ghost of a smile.

She turned her head in his direction and poked his arm. "What are you smiling at?"

"Everything. . . . Nothing."

Four days had passed since the *Enterprise* left the Galor system, following the unknown transport ship at a distance that tested the limits of the *Sovereign*-class starship's sensors—an action predicated on the fateful assumption that the transport was following the cloaked Breen warship. Their course had seemed to lead toward a region of unclaimed space on the borders of both the Breen Confederacy and the Federation.

If the captain's gamble proved correct, and the transport was dogging the Breen, then the advantage to the *Enterprise* would be that it had followed its target a great distance while remaining well out of sensor range. Worf could only hope that the transport's sensors had a great enough range that it was able to tail the Breen without being detected in return.

Choudhury nudged Worf. "Stop thinking about work."

He hated being so easily interpreted. "How did you know?"

His long-limbed paramour stroked his jaw. "You get this look in your eyes, like you can see through the bulkheads. And you tend to sigh when something bothers you."

"Good to know." He kissed her. "I'll remember that the next time I play poker."

A broad grin lit up her beautiful face. "It won't help you. I know all your tells."

"Such as?"

"As if I'd tell you." She rolled out of bed and sauntered toward the bath nook. "It's not my fault you wear your heart on your sleeve." She paused in the doorway and shot him a smile over her shoulder. "If that costs you money from time to time, that's your problem."

Hypnotized by the whisper-rush of the sonic shower, Worf drifted off for a few minutes, succumbing to days of sleep deprivation and overwork. Dreams came swiftly and swept him up, and all the visions bled into one another. He stood at the prow of a narrow seacraft with a dragon's head, squinting into the spray with each break of the surf. . . . Garbed in the robes of Kahless, he climbed the steps of a jungle temple as a teeming mass of Klingons cheered his name. . . . He stood alone and naked on a barren black island in a lake of fire and wondered if it was Gre'thor. Then he awoke with a start to see Spot, the cat who had claimed him for her own after Data's death, perched atop his chest and staring at him through half-closed eyes.

He admired the cat's brazen, direct approach to life. If she wanted food or attention, she accosted him until he granted her desire. If he tarried or resisted, she attacked him. Despite her small size and the human-pleasing aesthetics of her appearance, she was a predator. That was something Worf could respect. He petted the feline's orange head, then gave her a gentle pat on the back as her cue to get up and go wait by her food bowl. Spot reacted slowly and moved with obvious effort and discomfort as she jumped down to the floor, then trudged across Worf's quarters toward her feeding area beside the replicator. He got up and followed her, dismayed by the creature's increasingly obvious infirmity. She was roughly seventeen years old by his estimate, and despite the preventive care she received from the ship's veterinary medical specialist, she was showing signs of her age. With proper care and nutrition, she might live another decade, but he sensed in the cat a spirit almost Klingon in its fierce pride; he knew it would offend her dignity to prolong her life after its quality had expired. As he procured her favorite dietary formula from his replicator with the press of a button, he promised himself that he would safeguard her honor as he would that of any true warrior.

There will come a good day to die, my friend. But for you, this is not that day.

Choudhury returned from the bath nook wrapped

in a blue-and-white striped towel, her damp black hair tossed over one shoulder, and smiled at the sight of Worf tending to Spot. "At long last, I realize who your true master is."

"I should have thought it was obvious long ago."

He met her in the middle of the room and caressed her cheek with the back of his hand. She closed her eyes and leaned into his tender gesture, as if to prolong it. "That feels nice." Cupping her hand over his, she opened her eyes. "I want to say something."

Worf clasped her hand. "Speak."

"I want to thank you." For a moment, a bashful color warmed her face. "When the Borg were laying waste everything in sight, and I needed someone to cling to . . . you let me hang on to you. After it was over, and I needed someone to go home with me and help me start over, you were there." As if ashamed, she averted her eyes from his and bowed her head. "Later, when I got scared and thought I'd made a mistake, and I asked you for space, you gave it to me."

A tear rolled from the inner corner of her right eye, and as if by instinct, Worf reached out and with the slightest brush of his thumb wicked it away. Choudhury looked up at him with a bittersweet smile. "I feel like I've been stuck to a pendulum the last few years—swinging one way, then the other, pulling you close and pushing you away. But now . . . I finally feel like I'm back at the center. I've found my balance. I know who I am again, and what I want."

"And that would be . . . ?"

She traced the curve of his ocular ridge with her delicate fingertips. "I want to be with you. Like this: simply . . . honestly . . . in the moment."

Her declaration pleased him. But still his mind would not be at rest. "When I was young, I had a

Klingon mate, K'Ehleyr. When I was older and wiser, I took a wife, Jadzia. I loved and treasured them both. But I no longer desire such a permanent bond in my life. Perhaps one day that will change. But for now, that is how I feel. I tell you this not as a rejection of what you have offered . . . but as a statement of fact, so that there is no misunderstanding between us."

Choudhury kissed him and made it last.

When their lips parted, she looked contented. "As I said, Worf, I only want what we have now. Each other. No vows, no ceremonies, no children, no lies. I don't want to change you, and I don't want to be changed." She flashed an infectious smile. "Think you can live with that?"

He scooped her up in both arms and carried her back toward the bed. "Yes."

Leaning against an open doorframe, Jean-Luc Picard watched his two-year-old son René sleep peacefully and hoped the boy would stay that way. His son had suffered from bad dreams recently, and as a result it had become a bit of a chore putting him down each night. Most evenings the task fell to Crusher, but as often as possible, Picard tried to lend a hand.

Tonight he had been there, giving his wife a much-needed respite from the battle of wills with their precocious son. After dinner they had bathed René, fitted him with a night diaper, dressed him in pajamas, and tucked him into his bed. Then had come story time. A stack of children's books stood ready by René's bedside, and as Picard had begun the paternal duty of reading his boy to sleep, he had been impressed with his scion's growing vocabulary and seemingly insatiable appetite for narratives. By the time he cracked open the sixth tome of the evening's recitation, he began to question whether it would be unethical to let Crusher use a mild hypospray to hasten the boy's descent into slumber.

Never one to shirk from a challenge, Picard had held his ground, regaling his son in deep and dulcet tones with one fantastical tale after another, until, at long last, the child's eyes grew heavy and he drifted off, his breathing slow and regular, his face angelic and calm. With great care, Picard had set down the storybook, and then he had pulled up the covers over the curve of René's shoulder, kissed the top of the boy's head, and bade him *bonne nuit*.

He had planned to slip out of René's room and go catch up with Crusher, to see what she had been up to on this rare night of free time, but he had stopped in the doorway to look back and then found himself unable to leave. All he wanted to do was watch over his little boy, as if his presence would somehow shield the lad from the products of his own subconscious. But in his heart, he knew his motive for lingering was at least partly selfish; gazing at his son filled him with conflicting emotions of tremendous intensity. His fear of all the ills that might befall the boy in a harsh universe of cold realities clashed with all his hopes for what joys the future might bring; the pride that filled him when he saw some spark of himself in René was negated by the humility of realizing that his son was his own person, and that he could never truly know him, only love him and accept him and hope that respect was returned one day in kind.

His wife's hand fell softly upon his shoulder. "Addictive, isn't it?"

"More so with each passing day," Picard admitted. "And not just because I feel like I've already missed so many milestones in his life: his first word, his first step. I always seem to be elsewhere when he makes these great leaps forward."

Crusher draped a comforting arm across his shoulders. "It's not as if the day care team and I didn't record those moments."

"I know." He couldn't shake off a petty, nagging guilt. "But seeing it on a screen—or even in the holodeck—isn't the same as having been there. Part of me wonders if he'll always know, on some instinctual level, that I missed those key moments in his life."

She rested her head against his. "Trust me, Jean-Luc: in the grand scheme of things, your absence at those moments will mean far more to you than it ever will to him."

He snaked his arm behind her back and held her close at his side. "I want to do everything for him, and yet I can't think of anything to do. I want to protect him from everything, even when there doesn't seem to be any danger." The sheer immensity of what he didn't know made him laugh despite his transient melancholy. "I want to give him everything, but half the time I can't seem to discern what he actually wants."

"And that's parenthood," Crusher said.

La Forge was jolted out of his moment of nostalgic reverie by the voice of his dinner date, Doctor Tamala Harstad. "You're not even listening to me, are you, Geordi?"

Found out and called out, he did his best to feign attention and pretend nothing had happened. "Sure I was. I'm sorry. You were saying, about the . . ." He paused, hoping Harstad would show mercy and fill the conversational gap. Instead, she stared at him, her dark brown eyes piercing his pretenses and defenses with alarming ease. He raised his palms in surrender. "You got me. I lost focus for a minute there. I'm sorry."

The trim, dark-haired physician set down her fork

beside her plate of half-eaten vegetable stir-fry over jasmine rice. Then she reached across the table and laid her pale, slender fingers across the back of La Forge's large, callused brown hand. Her reassuring smile accentuated her already high, prominent cheekbones. "Something's bothering you."

"Not exactly," La Forge said. "The break-in, that android we chased on Galor IV, and now this Breen ship we're tailing . . . it all has me thinking about Data."

She seemed genuinely curious. "Anything in particular?"

"The stolen prototypes." La Forge realized that it was a relief to unburden himself, to let someone else hear the thoughts that plagued him, so he continued. "To Data, they weren't just failed experiments. They were his brothers. He used to keep them in a private cybernetics lab, inside his quarters here on the ship, along with the bodies of his older brother, Lore, his daughter, Lal, and his mother, Juliana Tainer."

Harstad waved one hand to interrupt. "Hold on—who? His daughter? His mother?"

"It's a long story, and it's late. Mind if I just hit the high points?"

She reached for her glass of white wine. "That would probably be best."

"Lore was Data's twin, but to be blunt, he was kind of a sociopath. He tried to betray the *Enterprise*-D to a crystalline life-form, stole Data's original emotion chip, and ended up colluding with the Borg before Data shut him down and disassembled him."

To his surprise, Harstad absorbed his first salvo of *Enterprise* crew history with aplomb. "So, you're saying his family has no shortage of drama."

"Pretty much." He sipped from his glass of zinfandel. "Around that same time, Data built an android, told us it was his 'child,' and named it Lal. She picked her own identity and seemed to fit in pretty well at first. Then some admiral from Starfleet tried to take her away from Data, and she got so panicked that her positronic matrix failed. She died later that day."

Harstad cringed in sympathetic horror. "God, that's awful. How could they do that to her? Or to him?"

"It was before the ruling on AI rights." He sighed, saddened by progress that had come too late for those who'd needed it most. "On a completely different tack, there's the story of Data's mother, Juliana Tainer."

She propped her elbow on the table and planted her chin on her hand. "I'm all ears."

"Data's creator, a scientist named Noonien Soong, loved a woman named Juliana Tainer. They married in secret while working together, and she helped make Data the person he was. Well, when she was mortally wounded and Soong couldn't save her, he copied her consciousness to a positronic matrix—then put it in an android replica of her body. He made it so it could fool sensors and let her pass for a human. It even made her age like a normal human, so she could grow old and have a 'natural' death." His heart grew heavy as he recalled the sight of his friend returning to the ship in mourning, bearing his mother's coffin. "Ten years ago, shortly before our last mission to Galor IV, she passed away." He leaned forward. "Ready for the weird part?"

A conspiratorial gleam signaled her interest. "There's a weird part?"

"A few days after Data brought his mother's body back to his lab . . . she vanished."

He could see in her eyes she'd taken the rhetorical bait. She was hooked. "How?"

"*That,*" La Forge replied with a theatrical flourish, "is a tale for another time."

Her enthralled gaze became a chastising scowl. "Enjoy sleeping alone tonight."

"All right—if you insist. Believe it or not, there is an immortal human being, a man who's lived several thousand years. If I told you some of the famous people he's been, you'd be amazed. When we met him ten years ago, he went by the name Emil Vaslovik. He'd reinvented himself as a professor of cybernetics—and he was Noonien Soong's mentor."

The doctor arched one elegant sable eyebrow. "Now I think you're putting me on."

"I'm completely serious. Do you want to hear this or not?"

She waved him on. "Continue."

He took another sip of wine to shed his inhibitions. "Vaslovik built a new kind of android, with a holotronic brain. He'd built androids before, for company, but never one like this. It took on a female persona and called itself Rhea McAdams. She seemed so human that she tricked us into believing she was our new chief of security. Long story short—"

"Too late."

"—Data fell in love with her, she fell for him, but then she left and broke his heart. I had to listen to him moan about her for *months* after she left. Anyway, Data always thought Vaslovik took Juliana's body because he hoped to resurrect her positronic matrix, even though that's pretty much impossible."

Harstad appeared to be speechless. For close to half a minute she sat in silence, looking in every direction, it seemed, except at La Forge. Then she looked the chief engineer in the eye. "Do you have a lot of stories like these?"

"You have no idea." He remembered how they had steered onto this topic, and his mood turned serious.

"Anyway, all this has had me thinking about Data's brother, B-4. As far as we knew, he was the last of Data's kin that was still functioning. He also has all of Data's memory engrams stored in his mind. But something's going wrong, and unless we find him soon, it might be too late to help him. . . . And that's what I was thinking about when you snapped me out of my trance a few minutes ago: how I plan to help B-4, assuming we get to him in time."

A look of concern darkened her countenance. "What is it you're not saying, Geordi?"

The truth of his situation was one that he dreaded speaking aloud. He had balked at it when Maddox had spelled it out for him, and when he'd read the protocols for the stabilization procedure, he'd felt physically ill. As desperately as he wanted to envision himself as a healer trying to bring relief to B-4, his conscience insisted on tarring him as an assassin.

"The only way I can save B-4," he said, "is to permanently erase Data's memories."

6

A bold orange star blazed at the center of the main viewscreen as Picard stepped out of the turbolift and strode to his chair. Minutes earlier, after several days of radio-silent, high-warp pursuit, the *Enterprise* had abruptly returned to impulse, and Worf had requested Picard's presence on the bridge. The captain took his seat beside Worf. "Report, Number One."

"The transport dropped out of warp as soon as it reached the edge of this star system." The XO relayed a tactical map from his command console to Picard's. "It appears to be taking cover inside the rings of the system's fourth planet, a gas giant. I've ordered Faur and Dygan to use the fifth planet's northern magnetic pole to mask our presence once we enter the system."

It was a tactically sound decision, and exactly the sort of precaution Picard expected from an officer of Worf's experience. He studied the map of the system and read its dry-sounding catalog identification aloud. "'FGC-38919.' What do we know about this system?"

"Not much beyond what is listed in the General Catalog. This system was mapped thirty-nine years ago using long-range sensors, but it has not yet been explored."

A titanic, pale blue gas giant with rings of varying shades of gray drifted into view from the left side of the viewscreen and soon dominated the ship's forward view. Piloting the ship into a parking orbit, Faur reported, "We're inside the planet's magnetic field."

Worf issued orders with cool confidence. "All systems to minimal power. Lieutenant Choudhury, monitor the system for any signs of starship traffic—passive sensors only."

"Aye, sir," the security chief replied, just before the bridge lights dimmed to standby mode and the rich thrumming of the ship's impulse engines faded to silence.

Minutes passed slowly, and Picard used the time to familiarize himself with the map of the star system. Seven planets orbited a K3V main-sequence star. Its three inner planets were terrestrial worlds. The first was a mostly molten chunk of lead and iron; the second was a Class-N world with a superdense, superhot atmosphere of sulfuric acid, carbon dioxide, and methane; and the third was a Class-L world with a barely breathable nitrogen-oxygen atmosphere, similar to Mars after its first several decades of aggressive terraforming. A wide, dense asteroid belt lay between the orbits of the third and fourth planets, separating the system's rocky inner worlds from its four Class-J gas giants of varying sizes and hues. Only one of the giants lacked rings, and each was orbited by no fewer than a dozen natural satellites in a wide range of sizes.

The system's most intriguing characteristic, however, was an unusually high level of docelerite particles in a six-billion-kilometer radius of its star, with an even more dramatic concentration in its asteroid belt. Docelerite was an exceedingly rare compound not normally encountered near main-sequence stars.

Its most troublesome property was that, when found at levels as high as these, it impeded warp travel by making subspace fields dangerously unstable.

Choudhury silenced a soft alert tone on her console. "We're picking up something near the third planet." She adjusted a few settings on her console. "A sudden surge in neutrinos . . . it appears to be a ship deactivating its cloaking device."

Picard was eager to see if his hunch had paid off. "Can we magnify that?"

Dygan keyed in commands at ops. "Optical sensors to maximum magnification."

The image of the third planet was small and hazy, and Picard found it difficult to discern any details of the gray-green smudge he assumed was a starship. Still, only moments later, he heard tactical officer Šmrhová declare from her post at the master systems display, "Analysis confirms that's the same ship we scanned in the Galor system."

"It's entering orbit of the third planet," Choudhury said. "We're picking up ship-to-surface comm traffic, and some high-energy emissions. Looks like a transporter beam."

Worf threw a hopeful look at her. "Can we get a lock on their transport coordinates?"

"Negative, sir. Not at this range with only passive sensors."

The first officer looked to his captain for direction. "Should we move closer, sir?"

"Not yet. Right now we hold the tactical advantage: the Breen don't know we're here." Picard stood and walked back to join Šmrhová at the MSD, and Worf followed him. "Lieutenant, have we made any progress on penetrating the cloaking device on that ship?"

Šmrhová summoned the latest updates on the large

screen in front of her. "Yes, sir. We've been refining the protocol since we left the Galor system. If we can bring even a few of our active sensors on line, we should be able to track this ship, and others using this older version of the cloaking device, when they're at ranges close enough for combat." She called up a different set of reports and tactical diagrams. "At longer distances—for instance, within a single star system—we could detect their emissions well enough to know generally where they are and how many of them there are, before they enter our firing solution."

"Excellent." He stepped aside with Worf. "Hold position here until the Breen ship cloaks. Once it does, its own sensors will be limited, and we'll engage active protocols to track it."

Worf signaled his understanding with a curt half-nod, and the two men returned to their chairs. As Picard expected, they did not have to wait long for the Breen ship to break orbit and raise its cloak. Turning back toward Šmrhová, Worf said, "Initiate tracking protocols."

"Engaged." Moments later, she added, "Captain, the Breen ship is heading out of the system at full impulse, on bearing two-six-three mark seventeen."

"Acknowledged." Picard looked to his left, at Choudhury. "Any movement by our stranger in the transport?"

The security chief shook her head. "Not yet. So far, it . . ." She let the sentence trail off and started working with increasing urgency at her console. Her mask of serenity slipped for the briefest moment; then she recovered her composure and met the captain's stare. "It's gone." Resuming her efforts, she added, "Correction: it's on a stealth trajectory through the asteroid belt, headed for the third planet."

Worf asked Picard in a confidential voice, "Should we overtake and intercept?"

"Let's not be hasty, Number One. The Breen ship made contact with someone on the planet's surface. Whoever that someone is, I'm betting they won't welcome visitors—which makes it useful that the transport can approach the planet far more discreetly than we can. It's also a *private* vessel; its presence might attract interest from the Breen, but it wouldn't be grounds for a military reprisal. Ours, on the other hand . . ."

The XO frowned. "Understood. How do you wish to proceed?"

"Covertly."

"Understood." Worf raised his voice and started issuing orders. "Lieutenant Šmrhová, track the transport ship as it approaches the third planet. If it lands on or beams anything to the surface, I want precise coordinates. Lieutenant Faur, watch for any sign of cloaked ships entering this system. Be prepared to exercise evasive maneuvers if we are detected. Glinn Dygan, inform all departments that all noncritical systems are to remain at minimal power levels, to reduce our sensor profile. If there is a Breen installation on the third planet, it might conduct random sweeps of this system. Do not underestimate their sensor capabilities.

"Lieutenant Choudhury, have Commander La Forge and one of your security officers meet us in the observation lounge in one hour. We have an away mission to plan."

"According to our sensors, the transport ship we followed to this system landed on its third planet roughly ten minutes ago." Worf enlarged a topographical map of the planet's surface on the main screen of the observation lounge's MSD console. "It touched down here, on the edge of a narrow valley surrounded by steep, jagged terrain. We have observed a massive industrial complex there, but it is protected by a scattering field, so we are unable to make detailed scans."

Choudhury and La Forge sat on either side of security officer Ensign Velex, a lean and sinewy young Troyian man whose bright green face was topped by close-cut coppery hair with a metallic shine. The three officers faced Worf, who stood on the other side of the table. Velex caught Worf's attention and nodded at the screen. "Sir, do we know what that complex is?"

"Not at this time." Worf updated the screen to show the best enhanced version of the intel, but the difference in detail was negligible. "All we know so far is that it is huge, the Breen transported something to it, and our unknown subject has landed his ship near it. For lack of a better lead, we are assuming that is where the Breen delivered the stolen androids."

La Forge wore a look of determined focus. "What's our next move?"

"The captain has ordered a covert away mission. Its risk factor will be high. If we are captured or killed, Starfleet will disavow us and our actions. No reinforcements or rescue teams will be sent in after us." With a tap on the console, Worf posted a mission summary and equipment loadout specifications on the screen. "We will be wearing solid black field combat uniforms with no rank insignia. Comm transceivers will be concealed inside our uniforms' collars and set for silent vibration to signal incoming transmissions. If you are hailed when you cannot respond safely, tap your transceiver once to send a silent response. To open a regular comm channel, tap it twice." Everyone nodded their understanding, so he continued. "Our mission is expected to be of minimal duration, so we will travel light: no rations—just canteens, civilian-grade tricorders, generic first-aid kits, and non-Starfleet sidearms."

Velex furrowed his metallic brows in a questioning manner. "Just sidearms, sir? Shouldn't at least one of us carry something heavier?"

Worf understood the impulsive young Troyian's desire for superior firepower; as a newly minted officer, the Klingon would likely have made the same request. However, he had since learned that sometimes entering a situation in possession of greater destructive potential could lead to more problems than it solved. "The captain's orders are clear, Ensign. We are to treat this as a covert recon op, not a combat mission. Will that be a problem for you?"

The emerald-skinned youth shook his head. "No, sir. No problem."

Satisfied with the ensign's answer, Worf moved on. "We will advance on foot into the valley from the western hills, survey the facility from a distance, and infiltrate it if doing so seems feasible. Our primary objective is to locate and recover the stolen androids. Our secondary objective is to figure out why they were taken. If we can, we are to learn the facility's purpose, map its exterior and interior layouts, and identify its personnel and defenses."

Choudhury studied the mission summary. "How long do we expect to be in the field?"

"Less than twenty-four hours," Worf said. "After we reach the surface, we will contact the *Enterprise* at six-hour intervals. If we miss three consecutive check-ins, or if the ship does, the mission is to be considered compromised and aborted. At that point, if we are still alive, we will become responsible for arranging our own escape from the planet's surface."

"Wow, this just gets better by the minute," La Forge quipped.

The security chief deadpanned, "You haven't heard

the best part." She looked at Worf. "Tell Commander La Forge and Ensign Velex the insertion strategy."

Worf knew that La Forge was not going to like what he was about to hear. "Because we must preserve plausible deniability for the Federation, we cannot use any Starfleet shuttlecraft to reach the planet, nor can the *Enterprise* risk orbiting the planet to beam us down." A few deft taps on the console filled the display's main screen with a schematic for a modified photon torpedo casing. "We will remove the ordnance packages and warp propulsion coils from four photon torpedoes. They will be fired toward the third planet at full impulse while the *Enterprise* uses the fourth planet's magnetic pole for cover, as the transport ship did. The torpedoes' shells will be wrapped with sensor-dampening materials and threaded with shaped microexplosives." He initiated a computer-generated animation that depicted the four torpedoes cruising into orbit of the planet and disintegrating. "The explosives will shatter the torpedoes' casings as they enter the planet's upper atmosphere. From there, we will make planetfall in radio silence, using orbital skydiving suits modified with sensor camouflage."

"I get it," Velex said. "We'll look like meteors breaking up at high altitude." A broad grin lit up his emerald face. "Damn, that looks like it's gonna be *fun*."

The ensign's enthusiasm put a deep frown on La Forge's face. "You say that now, but the last time we did something like this, my team and I got dropped into high-mountain terrain through heavy fog. One of my men never reached the ground alive." He cast sour glares at Worf and Choudhury. "You two weren't here for the Tezwa assault. This plan might sound clever in theory, but in practice it can go wrong faster than you'd think."

"I am aware of the risks," Worf said. "If you wish to withdraw from the mission—"

His suggestion seemed to offend La Forge. "Not a chance. But if we're being shot into orbit in self-destructing torpedoes, I plan on checking every square centimeter of those things myself. Same goes for the suits."

"I would expect nothing less." Worf switched the display back to its standby mode. "We have orders to deploy in ninety minutes. Assemble at 1340 hours in Torpedo Bay One for suit-up and final preparations. And do not discuss this mission with anyone—captain's orders." The others nodded in affirmation. "Dismissed."

La Forge was the first one up and out of the room, and Velex was close behind him. Choudhury lingered behind with Worf, interposing herself between him and the door. Her features telegraphed a mild air of concern. "I didn't want to say anything in front of Geordi or Velex, but I have a question about the mission."

Worf suspected he knew what was troubling her. "Ask."

"If the *Enterprise* can't risk approaching the planet, what, exactly, is our exit strategy?" When he failed to answer right away, she deduced the bad news. "There is no extraction plan."

He was unable to look her in the eye. "Not as such."

There was a rare note of anger in her voice. "How are we supposed to get off the planet?"

I owe her the truth. "If this mission goes as I expect? Any way we can."

For fifteen minutes that felt like a foretaste of forever, La Forge had lain cocooned in darkness, his breath hot inside the helmet of his orbital skydiving suit, his short but beefy form packed claustrophobically tight inside a modified photon torpedo that he was beginning to fear might soon double as his coffin. After a nausea-inducing rush of sudden acceleration had come the disorienting sensation of weightlessness, as he and the rest of the away team were shot from the *Enterprise* on their interplanetary journey to the third planet, which Choudhury had code-named Mangala, an homage to a deity of war in Vedic astrology.

Alone with his thoughts, La Forge pondered the ethics of the mission that lay ahead of him. Even if they reached B-4 before the inevitable collapse of his positronic matrix, he wasn't sure he could bring himself to erase Data's memory engrams from the android's brain. He knew that doing so was the only way to prevent the android's mental disintegration, which would result in the irretrievable corruption of Data's engrams in any case, but willfully expunging the last traces of his best friend's identity from the universe felt to La Forge as if fate itself was perpetrating a cruel joke upon him.

His bitter reflections ceased as the torpedo casing shattered and flew away in a storm of black shards and dimming sparks. The majestic curve of Mangala's reddish-brown northern hemisphere spread out beneath him, its albedo so intense that he had to squint until the polarizing filter of his suit's visor activated and cut the glare. Free at last to move, he extended his arms and legs to exorcise the stiffness that had accumulated during the short transit from the *Enterprise*. Then he powered up his suit's built-in computer and watched holographic information flicker into view on his virtual heads-up display.

Even as he watched details of the planet's barren, cracked-and-cratered surface speed by far below, he still noted no sensation of movement. *Not enough air resistance for us to feel our movement. We must not have breached the mesosphere yet.* He tapped commands into the simple interface built into the suit's left forearm and activated its low-power deflector screen, which would prevent him from burning up as he and the others made planetfall. Information appeared in ghostly greenish script, superimposed over his view of shredded wisps of cloud that girdled Mangala's equator. At a glance he was able to note his orbital velocity and declination, the distances between himself and the other three members of the away team, and various statistics about his suit's power and air reserves. *So far so good.*

Another quick tap activated the computer-assisted navigation circuit that would control his suit's thruster pack and guide his descent along a preprogrammed approach vector. As the team passed over the terminator line, the landscape below vanished into the cloak of night and the heavens above revealed a bounty of stars. The bright green projection of his suit's HUD blazed in sharp contrast to the enveloping darkness, and he felt the relentless hand of the planet's gravity take hold as the angle of his dive steepened.

All at once came an increase in air resistance, and with a deafening roar a fiery nimbus bloomed around him, held at bay by the suit's deflector field. For several seconds the glow of friction provoked by his plunge through the stratosphere overpowered his view, making it impossible to read his HUD. When it finally abated, he checked his altitude and confirmed that he and the rest of the away team all were still in formation and displaying steady vital signs as they dropped like missiles through the troposphere.

The helmet displays of the orbital skydiving suits boasted a number of helpful features, such as ultraviolet night-vision filters or topographical wireframe overlays, that La Forge was sure the other team members were using to good advantage at that moment, but thanks to the full-spectrum vision provided by his cybernetic eyes, he had no need of the suit's assistance. He engaged his innate UV frequency settings and surveyed the landscape as if it were lit by a spectral, frost-blue twilight. Jagged formations of rock stabbed threateningly skyward beneath the team, and from their current altitude the landing zone on the edge of the mountain range looked precariously narrow. He felt a twinge of anxiety as his suit's thrusters fired, then he relaxed as the HUD confirmed that his approach trajectory was correct. *Good thing the computer's driving. If I had to do this manually, I might not make it.*

A countdown appeared on his display. It reached zero, and his chute automatically deployed. He felt a bone-jarring jolt of deceleration in his back and shoulders as the black canopy snapped open above him. Following the textual prompts on his visor display, La Forge guided himself to a pinpoint landing squarely inside his designated drop zone, in the center of the mountain pass. He stepped clear as he released his canopy. The fluttering swirl of high-tech microfiber fell like a shadow on a cluster of sharp rocks at his back.

Within minutes, La Forge and the others had gathered up their parachutes, doffed their skydiving gear, and regrouped in a close huddle. Worf looked over the group. "Any problems?" The others shook their heads. "Good. Velex, dispose of the dropsuits."

"Aye, sir," the Troyian said. He retrieved and unfolded a small portable entrenching tool from his backpack, excavated a wide but shallow pit, and tossed his skydiving gear into it. La Forge, Worf, and Choudhury did the same. Velex stomped the gear flat, then took a canister of molecular acid from his pack and emptied it over the suits. As their gear rapidly dissolved, he used his miniature spade to bury the pit of slag.

While the ensign concealed the team's abandoned equipment, Choudhury stepped away and made a quick sweep with her civilian-model tricorder. After Velex had finished his task, she returned and beckoned the others toward a narrow trail that led upward. "There's a small plateau about a hundred meters up that path, beyond those rock towers. I'm picking up signs of metal that might be from our mysterious transport."

Worf nodded at Choudhury. "Lead the way." He looked at Velex. "Bring up the rear and guard our backs." Then he started walking as he added, "Move out."

Progress along the path was slow and difficult. At times the sheer cliff faces on either side drew so close that the team had to sidestep through them, and even then they succeeded only with great effort. Though the plateau was not very far away, it took nearly half an hour for them to reach it. They emerged from the pass to see the sleek, silver transport ship parked atop the plateau, away from its edge and nearly flush against the mountainside. Far from being smooth and empty, the plateau was dotted with dozens of small, dagger-like rock formations, each of which was more than large enough to conceal a large humanoid—or who knew what else. Beyond its edge lay an unparalleled view of the adjacent valley, which was dominated by a massive, sprawling factory whose steely depths glowed with dull crimson light.

Choudhury checked her tricorder and reported with a gesture, *No life signs.*

Worf issued orders with his hands, signaling in quick succession: *Keep your eyes open. Choudhury, flank left. Velex, flank right. La Forge, take shelter and cover us.*

Then the Klingon drew his sidearm and prowled straight ahead, through open ground and under the alien transport ship. The two security officers brandished their weapons and stole forward around the edges of the plateau, advancing from one formation to another in a stuttered pattern while covering each other. La Forge marveled at how quiet the three of them were. He couldn't hear their footfalls on the dusty ground; they were like ghosts in the night.

From behind him came the crunch of gravel under a boot. He spun and leveled his Orion-made blaster at a face both strange and familiar. The man looked just like Data, or Lore, or B-4, but his complexion was fully human, and his light-brown hair fluttered in the mountain breeze as he regarded La Forge with a beatific smile. "About time you got here. What kept you?"

The young man's voice sent a chill down La Forge's back. He sounded like Data, but his tone was cocksure and more than a bit arrogant—echoes of Lore's inflections. Unlike Lore, he had no malice in his eyes, and something in his manner spoke of a gentle humor. Drawn by the sound of his voice, Worf, Velex, and Choudhury came charging to La Forge's aid, and the three of them fanned out behind his back. A glance over his shoulder made it clear to La Forge that his compatriots all had their weapons aimed squarely at Data's peculiar doppelgänger.

With exaggerated slowness, the youthful figure lifted his empty hands, palms facing the away team. "I'm not armed. So maybe you could all take a breath and calm down."

Choudhury narrowed her eyes, struggling to make sense of the situation. "B-4?"

The stranger stifled a derogatory chuckle. "Not by a long shot."

Worf snarled and tensed his finger on his blaster's trigger. "Lore!"

"Sorry, no."

Velex stared at his tricorder display, perplexed. "Sirs? One second this guy registers as human, the next he scans as a Soong-type android, and then he doesn't show up at all."

La Forge took the scanner from Velex and studied the details it had recorded about the stranger's internal structure. "You're definitely a Soong-type android, but your body contains systems and components I've never seen before." He switched off the scanner and looked more closely at the man's bluish-gray eyes. "Who are you?"

The android offered his right hand to La Forge, who did not take it. "Doctor Noonien Soong. It's nice to see you again, Geordi. And you, as well, Worf." Seeing that his greeting had been rebuffed, he withdrew his hand with a disappointed half-shrug.

"I do not understand," Worf said. "Data told us you were dead."

"I wanted him to think I was. A boy doesn't really become a man until his father dies. But let's just say that when it came time to shuffle off this mortal coil . . . I had other plans."

Staring in disbelief, La Forge wasn't sure he could take this man at his word—yet everything he said rang true. He spread his arms as if to embrace the impossible. "How can you be Doctor Soong? And assuming you're telling us the truth, and you are who you claim to be—what the hell are you doing here?"

Soong smiled. "That, my friends . . . is a long story."

PART TWO
NOONIEN

2367

7

I look into my son's golden face. Data is a portrait of innocence—or should I say naïveté? His pale eyes stare back at me with wonderment, but I see that the truth of this moment eludes him, despite its copious visible evidence. I'm bruised and broken, propped up against the wall of my home like a marionette with its strings cut, the right side of my face aching where his older brother, Lore, struck me down like the invalid I've become. I feel the warm tickle of fresh blood on my forehead above my right eyebrow and on my fleshy, wrinkled jowls.

Heaven help me, I'll need to spell it out for him. I take a breath and muster my strength.

"Everybody dies, Data." I behold my ageless son and permit myself the luxury and vanity of hope. "Well . . . *almost* everybody."

Data kneels at my side, garbed in the drab brown Pakled rags his brother Lore had been wearing when he'd answered my homing beacon. That was an unforgivable mistake on my part, one I should have taken steps to avoid; damn it to Hell, why didn't I give each of my sons a unique homing-signal frequency? That was lazy of me. Lazy and stupid. But the damage was done, and once I'd realized Lore was awake and roaming the galaxy, I couldn't just let him walk out the door. Keeping him here had been easy; I'd just played on his emotions, which I knew to be primitive and easily manipulated, by telling him I was dying. Of course, Data nearly exposed my lie by asking me to elaborate on my ruse, and it was just dumb luck that Lore was so caught up in the moment that he failed to notice Data's blunder. Curse my cybernetic naïf for breaking down my disguise with his questions! But if I have to confess my sins, I'll admit this is why I love Data best: He's an unblemished soul. He's my redemption.

He studies me with great focus. "Do you believe that we are in some ways alike, sir?"

"In many ways, I'd like to believe." I don't have the strength in me to say the whole truth, and he doesn't have the time to hear it. His ship—which he hijacked to come here, in answer to my interstellar summons—is waiting for him in orbit with a mortally ill child aboard, one who needs to reach a nearby starbase immediately if he's to survive. If only I had more time, I would tell Data everything—a lifetime of secrets and regrets, of hopes and dreams. I would tell him that when I look at him I see all that is best in me: my curiosity, my ethics, my desire to learn objectively about the universe. I would tell him that creating him was my greatest triumph, that he is my gift to the people and culture that nurtured me and made my explorations possible.

But there's no time left. He needs to go, and I need him to leave.

He tilts his head in a way that makes me think of a small, confused bird. "Then it is all right for you to die. Because I will remain alive."

Is he truly exhibiting compassion? It seems unlikely since his brother absconded with his emotion chip, the one I built expressly for Data, packed with selected memories from my life, knowledge that I'd hoped to bequeath to the last of my sons as his birthright. No, I suspect Data is simply parroting words of comfort, pretending to feel empathy. It's just a part of his programming, no doubt the product of Juliana's contribution to his core software. Still, I find myself grateful that he's here, and that some small part of him wants to console me at my end. It takes a tremendous effort, because I'm so tired and my arm feels so leaden, but I reach up and with a feather touch I pat my son's cheek as if to assure him, *It'll be all right.*

My gesture seems to trouble him. "You know that I cannot grieve for you, sir."

Oh, that infallible truthfulness, both endearing and excruciating. I wish everyone were so transparent in their motives as my son. My wondrous son who underestimates himself yet again.

"You will—in your own way." I can see he doesn't know what I'm talking about. I can only assume he hasn't yet realized that, given time, he will internalize these events and that their details will become integrated into his future behaviors; that he will cope with this loss by keeping me alive through unconscious imitation, and that one day, when he least expects it, I will return to him in his dreams. Oh, he has so much left to discover! I wish I could be there to see it, to live through his eyes . . . but this is what it is to be a father. You welcome your children into the world knowing that if all goes the way you plan, you won't get to see the end of their story. It seems a sad notion until you realize that's what gives you hope for the future.

The last smile I offer my son is bittersweet. "Good-bye. Good-bye, Data."

He mirrors my expression, and it's so much like looking backward in time that it makes me want to weep like a child. He nearly breaks my heart as he says, "Good-bye . . . Father."

I reach out, fumbling with a palsied hand, and clasp his. "Go now."

"What shall I do with your corpse?"

Blunt and simple. You have to love him for that. "Leave me here. After my life signs fade . . . this place . . . will self-destruct. It's my . . . funeral pyre." I release his hand. "Go."

He stands and towers over me. "As you wish, Father." His hesitation is brief, but then he turns and leaves. I listen to his footsteps; I hear him stop a few paces outside my front door. There is no sound of a transporter beam; he must be monitoring my life signs with a tricorder, or perhaps he is having his ship monitor my vital signs from orbit—is there anything those starships can't do these days? As I expected, Data won't leave until he knows this is really over.

I close my eyes and let my pain drag me down. With a bit of extra effort I bite down on the capsule embedded in my lower left wisdom tooth, and its enamel surface cracks. I can't taste the drug that seeps from its core, but I can feel it working. My breathing grows shallow and the world melts away. Darkness surrenders to light, and a silver veil is drawn back before me. For a moment it's like staring into the sun but without the pain. Then darkness falls again—

—and when clarity returns, it comes in a torrent. I shudder to consciousness, victim of a chill down my spine. I glance at one of the dozens of antique clocks adorning the walls of my longtime secret abode, and I see that several hours have passed since I dosed myself with hypothoride. I can only hope my ruse has worked, and that Data and his shipmates have left orbit. I have much to do, and the last thing I need now is an audience.

I take my time getting up from the floor. My body is little more than a bloated bag draped over brittle bones, an assortment of aches and pains accumulated over the course of a sedentary lifetime consumed by research and slow experimentation. When I finally regain my feet, I'm short of breath, and my head swims. All my life I dreamed of spending my retirement someplace hot, mostly as a rebellion against a youth spent spelunking one frozen dead world after another at the sides of men like Emil Vaslovik and Ira Graves. Now, after years sequestered in the jungles of Terlina III, I'm reconsidering my decision. The air here is so thick with humidity and pollen that it's a struggle to pull a full breath into my failing lungs.

Crossing the room in doddering steps, I have too much time to think, and I curse myself again for letting Lore trick me, and not for the first time. I spent years crafting that emotion chip for Data; it was a labor of love, a singular achievement that I'd decided long ago would be the last great work of my mortal hands. Yet, as angry as I am, I can't bring myself to hate Lore, not even for this. He's still my son, flawed as he is. Juliana never liked him, of course; she said he embodied all my worst traits and magnified them: my selfishness, my ego, my vanity and insecurities. But she was blind to the better parts of me that live in him—my ambition, my creativity and gift for improvisation, not to mention my sense of humor.

What's done is done. It's time for me to let go of this, and so much else, and move on. I told Data the truth; even if I had more time in this life, I couldn't possibly make another chip like the one his brother stole. I sacrificed parts of my mind to imprint that chip, permanently erased several of my memory engrams in order to transfer them into its subprocessors, all in the hope that I might gift him with that spark of humanity he always seemed to think had eluded him.

The wall is my guide as I shuffle inside my bedroom, and then I use my dresser as a crutch as I sidestep around it. At last I come to an enormous wall tapestry, by far the largest in the house; it hangs from just below the ceiling and reaches to within a centimeter of the floor. It's thick and heavy, an intricate replica of Michelangelo's famous painting *The Creation of Adam* rendered in wool and silk, and it covers most of my room's south wall. A gentle tug frees its lower right corner from its anchor, and I slip behind it, sandwiched between the leaden drapery and the wall as I feel my way to the portal hidden behind it. It wouldn't be obvious to the naked eye, but I know where the security pad is, in the corner where a horizontal groove in the wall meets the seam between two prefabricated panels. I press my hand flat against it, and the previously opaque pad becomes translucent as a bright, ruby-hued biometric sensor scans my palm and fingertips and bathes me in its crimson light. It confirms my identity and opens a second panel directly in front of my face, revealing a retinal scanner. Ignoring the aching in my lower back, I lean forward and ease my right eye into place above the padded sensor.

I hate this part. The bright green light makes me want to squint, but if I do, I'll just have to start the scan over. For a few seconds the pulse leaves me half-blind and seeing purple spots. I hear the low clack of magnetic locks retracting, followed by the soft hum of the panel sliding aside. Luckily, I've kept the next part simple. All I need to do is step inside. Safely inside the small lift, I mumble, "Down." The door closes behind me, and the cylindrical pod descends.

By the time I reach my home's hidden basement,

most of the violet speckles have faded from my sight. My dimly lit workshop gradually brightens as its motion sensors detect my arrival. I hobble toward a rainbow-colored Gordian knot of cables and wires that ring a machine I've spent decades perfecting: my synaptic scanner. It was inspired by a spinning platform I once saw on Exo III, a device for imprinting a featureless, mindless android template with the physical appearance and consciousness of an organic being. That was an impressive piece of technology, but not without its flaws. It was excellent at reproducing the *details* of a person's body and mind, but not one's *essence*. The androids it produced lacked what my old pal Doctor Ira Graves would have called the "human equation"—a remarkably racist term, I know, but that was Ira for you.

My machine improved upon the Exo III device in a number of ways—most of which were my own inventions, plus a few I learned during my years as Graves's research fellow and one that I copied from an ancient artifact Starfleet once secretly hired me to study on Camus II. First and foremost, my machine doesn't spin. Porting one's consciousness into a synthetic brain must be traumatic enough; who wants to wake up from the experience feeling like they've been on an amusement park ride run amok? Not me, thank you very much.

I activate the synaptic scanner's master console with the merest brush of my hand. Every system in the basement purrs to life, and the charge in the air is electric, a tangible sensation of excitement. Tendrils of radiant plasma creep around the machine's edges and fill the air with the tang of ozone; so much power is coursing through that thing it's all but impossible to insulate it fully without making it overheat.

Lying on one side of the scanner, fully prepared and awaiting my arrival, is the most advanced android I've ever built. For the past thirty-four years, every waking moment I could spare from my work on Data's emotion chip has been devoted to building this, an android that incorporates all I've ever learned about cybernetics and artificial intelligence. Its positronic brain is configured for the native expression of human-style emotions, and unlike all my previous creations, this one has no homing beacon, no off switch, and no hidden surprises. It also incorporates a more compact energy source, greater memory capacity and computational power, a built-in subspace transceiver, and a few concealed gizmos and repair kits—always handy.

Looking into its youthful face—*my* face, as it looked sixty years ago, when I was a young man—reminds me of what my ex-wife Juliana always used to ask me, "Why do you always make them in your own image, Noonien? Is it because you like playing God?" I never bothered to answer her when she went on those rants; I didn't see the point of explaining myself, because I was certain she would never understand. I *made* my sons for the same reason a painter paints: because I needed to do it. I didn't make them to serve a function or play a role; I made them just to be, to live, to think and feel, and to choose their own fates. The reason all my androids *looked* like me was because I've spent my whole life working toward the moment when one of these androids would become me—or, to put it more correctly, when I would become one of them.

Now that day is here, and I can hardly keep my hands steady enough to key in the final activation sequence. I'm on the verge of accomplishing what Ira Graves tried but failed to do (a blunder that nearly destroyed Data in the bargain, for which I still curse Graves's memory), and unlike Ira, I already know my plan will work—because I've done it before, thirty-one years ago, when I used an older model of this machine to save Juliana's life by transferring her consciousness into a perfect android replica of her body. I'd had no choice, then. The wounds inflicted by the Crystalline Entity's attack on Omicron Theta had left my beloved wife trapped in a coma by the time I'd flown our escape ship here. I couldn't let her die, so I transitioned her mind into a cybernetic shell. I knew she would've hated me for it, so I programmed her to think she was human, and I built her so well that the rest of the galaxy would believe she was.

Not long after she "woke up" she left me, filed for divorce via subspace text message, and abandoned me to my work. I've had decades to think about my mistakes. To be honest, I'd known for a long time that I was losing her, that we were growing apart. But even though I saw it coming, I refused to believe it. In the letter that came with the divorce decree, she spelled out all the ways I'd disappointed her as a husband. I don't know why I didn't try harder to show her how much she meant to me. All I know is I've had three decades to live with my regrets.

That's about to change. She's still out there somewhere, living her life, oblivious of what she really is. But now that I'm about to follow her across the threshold into a synthetic existence, I can tell her the truth—about what she is, and why I made her the way I did, and how I really feel about her. I'll be able to roll back the clock on her aging, give her back her youth. We'll have eternity to learn how to be happy together.

Not that I plan on giving up my research. After all, what's the point of making myself functionally immortal if I don't continue my work? There are far too many people who need me to continue, whether they know it or not: Juliana, Data, the Federation, and who knows how many artificially intelligent synthetic beings yet to be discovered. I owe it to them to preserve myself, my knowledge, my unique talents, for as long as possible. There's so much left to do.

I sit down on the empty side of the synaptic scanner and ease myself onto it. Deep aches and pinched nerves throb inside my joints, and my spine feels as if it's ready to snap as I fight to lie flat on my back so that the cortical nodes will be at the correct points around my head. The machine pulses and hums; it's holding in standby mode until it senses I am in position. Unable to resist the impulse to anthropomorphize, I chuckle at the fantasy that the machine is impatient with me and is silently urging me to hurry up and get comfortable.

"Hold your horses," I grumble under my breath.

Then I'm settled, and I feel the soothing effects of delta waves being projected into my brain—not enough to render me unconscious, just enough to relax me and keep me calm during the transfer process, which is about to begin. The rest of the lab goes dark as all available power is funneled into the synaptic scanner. I've crossed the Rubicon now. No turning back.

If I had more time—say, another lifetime (or two, or ten)—to work out all the pesky details, this isn't the method I'd choose for transitioning to synthetic consciousness. The truth is, I'm worried even now that I've made a huge mistake, but I see no other way forward. Part of me wonders, *What if this isn't a transfer of consciousness but just a duplication? What if the true me dies on this table and the me that gets up inside that android body is just a clever copy? Will I really have cheated death—or merely created a new being that thinks it's me?*

Thoughts like these have kept me awake more nights than I can count. In a perfect universe, I would create nanomachines that would replace my organic brain cells one by one, duplicating their function and memory content. I'd notice no change in my consciousness during the process of the change. And then, one day, the last of the organic cells would be replaced, and all that would remain would be the synthetic brain, a positronic matrix built in the image of my original brain. Then all that would remain would be to gradually replace my limbs and organs and other tissues with cybernetic components, until I achieve completely artificial status.

But I have neither the technology to make that dream a reality nor the time to invent it from the vapors of my imagination, so this cobbled-together masterpiece of ancient artifacts and cutting-edge technology will have to suffice. I take a deep breath and fix my eyes on a photo of Juliana that I've tacked to the ceiling directly above my side of the machine. If this turns out to be a fatal error, I want her face to be the last thing I see.

I feel a rush of something like vertigo as the synaptic scanner starts the transfer. My eyes lose focus for a moment, and my proprioception becomes confused. When I blink I feel two sets of eyelids moving; I swallow to choke back my fear, and it's as if I have two mouths. Paralysis sets in, and I remember that I programmed a variant of the annular confinement beam used in transporters to keep myself steady on the platform, to prevent myself from sitting up in fear mid-transfer and erasing my biological mind with a feedback pulse before my new positronic brain is finished receiving my consciousness. I fight to clench my right hand into a fist, and I'm rewarded by the uncanny sensation that I have two right hands, one old, one new, acting in synchronicity.

My sight grows dim, and I fear I'll lose the image of Juliana. I refuse to let myself blink. Then I'm seeing two places at once: the patch of ceiling graced with her photo, and a blank gray slab of concrete directly above me. Next comes the most disconcerting but strangely intriguing sensation: I am in two places at once, occupying two bodies with one mind, conscious in both. It's wondrous, but how do I explain it to you? You're basking in the sun while running through the rain; you're listening to jazz inside a crowded, smoke-filled nightclub while squinting at the sun from atop a mountain's snow-capped peak. It's like that.

My bivalence is brief, a fleeting moment of duality that slips from my fingers. Perception and sensation coalesce into a singular point of view once more, and as I inhale, I feel whole again. One body, one pair of hands, one pair of feet. The machine's eerie droning cycles down into silence, and I sit up. Looking down, I see I'm now living inside the android body.

I roll off the slab and land on my feet. The difference is incredible: I've never felt this strong, this sure-footed, not even in the prime of my youth. Even more impressive, all my sensations seem the same: my lab looks and sounds as I remember it; its odors of chlorine and ammonia are as astringent as they are familiar. The sultry heat radiating from the machine warms my skin as I circle it to check its activity log on the master console.

Every nanosecond of the transfer has been recorded; I can see exactly which neurons, engrams, and synaptic pathways were copied at each moment, note when each was successfully duplicated into my new positronic matrix, and when its corresponding biological original was erased from my old brain. Only after I've reviewed all the data do I realize I've done it in a matter of seconds—as a mere human, it would have taken me weeks to read all this. What's more, I have perfect recall of every iota of what I've read.

A quick scan of my old body confirms it's dead, and its brain appears to be completely erased of memories and synaptic connections. I want to shout, "It worked!" I want to dance around my lab and rejoice, but some part of me still doubts this is real. Despite the fact that I was conscious throughout the process, regardless of the fact that I existed in both minds at once before settling into my new body, I can't free myself of this seed of skepticism—or is it guilt? Indulging my penchant for melodrama, I wonder for 0.0003 of a second whether I'm a murderer. Then I realize that if I am, I'm actually a suicide, and this perfect replica I've become is merely a witness, a blameless bystander to a mad old man's misguided self-destruction.

Satisfied that the transfer is complete and successful, I run a self-diagnostic. All my systems are in working order; all my circuits are functioning perfectly. I key in the self-destruct sequence for this house and head for the lift. Half a minute later I'm striding through my house, memorizing its eclectic conglomeration of ancient books and atlases, miniature replicas of dinosaur fossils and animal skeletons, my bronze bust of Shiva, and all my tapestries and antique clocks and high-tech-looking knickknacks of dubious purpose. This has been my sanctum for more than three decades, my refuge from a society that spurned me and a galaxy that seemed hell-bent on killing me. I have done some of the finest work of my life in this place. I pause in my doorway and look back at the spot where, only hours earlier, I said good-bye to my son.

"Good-bye," I say, this time to my life as it was. It's over now, and I need to go.

I run through the jungle to the concealed vessel I've prepared for this journey. As I clear the brush and camouflage from my sleek, well-equipped, and warp-capable starship, I recall what I told Data earlier today, before Lore's arrival, when I explained how I survived the Crystalline Entity's attack on Omicron Theta when all the other scientists there didn't: all my life I've made certain, no matter where I was or what I was doing, to leave open a route of escape.

Obstacles cleared, I open the port-side hatch and walk up the gangway, inside the ship. The ramp retracts and the hatch slides shut behind me, and my state-of-the-art craft powers up with the press of one button on its main console.

Then a distant explosion shakes the ground, and a bloodred mushroom cloud of fire rises into the night sky, blotting out the stars. I permit myself a few seconds of nostalgia and watch my past literally go up in smoke. In a few days, a recycling company I've hired will arrive to collect my fusion generator. Next month, an ecological preservation team I've kept on retainer for the past several years will mop up the scorched mess my exit has left behind.

By then, of course, I will be long gone and far from here.

I initiate the liftoff sequence . . . and leave Terlina III a new man.

8

It's been months since my "death," yet I've never felt so alive. A breeze delights me with the briny perfume of the ocean and the aromas of alien delicacies wafting from beachfront restaurants. Sunlight warms my face. The crash of surf on sand underlies the music of laughing children. I'm immortal, incognito, and dwelling in paradise.

As I stroll the boardwalk of a seaside resort on Pacifica, none of the passersby know me. Today my name is Nomis Sutay, and thanks to a few simple cosmetic tweaks—some epidermal spots and a subtle darkening of my hair—and a few changes to my biofeedback circuit, I'm a young Trill business executive on a vacation. I have dozens of these identities ready for use, each complete with its own retinal patterns, fingerprints, and official documentation. It's amazing what one can do when one knows how to manipulate the systems and records of the civil government. Of course it also helps that I had decades in which to prepare and establish these alter egos—decades in which I worked under other aliases as an off-site contractor, writing security software to prevent exactly this kind of subterfuge.

Waves collide and collapse into foam, smoothing the

white-sand beach into a tabula rasa as they recede. The ocean calls to me like a siren, and I can't resist its lure. I kick off my sandals, pick them up, and carry them as I leave the boardwalk and pad toward the water. The sand is hot and soft under my feet, almost like regolith. It seems unnaturally fine. Perhaps the resort uses a processed, artificial sand as a top layer for its beach. They wouldn't be the first. Not that I'm complaining—I have no standing to criticize others for seeking perfection in the synthetic.

Sea foam surges over my feet, and bits of seaweed tickle my ankles.

For a moment I consider staying on Pacifica. It's so beautiful that I can almost imagine spending aeons savoring its natural wonders—a brilliant azure sky painted each evening with a sunset so exquisite that it breaks my heart; endless expanses of open sea, all of it so clear and blue that I almost can't find the horizon, because sea and sky become one in the distance.

Alas, I know I can't stay. It's dangerous for me to remain in any one place for too long. As it is, I need to avoid most of the Federation's core worlds. Too many automated facial-recognition sensors in public spaces. Most of the time they're just passive collectors of intelligence, but the last thing I need is to be recognized by some computer as one of my sons.

That might be the worst part of my ongoing charade: I desperately want to contact Data to tell him I'm alive and share the news of my transformation, but the risks are too great. He would probably feel duty-bound to reveal my secret to Starfleet, and then there'd be no end to my troubles. Despite his success at persuading Starfleet to recognize his legal rights, Data's status under Federation law is still unclear—which means that my status is now likewise hard to define. As a human being I had significant protections for my person and effects. Do I still? Or did I surrender those rights when I gave up my organic existence? These might be fascinating legal quandaries for someone to debate and resolve in a court of law, but not when my life and freedom are on the line. I refuse to put up my existence as the stakes in that gamble.

No, the smart thing to do is to stick to my plan. I have many personas to establish on dozens of worlds, so that I can ensure my very long future will be secure—from both financial concerns and inquisitive minds. Once I've ensconced myself somewhere safe, I'll trigger Juliana's homing beacon and bring her home to me. Then I can rejuvenate her body, deactivate her planned senescence, and revive her. Of course, then comes the hard part: explaining to her what she really is, and why I had no choice but to preserve her life that way. Ever since she left, I've been afraid that she won't forgive me when I reveal the truth to her. I keep hoping she will, and that we can be together from then on, both of us forever young . . . but what if she can't accept a synthetic existence? What if she hates me for what I've done to her? Such questions haunt me. On those rare occasions when I still dare to shut myself down for a few minutes to let myself dream, my subconscious conjures anxiety plays, almost always on this theme.

The surf is up to my knees when I finally tear my gaze from the sunset and start back to the boardwalk. I'm still suffering an alarming number of odd moments as I learn to control my new sense of time. Knowing that I have eternity ahead of me, I'm often content to let hours bleed away while I do nothing; it feels sometimes like time is rushing past me in a blur. I imagine I must look like a statue when that happens.

At other times, when I need to take in a lot of information and react quickly, I'm able to perceive the passage of picoseconds. I can think far faster than my android body can act, and that's no small boast, because I can be faster in my actions and reactions than just about any organic humanoid known to science. Data is almost fast enough to catch an old-fashioned chemically propelled projectile known as a bullet; I'm more than fast enough to do it. Not that I would have to, as most ordinary projectiles won't pierce the armor mesh that protects my core systems, or the armor plating that shields my positronic brain. And nothing less than a heavy stun setting from a phaser would even get my attention.

Dusk is settling on the resort as I step up from the now-cool sands onto the vintage-style boardwalk. I put my sandals back on and whistle a chipper tune to occupy my thoughts—and keep myself rooted in real time—during the walk back to the Crown Star hotel.

The Bolian doorman smiles as I pass him at the entrance. "Welcome back to the Crown Star, Mister Sutay."

I throw him a jaunty salute. "Good to be back."

On my way past the front desk, the night manager, a comely female Bajoran, waves at me. "Good evening, Mister Sutay."

"And a lovely one it is, Syrinna." I wink at her, and she blushes.

Yes, I've styled this cover persona as a shameless flirt. A man has to have some fun if living forever is going to be anything other than a dreadful bore.

I return to my room, shower, and change into fresh clothes for the evening. To my chagrin, I'm running a few minutes late; I have dinner reservations at one of the town's more acclaimed purveyors of nouvelle cuisine. I don't need to eat for sustenance, but it's imperative I maintain appearances. If someone should ever make a detailed inquiry into the background of this character I've invented, it will seem more than a trifle suspicious if he never took a single meal during a two-week sojourn. Or never dallied with any of the many available young women also staying at the resort. What can I say? I'm just demonstrating a keen attention to detail.

Tonight's details include an appetizer of Pacifican lump crab meat served over crunchy sea greens dressed in Argelian sesame oil; an entrée of sautéed deep-sea scallops over a savory puree of white beans and garlic, garnished with local edible flower petals and accompanied by a side of peppery greens lightly dressed with a balsamic reduction; and two glasses of a crisp white wine with a pleasantly mineral quality, a Vermentino imported all the way from Sardinia, on Earth. Not wanting to play the part of a glutton, I skip dessert. I leave a generous tip and resist the impulse to make a pass at my Deltan waitress on my way out of the restaurant.

Not much feels different since my change, but two things I miss are the sensation of being pleasantly stuffed after a big meal, and basking in the warm glow of alcohol after a couple of drinks. Wine still tastes the same, maybe even better. The chemical receptors in my new mouth are far more numerous and precise in their sensory capacities than what I had before. I can *taste* the alcohol in my drink, I simply can't feel it in my body. It saddens me to know that my consumption of spirits has been reduced to an aesthetic exercise. I can play the parlor game of vivisecting the bouquet, flavors, and "mouthfeel" of a wine better than ever before, but it feels like a hollow pursuit now that I'm immune to the consequences of my appetites.

It's a short walk back to the hotel. Actually, it seems

like a short walk to everything around here. The resort was obviously designed as a bit of a tourist trap; its few square kilometers are packed with points of interest and distraction, all dispersed or camouflaged just enough that one never loses the illusion of being in a tropical retreat, but all close enough that one never sees any need to use mechanized transportation—which, of course, might tempt a person into leaving the resort and visiting the rest of this gorgeous planet.

Faint echoes of footsteps trip down the alleyways behind me, and I stop to listen. The soft reports of footfalls cease. I spend several seconds listening to a zephyr disturb the fronds of the transplanted date palms that line the resort's main street like sentinels. I discern the voices of other people in my vicinity, the nocturnal chittering of insects in the beach grass, laughter from the terrace of a house ahead of me, a harp's ethereal music from a farther room. Not sure of what I expect to find, I look back along my path from the restaurant. I see nothing amiss.

Quickening my steps, I resume walking. I'm hyperalert now. My eyes scan the windows of buildings on the other side of the street, seeking the tiniest reflection that might betray a stalker in my shadow. I pay attention to olfactory cues, as if an enemy might be flushed out by his overuse of cologne. Most of all I listen, analyzing every bit of audible noise I receive for patterns. Then my diligence is rewarded—I hear the echoed footsteps again.

They are not my own steps coming back to me, of this I'm certain. The intervals between steps deviate from my own by as much as nine-hundredths of a second, and as little as four-hundredths. It is the ostensibly random variance of another person tracking my movements.

Who would be following me? Who could know who I am? Or why I'm here?

As urgently as I wish to know the answers to those questions, I can't risk a confrontation. If I'm wrong, if this is just a mistake, I'll do more harm than good by forcing a conflict. No, the best response is the one I'm prepared for: evasion and escape.

I hurry past a sprawling lawn with a white gazebo and past the next building ahead, which claims to be a museum devoted to Pacifican aquatic archeology but which I can tell with a glance inside its lobby is little more than a slapdash fraud devoted to fleecing tourists. I turn the corner and hope I'm at least momentarily hidden from my stalker's line of sight. I kick off my sandals and start running. Barefoot, I move much faster than in those awkward flip-flops, and more quietly. At my first opportunity I cross the road and veer off across a dark lawn. Then I pick up speed. In the darkness I hear my would-be spy racing to catch up with me. I leap over a tall hedgerow and roll through a somersault as I land on the other side.

It's a short distance now to the Crown Star, but if I'm being tailed, there might be hidden surveillance devices watching my lodging. Walking in the front entrance suddenly seems like a bad idea. Fortunately, I took the precaution of checking into the adjacent Royal Pacifican Suites under another of my identities, in the unlikely event of a situation such as this. In the twenty seconds it takes me to reach a small copse of palm trees near the Royal Pacifican and take cover behind their broad fronds, I've banished the Trill-style spots from my skin, lightened my hair to a dirty blond, and changed my eyes from brown to green. It took me ten years to perfect the chameleon circuits in this body, but right now I feel that was time well spent.

Whoever is searching for me will likely soon return to this island's strip of hotels in the hope of reacquiring me as a target. My Watcher might already be here. I look at my cranberry tropical-print shirt and baggy beige shorts. These are common-enough clothes on this island, but I can't risk drawing the Watcher's attention by waltzing out from cover in a shirt that sets a new bar on the concept of *loud*. I might as well just jump up and shout, "I'm over here!"

How do I cross the last few meters to the Royal Pacifican without drawing undue attention? I see a honeymooning young Betazoid couple stroll past on their way to the hotel, and I see my chance. I strip off my clothes, distend my abdomen to feign a potbelly, and, as nonchalantly as possible, fall into step a few paces behind the naked newlyweds. Just as I hope, most of the more prudish types in the vicinity avert their eyes, and the rest pay all their attention to the two gorgeous specimens ahead of me. Who wants to stare at a naked fat man?

I walk through the lobby of the Royal Pacifican with my head up, confident, as if I owned the place. The front desk clerk obviously wants so badly to laugh at the sight of me that it's killing him, but he plasters a stiff, crooked smile on his white-mustached Efrosian face and beholds me with wide, frost-blue eyes as I step up to him and nod. I greet him in a deeper voice than the one I've been using next door. "Good evening."

"Welcome back, Mister Tasker."

My direct eye contact makes him uneasy, so I refrain from blinking, just to make it worse for him. "Thank you, Kinett."

He swallows nervously and blinks twice in quick succession. "How may I help you?"

"Any messages for me?"

A shake of his head. "No, sir." He purses his lips so fiercely they blanch.

"Ah. Too bad." I press my hands comically to my bare chest. "I'm waiting for a suit to be delivered." I gesture at myself and shrug. "Laundry day." I walk away toward the guest elevators. "If and when my tailor sees fit to arrive, send him up to my room, will you?"

"At once, sir."

I step into the lift and press the button for the twenty-third floor. My ride up is quiet and uneventful, thanks to the discreetly averted stares of the Bolian couple and their three young children who are sharing the elevator car with me. They step out onto the nineteenth floor, and I finish the last few seconds of my ride alone.

The doors open again, and I sprint down the hallway to my room. I adjust my palm print, retinal patterns, and biofeedback profile to the presets for this identity, and step into range of the automatic sensors for the door to my room. "Liam Tasker. Unlock and open." The door slides open with a soft hiss, and I rush in. Within minutes I've garbed myself in a dark suit with a black shirt, and a pair of immaculately polished black shoes. From the drawer by the bed I retrieve a locked duranium case that opens for only one thing: an encrypted, short-range signal transmitted by my positronic matrix. The box springs open, and I retrieve the backup remote command unit for my ship, the *Archeus,* and its feminine-persona AI, whom I've named Shakti.

The device is small and rectangular, sixteen centimeters by nine square, and only five millimeters thick, but it's my lifeline to my ship—and my ticket to a fast escape. I've made only two of them, and I always try to have one with me and the other hidden nearby. With a few simple taps on its smooth interactive surface, I direct the *Archeus* to beam up all my personal effects from my room at the Crown Star, and then my supplemental baggage from here at the Royal Pacifican. Then

I open a subspace channel to the ship. "Shakti, are you there?"

Her silken voice is sympathetic. *"Yes, Noonien. You sound upset. Are you all right?"*

"I'm fine, but I need you to do a few small favors for me."

"I understand."

"First, power up the warp drive and plot a course away from the Federation."

I hear the skepticism in her tone. *"Do you have a particular direction in mind?"*

"Start by taking us toward the Taurus Dark Cloud. I'll adjust the course en route."

"As you wish. What else can I do for you?"

The mellisonant hum of a transporter beam turns my head, and I watch my bags and other personal items vanish from my decoy hotel room. I key in new commands for *Archeus* via the remote and lock my ship's transporters onto my coordinates. "Please call the front desks at the Crown Star and Royal Pacifican hotels for me. . . . Tell them I'm checking out."

Hours later I'm light-years away, and only now do I stop and wonder if I might be the slightest bit paranoid. Reviewing my eidetic memory of the evening's events, I realize that I never actually saw my Watcher. Footsteps alone were enough to send me on a mad dash. At the time, my analysis seemed reasonable to me, but now I'm doubting myself.

It seems implausible that my positronic brain could have manufactured an auditory hallucination. I tested and refined this body's sensory components for years; their reliability seems beyond reproach. All my internal diagnostics confirm my systems are free of error or malfunction, but what if the glitch is in my mind? Not a simple misfire, mind you, but one more fundamental and insidious. If I made an error in the structure of my synaptic network, I might have left myself prone to any number of maladies—paranoia being the least of them. Even if I wasn't mistaken about what I heard, I might have drawn profoundly flawed conclusions.

I open my left parietal flap for access to the diagnostic port of my positronic matrix, and then I unwind an isolinear data cable that is connected at one end to *Archeus*'s main computer. "Shakti, I'm patching in. Would you be a dear and please run a level-one diagnostic on me?"

"I'd be happy to, Noonien."

Sometimes an objective perspective is what's needed to make an accurate diagnosis. I insert the cable's prong into my diagnostic port. "Ready when you are."

There is no physical sensation to the exam, but I am keenly aware of the test pulses pinging my various circuits and subprocessors. A swift and steady flow of information courses through me like thread through a needle's eye. I avert my eyes from the situation monitor on the cockpit's starboard console; I don't want to bias the results by observing the intermediate benchmark data. After several minutes of silent probing, Shakti rewards me with her gentle bedside manner: *"Just a few moments longer, Noonien. We're almost done."*

"No hurry. It's not as if I have someplace to be."

The digital flood abates nanoseconds before Shakti says, *"Diagnostic complete."*

"And? What's the verdict?"

"All systems operating within normal parameters. No errors detected." With a smidgen of mockery, she adds, *"You're fine, you old hypochondriac."*

Why I thought that programming my ship's AI with

a colloquial dialogue subroutine and a full range of humanoid idioms was a good idea, I'll never know. I unplug the test cable from my diagnostic jack, coil it, and put it away. I am reassured by the results of the independent test, but doubts linger. How would I even test for a fundamental design flaw? All that *Archeus* and Shakti can do is measure my systems' performance against the parameters that I defined as normal. But what if those parameters themselves are wrong? I might never know.

For now, I'll have to proceed on faith. If I'm not paranoid, and I was being followed by someone on Pacifica, then maintaining a state of heightened awareness and increased discretion is the best response from now on. If I'm wrong, such precautions won't do any harm.

I leave the cockpit, head aft to my small cabin, strip off my clothes, and step inside the cramped head. Though I have no need of a lavatory, and briefly considered removing the one on *Archeus* to make room for some additional storage, I decided to keep it in case I ever need to pass myself off as an organic traveler, or find myself accommodating a biological passenger. Regarding my reflection in the mirror, I watch myself transform with a few simple bits of cybernetic wizardry. I adjust the pigmentation settings in my synthetic follicles, turn all my hair gray from head to toe, then accelerate the growth rates of my facial follicles until I sport a moderately robust gray beard. By strategically deploying synthetic collagen, I simulate the ravages of age upon the circles under my eyes, the skin of my forehead, and the droop of my jowls. My eyes become a hazel mix of gold, green, and brown, and then I shift my skin tone to a warm honey-brown by means of some simple catalytic reactions.

The *pièce de résistance*: some subtle ridges at the top

of my nasal bridge. My Bajoran persona, Taylen Jull, comes to life. I smile at myself. "Hello, there. Nice to meet you."

Yes, this will do nicely.

I return to the cockpit, walking with a slight limp in my left leg—the lingering aftereffect of an injury poor Jull suffered as a slave of the Cardassians during the occupation, before he escaped and made a new life for himself in the Federation, amassing a significant fortune in the process. "Shakti, please set a new course." I ease my body into the pilot's seat with the stiff and measured movements of a man in less than prime condition. "Our new destination is Tessen III."

"Laying in the new course now."

Tessen III, a remote but populated Federation world, is where I will begin fortifying the virtual "paper trail" for my latest *nom de voyage*. I need to make sure there are acquaintances and business associates for people to contact when they investigate this persona, so that I can use it to establish a long-term cover without arousing personal or governmental suspicions.

It will be the first of many stops I need to make over the next few years. I've planned my itinerary with great care. Each world on which I build a part of my ersatz history needs to be sophisticated enough that its records are accessible from elsewhere in the Federation, so that my stories can be confirmed with a minimum of effort. However, each world must be remote enough that no one is likely to make the effort to visit it in person, and it must not be so saturated in security technology that I risk having my biometric profile recorded and disseminated.

If I have learned anything from my brush with exposure on Pacifica, it's that the time for vacations is over. I need to be more careful and less visible. Tempting as it might be to roam the galaxy like some carefree interstellar vagabond, that is not the road I have chosen. I created a legion of disposable identities as a means to an end, and now I must put them to use.

The time has come for me to disappear and let my fictions take on lives of their own.

2368–2369

9

Until I became postorganic, it would never have occurred to me that I might have a day that lasts three years, but that's the sort of thing I've come to take for granted as my paranoia intersects with my artificial body's lack of a need for sleep. It's sort of surreal, to be honest. Deep night and daylight blur from one to the other and back again, and I hardly notice the difference. Of course, I spend most of my time sequestered like a lucifuge, expending absurd degrees of effort on not being noticed or recognized. It's fortunate that most of what I need to do can be accomplished with a minimum of personal contact. I rarely need to risk showing my face in major cities anymore. Usually, it's enough on most of these lonely balls of rock to check in at some satellite office in a remote territory. Once some underpaid out-of-the-loop minor bureaucrat verifies my credentials, his superiors never even think to question him.

Most of what I'm doing these days is setting the stage for the future. Opening accounts. Moving credits around. My research wasn't free, after all; it took decades to amass enough credit to live in isolation. I earned a small fortune developing the sophisticated algorithms that govern interstellar credit fluctuations in an economy that has no cash and few fungible commodities. It was an even more boring task than it sounds, but I knew it would pay dividends—both figuratively and literally—as the Federation expanded and opened its borders to foreign investment. Every time the Ferengi carp that the Federation's economy is "primitive" and in need of their expert guidance, I laugh. The system I helped the Interstellar Commerce Commission put into place was designed to blindside the Ferengi over the course of decades. By the time they realize what has happened, their future will be linked forever to the Federation's.

And the profits from that transaction will accrue to the Ad Astra Finance Corporation, which is a wholly owned subsidiary of the Ceres Finance Group, which in turn is controlled by the Cygnus Capital Group LLC, which is roughly twenty or thirty shell companies removed from the Soong Partners Holding Corporation, to which a staggering amount of interstellar credit flows on a regular schedule. Part of crafting a plan for immortality was realizing that, in the mind of the public, no person lives forever—but corporations go on and on.

I admit, I felt at first like I was doing something wrong. Nesting corporations within one another and hiding the connections in such notoriously secretive banking entities as the Bank of Bolarus, the Orion Depository, or the Ferengi Central Reserve seems on its face to be at least questionable if not blatantly criminal. But the system permits their existence, so I see no reason not to exploit it. After all, what's my alternative? Should I surrender myself—the first truly self-made man—to the government for analysis and potential vivisection? Don't be ridiculous.

Instead, I wander the fringes of Federation territory,

tapping into its communications and financial infrastructures from the most far-flung and least-monitored points in its domain. One careful trade and transaction at a time, I lay the foundation for a brighter future, for a fortune that will grow and pass from one manufactured identity to another in perpetuity. Don't misunderstand my intentions; this is not about greed. It's about security. I need to do this so that I can live a private life while wielding subtle influence on the direction of science and politics, to shape a future in which sentient artificial intelligence and synthetic beings can live in harmony with organic beings, enjoying the protections and recourse of the law, and thrive without the burden of discrimination based upon the nature of their origin. It's a crazy dream, but I believe in it.

But I digress. My mind is a maelstrom since the transition. I can harbor so many trains of thought that I distract myself. One part of me continues as if on autopilot, navigating rote tasks or executing the rigmarole of daily life, while other parts of my consciousness carom away on wild tangents. The result is that I sometimes feel only half-invested in my present moment. My disjointed time-sense, my fine-grain perception and ultra-long-term perspective, feel jarring to me. Time simultaneously streaks past and creeps in its petty pace, leaving me lost in the present. Perhaps it would feel different to me had I been born to such a consciousness, but having spent the first eighty-odd years of my life as flesh and bone, I find this new state alien beyond words.

I blink and I'm on Antos IV, incorporating a dummy company under an assumed name.

A blur of names and faces, a flurry of shaken hands and empty smiles, and I'm on Megara, passing my time on a park bench, waiting for an appointment that doesn't happen for another eight hours. I spy a tree not unlike a willow with its great crown of drooping boughs, and it triggers a deep memory, of the spot on Omicron Theta where I met my Juliana and knew in the span of a breath that she would be the love of my life.

Even now the details of that memory are hazy, the product of inexact organic engrams that rely on associative triggers—one of the strengths of biological memory, but also one of its great flaws. Tying information recall to sensory triggers creates powerful mechanisms, but it also leads to unexpected activations. Worst of all, the chemical nature of organic engrams leads to inexact recall at best. I compare the lucidity of memories formed after my transition to those from the life I lived before, and there is no comparison. My new brain records its experiences with far greater fidelity and clarity than my human brain ever did, and I am able to relive my post-transition moments down to the finest sensory details. By contrast, my human recollections are like blurry snapshots of frozen moments recorded through a mud-covered lens.

And yet . . . my memory of Juliana is so clear, like spring waters. The shocking blue of her eyes, the sweetness of her Irish lilt, the burnished copper hue of her hair, the rosy flush of her cheeks are all so vivid. Her essence was a firebrand, making its mark in my psyche from the first moment I met her. She was indubitably unique in the universe, brilliant and special and difficult and so much more. How could I have helped but be smitten?

It pains me now to think how many of those moments must already have been lost to the imperfections of my former human brain. I try to dredge up those long-past days and give them new life, but it's as if the pages have been ripped from my book of memory, leaving only dead-end listings in an index of regrets. Only the palest snippets of those days stay with me. I remember flashes of the afternoon we spent in a park, in the capital of Marvala IV, right after we got married in a secret ceremony. It was cool and sunny, early spring, and children were racing model sailboats on the rectangular pond. The trees had just recovered their leaves after a hard winter. We sat on a blanket, sharing a bottle of white wine, and I snapped a photo of us by holding my pencam at arm's length. It was an awkward photo that overemphasized my nostrils, but it was one of the few pictures ever taken of us together, and I treasured it right up till the day the Crystalline Entity laid Omicron Theta waste, along with my lab and that precious photo, which occupied a place of honor on my desk, beside my workstation.

There were other moments, of course. Outside her window there was a nest of rock doves, and when our romance was in its early days, I lay awake many times beside her, enthralled by the soft cooing of the birds in the blue-gray dim of the predawn hours. That recollection unleashes a flood: a night we cooked Polish sausages and sauerkraut with beer on her stovetop because the replicator was broken; the time she asked me to sing to her when she felt ill, and the only song I knew well enough to attempt solo and a cappella was the centuries-old comic ballad "Rocky Raccoon"; we made a habit of sleeping late on Saturdays and then treating ourselves to a brunch that always included raisin bread and mimosas.

And then I wince at the memory of her falling, stricken by the devouring energies of the Crystalline Entity, and her sightless stare as I carried her inside my escape ship and fled that world for my secret redoubt on Terlina III. I used every trick I knew to keep her alive, to cheat death, but I felt her slipping away from me a bit more with each passing day. And so I turned my great secret project, the synaptic scanner and the blank android prototype, to the task of saving the only woman who has ever mattered more to me than myself.

The scanner and her new positronic brain were ready before her new body was. I hadn't realized before I started how mind-bogglingly difficult, verging on impossible, it would be to capture the totality of her, to remake her in all her perfection, all her imperfection, all her fathomless humanity, all her peerless beauty and infinite subtlety. Fortunately for us both, I was just deluded and desperate enough to try. But it was so slow to come to fruition, and while I was tinkering and refining petty details, her life ebbed. Out of time, I put her in the synaptic scanner and ported her mind into its new form, but then I left her inactive so I could finish my work.

Even though I'd known she was not really gone, that the quintessence of her had been preserved and was only sleeping, I couldn't help but feel I was lying to myself, that my beloved had died on that table, never to return. It didn't matter how many times I told myself her mind, memories, and soul were safe inside a positronic matrix waiting to awaken; I still wept as I dug a grave in the jungle and interred her native form. My tears mixed with my sweat as I hacked through roots and manually excavated that pit until it was two meters deep, and when I dropped that first shovelful of loam atop her shrouded corpse, it felt so real, so final.

It took me nearly two months to finish refining her new body so that it would fool even her. I hoped that any details I might have missed could be explained away as products of imperfect tissue regeneration, stemming from the injuries the Crystalline Entity had inflicted. For the eight weeks I spent reincarnating my beloved Juliana, I left my lab each night in tears. When I went to bed I'd lie awake, staring at the emptiness on her side of the bed until I shuffled over and slept there myself so I wouldn't have to look at it and know she was gone.

The day I roused her, like a prince breaking the spell of slumber on a hexed princess, was one of the happiest of my life. Juliana awoke with no suspicion that she was anything other than what she'd remembered being. I'd told her she had languished in a coma since the Omicron Theta tragedy, and she believed me without hesitation. It felt to me like a miracle.

Not long afterward she left me, for all the reasons I'm sure the original Juliana eventually would have, and I wondered if perhaps I'd made her too well.

Now I'm in motion, and the endless night of stars drifts past me, a steady stream of space and time, an unbroken continuity hypnotic in its homogeneity. At high warp, the stars seem claustrophobically close together. It's an illusion, a trick of perception, but then so is reality, when you think about it. Reality is what we perceive, what we experience.

I'm leaving a bank on Argelius, aglow with success after securing a very generous line of credit for a new interstellar shipping company. It's a more pedestrian enterprise than many I've inaugurated under my myriad corporate umbrellas, but one I suspect will be eminently useful when it comes time to move resources and equipment without having to answer awkward questions or fabricate convoluted explanations. As I cross the lobby, I spy through an open door a conference room and a long table on which rests a large sheet cake—or, rather, what remains of it now that the partygoers have descended upon it like locusts. At the center of the festivity is an older man, a white-haired and dignified Trill gentleman who looks abashed at the attention. A paper banner on the back wall of the room is emblazoned with metallic-red letters: FAREWELL.

It's a retirement party. I've seen dozens of these. Pathetic affairs, to the last.

I've avoided spectacles like this my whole life. I made a point of never retiring precisely so I'd never have to sit and smile through one of these stale-cake and cheap-sparkling-wine fiascoes. I've hated them ever since the farewell party the faculty threw in absentia for my first cybernetics professor, Doctor Emil Vaslovik, Ph.D. He was one of the most brilliant men I've ever known; he taught me more about robotics, cybernetics, artificial intelligence, biomechanics, and computer programming in one summer internship than I learned during my next eight years at the Daystrom Institute as an undergraduate, and then as a graduate student and a doctoral fellow. Some of my most ambitious ideas were the product of his teachings.

I know Vaslovik didn't retire. He simply vanished, along with all the artifacts we found on Exo III. He had been bursting with ideas, many of which became touchstones for his graduate assistant, Ira Graves. None of the other faculty at my dissertation defense got a word in between me and Graves as we peppered each other with the latest cutting-edge ideas in AI and cybernetic design. To tell the truth, I think most of them were convinced my dissertation was hogwash. There I was, some cocky twenty-six-year-old, telling them how I planned to revolutionize AI by creating positronic brains, even though everyone else in the field had "proved" it was impossible. If it hadn't been for Graves, they probably would have refused to grant me my doctorate.

I've always wondered what became of Vaslovik after

he vanished. I've long imagined he did it so he could finally work in peace, away from all the naysayers. That made him my hero, and I promised myself one day I'd do the same, as soon as I proved my theories about the positronic brain. Of course, after Graves also left the Institute, the ridicule began.

"Soong's folly," my detractors said of my research. Not even Graves—who by then was well on his way to becoming a superstar in AI, with all his research projects grotesquely overfunded by the confluence of Federation grants and private investors—believed in me. He smugly suggested I ought to come work for him instead of "making a damn fool" of myself.

Yes, I admit it. I despised him. He was brilliant. He did revolutionary work. I had great respect for his achievements. But the man was an egotistical, misogynistic troglodyte. Imagine, if you will, a hormonally imbalanced Neanderthal who is inexplicably graced with a brilliant gift for computer engineering and artificial intelligence programming. A being that can craft an elegant virtual sentience by day, and go on drunken howling sexual rampages by night. That monstrous hybrid of genius and savagery was Ira Graves.

Perhaps I've exaggerated his faults ever so slightly. But you get my point.

There were times I doubted myself. I spent years trying to unlock the secrets of several half-sketched ideas I'd once seen in Vaslovik's notes: proposals for circuit pathways and isosynaptic structures that would give rise to human-style emotions natively in an artificial intelligence. The promise of such technologies fascinated me, but I could never figure out how to reconcile them with my own designs for a positronic matrix. It was maddening to see such a tantalizing possibility shimmering like a mirage, only to have it ripple and fade when I tried to render it in concrete terms as a prototype. I doubt even Vaslovik knew how to porter those ideas over the threshold separating the theoretical from the practical. But he was like that—always concocting ideas for grandiose technologies that no one could possibly have the resources to build, or the wisdom to use properly if they did.

Vaslovik was probably the only person I ever knew who believed I would succeed in my dream of creating a stable positronic matrix. At least, he made *me* believe that he believed in me.

Months seem to pass like hours as I work my way from Benecia to Evora, alighting on multiple worlds just long enough to establish new shell corporations, complete with encrypted subspace comms that shuffle incoming messages from one to another in endless loops, masking both the origins and destinations of their signal traffic. Cloaked in a different alter ego on each planet, I build a network of shadows, a web of phantoms that will surround me like a fortress in the years to come. From the lush Summer Islands of Deneva to the blustery boulevards of Nokolu, Fellebia's metropolis of commerce, I roam the Federation's core and periphery with a singular purpose. I pass my time between stops reading all the science journals, political news, and heartbreaking works of literary genius that I never had time for during the past sixty years. Ultimately, I'm forced to conclude I didn't miss much.

I'm on Hanolan, my business concluded, admiring the perfume of wildflowers on a summer wind as I am ferried back to the open-air starport outside the sprawling colony's city limits. The hovercraft makes a scheduled stop and picks up a few new passengers bound for the landing fields. Among them are a pair of twin brothers, young Efrosians with golden manes and their culture's traditional drooping mustaches and upswept eyebrows. As the two men converse in a discreet hush, I note how well they mirror each other in every glance, laugh, and gesture.

Seeing them together reminds me of my boys, though they never got the chance to interact like this at the Omicron Theta colony. After the debacle of Lore threatening the other scientists, I had been forced to shut him down and disassemble him. I knew it had to be done, that it was the right thing to do, but still it broke my heart. He was my son, a part of me, yet we took him apart as if he were nothing but a broken appliance. Juliana said it was my fault for trying to realize Vaslovik's designs for emotional emulation circuits in an incompatible technology, and I knew she was right. I even admitted it—a rare concession on my part.

That wasn't enough to earn Juliana's forgiveness, though. She resented me for making a new android after our first three prototypes had all failed so dramatically. "Miscarriages" she'd called those first three, and the grief in her eyes told me she wasn't being facetious. She begged me to abandon my research into androids and focus on pure AI instead. I couldn't tell her that even then I was planning the greatest escape of all time—a swindle of the Grim Reaper, an indefinite extension of my lease on life through the miracle of synaptic scanning and cybernetics.

What I never told Juliana, or anyone else, is that Lore—and later, Data—would not have been possible without B-4. I had to design him in secret, outsource the fabrication of his components to private laboratories across the Federation, and then assemble him in a rented lab on a small rock called Draken IV, on the edge of the Romulan Neutral Zone. It's not how I wanted that breakthrough to happen, but Juliana's intransigence made it necessary. The deaths of the first three prototypes had been simply too much for her to take. And it wasn't that I didn't grieve for those early cybernetic stillbirths; on the contrary, I wept for them just as bitterly as she did, if not more so. I was simply more driven to find the solution than she was. I couldn't let my sorrows stand in the way of my dream. And so I took a short leave from Omicron Theta, under the pretense of auditing a seminar at the Vulcan Science Academy, and continued my work alone. I knew I was on the verge of success, and I refused to stop short.

On a windy, gray, and finger-numbingly cold winter morning, B-4 awoke full of questions and innocence. His positronic matrix was primitive but stable, and he hungered for knowledge, for input. I did my best to accommodate his need for education, but before long I understood that his ability to grasp complex concepts and interpersonal relationships was far too limited for him to ever become more than a good-hearted simpleton. He was my son and I loved him, but I didn't let my affections blind me to his shortcomings.

Tears stung my eyes as I lied to him. "You're going to sleep for a while."

He cocked his head and stared at me with wide eyes devoid of guile. "Why?"

"Because I need to do some work on your systems, and you need to be off line while I work. When I'm done, I'll wake you up again. I promise." Then I reached around his torso and found his on-off switch. I pressed it, and his chin dipped against his chest. His childlike gaze went flat, and his face—my face, rendered in metallic hues—went slack. I packed him away in a carton deliberately mislabeled as "laboratory equipment," and I turned off the lights and computers on my way out the door. I left a deposit covering the rental of the lab for the next few decades, and I convinced myself that one day I would go back for him.

I went home to Omicron Theta, enriched with the knowledge of how to stabilize a positronic matrix. Having done the impossible once, I resolved to apply the lessons from B-4's inception to more advanced prototypes. Juliana still resisted my pleas to build more androids, as I'd expected. It took me several days to explain my new method of stabilizing the matrix, and to convince her it was worth trying. Of course, I dared not tell her about B-4. She would have been furious had she learned I went behind her back and risked another failure without telling her.

Reassured by my new confidence, she helped me construct a new prototype. When she saw its matrix stabilize, all her old misgivings faded away; I'd never seen her so happy. Our new son opened his eyes, looked at the two of us . . . and smiled.

He was a triumph beyond my wildest hopes. I named him Lore.

Reveling in my success, I wasted no time starting design and fabrication for yet another prototype, one whose systems would incorporate a few minor improvements over Lore's. I had just started designing its brain when the other scientists at Omicron Theta started complaining that Lore had intimidated them, or threatened them. Like any father, I refused to believe them.

One of them, a quantum chemist named Kim Volonakis, became so incensed at Lore's behavior that she cornered me in my lab one night and seized me by the collar of my lab coat. "He's a menace, Noonien! Do something about him, now, or I will!"

I wanted to believe my scion was simply misunderstood, but eventually even I had to admit something was wrong with him. He was rich in intellect but poor in empathy; he had great ambition but no compassion with which to temper it. The more he learned, the more arrogant he became. In the end, his contempt for all of us was naked and unsettling. As much as I wanted to keep his mind active so I could study it and try to discern what had gone wrong, Juliana demanded I shut him down and disassemble him.

For the second time in my life, I willingly betrayed the trust of one of my children, and I used a remote control padd to turn Lore off. I disassembled him with Juliana's help, and we locked his components in a secure storage vault. As I nudged his eyelids shut, I vowed that if I ever had the opportunity and the means, I would fix him. I owed him at least that much.

Meanwhile, over Juliana's objections I had activated Data, but only after acquiescing to the other colonists' demand that he not be invested with human emotions as Lore was, and that his programming be modified with certain safeguards, to prevent him from turning against us. I hated neutering his psyche in this manner, but after the havoc Lore had wrought, I was in no position to argue against it. In some ways, Data reminded me of B-4. I don't mean that as an insult; Data was obviously far more intelligent, though he suffered at first from motor-control issues and intermittent episodes of sensory-input overload. No, the similarities lay in their shared innocence. Like B-4, Data lacked a sense of shame about his body, he had no grasp of social niceties, and he didn't consider any topic of inquiry taboo—traits that led Juliana to insist we create a "modesty subroutine" to augment his ethics and morality programming.

It was ridiculous, really. I'd envisioned Data as a fully realized synthetic sentient being, and my peers wanted him to be a passionless drone.

Those early days, when I spent my every waking moment helping Data adjust to consciousness and learn about himself and the universe in which he lived, were some of the happiest I'd ever known. I felt like a real father, guiding my fragile, impressionable son through the perilous first steps toward independence.

One morning I strolled into my lab, looking forward to a new day of parenting and discovery . . . and discovered Juliana had wiped Data's memory. I flew into a rage, called her horrible names, and hurled beakers and Erlenmeyer flasks against the walls, showering the floor with a million glittering shards.

She fled from me, genuinely confused. "Noonien! What's wrong with you?"

I kicked over a portable light stand. "How could you do this? *Why* would you?"

"What are you talking about?" She raised her hands and struck a defensive pose. "I left all his learned skills intact, his programming's unchanged, and his matrix is still stable." Modulating her voice to project calm, she asked, "Why are you so angry?"

She was never going to understand that she'd robbed my son of his childhood. All his hard-won lessons, the confidence that came with experience over adversity—it was all gone, erased by a touch on a polymer companel. In a matter of seconds, she'd erased weeks of work.

No, that's all incidental. None of that really mattered. What left me quaking with rage was that she had erased *me* from Data's memory. She'd robbed me of my fatherhood, obliterated what would have been the foundation of my relationship with my son.

All I could say was, "Why?"

"I wanted him to have a clean slate." She lowered her hands slowly. "Now that he's past his awkward phase, I saw no reason for him to have to go through life remembering all those embarrassing moments. After all, how much of our childhoods do we really remember? How much would we ever want to? But he can't forget unless he makes a conscious decision to erase part of his memory—something you've programmed him never to do."

I was heartbroken, but I couldn't fault her motives. She'd had no idea what she was really doing to me, to him, to us. From her point of view, this had been a kindness. What could I say? I rubbed the tears from my eyes and sighed. "That's it, then."

Remorseful and fearful, she edged toward me, one hand outstretched. Her touch was tentative and uncertain as her fingertips brushed my arm. "I'm sorry, Noonien. If it helps, I was actually preparing a surprise for you and Data—a gift, of sorts." I looked up at her, and she offered me a sad smile. "Come and see?"

She led me to the master console beside the slab on which Data lay. A few taps and she called up a directory full of raw information. "These are the logs of all the other colonists here on Omicron Theta. And some of them even contributed scans of their memory engrams."

"They donated all this willingly?"

Juliana blushed. "I may have made a few heartfelt appeals." She brightened her mien and took me by my shoulders. "Think of how rich his perspective will be with that much life experience to build upon! And maybe if he has memories of lives seen through other people's eyes, he'll find it easier to empathize with them, and understand them."

Beneath, between, and behind her words, I heard what she'd meant but hadn't said: *Unlike Lore.*

"It's a lovely idea. How long will it take to upload all this?"

"A few days, and a few more after that to compile them into his matrix."

I nodded. "So, we can reactivate him on Saturday?"

"Yes, I think he'll be ready by then."

Of course, Saturday never came—the Crystalline Entity did, on Thursday. It laid waste the entire planet and scoured it clean of every last microbe.

I tried to save Data. I wanted to, but Juliana kept shouting there was no time as she dragged me away from my lab toward our escape ship. Fueled by adrenaline, she was stronger than I was, and I lost that tug-of-war as soon as it began. Looking into her eyes, I saw abject terror, and as the first tendrils of energy from the Crystalline Entity struck her down, I felt the icy hand of fear as well. Cradling my wounded beloved in my arms, I knew there was no choice.

I ran.

And for the third time in a matter of months, I abandoned my children—and this time, I knew I had orphaned the best part of me on that doomed world. In the name of love, I ran and never looked back, forsaking everything and everyone I'd ever known to save Juliana—never suspecting that our love was just as doomed as the colonists and sons I left behind.

Now I hurtle alone through the night, a pilgrim between the stars, my heart and mind set at last on the same mission: to win back the love I lost, no matter the cost or how long it takes.

Perhaps I'm on a fool's errand. If so, I can live with that.

If you ask me, the universe could use a few more fools.

JANUARY
2370

10

After more than six months on this planet, I still can't get a straight answer from any of the locals as to whether I should call it Velestus, Centaurus, Al Rijil IV, or Alpha Centauri IV. Opinion, apparently, is somewhat divided on the matter. Whatever its name really is, it's quite a beautiful planet. Ensconced in the top-floor corner suite of an office tower I've purchased, I marvel at twin suns sinking into a brilliant orange-and-lavender dusk. Neither of the planet's two small moons has risen yet, but its prismatic ring is reflected on the endless reach of the sea surrounding this verdant tropical island. That's another thing I love about this planet: coastal real estate is dirt cheap because they have so much of it. Thousands of tiny islands make up hundreds of clusters and archipelagos on the planet's surface. If you like beaches, this is the planet for you.

I equivocated for some time about establishing my primary residence on a world literally in the heart of Federation space, less than five light-years from Earth. It seemed like an invitation to calamity, a foolhardy tempting of a universe I know to be capricious and without remorse. Then I came here and realized its society was as scattered as its landmass. I have surprisingly little contact with other people, and in a postautomation society powered by clean fusion and serviced by replicators, no one sees this as the least bit unusual. In a core system populated by more than three billion sentient beings, I've managed to find a remarkable measure of true anonymity and isolation. I couldn't have planned it better.

Funny thing about living alone: when I first tried it, it felt strange. It took me a while to get used to the silence, to having no one else to help me keep a conversation going. But once I acclimated myself to it, I liked it. Suddenly, interacting with more than a handful of people at a time became a nuisance, an inconvenience to be avoided at all costs. But I craved information, a steady diet of news delivered via subspace networks from every corner of creation. I became addicted to it; it reached a point within a few years where I interrupted my work every few minutes so I could look at news feeds and see if anything had happened worth knowing about. Juliana insisted I have an attention disorder, probably as a subconscious manifestation of my loneliness. What rubbish. How can I be lonely when I hate people?

Eventually, in the interest of getting things done before I ran out of life, I broke myself of my information addiction . . . with one notable exception: Data.

I've been keeping tabs on my boy for a long time now. Roughly two years after Juliana and I left Omicron Theta and took refuge on Terlina III, she left me. She did it without fuss or drama. I woke up one morning to a fresh-brewed pot of chai and a letter declaring our marriage dissolved. I vaguely recall passing that entire first day sitting at my dinner table, my mug of tea cold in my hand as I stared out the open door and hoped she would come to her senses and walk back in with a grand show of contrition. Night fell, and I was still alone, so I went back to bed.

The next day, I was so desperate, I thought of going back to Omicron Theta for my sons. Ever a pragmatist, I did some research first. Using some backdoor codes I'd left behind in Starfleet's comm network while doing some contract work for them in my youth (a handy shortcut my old mentor Vaslovik taught me during that internship), I looked up the latest reports about the planet and the colony. It was irrational to think that anything could have survived the onslaught I witnessed there, but hope rarely listens to reason.

Imagine my surprise upon reading in the logs of the captain of the *U.S.S. Tripoli* about the recovery of an apparently sentient android who had no memory of the calamity that had claimed the planet and all its denizens—including, they all thought, his creator.

My boy had slept through an apocalypse, and within a day of being woken up had hitched a ride on a starship and filed an application to Starfleet Academy. I knew then that he was prone to making rash decisions, just as I am, and I've kept a careful watch on his life ever since. Of all the possible paths in life, why did he have to walk down that one? I wasn't above doing occasional work for Starfleet and the Federation, but I never let them get anywhere near my cybernetics research, and with good reason. From the very start they failed to respect Data for what he truly was: a new lifeform. As soon as he applied to their overhyped Academy, some young snot named Bruce Maddox opposed his admission on the grounds that he's not a sentient being. I'm not saying Starfleet doesn't serve a purpose or do its share of good in the galaxy, but I'm no fan of the military, especially not its more regressive elements. And don't delude yourself; as "enlightened" as

Starfleet pretends to be, it still harbors a reactionary core.

Through the years—during Data's first posting on the *Starship Trieste,* his slow climb through the ranks, and now his service on the *Enterprise*—I found it tedious to try to monitor him constantly, so I simplified my task by creating a specialized AI, a news daemon whose sole function was to scour all Federation news and internal Starfleet communications for any mention of Data or the ships on which he served. It helped that he soon became a pseudocelebrity in cybernetics circles; at least once a year someone tried to polish up their bona fides by publishing a paper about him. Looking back, I realize I moved slowly all those years not because I was old but because I was towing half the scientists in my field on my damned coattails.

I also took to perusing Data's personal logs in a digest format on a monthly basis, but I soon fell far behind on that reading—Data can at times be excruciatingly verbose.

Yes, yes, I know. Call it a family trait and let's move on, shall we?

These days, I indulge a new obsession: my search for Juliana.

It would be easier had I started tracking her as soon as she'd left Terlina III, but at the time I'd wanted to respect her privacy. Now those records are decades old. You wouldn't think that would matter in an information-based society like the Federation, but some worlds expunge what they consider to be trivial records after as little as a few years. It depends a great deal on the local laws and customs of each world. On planets like Earth and Vulcan, whose peoples treat information archiving like a religion, mundane records can stretch back centuries—a baffling practice on its face, but perhaps useful if one has long-term plans to meddle in time travel. Other peoples, such as the live-in-the-now hedonists of Risa or the privacy-minded Neuvians, barely maintain records of any kind when they cease to be immediately useful.

By necessity, my search began with old travel records dating back more than three decades, to the period during which Juliana left me. I first checked the files on worlds within ten light-years of Terlina III; finding no leads, I widened my search radius to fifteen light-years. Each expansion of my search range multiplied the number of possible worlds and starports and space stations that might have hosted Juliana on her travels, however briefly. Unfortunately, the more worlds whose records I needed to plumb, the longer each step of the search took.

Eventually, the search process became too tedious and time-consuming; with apologies I foisted it off on poor Shakti aboard the *Archeus*. When I'm not traveling, it's pretty much all she does. Every now and then she scares up a promising tidbit of information. A few times it's been a red herring, but she's had her share of successes, so I continue to let her take the lead while I tend to the unglamorous realities of running a multipronged interstellar corporation with more than eight dozen subsidiaries—but fewer than a hundred actual employees. When I have need of actual labor for anything, whether it be fabrication or moving cargo, I subcontract. It simplifies the paperwork and adds yet another layer of insulation between me and the universe at large.

The sun has set, and the sky outside my windows darkens to a royal purple richer than the dreams of Croesus. On dozens of worlds across a vast swath of local space, my businesses thrive. Today, at least, my grand scheme remains on schedule. I'm tempted to celebrate.

Then I hear Shakti's voice via the secure internal comm from *Archeus.*

"Noonien?"

I rub my eyes in a pantomime of anxiety. "Yes?"

She strikes an apologetic note, never a good sign. *"I hope you'll pardon the interruption, but I've found some news of interest regarding Juliana."*

At once my attention is fully engaged. "More travel records?"

"Several. I can document her movements from Ronara to Kenda II, and from there to Epsilon Canaris III by way of Beltane IX. However, her journeys as Juliana O'Donnell appear to have ceased following her arrival on Atrea IV in May of 2343."

Damn this emotionally intuitive AI with which I've afflicted myself; her omissions in the name of mercy are as devastating as Data's oblivious bluntness once was. "What're you saying, Shakti? Did something happen to Juliana on Atrea IV?"

"I'm afraid so, Noonien. . . . She got married."

If I were still made of flesh, that news would stir the acid from my gut and poison my esophagus with hot, sour bile. I can be grateful that my android form spares me that indignity, but I still feel a flush of warmth from my anger; my mechanical pulse quickens, and the only check on my erupting bonfire of rage is a smothering tide of despair.

My Juliana's remarried. I understand why she left me, but how could she replace me? How could anyone ever take my place in her life? It just doesn't make sense. I need to know more before I can get a handle on this. "Married to whom?"

"An Atrean scientist," Shakti says. *"Noted geologist*

Doctor Pran Tainer. Their public marriage notice indicates that she worked with him as his assistant prior to their engagement."

And just like that I regret making my android body impervious to the effects of alcohol. I slump forward and bury my face in my palms; I need to shut out the rest of the universe for a moment so I can cope with this. It's so unfair. I gave Juliana more than she can possibly know; I spared her from death's sting, and I even let her leave me because I believed that one day she and I would be together again. Sure, I programmed natural aging and mortality into her body, but that was partly as a safeguard against the possibility that I might not live to see a reunion. It was always my plan to free her from that curse, break the spell of aging, and live with her forever.

Has all this been for nothing? I was prepared to romance her, to court her from scratch and prove my love for her—but I hadn't counted on having to woo her from the arms of a spouse. What if she truly loves this Pran Tainer? What if she loves him more than she loved me? What if he's her soulmate? Dammit, just asking these questions makes me sick to my artificial stomach, like I'm in free fall and wearing a blindfold. My mind works at superhuman speeds, executes more operations per second than any humanoid brain in history, but I can't reason my way out of this haze of confusion. I trace the activity in my neural pathways and see the same thoughts making wild loops, going around and around without resolution, and I feel circuits rerouting in automatic response to the threat of my matrix becoming snared in an infinite loop.

It's not as if there aren't numerous other tasks into which I could submerge myself and hope to drown my grief with distraction. I could build a new basic-emotions chip for Data in a fraction of the time it took to produce the first one. It's like mastering a piece of music: before you know it, it's a mystery; after you learn it, performing it again is almost like muscle memory. It's not as if I don't have the resources to make a new chip; it just wasn't how I'd planned to spend my second life. Besides, as much as I'd like to do Data this service I owe him, there's another, far greater debt pressing on my mind: his brother, Lore. Before I do anything else, I need to sort out that error in my judgment. I never should have turned my back on him, never given him the chance to leave my sight and impersonate Data. Hell, the only reason I conned him into staying on Terlina III was because I hoped he could still be reasoned with—and, failing that, contained. But I made him too much like me. Too crafty, too sly. I should have known.

Yes, this is where my focus needs to be right now: on my boys.

"Shakti, has there been any recent news about Data?" These days, the news daemon I built to monitor Data is an integral part of Shakti's programming.

My query is met by an uncommonly long silence. Perhaps I'm projecting my anxieties onto my AI assistant, but I might almost describe this brief lacuna as *awkward*. I look up and lift my voice. "Shakti? Did you hear me?"

"I heard you." After another pause she adds, *"There is a new digest of logs by Lieutenant Commander Data, covering stardates 46982 through 47025."*

In nanoseconds I translate that into calendar dates, and then my anger flares. "You've been sitting on those logs for over two weeks? Why didn't you tell me when they came in?"

"At the time, it seemed imprudent."

Some days, I just can't fathom how Shakti thinks.

Now, before you snicker and point out that I created her, so therefore it must be my fault, think of all the parents in the galaxy who find themselves vexed by their biological offspring. Mine is a universal problem, apparently.

"Why did it seem imprudent?" This inquiry provokes naught but more silence, leaving me to reason this out on my own. I intuit a possible explanation, but it's far from exculpatory for my troubled young AI. "Shakti, how long have you known about Juliana's marriage to Tainer?"

There is shame in her synthetic reply. *"Twenty-five days, nine hours, and eight minutes."*

This is making more sense by the moment, but I remain unhappy about it. "Why, then, did you choose to tell me about it tonight?"

"I'd calculated a ninety-eight-point-seven percent chance you would inquire about Data's logs within the next local day. I'd hoped that shifting your attention to Juliana might delay that request, even if only briefly." Welcome to the chief drawback of interrogating an AI; they are programmed to deliver truthful and accurate responses, but not necessarily helpful ones. I ask why she did these things, and she explains her reasoning pattern but omits her motive.

Bereft of alternatives, I play along.

"And why did you wish to delay my receipt of Data's logs?" More of the silent treatment. How in blazes did I manage to make a *bashful* AI? I see I'll have to draw her out by degrees. "Is it because this latest digest contains bad news?"

The guilt in her voice is laced with sympathy. *"I'm afraid so, Noonien."*

"Enough stalling, then. Upload the logs to my station. Now." If I wanted, I could have had her transmit the files directly into my positronic matrix, but as useful as such a feature seemed when I designed it, it struck me as far too hazardous to use once I had to live in this body. What if someone loaded a virus or malicious program directly into my mind by using an ordinary transmission as a Trojan horse? That's just not a risk I'm willing to take. The only direct interface I'll allow is with systems and software of my own design that I know are secure.

Data's logs appear on my holoscreen. Some of them are entered as plain text; others are audiovisual recordings he made in his quarters aboard the *Enterprise*. There's not much difference in tone between text and Data; he usually exhibits the oratorical skill of a houseplant. I choose to watch his recordings not for his rhetoric but just so I can see his face. As impatient as ever, I decide to start with the last entry.

The screen snaps to a head-and-shoulders shot of Data. He looks directly at me, as if we're conversing across a dinner table, and he tells me in his innocent monotone about his day.

"At 1732 hours and forty-one seconds today, I disassembled Lore. I have stored his constituent parts in separate containers within my private cybernetics laboratory, here inside my quarters. I have also taken special precautions to ensure that Lore's brain remains inactive, as he can never again be allowed to threaten others. Though I succeeded in removing the emotion chip from his brain after subduing him, it appears to have been damaged by the phaser blast that initially incapacitated him. I do not know if it will be possible to repair the chip, but a more pressing concern for me is whether I should. The emotions Lore transmitted to me during the confrontation with the Borg rendered me highly unstable and susceptible to his suggestion

and manipulation. While I doubt that Doctor Soong's original chip would have produced that effect had it been installed as intended in my neural net, I am left with troubling questions as to whether the introduction of emotions to my positronic matrix would make me unfit for duty in Starfleet. Conceivably, such a change to my core systems and software could be grounds for Starfleet Command to deem me a different person than the one I currently am. At my next opportunity, I will have to discuss these possibilities with Geordi and Captain Picard."

The log entry comes to an abrupt end. I recline my chair, stunned silent.

Lore is dead.

Suddenly, I need to know everything, all the details, and I can't be bothered to sit and wade through all of Data's long-winded narratives. I call up the text transcripts of his logs and parse them as swiftly as my android perceptual abilities will allow. In under two seconds, I have the full account of Data's final confrontation with Lore. It was an unmitigated horror show; I knew Lore was disturbed, but I'd never have thought him so unhinged that he would ally himself with the Borg. But what did I expect? Even before he gummed up his matrix with an emotion chip that was never meant for him, he was fool enough to strike a bargain with the Crystalline Entity. Is one world-slaughtering alien menace really so different from another? But the details are ghastly. Lore decided to help the Borg transition to a fully synthetic existence. The only part that eluded him was the secret of synaptic transfer. To find it, he nearly turned poor Geordi La Forge's brain into Swiss cheese. There's no denying the obvious now: my son really was a monster, a boundless sociopath. If Data hadn't stopped him, he'd have killed millions—perhaps even billions. The sum of his evils would have been incalculable.

Yet the thought that echoes in my dry old brain is, *My son is dead.*

The horrible truth of this moment is that I don't know whether to grieve or celebrate. He was a menace, I see that now. But he was my boy, made in my image. In the end, all I feel is numb. What else can I do? Lore tried to kill Data. After all the times he wronged his younger brother, and then corrupted him by force, Lore was ready to let his envy drive him to murder. I can't forgive him for that. Part of me wants to take the blame, but I have to hold Lore to the same standard I would expect for anyone else. Lore has no one to blame for his actions but himself.

If I'm to be truthful, this has been a long time coming. When I heard the news that Data had been discovered in the ruins of the Omicron Theta colony, I checked every source and account I could find for any mention of Lore. When I found none, I assumed—let's be honest, I *hoped*—that his body had been destroyed by the attack of the Crystalline Entity. I knew it was unlikely, especially since Data had survived, but even then I knew no good would come of Lore's return, especially now that I was in no position to repair him. Believing he had been destroyed enabled me to get on with my life and work on Terlina III.

Of course, I lied to Lore after he responded, as Data had, to the homing signal I sent a few years ago. I told him I didn't know he'd been reassembled, but that wasn't true. I'd read all of Data's logs about discovering Lore in a buried lab on Omicron Theta in 2364, and Lore's subsequent attempt to betray the *Enterprise* to the Crystalline Entity, but I couldn't just admit that to his face. What I told him about the years between my departure and his reassembly had been true, to a point. Had I been certain that Lore survived the attack on the colony, I might have gone back for him. What I was careful not to say was that if I'd done that, I'd have erased his mind, his programming, and all his memories, and just started over, probably with a copy of Data's matrix as a new template. If I'd admitted that, he would have made certain to kill me, instead of merely beating me to within an inch of my life and leaving me for dead.

No, I can't feel sorry for him. Not after what he's done.

I feel sorry for myself. It sounds selfish, but isn't that the guilty secret of mourning? We know the departed are beyond sensation, beyond recrimination or suffering; they no longer need our pity or compassion. So we give it to ourselves, and not in small measures but in waves. Staring at words on a screen telling me my first great creation has perished, all I can think about is that a unique and vital facet of my legacy is gone forever, taking a piece of me with him.

Only one part of my sorrow is of a generous kind, a product of empathy. I created Lore; it should have been me who unmade him. Now this black stain of fratricide will haunt my noble youngest son forever. If Data ever makes that emotion chip work properly again, and dares to install it into his neural net, he'll suffer for this day in ways he can't imagine. Guilt and loneliness are two of the most devastating emotions, and someday he'll have to endure their agonies . . . for no better reason than that his father was a coward.

JULY
2370

11

I step out of the lift onto the top floor of a residential tower where I reside on Centaurus. I mean, Velestus. Or . . . never mind. It's on the same island as my office, just a few minutes' walk away. I've been offworld for business the last few weeks, and I'm looking forward to being home. I beamed down my luggage from *Archeus* while I was still in orbit, but the ship is due for basic maintenance and refueling, so I locked down its main computer to keep anyone from discovering Shakti, landed *Archeus* at a rented berth in the island's tiny commuter starport, and walked home with no burdens but my cares.

Outside the door of my penthouse suite, I pause just long enough for the biometric sensors to verify my retinal pattern, body-mass distribution pattern, and heat signature. An artificial voice from the security panel challenges me: *"Voiceprint identification, please."*

"Eamon Cattura."

"Thank you, Eamon." The security system opens my door for me. *"Welcome home."*

Two steps inside the spacious, split-level main room, I stop. Everything is dark. I've programmed the lights to brighten to one-third when I enter at night, even though my cybernetic eyes don't actually need the illumination. By reflex, I survey the room while tuned to infrared with my left eye and ultraviolet with my right. Nothing looks amiss; all is quiet. My olfactory sensors detect no odors such as I'd expect from a biological intruder, but there are unfamiliar trace particles in the air. Synthetic fibers, I believe, and faint hints of silicon, as well as a few exotic and mildly radioactive substances. I emit an ultrasonic pulse and compare the echoes against my memory. There is someone on my left, just out of sight around the corner.

I start to back up, planning to make a break for the lift, which lingers open behind me in the penthouse lobby. A man's sour, taunting voice from inside my suite arrests me.

"Where do you think you're going, Noonien?"

My instinct for self-preservation tells me to run, but I have to know who this person is and how he knows who I am. Damn this insatiable curiosity! I take a few more steps inside the suite and let the front door slide closed behind me. I look toward the corner and raise my voice in a feeble attempt to sound brave. "Show yourself."

The visitor—a less charitable narrator might call him an intruder—steps into the room with me. He's tall and thin, at least fifteen centimeters taller than I am, a trim silhouette in front of the wall of floor-to-ceiling windows that look out upon the moonlit swells of the sea. As he draws near, I see his face in the frost-colored twilight of night-vision. His face is surprisingly human except for its upswept, almond-shaped eyes and the angularity of his cheekbones and orbital ridges. He stops and looms over me, his countenance inscrutable. "I'm Tyros."

"I'd introduce myself, but you already seem to know who I am."

"You're a hard man to reach, Noonien. We could have had this conversation a few years ago on Pacifica if you hadn't been so skittish."

I replay my vivid memories of fleeing a shadow. "That was you?"

He takes a comical bow with his arms spread, then gestures toward a pair of facing chairs with high backs and comfortably upholstered armrests. "Shall we sit?"

I shrug one shoulder and stare at him with keen suspicion. "If you like." He leads me to my own reading chairs and takes the one to our left. I ease myself into the other but remain coiled, ready to spring into retreat or attack. "What're you doing here? What do you want?"

"Hard as it might be to believe, Noonien, I'm just here to say hello."

It might be a trick of the shadows, but I could swear the bastard is smirking at me. "You're right, it is hard to believe. And since I don't know you, you can call me Doctor Soong."

"If you prefer, Doctor. It's all the same to us."

"Us? Who's us?" The more he says, the less I like him.

He folds his freakishly long, bony fingers together in front of his chest and leans forward. "I'm an envoy from an ancient galactic fellowship. We've been watching you for a long time, Doctor—ever since your excursion to Exo III with Doctors Graves and Vaslovik."

My jaw drops open with shock, and I know I must look like a jabbering fool. "Exo III? Are you kidding me? That was nearly sixty years ago!"

"Sixty years?" Those words seem to amuse him. A taut smile deepens the creases of his cadaver-like visage. "A mere wink in the gaze of eternity, Doctor."

I'm beginning to suspect my uninvited guest is more

than he appears. "What, exactly, is the nature of this 'ancient fellowship' you claim to represent?"

Tyros unclasps his fingers and leans back, hands planted on his chair's armrests. "I didn't claim to represent the fellowship. I merely said I was its envoy. As for its nature, it's a loose collection of peers who travel the galaxy—sometimes alone, sometimes together in pairs or groups—and reconvene at irregular intervals to share their experiences and compare them."

It's a wonderfully evasive answer, no doubt truthful and accurate but not exactly helpful. Watching stray tachyons and neutrinos flee from his narrow skull, I crack my own knowing smile. "That's very interesting, Tyros, but it's not what I was asking."

"I know what you're asking. You want to know what kind of life-forms belong to the fellowship, correct?" He waits for my prompting half-nod, then he continues. "It's composed of people like us, Doctor. In a word . . . *artificial*."

Suddenly, my life's work and future ambitions seem dwarfed by a reality I'd never dared to think could exist. I knew some past civilizations in this region of the galaxy had, in the past, produced other sophisticated androids, but I thought they had all long since gone extinct.

"What do you want with me?"

"Isn't it obvious?" He leans forward, his mien conspiratorial. "You're one of the first new creators of complex, sentient artificial life the galaxy has seen in a long time. None of us in the fellowship possess gifts like yours. We'd like to learn from you."

I get up and shake my head in disgust. "I'm done teaching."

"Are you sure? I can promise you've never had students like us before. No biological pupil would ever be capable of learning as quickly as we can—nor would any of them ever be as motivated as we are to master your lessons."

His offer is enticing enough to make me stop and look back. "I'd be lying if I said I'm not tempted. But telling someone you've been spying on them for the last sixty years isn't exactly a great way to start a recruiting pitch."

He chuckles, and it sounds like genuine amusement. "Very true. We don't often deal with organics, so we forget sometimes they can be sensitive to observation. Not that I have the authority to speak for the fellowship, but, for what it's worth, I apologize."

"Apology appreciated but not accepted. Not yet, anyway." A twinge of fear makes me assume the worst. "I guess I should ask: Do I have the option of refusing this invitation?"

He recoils, ostensibly offended by the question. "Of course. We're not in the habit of abducting our own kind. As one of our members likes to say, 'We're kind of like a wine club.' By which he means we're a loose affiliation rather than an organized entity. We just want to invite you to the meetings, is all."

"That's kind of you, but I think I'd prefer to remain on my own awhile longer."

Tyros stands and stuffs his hands in his pants' deep pockets. He looks disappointed but not upset. "I understand. It's a lot to process. Maybe someday you'll change your mind."

I fold my arms. "Then again, maybe I won't."

He takes his right hand from the pocket. There is a small device in his hand, a black wedge with one green button. For a fraction of a second I wonder if it's a weapon. Then he opens his hand and extends it toward me, the device resting on his open palm. "In case you change your mind, take this."

I remain still, so he lobs the tiny device toward me. Damn my android reflexes, I catch it before I even think to let it simply fall to the floor; another of my life's missed opportunities. I turn it over and around in my hand like a child's toy. "What is it?"

"A quantum transceiver. If you ever want or need to make contact with the fellowship, just press the green button and wait. We'll be in touch."

I stuff the transceiver into my pocket. "Don't hold your breath."

"I don't breathe." Before I can sigh in exasperation, he adds, "But I get your idiom." He walks past me and heads for the front door, which opens ahead of him. I wait for him to stop at the threshold, look back, and offer some witty parting bon mot. Instead, he continues through the doorway, and the portal shuts after him.

Alone now, I reflect on the encounter. It seemed nonthreatening. Taken at face value, this fellowship of artificial intelligence seems benign enough. On the other hand, they found me here, despite my best efforts at identity camouflage.

In four-point-one seconds I make my decision.

I pack my bags, leave Centaurus, and never return.

AUGUST
2371

12

Until this moment, I never knew true boredom. I've committed one of the great conversational blunders of modern times: I've let a Ferengi start talking to me about money.

"The fundamental error of Federation economics is the assumption that it's a system in equilibrium," my dining companion mumbles through a maw of half-masticated tube grubs. He swallows hard and continues with rising volume and passion. "If you want to take advantage of new niches and emerging markets, you need to embrace out-of-equilibrium dynamics. Even if you factor in the Federation's economics-of-surplus model, there's room for greater profit."

I salute Prak with a dip of my chin and a lifting of my wine glass. "If you say so." Hoping he'll take the hint and change the subject, I sip my Denevan Sangiovese. A quirk of the light turns the spicy, dark purple wine a deep shade of ruby around its edges.

"The real innovation I want to bring to the Federation is the concept that spontaneously evolving economic structures can be given analytical and deterministic representations." Prak spears a jellied gree worm with his telescoping-handle fork, which is at full extension. "My current models suggest that inherently unpredictable events can be explained or understood in terms of endogenous economic forces." He retracts the fork's handle and devours his treat.

Our waiter arrives and sets our entrees in front of us. Prak is feasting this evening on soft-shelled Kytherian crabs and a side of pickled seaweed. I've ordered the filet mignon, medium rare, with roasted root vegetables. The momentary interruption is a godsend, in that it gives me a chance to steer our discussion back to the reason I arranged this meeting. As soon as the waiter steps away, I smile and look Prak in his beady, red-ringed eyes. "So. The casino."

"Must we talk business right this second? Our dinners will get cold."

I slice into the tip of my filet to check the color. As one would expect from the chefs of the most opulent and acclaimed luxury hotel on Risa, it's perfect. "Talk between bites," I tell Prak, just before taking my first bite of steak. Its salty, savory decadence is just as satisfying to my artificial palate as it once was to my human taste buds.

"Well, as I said, it's a franchise." He swallows and washes down his latest mouthful with a swig of Slug-O Cola while I do my best not to wince. "The biggest casino chain on Ferenginar. Our patented probability algorithms make ours the most profitable gaming houses in the galaxy."

It sounds promising, but I'm not sold yet. "How profitable?"

He bites a ragged crescent through another struggling crustacean, ending its suffering. Between wet chomps, he splutters out, "Quarterly? Eleven percent, guaranteed!"

That's not bad, but it's not enough for my purposes.

Fortunately, I'm sure I can improve on the Ferengi's overhyped algorithms, and I have my own plans for increasing revenues. "Sounds good. How soon can we set up the deal?"

He sleeves wet flecks of shell and crab from his chin, leaving a greasy smear down the arm of his jacket. "Depends on the details. How many locations? And where will they be?"

"Just one location. The Orion homeworld, in the capital."

I recognize the look in Prak's eyes. It's one I used to see from my colleagues throughout my years at the Daystrom Institute. He thinks I'm out of my mind.

Prak shakes his head—slowly at first, then with increasingly vigorous denial. "No. No, that's absurd. We've wanted to open there for decades. The numbers never work out."

"They will for me. I own the property it'll sit on."

He waves off my argument. "Doesn't matter. The taxes on Orion gaming houses—"

"Don't apply inside foreign embassies."

I admit to deriving a perverse degree of satisfaction from watching Prak process that revelation. "That's pretty clever for a *hew-mon* with such small lobes. I'll have to remember that trick." He leans across the table, bares a sawtooth grin of avarice, and lowers his voice. "Just out of curiosity: Whose embassy do you plan to work from?"

"The Nalori Republic's."

My poor Ferengi guest looks baffled. "But the Nalori and Orions hate each other."

"All the more reason they need good diplomatic channels." Which is exactly what I told high-ranking officials from both powers—shortly after I'd used a shell corporation to purchase sixteen square blocks inside the Orions' capital, demolished the lot's existing structures, and erected a walled compound of high-rise towers. Once the Orions invited the Nalori to send an ambassador to their capital for the first time in nearly a century (thanks in no small part to some financial incentives I offered), I persuaded the Nalori Republic to sign a dirt-cheap hundred-year lease for a spacious, high-security residence on my property, in exchange for putting the entire compound under its diplomatic protection and authority, while leaving its administration to me. In exchange for a cut of the casino's profits, naturally.

Prak's eyes narrow to slits. He must sense profit is in the offing. "What percentage of the compound's floor space will be devoted to casino operations?"

"Sixty-eight percent of fifteen high-rise towers, with the other thirty-two percent for the hotel, dining, and entertainment spaces. At an average height of a hundred floors per tower, we'd be talking about 707.2 million square meters of casino floor space, operating around the clock, every day of the year. Most of our games would be designed for winners' payouts at ratios of five-to-one—but the players would already be laying eleven-to-one."

Prak takes a minute to cogitate. He grinds another crab into paste with his teeth while the figurative gears inside his head crunch the numbers implicit in my proposal. "Tempting. Very tempting. But risky. The Orion Syndicate will try to shut you down."

"Let them try. With your support, fifty percent of my start-up capital and all my gaming equipment would be provided by Prak-Tikal Games Incorporated, and my security would be provided for free by the Nalori Commandos. As for food and other commodities, let's just say I have my own supply network and leave it at that. It's a sound business model."

He still seems resistant. "You'd face a lot of competition on the Orion homeworld."

"Imagine you're a traveling businessman from the Federation," I tell him, in my best fairy-tale storyteller's voice. "You've come a long way to Orion. Maybe you love it there, maybe you hate it, but either way you're tired after a hard day of haggling with the merchant princes. You could go back to your ship, but if you're like most tourists on Orion, you want to catch a show. See some dancing girls, play a few games of chance, have a rich meal. But you've heard the Orions' gaming houses and red-light districts are dangerous. Is it really worth the risk? But, wait! There's another option! A professionally run gambling mecca in the heart of the Orion capital! An endless variety of games and entertainments and restaurants to suit every taste. Best of all, this cornucopia of entertainment is safe and clean. . . . Where are you going to take your crew—who might also be your family—for a night on the town?"

I can't say whether my spiel has swayed Prak, or if he's just tired of hearing someone talk as much as he usually does. "All right, we'll back you, but we'll need time to pull it all together. You've just described the largest single gaming house in the quadrant. It might take up to a year to get that much equipment together, not to mention the security systems."

"That's fine. I need another eight months to finish building and furnishing the towers. But don't worry about the security system for the casino. I'll be using one of my own design."

"Suit yourself. But there's one more thing: for a risky venture like this, I won't guarantee an eleven-percent profit margin. At best, I'll guarantee nine percent."

"In that case, I need my franchise fee reduced to six percent per annum."

"Seven."

"Six-point-five, or I'll take this offer to your old friend Venk."

Hearing me invoke the name of his rival puts a bitter scowl on Prak's already prune-like face. "Fine, six-point-five. I'd swear you were part Ferengi if your lobes weren't so small."

I raise my glass in a mock toast. "I'll assume you meant that as a compliment." I savor another taste of my wine and put down the glass. "How soon can I expect the contracts?"

He takes a small portable comm from his coat pocket and starts tapping its touchscreen. "I'll have my assistant make the amendments now. You'll have the revised deal before dessert."

"Splendid." I pick up my fork and knife to carve off another bite of my filet, only to be interrupted by the soft electronic chirping of my own comm device. "Excuse me." I tap the screen and accept the incoming signal from Shakti, who I know I can trust to remain in character as my assistant and adhere to our current *noms de voyage*. "Yes, Bree, what is it?"

"Sorry to interrupt your dinner, Mister Miller, but there's breaking news you need to see." The screen of my comm switches to a live report from the Federation News Service. For the sake of discretion, Shakti has taken the precaution of muting the vid's audio, and with good reason. I'm looking at a stunning vista of scorched earth and wreckage, a smoldering scar cut across the surface of some barren world, a geological wound leading to the battered remains of a *Galaxy*-class starship's saucer half-buried in a hillside. The banner headline across the lower third of the image: USS ENTERPRISE CRASHES ON VERIDIAN III.

Suddenly my brilliant business deal means nothing. All I can think about is Data.

"Thank you, Bree." I switch off the comm, push back my chair, and stand, then shoot Prak my most apologetic look. "Forgive me, but I need to attend to an urgent matter of business. I'm sure you understand."

"Profit waits for no one." He waves me away. "Go, already. Time is money."

"Thank you. Don't forget to send the contract."

I leave the restaurant in haste, fighting the urge to sprint across the lobby to the lifts, even though that would make a spectacle of me—an error I can ill afford right now, or ever. The lift takes forever to arrive, leaving me to stare at the reflection of my latest disguise on the lift doors' mirror-perfect exteriors. My close-cropped gray-white beard looks like a natural extension of my snowy tonsure and sideburns. I'm wearing the visage of a man in late middle age, pale and wrinkled with dark gray eyebrows in need of a trim. Even my eyes are a steely gray. If not for my midnight-blue suit and smartly patterned gold-and-crimson tie, I'd be all but colorless.

The lift doors open, and I hurry inside. Its AI intones, *"Floor, please."*

"Sixty-three." The doors close, and I shut my eyes for the ride upstairs.

Four hours later, I've used every trick I know and exploited every back-door code I have into Starfleet's communications, yet I don't know much more than I did while I was sitting in the restaurant, looking at silent video of the *Enterprise*'s devastated saucer. It's as if someone on the *Enterprise,* or at Starfleet Command, is going out of their way to bury the details of whatever happened at Veridian III. All I've found so far are vague reports of a madman named Soran, who Starfleet calls a terrorist who unleashed "antistellar munitions" inside

Federation space, though I'll be damned if I can find any explanation of who he was or what he hoped to accomplish.

I try searching for any new log entries by Data, but there are none. In fact, there are no new logs on file from any of the *Enterprise*'s crew. Apparently, whatever logs are stored inside the ship's main computer will be retrieved manually after the computer core is transported home to Utopia Planitia for forensic analysis. This strikes me as odd, too. If the core is intact, why not recover the logs on-site? I have to conclude that whatever really happened out there, it's something so top-secret that Starfleet doesn't want to risk transmitting its details via subspace.

I'd call them paranoid if I weren't tapped into their network.

The only information I've found so far—other than the pabulum Starfleet Command is feeding to the press, which laps up the spin-doctored official statements like a hungry dog begging scraps—is an after-action report filed by Captain Jean-Luc Picard. He notes that a crew of rogue Klingons abducted his chief engineer and hacked the man's VISOR, enabling them to acquire intelligence that they used to compromise his ship's defenses.

If I were still organic, this would make me sick. An obsolete bird-of-prey shot down one of the Federation's most advanced starships. It would be funny if it weren't such a disgrace.

I forget about that. All I want to know right now is whether my boy is alive. His name's not on Picard's roster of verified fatalities, and he's not one of the crew's four MIA personnel. Reassured, I skim the rest of Picard's report and stop when I find mention of Data. To my relief, he is apparently unhurt, but this sentence troubles me: "However, Lieutenant Commander Data's behavior since installing his repaired emotion chip has been unpredictable."

It catches me by surprise, so I reread it three more times until it sinks in. Data repaired his emotion chip on his own. I breeze through the rest of the report and discover he had help from his friend La Forge, but that doesn't diminish the greater aspect of Data's accomplishment: he repaired his emotion chip *without my help.* I had no idea he'd come so far. Sure, he unlocked his dreaming subroutine on his own, but that was pretty much an accident, a real-life bolt from the blue. But this is different. If he can do work of this caliber and complexity, he's already decades ahead of where I was at his age.

After I get done basking in my pride over my son, I dredge up another enlightening tidbit: a salvage and cargo manifest prepared by the Starfleet Corps of Engineers team sent to recover the *Enterprise*'s wreckage. It's a full inventory of matériel and personal effects retrieved from the saucer, packed up, and sent back to Utopia Planitia. It's cross-indexed by property type and owner, so I skim all the cargo attributed to Data. Salvaged intact from his quarters are a handful of paintings; a Lorcan wisdom mask; my first three failed prototype androids, which Data recovered from Omicron Theta after Juliana told him where to find them; the body of Data's own failed experiment, the daughter he named Lal; and all of Lore's components . . . except one. The vault in which Lore's brain had been stored self-destructed automatically when it was compromised by bulkhead damage. Lore's positronic matrix was reduced to vapor.

I thought I'd already grieved for Lore, hardened my soul to his loss, but this news still fills me with sadness. As irrational a desire as it might be, I think part of me had secretly wished that one day I might still repair Lore's damaged mind. Maybe I could have fixed him, maybe not. Now I'll never have the chance to find out. There's nothing left of him to fix.

Picard seems uncertain whether Data will leave his emotion chip activated. For my son's sake, I hope he does. He's lived a good life so far with only the pure emotions of a machine to drive him. Yes, you read that correctly. It was always a bit of an exaggeration to say that Data had no emotions. He had to have *some* kind of emotions, or else he never would have done anything except what he was told—and what damn use would he be then? What he'd lacked were *human* emotions, and maybe that wasn't such a bad thing, in hindsight. Curiosity, loyalty, a need to be useful, a desire to live in harmony with other beings—those are all emotions. I mean, what is an emotion, really? It's a motive. A reason to act. Data has plenty of those: a sense of duty; an innate desire to acquire and accurately share knowledge; a drive to improve himself.

With just those emotions, he's made me proud (despite his insistence on remaining in Starfleet, a decision I continue to find disappointing, no matter how hard I try to accept it). But when I think of the broader vision of the universe he could possess with a wider range of emotions, I dare to hope. He's been a good and just person with only his ethics and morality programming to guide him; how wondrous a being could he become if he had true empathy? I think he, and the rest of the universe, deserve to find out.

The official news isn't good for much, in my opinion, but at least it tells me now that all the members of the *Enterprise*'s crew are on extended leave pending new assignments. Two overstyled talking heads—a male human and a female Trill—smile obsequiously at each other and trade rumors. *"Anonymous sources inside Starfleet Command have hinted that one of its new* Sovereign*-class starships might be renamed in honor of the* Enterprise,*"* he says.

"There's no official confirmation on that from President Zife's office," she says with a twinkle that makes me want to punch her, *"but one high-ranking member of the Federation Security Council assures me that the rewrite of the new Starfleet appropriations bill announced this afternoon might not be a coincidence, after all."*

Rather than vent my rage by destroying a useful piece of equipment, I turn off my hotel room's vid panel and resolve to get some sleep. It's been months since I let myself have an hour off to dream. I adjust the privacy setting at my door to DO NOT DISTURB and settle in for a long-overdue plunge into the arms of Oneiros. I hope to dream of my son—and I hope that wherever he is and whenever he next lays his head down to rest, he might continue to dream of me.

NOVEMBER
2372

13

"Mister Miller? Prince Xifal and Chairman Molob are here for their scheduled appointment."

I thumb open the reply channel of my intercom. "Thank you, Laryn. Send them in."

Courtesy dictates I should stand and emerge from behind my executive desk to greet these distinguished visitors. I recline my chair and steeple my fingers as the door opens.

The two forty-something Orion men step through the doorway into my office, and they squint against the harsh glare of the morning sun, which streams in over my head, through the window at my back. While my guests' eyes struggle to adjust, I size them up.

Prince Xifal has the lean and polished look of modern royalty, born to the spectacle of endless media scrutiny. He's lean and toned, more by athletics than by combat from the look of him. His skin is a bright shade of emerald; his short black hair has been styled into a slick crown. I admire his taste in clothes: robes of Tholian silk in hues of cerulean and charcoal, with accents of purple, and hand-tailored soft leather boots that hug his calves. Everything about him marks him as a man of wealth and status—in particular, his hard stare of haughty contempt.

That intimidating gaze is all he has in common with the man beside him. Where Xifal seems to glide into the room, Chairman Molob lumbers, a prisoner of his own fearsome mass. Molob is a hulking, dark-green brute with a shaved head and a bespoke suit. His raiment is no less custom-made than the prince's, but he has dressed to emulate the fashions of the Federation and, to a lesser degree, the Ferengi, eschewing his people's traditional garb. Even though he is careful to stay half a step behind the prince as they approach my desk, I can tell he is unaccustomed to showing such deference. In fact, his secondary status here seems to rankle him.

They halt in front of my desk, and the prince favors me with the ghost of a nod. His voice is rich with educated inflections. "Thank you for seeing us on such short notice, Mister Miller."

"My pleasure, Highness." I gesture to the chairs facing my desk. "Please, sit."

Xifal gathers the slack of his robes in a practiced flourish as he sits down. Molob plants himself on the other chair with all the grace of a collapsing building. While the chairman squirms and fights to shoehorn himself between his chair's arms, Xifal ignores him and proceeds to business with an air of unctuous charm. "Your builders have been rather busy, I see."

"Yes. I'm quite pleased with their progress."

The prince's charm fades. "We're not." He gestures toward Molob but maintains eye contact with me. "Chairman Molob and I feel that—"

"Excuse me," I interrupt with a raised hand. I look away from Xifal to stare at Molob. "I'm afraid I'm still unclear on what, exactly, you're the chairman of."

Molob's voice is every bit as rough as Xifal's is smooth, and twice as deep. "I represent a number of prominent Orion business interests."

"*Syndicated* interests, no doubt." His frown informs me that my innuendo regarding the criminal outfit known as the Orion Syndicate has hit its target. I return my attention to the prince. "My operation isn't even open yet, so I find it hard to imagine you already have a complaint."

My challenge elicits a cold smile from Xifal. "Are you aware of the impact your casino will have on the local economy, Mister Miller?"

"To be honest, I haven't given it much thought. Your economy isn't my concern."

The prince's cool façade gives way to irritation. "It should be, since you live in the midst of it. My economists paint a grim forecast. How attractive a destination do you think this resort of yours will be if you turn the neighboring districts into slums and ghost towns?"

I chuckle at his melodramatics. "Forgive me, Highness, but I think you're overstating the matter. At worst, the competition my business poses for your established gaming and hospitality sector will force a minor downward trend in what had been a wildly inflationary market."

Molob narrows his eyes. "So, you admit you'll be costing us money."

"That's the objective of business, isn't it?" Once again, I snub the chairman and direct my words to the prince. "Why don't we skip to the bottom line, Highness? What do you want?"

He adopts a thoughtful affect. "An annual token gesture of appreciation and support for the local community would go a long way toward easing any lingering resentments. Call it a charitable donation, if you will." He reaches inside his robe, takes out a business card, places it facedown on my desktop, and pushes it a few centimeters toward me. "Something in this range."

Curious to know how high a price he expects me to pay for the privilege of doing business on his planet, I reach over and slide the card to my side of the desk. Then I lift its edge and peek at the amount written there. Xifal, Molob, and their cronies have done their homework; it's a large number, but not an impossible one for me to pay. I leave the card on my desk. "No."

"You should reconsider," Molob says. "Otherwise your grand opening might run into . . . difficulties." His round face is grim and slack, adding weight to his threat.

"Such as?"

Xifal tries to sound nonchalant, as if he's merely speaking in hypothetical terms, though we all know he isn't. "An operation as large as yours needs manpower, Mister Miller. I know the Nalori are providing you with gratis security services, but they can't run your gaming tables, or serve customers in your restaurants. You could bring in workers from offworld, but then you'd have to house them in your hotel, reducing your profits. And they'll cost you more in wages than Orions will. You need Orion labor. But if my government bans Orions from working here . . ."

"That would be a curious strategy on your part, considering you profess to care so deeply about the effect of my resort on the local economy. How much worse will that effect be if you cost this region tens of thousands of high-paying jobs simply out of spite?"

Molob's voice is low and ominous. "You don't want to find out."

"We'll see. It's an interesting scenario." I pick up Xifal's business card and fold it into an origami crane. "Unfortunately for you, it's based on a faulty premise."

The prince watches my eyes, not my hands; he's a shrewd one, I can tell. "Faulty?"

"Afraid so. You see, Highness, most of my operation is automated. The cleaning and laundry are done by machines. Most of my single-player games require no direct supervision. The multiplayer tables are run by holographic dealers and croupiers. My restaurant servers and spa therapists are also holograms, as are the bartenders and hosts. Instead of a pit boss, my gaming floors are overseen by the most sophisticated casino-management AI ever designed. I employ only a handful of specialists, most of them chefs, to provide gourmet dining experiences for those customers whose palates and budgets have evolved beyond replicated fare." I flash a devil-may-care smile and recline with my hands behind my head of white hair. "So ban your people from working here, it won't matter to me." I shoot a glance at Molob. "Besides, I never saw any reason to give your people easy access to my operation. I'm not going to start now."

The chairman launches himself from his chair and lurches around my desk. I stand and meet him halfway. He towers over me, so close that I can smell his cloyingly sweet spice cologne and sour-mash halitosis. Murder burns in his eyes, yet something keeps the lummox from finishing what he started. Maybe he's not as stupid as he looks. He seems to understand that even though I don't look like a match for him, there must be a reason I'm not backing down. I almost hope his temper gets the best of him; I can break him like a twig if I choose to do so.

Xifal's voice is an icy knife cutting through the heated moment. "Molob. Sit down."

The chairman stands frozen a moment, then backs away from me. "I was just leaving."

As Molob heads for the door, the prince keeps his eyes on me and does his best to feign polite disappointment. "A pity. I'd hoped we might be friends."

"You came here with a purpose, Highness, but it wasn't friendship." I pick up one of my business cards from a small silver stand on my desk, and hold it out toward him. "But that doesn't mean we need to part company as enemies."

He radiates suspicion as he looks at the proffered card. He inches toward me like a wild animal creeping up on something it thinks might be bait. Then he gingerly plucks the card from my hand, turns it over, and peruses my counteroffer. "This is half what I asked for."

"I could give you nothing." I savor his scathing glare, then add, "But if you're willing to accept my counteroffer, I could arrange to have some of the resort's noncritical support services outsourced to the local community. For instance, all our laundry and off-site cleaning, as well as our food-and-beverage procurement and live entertainments."

The prince mulls my terms. I can tell he's unhappy with them, but he seems smart enough to understand that this unpleasant compromise is preferable to waging a mutually self-destructive conflict. "What should I tell Molob?"

"I'd be honored to offer the chairman a seat on my board of directors. A position that comes with a considerable stipend—and no actual responsibilities. Not even attendance."

Xifal puts on a sour look of resignation, then pockets my card. "I'll talk to him."

"I look forward to hearing from you, Highness, and hope you'll both be my honored guests at the grand opening next month." We shake hands, then he leaves without offering me the customary valedictory pleasantries. It's just as well. I'm happy to see the back of him.

I return to my desk, drop into my chair, and let it

swivel to face the broad window. Outside, the sleek vista of high-tech high-rises and dense blurs of air traffic are bathed in golden morning light. I'm surrounded by modernity, yet the ways of business remain unchanged since the age of barter and battery. I should be appalled, but I'm exhilarated.

So sue me. I may be an android, but I'm still a man.

MAY
2374

14

Few experiences are so thoroughly satisfying as seeing one's plans come to fruition even more perfectly than expected.

It's been less than eighteen months since I opened the Imperial Star Resort here inside the Nalori diplomatic compound. As my calculations predicted, the Ferengi seriously undervalued the house's edge, but that's only partially their fault. They were notoriously pessimistic in their forecast of the resort's prospects in the face of resistance from the entrenched Orion interests, but that accounts for only a small fraction of the Ferengi's error. There was no way they could have known the advantage I would enjoy by using holographic gaming personnel controlled by a security system of my own design—one that measures real-time biometric data from all players at all points in the resort, observing their responses for signs of deception, while simultaneously analyzing the outcome of every wager for any sign of variance from the normal range of gaming probability. Most modern casinos employ systems like it, but none are so sophisticated as mine, and none are even a hundredth as fast. While other systems blunder along on isolinear cores linked by FTL optronics, I've deployed a holographic AI matrix that processes information in fields of exoquads—orders of magnitude beyond anything else in known space.

It also helps that business has been good. After the outbreak of the Dominion War five months ago, tourist traffic inside the neutral Orion Colonies saw a sharp increase. No place inside any of the territories surrounding the Orion Colonies is safe—the Federation, the Cardassian Union, and the Klingon Empire are all swept up in this martial madness. The only spot for a hundred light-years where people can relax without fear is here, among the Orions.

The uptick in recreational traffic has had another beneficial effect, from my point of view: it's keeping the Orions busy, flush with profit, and off my back. They appear to be mollified by the deal I struck with Prince Xifal and Chairman Molob. There's plenty of tourist money to go around, so for now they're minding their own business and letting me do the same.

Walking the ground floor of the resort's central tower, I drink in the sound of pleasure transformed into profit. The electronic singsong of automated gaming machines mingles with the susurrus of conversation, punctuated by bursts of laughter and whooping cheers of elation and surprise. Holographic servers deliver drinks and snacks to the high-rollers, winners and losers alike, ensuring there's no reason for anyone to leave his or her ergonomically designed chair at a table. I pass the blackjack tables and smile at the musical percussion of clay chips as they're committed to the pot. One glance at the table and already I can tell who's going to double down and be sorry for it, who's going to stand when they ought to hit, and who should not be there to begin with. The clack and rattle of roulette wheels is almost drowned out by the exaggerated feedback sounds from the dabo wheel. It's in midspin, moving too fast for most humanoids to gauge, but I can see that no one has made the winning bet of triple over. Their loss, my gain.

I cross the opulent atrium on my way to check the restaurants that serve as my resort's crown jewels, and I'm intercepted halfway across by my hotel's general manager, Katja Tangano, an attractive but stern human woman from one of the Rigel colonies. I can tell by her rigid posture and pinched features that something is less than optimal, and it must be significant in order to merit my attention. She falls into step beside me without making eye contact, a data padd clutched to her breast, and her chin held high. "Good evening, Mister Miller."

"Katja. What's on your mind?"

"Security breach." She hands me the padd. "A saboteur introduced malicious code into our replicator database while trying to use it as a backdoor to the casino's security system."

I've wondered when something like this would happen. I can't say it's unexpected, but it's tedious all the same. I hand back the padd without looking at it. "Sum up for me."

"Breach detected and contained within twenty seconds, perpetrator arrested."

I lead her inside the Terran-Vulcan fusion restaurant, whose ruddy lighting and spice-scented atmosphere provides a welcome respite from the bright, chilly noise of the gaming floor. I take a circuitous path around the busy dining room to the kitchen. "Who's our hacker?"

"A Yridian named Lokos. We're running an ID check to see if that's an alias."

"I can almost guarantee it will prove to be. How much damage did he do?"

She checks the padd. "He corrupted the replicator patterns for ninety percent of our most popular level-one menu items. We have a growing backlog of unfilled orders, and cancellations are starting to come in."

I round the corner into the kitchen with Katja close behind me. I ask over my shoulder, "How long to restore the database?"

"Six hours."

"Mark down all level-two dishes to level-one prices and offer all customers with backlogged orders free drinks or desserts."

"Done." She peels away, relaying my instructions via her earpiece comm as I taste-test the latest creations of chefs David Auerbach of Earth and T'Nal of Vulcan with a discerning palate and an approving nod. "Excellent work, gents. Dave, the jambalaya needs a touch more heat. T'Nal, I'd suggest a pinch of Andorian cilantro for the plomeek-miso soup." Both chefs fix me with evil stares of contempt for daring to tell them their business, and I pretend not to notice as I leave via the rear service exit, into the support corridors hidden from public view.

Setbacks and petty incursions notwithstanding, the resort is proving more profitable than anything I'd ever imagined. At this rate, it will have paid for its own creation within another two months. Everything after that will be pure profit, on a scale to rival the gross domestic products of a few of the smaller interstellar nations in local space.

With all this talk of profits, you must think I sound like a Ferengi. But unlike me, those avaricious little opportunists acquire assets for their own sake—for bragging rights or, in the case of the more superstitious ones, to buy themselves a better afterlife when they face the Blessed Exchequer. I, on the other hand, have more concrete motives for amassing this type of obscene wealth. You see, it costs a great deal of money to buy a planet.

I'm not even talking about a particularly lush Class-M planet, either. Anyone of generous means can buy an island. More than a few have even laid claim to continents. One person in a trillion might have the resources to buy a small moon. But purchasing a whole planet, *any* planet, requires a vast fortune. Many well-financed corporations, both public and private, have leased mining rights or staked resource-development claims on worlds, but that's not the same thing. To acquire a world outright, so that it becomes a private and sovereign possession, is a capital investment the likes of which has been accomplished only a handful of times throughout recorded history. In fact, I can find evidence of only three people who have ever done so, all of whom conducted the transactions through shell corporations.

Why buy a planet? For one thing: privacy. When you own a world free and clear, you no longer need to worry about explaining yourself to anyone. Sequestered on my own private planet, I can make up new identities at will; I can become anyone I want at any time. Free of the surveillance state and its cumbersome rules, I will be free to face my nigh-immortal existence on my own terms. And it will be a perfect hideaway for the new life I've planned with Juliana.

I still have no idea how to woo her from that husband of hers, and that realization troubles my thoughts as I board a service lift that will take me back up to my office suite. I appease the biometric security system with my voiceprint and retinal scan before directing it upward to my sanctum. As the lift car hums along, I imagine several scenarios by which I might win back Juliana's heart. The craziest, of course, would be to tell her the truth. I could explain what happened to her on Terlina III, what she really is, why I did this for her, and how much more I can still do. I'd like to believe she'd reward such honesty, but experience tells me otherwise. The truth will have to come out sometime, but the timing will be a delicate matter.

Ah, well. There'll be time to sort all that out soon enough. One step at a time, as my old mentor used to say. Solve the problem in front of you, then move on to the next.

The lift stops, its doors open, and I step out and pass my secretary's desk. I catch the fetching young Trill lass's eye on my way into my office. "Laryn. Any messages?"

"A few dozen. All waiting on your private comm."

"Very good. Hold my calls unless there's an emergency."

She confirms the instruction with a demure smile and the hint of a nod.

My office door closes behind me. I stroll behind my desk and take in the view of the Orion capital at nightfall. The city's grid is a constellation of light, with my resort at its center. For a few moments, the universe feels like a machine tuned to my purposes, a pliant servant bending graciously to my will. It's almost as if I can see the future shaping itself to suit me.

Then the unthinkable happens.

It's a tiny thing, a fleeting signal of less than a microsecond, resonating inside a dedicated circuit in my positronic brain. Inside that circuit is a single quark, quantum entangled with a distant partner. It's reacting to a pulse from its mate, somewhere else in the galaxy.

The signal is simply the binary code for seven: 111.

That's Juliana's code. The one I programmed into her termination circuit, to notify me if anything ever happened to her. For decades I monitored that circuit in my lab, praying it would never activate. I installed it into my own android brain so that I could never be parted from it.

No, this has to be a mistake. This can't be true. It's a malfunction.

I open an encrypted channel to my ship. "Shakti, search all news from Atrea IV, anything related to Juliana Tainer. Do it quickly."

She reacts to my panic by striking a calming note. *"Hang on, I'm checking."* Seconds pass in silence as all my processors spin and loop on one morbid thought, on the possibility that Juliana really is gone. I don't want to think about it, but it floods every cell of my consciousness. Then Shakti speaks, and I'm grateful to have her voice break my spell of mourning. *"I'm sorry, I found no recent news about Juliana Tainer."*

"No, of course not. It's too soon. . . . My God. I might be the first person who knows she's dead." Suddenly, my imagination takes a cruel turn: What if she's been the victim of foul play? What if someone conducts an autopsy and discovers what she is? I can't rest until I know what's happened. "Shakti, prep *Archeus*. I need to get to Atrea IV as soon as possible."

Less than seventy-two hours later, I'm on the surface of Atrea IV, in the heart of Mainzeros, one of its more picturesque highland cities. Shakti scoured the local news when we made orbit, and found prominent public notices regarding Juliana's demise. Apparently, she and her husband are figures of local notoriety. They lived in a suburb not far from here, one with lots of stone-paved streets and quaint buildings marked by an archaic flavor. Even here in a so-called city, there's little technology in open view; the Atreans like to pretend they still live in simpler times.

Hacking into the civilian health-care system's database proves simpler than I'd expected. Within minutes of reaching the surface, I confirm that Juliana's body has been brought to the morgue in the Kessatol Medical Center in Mainzeros. Fortunately, because the initial on-site exam of her body indicated no signs of wrongful death, she hasn't been scheduled for autopsy. I just hope I can get to her before they do anything drastic; the Atreans have little regard for their dead, and eschew such funerary practices as burial or viewings of the corpse. As a general rule, they cremate their dead as soon as it's practical to do so, and conduct their memorials at home.

Even though my current disguise isn't an Atrean, I draw scant attention as I walk among the locals and ride beside them on maglev streetcars. As a full member of the Federation, Atrea IV sees its fair share of offworld visitors and alien permanent residents. For this trip, I've divorced myself as profoundly as I can from my casino-magnate persona. The greenish cast of my complexion, the elegant curves of my upswept ear tips, my steep brows, and my atrociously bowl-cut sable hair mark me unmistakably as a Vulcan. I've kept my attire simple, just a black jacket and trousers with a dark gray shirt and black shoes. I don't want to attract attention or be memorable. My aim is to be forgettable.

It's midday when I reach the medical center. My positronic brain translates its Atrean signage automatically, and I navigate the sprawling complex's labyrinth of corridors with ease. Along the way, I pass several members of the hospital staff, who appear to hail from a wide variety of Federation species. This world has become more cosmopolitan in recent years than I'd realized. Good; that will be useful.

Soon, I spy an empty staff lounge with some free-standing lockers. I slip inside and walk to the lockers. Examining the security keypads with my visual receptors adjusted to microscopic settings, I see patterns of genetic material on the keys that suggest their security codes are only four digits long, and based on the visible technology, their locks require no biometric data. Normally, a ten-digit keypad using a four-digit code means any given lock might be using any of ten thousand possible combinations. But if you know which four digits to use and only their order is left to be determined, there are only twenty-four possible combinations.

Putting my android body's dexterity, visual acuity, and reflexes to good use, I start entering each of the twenty-four likely combinations for the closest locker. In 4.6 seconds, on my eleventh attempt, the locker door opens. I am in luck; inside I find a doctor's blue lab coat, standard garb in Atrean hospitals. I put it on and grab a data padd from the locker's top shelf. Now I can be even less conspicuous, just another staff member in a large medical center. I slip out of the lounge and walk at a leisurely pace to the nearest lift, which I take to the morgue sublevel. As I'd hoped, when the lift stops at an intermediate floor to admit an Atrean nurse, she acknowledges my presence with a polite smile and an averted gaze. Playing my part as a Vulcan, I respond with the most minor dip of my chin and no change in my expression. She pays me no heed and continues to ignore me as I step out into the sublevel and continue on my way.

Like most such facilities, the morgue in the Kessatol Medical Center is populated by only the most minimal staff. There seems to be little need for forensic medical investigation on this planet; that, coupled with the Atreans' preference for post-mortem cremation, means most of this facility is likely unused at any given time.

The drawback to this is that an unfamiliar person will be far more noticeable in the morgue than in other areas of the hospital. I need to be more careful from this point forward.

I observe the activity in the morgue from a safe distance down the corridor. Two people, an older Atrean man and a young female Trill who I think might be a medical student, seem to be the only ones working here at the moment. I listen in on their conversation and deduce that they are on their way to run tests in their adjacent laboratory.

They head to the lab through a connecting door, which closes behind them. I hurry inside the morgue and find an unsecured computer terminal. Its access is limited to morgue records, but that's all I need at the moment. I find Juliana's record and transfer a copy to my stolen padd. Then I note which stasis drawer her body is in, and I move off through a different door into a large space of gleaming metal, cold tile floors, and pale blue light that can drain the color from any face. The air is sharp with antiseptic. Counters along two walls are lined with analysis machines of various kinds, computers, and safe disposal boxes for medical waste. Lined up in the middle of the room are several autopsy tables. They're simple things: metal platforms with raised edges, vented grid plates suspended in frames above shallow basins that feed deep drains, faucets at the head to provide hot and cold running water, and flexible hoses to direct water or compressed air as desired. Next to each table is a tray loaded with medieval-looking surgical instruments. Above each table is a movable bank of lights. This room looks as if it hasn't been used for an actual autopsy in months, but I still get a shiver from being here.

Eager to be gone, I move at a brisk step beside the room's far wall, which is a grid of recessed stasis pods.

I find the one the computer says contains Juliana. The metal hatch folds down and opens at my slightest touch, and the slab on which her body rests slides out for examination. I lift the pale gray sheet from her face and draw it back. Then I freeze. She has aged, of course—I designed her to—but she's just as radiant as she was when I knew her, so long ago. Grief wells up within me, and I fight to choke back my emotions. There is too much to do. I can't let my anguish sidetrack me, not now.

I find the edge of the flap beneath her hair, over her temporal lobe. I press it in and give it a firm nudge until it flips open. Then I set down the padd and take some precision tools from my pants pockets. A few quick tests confirm the worst: this is no mistake, no malfunction.

She's dead. My lovely Juliana is gone.

Her biofeedback circuit is still active, masking her true nature from scans; that much at least has gone right, but I'm paralyzed with confusion. How can she be dead already? In this day and age, when humans routinely live two or even three decades past their centenaries, why would Juliana's android body decide to shut down when she was only in her seventies? Her chart offers no explanation; all it says next to CAUSE OF DEATH is "natural causes." Utter garbage.

I run a few tests of her biofeedback logs, determined to find a better answer. It's slow going now that her positronic matrix has completely succumbed to cascade failure. I have to work around dead pathways in my search for the truth.

Then I hear footsteps heading in my direction: more than one person. They are still a couple of rooms away; yet again I'm grateful for the sensitivity of my aural receptors.

I press shut the flap on Juliana's head and return her

body to the stasis pod with a gentle nudge. The hatch automatically lifts closed with a barely audible hum. I pick up my stolen padd from the floor and take stock of my options. I can't leave the way I came in, since that's where the steps are coming from. There's an open doorway on the other side of the room, so I steal toward it, taking care to step lightly. I slip inside, and duck around a corner, using my night-vision filter to assess my surroundings. It's a small antechamber, a washroom for the staff. There's a long trough sink, some sanitizing-field emitters, bins for soiled work garments, and what I presume are toilet stalls. Hiding next to the doorway with my back against the wall, I can observe the examination room thanks to a mirror opposite me, facing the open doorway.

The Atrean coroner enters first, trailed by his female Trill student.

Following them into the room is Data, in his Starfleet uniform.

I cease respirating and halt my synthetic heartbeat. Every system in my body goes silent. For all intents, I'm practically a statue. Data's hearing is nearly as sensitive as mine; I can't take a chance on him detecting my presence, so I begin shifting the color of my complexion to a darker hue, to minimize the possibility of his catching my reflection inside the darkened room.

Fortunately for me, all his attention seems to be on the doctors as they lead him to Juliana's pod. They open it for him, and his face seems to age years in a moment as he looks down at her. He reaches out as if to touch her cheek, then stops just shy of contact.

"How did she die?"

The coroner checks his padd. "The test I just ran indicates it was a severe stroke. I was just getting ready to update her file."

Data looks bewildered. His voice goes flat; I think he's in shock. "I was not aware she was at risk for such an event."

"Normally, she wouldn't be. But I think it was triggered by some natural compounds found in Atrean produce interacting unpredictably with a quirk of her human biology. Some of the medications she was taking for hypertension might also have played a part."

Damn my perfectionism! I made her biomimetic circuit too well. I knew it would have been too suspicious to give her the appearance of flawless health as she grew older, so I designed her biofeedback system to adapt dynamically to her diet and environment. It never even occurred to me that I might condemn her to an early grave because of some freak confluence of factors.

The coroner seems ill at ease standing beside Data. I think it might be because Atreans are unaccustomed to someone standing so enraptured over the body of a dead loved one. As if trying to cue Data, he says with practiced sincerity, "I'm sorry for your loss." When Data doesn't move or respond, the coroner and his student exchange flustered looks. Then the coroner asks, "Do you need anything else, Commander?"

"A few minutes." Data fixes the coroner with a frank stare. "May I have a few minutes alone with my mother?" His tone makes it clear he's giving an order, not asking permission.

The coroner nods and ushers his student out ahead of him. "We'll be outside."

As soon as the pair leave, Data surveys the room, his face a mask of suspicion. He looks up and around, perhaps searching for surveillance devices but finding none. He reaches down and strokes Juliana's hair, and his eyes shine with the promise of tears.

Then he gently presses the side of her head. What is he doing? Does he know about Juliana? My God, he must. He opens the flap over her temporal lobe, just as I did. He draws a tricorder from a holster on his belt and scans Juliana's defunct positronic brain. He frowns, then shuts off the tricorder, holsters it, and closes the flap on his mother's head.

I know from his logs that he met her a few years ago, but I had no idea he'd discovered her true nature. He and his friends on the *Enterprise* must have redacted the information from their records to protect her privacy. For that matter, they must have concealed the truth from Juliana, or else she'd have gone into cascade failure years ago. I wonder if Data found the message chip I left embedded inside her brain. Wouldn't that be something?

My runaway train of thought is derailed as Data calls out, "Doctor!" The coroner rushes in, and Data adds, "My mother's husband, Pran Tainer, has released her remains to me. You will find the necessary authorizations on file with your administrative office."

"Yes, Commander. We've been informed. They finished the *tai-lun* yesterday."

Data takes another look at Juliana, then he walks away and rejoins the doctor, who follows him out as he says, "Have her body prepared for transport and loaded onto my shuttlecraft. It is currently parked on the hospital's secondary rooftop landing platform."

The door closes behind them, leaving me once again alone with Juliana.

Had I known Data was planning to claim her body, I wouldn't have risked coming here. My plan had been to liberate her body from this place by beaming it up with me to *Archeus*. Now I can't even consider doing that. I know Data too well; he's a relentless investigator once his curiosity is engaged. And though I have plans for his future, I'm not yet ready to reveal myself to him. No, it's time to go.

I ditch the doctor's jacket in a laundry bin and abandon the padd in one of the toilet stalls. Then I key my subdural transceiver. "Shakti, do you read me?"

"Yes, Noonien. Are you ready to beam up with your cargo?"

"It'll just be me. Get the ship ready to fly. We have to go."

"Understood. Stand by. Energizing . . ."

For a moment I consider trying to follow Data's shuttlecraft in *Archeus,* but what would be the point? Data might be arranging some kind of memorial for Juliana aboard the *Enterprise,* but it's not as if he plans on burying her in space afterward. No, he'll almost certainly inter her remains in his mausoleum of my failures, beside the three miscarriages, his daughter, and the lobotomized husk of Lore. Still, it could be worse. At least she'll be with family.

I bid a silent farewell to Juliana as the transporter beam enfolds me.

Fais de beaux rêves, ma chérie.

What should have been a short jaunt home has turned into a nearly three-week-long debacle. I'd plotted what I thought was a safe and relatively direct course back to Orion, only to find that a recent offensive by Dominion forces and their Cardassian allies has turned the sectors between myself and the Orion homeworld into a bitterly contested war zone.

To get home without the risk of becoming collateral damage, I've been forced to detour "south," nearly a hundred light-years beneath the central regions of the galactic plane, in a loping elliptical path that I and other civilian traffic have been assured will keep us clear of the fighting. Having learned over the years what Starfleet's promises are worth, I fully expect to be waylaid by a Jem'Hadar warship at any moment.

If there's any benefit to this roundabout path, it's not so much that it's safer as that it's given me a forced vacation from my life. It occurs to me that much of my time in recent months has been spent running the resort and planning for a future with Juliana—a future that's no longer possible. All that's left of it is the collapsed wave function of my unfulfilled hopes.

Even though it no longer matters, I still can't help but wonder how I would ever have rekindled our old love. Now that she's gone, it feels easier to admit to myself that she had long since moved on. When I'd first left Atrea IV after saying my farewell, I put *Archeus* on autopilot and tried to silence the chaos in my neural net by letting myself sleep. As soon as my conscious functions went off line, I dreamed of open water, a dark expanse of ocean under a hostile sky ribboned with lightning. I was swimming out to sea and had passed beyond the point where I could hope to touch the bottom. Above me was fire and thunder; beneath me, an insatiable abyss. Flashing forks from the heavens stabbed at the rolling waves, and I knew that it would be only a matter of time until one of those thunderbolts found me. All at once, swimming felt futile. There was no land in sight, no thought of rescue. It would be so much easier to stop struggling and let my weight drag me down into the darkness. Yet . . . I kept on swimming.

Some dreams are simpler to interpret than others. The subconscious is not always subtle.

After I awoke, I let my thoughts turn toward nostalgia. Before long, my reminiscing turned maudlin, and

I found myself reliving my memories of the lost and departed: my old colleagues, not least of them that arrogant but charming windbag, Ira Graves; all my failed sons—the three who never gained sentience, and the one whose mind became twisted by envy and ambition into something violent and ugly; and now, unkindest cut of all, my Juliana.

I've let myself wallow in my brooding long enough. I've relived years of memories in a matter of days, poring over every engram and reconstructing the details from my journals and holographic recordings to build a better mental archive of my life. It's time to think of something other than the dead. I still have one living son; he should be my focus now.

The optimist in me wants to believe I still have two sons, that B-4 might still be out there somewhere, but the cynic in me knows that's unlikely. It was early 2335 when I left him on Draken IV and went back to Omicron Theta to assemble Lore and Data, using the techniques I'd perfected on B-4. Master of procrastination that I am, it took me more than twenty-one years to return to Draken IV. I arrived one freezing-cold night to find my old rented lab ransacked, and all its valuable equipment stolen . . . along with B-4. If only I'd fitted him with a homing beacon and recall circuit, maybe I could have tracked him down. But what was done was done, and I resigned myself to the fact that my son was gone, probably disassembled in some government-backed laboratory, far away in some forsaken corner of the galaxy.

Some father I turned out to be; I abandoned all my sons. Data's done well enough for himself, but poor B-4—how long has he been missing? At least eighteen years now, maybe longer. The shame of what I did over the course of my biological lifetime weighs heavily on my conscience, and now I can't help but think I've failed Juliana just as gravely, by making her the victim of my perfectionism and obsessive drive to make my androids as "real" as possible. Why did *real* have to mean fragile? Or mortal? Wasn't it enough to make them in my image? Did I also have to curse them with my own limitations? I didn't see any reason to burden my own new vessel with those shortcomings, so why did I handicap my sons and the love of my life?

I shake off my self-recrimination with a flush of anger and a surge of determination. I need to think about Data now. He is the last part of me still thriving openly in the universe. It's time I turned my resources to his benefit. I need to understand him and his life better than I do, and then ask myself what I can do to improve his existence. It's time I was more to my son than a creator figure, distant in time and memory; it's time I started acting like his father.

Archeus is close enough now to Federation space that I'm able to tap into one of Starfleet's automated long-range comm relays. One of the fringe benefits of the war is that there's so much signal traffic that my occasional snooping sessions get lost in the torrent. I'm also close enough that I can use my backdoor codes to access Data's newest logs, and see what he's been up to since he claimed Juliana's body on Atrea IV. It takes several seconds to make a connection that can't be traced back to me, a few seconds more to download the logs, and then I cover my virtual tracks and terminate the comm channel before anyone gets curious about it.

This batch of entries is more numerous than I'd expected, and of greater length and detail than usual. It must have been an eventful three weeks for Data. I open the files, have Shakti scan them to make sure they contain no harmful code, and then I download them directly into my positronic brain. Precisely 3.782 seconds later, I sit back, stunned. *Eventful* is an understatement. Data and his shipmates unraveled a five-hundred-thousand-year-old mystery and uncovered the secret history of artificial intelligence in the Milky Way—exposing a web of interconnectedness that includes not only myself but also my friendly rival Ira Graves, our visionary mentor, Emil Vaslovik, and our ill-fated 2304 joint expedition to the caves beneath the surface of Exo III.

You probably think I'm exaggerating. I'm not. I'll concede that Data's account of events strains credulity, but I've never known him to lie. Omit facts, yes. But never lie.

His latest adventure seems to begin with a violent attack on the Starfleet lab at the Daystrom Institute Annex on Galor IV. Captain Bruce Maddox—yes, the same cretin who tried to take Data apart in the name of "science"—was found nearly dead. A shame his attackers didn't finish the job. But I digress. It seems his life was saved by Vaslovik, who in turn faked his own death and escaped with a prototype android he had been developing for the past two years with Maddox and his collaborators, Admiral Anthony Haftel—yes, the clod whose meddling hastened the cascade failure of Data's precious daughter, Lal—and two holographic systems experts, Doctor Lewis Zimmerman and Lieutenant Reginald Barclay.

This prototype android sounds remarkable, even though there are no schematics or even rudimentary scans. My old mentor, the "father of neurocybernetics," and his new minions used a holographic matrix to stabilize a nascent positronic brain, thereby protecting it from cascade anomalies and fostering more rapid formation of new cybersynaptic pathways in its neural net, greatly accelerating its development, learning capacity, and processing speed. It's an elegant proposition, and if what Data says is true, they made it work. I can tell right away this is a stroke of pure genius, because I'm already fuming with envy and wishing I'd thought of it first.

The *Enterprise* crew investigated the attack, and to make a long story short, got drawn into a rather violent kerfuffle involving more sentient AIs than anyone in Starfleet has ever seen before. Data, not surprisingly, ended up in the midst of the fray and emerged somewhat worse for wear. Along the way, he writes, he and his comrades made some remarkable discoveries.

It seems my son shares my gift for mind-boggling understatement.

They uncovered incontrovertible evidence that my old mentor, Emil Vaslovik, is actually a six-thousand-year-old man, some manner of unique mutant, an immortal who remains in the prime of his adulthood. Data says Vaslovik has lived under countless aliases through the millennia. You might have heard a few of his names mentioned in passing: Leonardo da Vinci, Alexander the Great, Johannes Brahms, Solomon, Lazarus of the rock, Merlin . . . and no doubt a hundred other names lost to antiquity.

This immortal genius of innumerable names had a penchant for creating and nurturing sentient artificial intelligence, perhaps because he hoped to create a companion he wouldn't so easily outlive. His latest work of art, this holotronic android, apparently shares his talent for assuming identities and deceiving people. Templated as a human female of mixed European and Japanese heritage, she adopted the *nom de guerre* Rhea McAdams and, with Vaslovik's help, insinuated herself as the *Enterprise*'s new security chief within days of being activated.

A week after Data was first activated, he could barely tie his shoes.

Now this brilliant, absurdly powerful holotronic android is at large, traveling as a guest of the same fellowship of artificial intelligence whose overtures I rebuffed a few years ago. And Vaslovik? Vanished without a trace, leaving behind countless unanswered questions, a swath of destruction, and no doubt his most recent identity, shed like a reptile's worn-out skin.

But all these details, as monumental as they might appear on their face, are incidental. They are overshadowed by a matter of far greater importance, a trend in Data's personal logs.

My son has fallen in love. With Vaslovik's android, Rhea McAdams.

Imagine my relief to read in Data's own words that the attraction is mutual. She's as smitten with him as he is with her. And now he's pining for her, patiently awaiting her return.

My eyes tear up, and a flood of mixed emotions trembles my lower lip even as a goofy smile contorts my features. I'm overcome with joy for Data and envy for Vaslovik. For forty-one thousandths of a second, I don't know which emotion to indulge. Then I decide, *What the hell; I am legion.* I surrender myself to both feelings at once. *My boy is in love.*

15

I'm a day's travel away from Orion and clear of any threat from the sprawling war zone known colloquially as the Alpha Quadrant. Shakti is compiling the latest updates from the resort so I can go to work the moment we arrive, and I'm passing my time trying to imagine how to stabilize a positronic brain inside a holographic matrix. To fill the empty spaces in my thoughts, I'm listening to a recording of Igor Stravinsky's suite from *The Firebird*. *Archeus*'s narrow confines roar with the thunderous beauty of the classic Russian ballet, which fuses the myth of a bird of fire that's both a blessing and a curse to those who dare to possess it, and the folk legend of Koschei the Deathless, a man who cheats death only to pay dearly in the end for his hubris.

Doing things the hard way has never been my first choice, though I've never let difficulty dissuade me from pursuing an idea. Naturally, my first step in attempting to duplicate Vaslovik's holotronic technology was to try to steal it remotely from the computers of the Daystrom Institute Annex on Galor IV, using a number of custom-built, self-replicating viral programs that I uploaded to their mainframe via the Federation's comnet. To my dismay, Vaslovik had wiped the Annex's computers of all information related to his new android. There was literally nothing left for me to steal. So, I started from tabula rasa, with just the idea itself to guide me.

One week later, that's still all I have. That and a festering resentment of Vaslovik.

I suppose I should be grateful. I've spent the past few days alternately giddy for Data and stewing with jealousy toward my old mentor. Mostly the latter, actually. I've hardly had time to be depressed about Juliana, though I continue to be haunted by endless hypothetical situations I can never test: *What if I hadn't programmed her biofeedback circuit so well? What if I had told her the truth of what she was twenty-six years ago, when I first activated her? What if I had thought to make two copies of her mind and keep one safe, in case of something like this?*

Empty queries such as these are ridiculous, a cruel waste of my time, yet they consume ever-increasing blocks of my neural network. Why can't I break free of this pattern? It always seemed so simple to tell other people to "let go" or "move on" or "get back to living," but now that I'm the one with a huge hole in my life where Juliana used to be, I see it's not so easy.

Shakti lowers the volume on the music to give me a routine update. *"Noonien? Orion's space-traffic control network has sent us an automated hail. They're asking for our approach vector and final destination. Shall I reply with our flight plan?"*

I'm about to approve her suggestion when an infinitesimal anomaly in my neural net arrests my every thought. It's a flash of action in my quantum entangled-particle circuit lasting less than four picoseconds—an event so brief, it can barely be said to have happened at all. But it did happen, my synaptic activity log confirms it. A single iteration of binary code from the entangled particle, an unmistakable message: 111.

It had to have come from Juliana's positronic matrix, but that shouldn't be possible. Once her matrix collapsed into cascade failure, triggering her entangled-particle circuit, that should have been the end. No technique known to science can rouse a failed positronic mind. Once its pathways degrade, they and the mind they harbored are gone forever, irretrievable and irreparable. But if that's true, what tripped her EPC? The only event I can conceive that might do so would be a spontaneous re-formation of her matrix, but that's an impossibility. Such an event would be nothing less than a thermodynamic miracle of the highest order.

Might Data have surpassed me in his knowledge of cybernetics? Is it possible he claimed Juliana's body because he had some plan for her? If he's revived her, he'll have to explain to her what she really is. I should be there for that discussion. Secrecy and safety be damned; if this was just a misfire caused by a failed repair attempt, I'll stay in the shadows, but I have to know.

"Change of plans. Shakti, fire up the sensors. I need to get a lock on Juliana's homing beacon without actually triggering it. The frequency is in the secured computer core."

"I have it." While Shakti engages the ship's sensors, I turn off the music and monitor the master control console. Minutes later—an interval that feels like an eternity to me—she presents a star chart on the navigational console. *"I detect a faint signal on the designated frequency. Bearing two-eight-four, mark one-nine. Range, four hundred sixteen-point-two light-years."*

I stare dumbfounded at the star chart. "That can't be right. The *Enterprise*'s logs report its last heading in the opposite direction, and it can't be more than ninety light-years from here."

"I've checked the readings, Noonien. They're confirmed."

This is insane. Aside from transwarp, I can't think of a known propulsion system that could have covered that much distance in so short a time. And if Data and the *Enterprise* are headed toward the Cardassian border, why am I detecting Juliana's homing beacon in the Beta Quadrant, far beyond the bounds of explored space? Who would abduct her body? For what purpose? And who would have the expertise to even attempt the reactivation of . . .

I form a hypothesis of what's happened, and I don't like it at all.

"Lay in a direct course on that heading—maximum warp."

A nagging voice deep inside my head warns me not to do this. I ignore it.

I have to know.

Sixty-one days, nine hours, and thirty-seven minutes later, I guide *Archeus* out of warp and pilot it into a circumbinary system—a red dwarf orbiting a small, yellow main sequence star, both encircled by six planets orbiting the two stars' combined gravitational center. The signal from Juliana's homing beacon is originating on the fourth planet, a small Mars-like world—I think the official designation is Class K—with a tenuous nitrogen-oxygen atmosphere. Not that I have any need of air, but it suggests to me that whoever brought Juliana here does.

I approach the planet at impulse and run multiple scans of its surface. No sign of habitation or automation, no artificial signals or power sources other than

Juliana's beacon. As I expected, it's a desolate rock-ball. Locking in the coordinates of the homing beacon, I begin my descent into the atmosphere. *Archeus* is surrounded by a blazing nimbus of air superheated by the friction of my ship's passage, forcing me to rely for a few minutes on instruments alone for navigation. When the fiery turbulence fades, a barren wasteland of cinnamon-colored desert stretches out beneath me. The ground passing below grows thick with jagged formations of rock, which are soon replaced by vertiginous mountain ranges.

Day gives way to night as I follow the beacon's signal into the mountains. I discover a vale surrounded by steep cliffs and forbidding peaks. The signal is emanating from there, so I make a slow circle of the area, gathering sensor data while performing my own visual reconnaissance. I think I'm supposed to be surprised to see, jutting from one mountain's side, a Gothic castle—complete with towers, parapets, and flying buttresses—carved out of the living rock. Instead I nod, as if this makes perfect sense, and then I land *Archeus* in its courtyard.

"Shakti, keep everything ready for immediate lift-off." I get out of my chair and head for the port hatch. "And don't let any strangers inside the ship."

"Understood. Be careful, Noonien."

I take a hand-scanner with me on my way out the hatch. It's been set to zero in on Juliana's beacon, which it's telling me is inside the castle. I take a moment to look around the courtyard. It's empty except for me and my ship. There are several doors leading to different areas of the castle, and all of them are either wide open or ajar. Because no one has challenged my arrival or my decision to park my ship inside its walls, I decide it's probably all right to let myself in for a look around.

Following the beacon's signal, I walk through an open door and continue down a long and outrageously high-ceilinged hallway.

There's nothing to see except naked stone beneath a heavy layer of dust. Mine are the first footprints this corridor has seen in ages—or perhaps ever. If someone brought Juliana here, they might have beamed directly to an inner chamber, obviating the need to walk these halls.

At the end of the hall is a closed door. The scanner says Juliana's beacon signal is coming from the room on the other side. I hesitate for the briefest moment, unsure of what I might say to her after all these years, and then realize I might be getting ahead of myself. Calming myself as best I can, I push the door open and walk inside, prepared for whatever awaits me.

Nothing does. The room is empty, a literal and figurative dead end. There are signs of activity in here, though. I note two sets of footprints on the dusty stone floor; one is significantly larger and wider than the other. The floor is rich with evidence that there has been heavy equipment in here—gouges in the stone where things were dragged, empty bolt-holes where some devices had been secured, and microscopic traces of advanced alloys.

In the center of the room is a large banquet table of polished onyx. Unlike every other surface I've seen so far inside this castle, the tabletop is immaculate. Free of dust, it's so perfect that I can use it as a mirror. I suspect this is a workbench until I see the glint of high-tech debris on the floor beneath the table. I squat and reach under to grab it. As soon as my fingers close around it, I recognize it as my own handiwork. I lift it up and regard it with a tired sigh.

It's what's left of Juliana's beacon and entangled-particle circuit.

Both have been excised from her body by the deft touch of an expert. The severances are beyond surgical in their precision. The person who did this knew how to navigate the complex circuitry of a positronic brain and manipulate its elements with unerring dexterity.

Right away, I can rule out numerous suspects.

This was not Data's doing. If he were going to awaken Juliana, he would have done it aboard the *Enterprise,* probably with the aid of his friend, Geordi La Forge.

Admiral Haftel, Captain Maddox, and their colleagues Barclay and Zimmerman all are exonerated by the simple fact of their sheer ineptitude, both individually and collectively.

But I don't need the deductive reasoning of some great detective to know who's responsible for this. I've known since the moment I felt the spark that heralded her resurrection.

Vaslovik has stolen my Juliana.

AUGUST
2375

16

It's easy to forget just how vast the galaxy really is until you try to find one person who could be anywhere in it. Measuring more than a hundred thousand light-years across and containing nearly four hundred billion stars and trillions of planets, the Milky Way offers a determined recluse more than a few good places to hide.

When I first left the nameless orb where I'd found Juliana's discarded homing beacon, I was at a loss. How could I track her? If she's inactive, if the signal I'd received was just a surge from her EPC as it was being removed, then she's nothing more than a mass of unremarkable elements and compounds, a mote in the endless sea of stars. On the other hand, if she has been reactivated, she can't be navigating the uncharted waters of her second life alone. She would stay with Vaslovik and depend upon him to steer them toward safety.

By the time I'd piloted *Archeus* back into Federation space, I'd concluded that my only hope of finding Juliana was to find Vaslovik. But how does one trace the steps of a man who's spent six millennia learning to be a ghost among the living? I thought about little else on the way back to Orion. After I'd settled back in at the resort and handled the hundred-odd crises that my staff had mismanaged in my absence, I sequestered myself as much as possible from its daily operations and began my investigation into the former lives and methods of Emil Vaslovik.

I began by exhuming a trove of secrets from Starfleet's archives. In addition to their recent dealings with him in his Vaslovik persona, they had at least one prior documented encounter with him, in the last century. It seems he once lived as the enigmatic financier Micah Brack. Later, reusing that name as an alias, he bought his own private planet—Holberg 917G in the Omega system, where he then lived as Flint. It's unclear how many names he's used since then, when his encounter with the crew of James Kirk's *Enterprise* forced him to abandon that identity. All I know for certain is that he surfaced decades later as Emil Vaslovik and embarked upon one of history's most brilliant careers in cybernetics and artificial intelligence.

How ironic. I didn't know that Brack was one of Vaslovik's past incarnations, but his purchase of a planet was one of the chief inspirations for my own post-change plan. Even now, I seem to be lagging more than a century behind Vaslovik—in both genius and guile. All the schemes I thought so novel, all the research I thought so groundbreaking, he pioneered decades before I was born. It's almost as if I'm his shadow brought to life, echoing his every move.

A note in Data's log of the events on Galor IV caught my attention one night. The holographic expert Barclay had mentioned Vaslovik wielding unexpected influence with technology corporation Brock-Cepak when the holotronic android project was in need of cutting-edge hardware that was in short supply and heavy demand. It occurred to me that Vaslovik might be a shareholder in the company. A review of its public filings didn't turn up his name—but what if the corporation knew him under a different identity? He told Kirk that he had been born in Mesopotamia as Akharin. That, too, failed to show up on Brock-Cepak's shareholder list, but I sensed I was on the right path, that I would need to look backward before I could go forward.

I started with every last shred of documentation regarding the purchase of Holberg 917G. That led to a web of holding companies and shell corporations, all of which were tied to other aliases without apparent origins or endings. I catalogued every name that had even a tangential connection to the Immortal's many possessions. Weeks of research turned up financial records dating back more than two centuries, from banks and financial institutions on several worlds throughout the Federation. Sudden influxes of cash linked corporate entities that I would otherwise never have imagined shared a common factor. I followed the money all the way back to Earth, where the Immortal first amassed his multimillennial fortune. The chain of information ended abruptly in the early twenty-first century; many financial records predating the 2030s have been lost. Even so, I had compiled a staggering volume of information about the Immortal—enough from which to begin profiling his financial tactics and strategies.

As the economies of Earth and its neighbors evolved in response to interstellar flight, the Immortal's means of manipulating them and concealing his finances changed with them. A few elements of his modus operandi seem to have remained consistent, however. He tends to reuse names from his past, sometimes with minor changes in spelling, or with inversions of surnames and given names. He also appears to be fond of anagrammatical names—turning "Danforth" into "Thanford," for instance. Also, as much as he tries to be a recluse (whether out of misanthropy, fear, or pragmatism), his abodes never range far from the edges of Federation territory. The financial and technological empire he's built over the centuries still exists, most of it operating now independently of his control but still at his disposal whenever he needs it, which suggests that he continues to have a need for it. No matter how earnestly he tries to divorce himself from the peoples and affairs of the Federation, he continues to rely upon it, however indirectly.

That narrowed my search radius to the periphery of the Federation. Before you mistake that for progress, however, I should point out that there are several million unpopulated star systems abutting the Federation's territory—the Immortal has a marked preference for taking refuge in uninhabited areas—and there was no practical way for me to search all of them. I couldn't limit my inquiries to systems with Class-M worlds, because Data recounted that his recent brush with the Immortal took place on a cloaked space station, constructed by sentient AI robots called exocomps, and orbiting a gas giant populated by vast clouds of sentient nanites.

I couldn't even be certain the Immortal had situated his new lair in orbit of a planet or a star. What if he'd placed it in interstellar space, near anomalies that would discourage the use of the region for shipping? He could dwell in the darkness, invisible and untouchable, for eons. No, if I was going to track down this man who's proved as elusive as a fistful of water, I would have to think as he does, envision the life he leads, and then use that insight to find some errant clue that's escaped his notice. I would have to find a mistake by a man who doesn't make them.

Fortunately, I have the luxuries of being very patient and all but immortal myself.

I began several months ago by meeting with Chairman Molob to discuss a business proposition. In exchange for my making generous donations to selected Orion "charities," he had his associates in the Orion Syndicate send some of their disreputable experts to infiltrate the Immortal's numerous extant business interests, as well as the financial institutions through which he disguises his transactions. Without knowing they were acting on my behalf, those operatives insinuated several pieces of software I've designed that will enable me to monitor all internal and external communications from those organizations. Then I began the laborious process of analyzing that daunting crush of raw intelligence for patterns and commonalities. There were more than I expected; the close relationships between many of the Immortal's corporations have led to a variety of partnerships and joint ventures unrelated to his efforts.

Over time, however, I found evidence of directives and transactions at many of them that originated from the same external agent. Requests for raw materials, arrangements for discreet and anonymous shipping and storage of those materials on a handful of planets in a fringe sector of the Federation, and the liquidation of assets to pay for all of it. All the instructions arrived via encrypted subspace messages that had been routed through hundreds of different comm relays to conceal their point of origin. It took months to recover all those comm logs and trace the signals.

Reassembling those traces has led me to a most unexpected destination.

In a star system known to the Federation only by its catalog number, a Class-M planet orbits an unremarkable F2V star of middling size. Except for the signals that I've tracked back to this planet, no artificial signals or energy signals emanate from its surface. By all accounts it's an unpopulated world, one not under consideration for colonization because Federation scientists believe its ecology is too fragile to survive the disruptions large-scale development would cause. It's exactly the sort of world the Immortal would have selected a century ago. Perhaps his cloaked space station was a unique construction, one he's not prepared to duplicate so soon after its destruction; maybe he simply prefers to live with grass beneath his feet instead of steel.

Regardless of what led the Immortal to this planet, I knew I needed to be cautious. He probably monitors the entire sector for threats of any kind. To pay him a visit, I had to conceal my approach and my presence. To that end, I equipped *Archeus* with a cloaking device, built from schematics acquired by my ever-helpful Orion friends, and "borrowed" a Starfleet-made isolation suit, which uses holographic illusions to render its wearer all but invisible, from the Xenology Department at my alma mater, the Daystrom Institute of Technology.

And now I'm here, on the planet's surface, standing less than thirty meters from a large and beautiful Tuscan-style villa that's nigh-undetectable from space. It stands at the top of a cliff, on the edge of a rain forest, looking down upon a lush valley where six-legged herbivores gambol through waving fields of tall grass.

It's a few minutes before sunset, and this world's white star has been turned pink by atmospheric haze as it sinks into the horizon. Vaslovik stands on the villa's covered promenade, garbed in a pristine white toga, swirling dark purple liquid in a Bordeaux glass with his right hand. He observes the day's end with a wistful gaze, his bearing proud but serene.

He doesn't look a day older than when I first met him, when I was barely nineteen years old, a naïve undergraduate awed by his reputation and his pompous self-assurance.

The sight of him fills me with toxic rage. I fantasize about seizing his head in my hands and crushing it into pulp. I want to drown out his howls of agony with cruel laughter.

I know better than to try. He possesses ancient secrets and terrible power. The forces at his command aren't obvious, but by all accounts he's not a man one should challenge rashly.

Then she appears, and all my anger melts away. Juliana drifts out of the villa, onto the promenade, a vision bathed in the ruddy glow of dusk. She's young again, her wild mane restored to its dark coppery luster, the lines of her face elegant and youthful. I'm snared by the sight of her as she was when we met, when our lives were full of hope, before decades of broken promises and buried resentments drove her from me.

She joins Vaslovik at the promenade's low wall, entwines her arm around his, and rests her head against his shoulder while she admires the sunset. They don't speak. Affectionate glances pass between them. I can see it in their eyes: they are beyond the need for words. It's an image of perfection, of blissful companionship . . . and all I can think is, *Damn you, Vaslovik.*

He's bested me in every respect. It wasn't enough he made my work obsolete with his holotronic android, he did the impossible by reanimating a dead positronic brain, and then he restored my Juliana as I'd hoped to do. He's given her everything I could have—the truth of her existence, eternal youth, and a private paradise for two—and more: the gift of resurrection.

I couldn't imagine how to win her heart from an ordinary man; how can I hope to seduce her from the man who rescued her from Death itself?

Minutes elapse, the sun passes from view, and the sky becomes a study in indigo. Vaslovik and Juliana head inside their home, hand in hand.

All I can do is stand and watch. There's nothing left to say.

Darkness falls, and I watch the lights inside the villa switch off.

Then I walk back to *Archeus,* thirsting for a revenge I have no idea how to take.

An hour later, I'm at warp speed, pushing my ship to its limits, desperate to outrun my shame and sorrow. I can't get the image of Juliana and Vaslovik out of my mind. All I want to do is scream and smash things, to feel something break beneath the force of my anger, but this isn't the time or the place. Damn it, I wish I'd put a holodeck on this ship!

Juliana's lost to me forever. I know it in my heart. But the farther I get from Vaslovik's new Eden, the more my thoughts turn to an even sharper loss: my former mentor has eclipsed my legacy. He's done something I never dreamed possible. But now I know it is. I've seen it.

I can't pretend it doesn't infuriate me. How long has he had such knowledge? How did he acquire it? I can't take it from him by force, but maybe I can duplicate his achievements—and advance beyond them. Yes, that's what I'll do! If he can resurrect a collapsed neural net, so can I. If he can build a holotronic brain, I can make a better one. I revolutionized the science of cybernetics once; I can do it again.

To hell with Vaslovik. Let him hide on the edge of civilization.

I'm going home. I have work to do.

OCTOBER
2376

17

I admire the view from the mountaintop. Hundreds of meters below, beneath a ragged blanket of gray mist, the densest jungle I've ever seen sprawls away in every direction to the horizon. A dark-striped and rainbow-ringed gas giant, this Class-M moon's parent world dominates the lavender sky. Warm breezes waft up from the jungle's canopy, rich with the perfume of fruit blossoms and the stench of rotting organic matter.

Turning my back on the verdant splendor below, I regard the quaint village that occupies the manmade plateau carved from the mountain's bare peak. Dozens of attractive little houses stand in orderly rank and file around a central green space. In the middle of the dark green lawn ringed by well-groomed shrubberies are a gleaming marble statue of the village's founder and a charming gazebo. This was a private research colony founded four decades ago and operated at a significant financial loss by a collective of ecologists, geologists, botanists, and various specialists in the disparate sciences of living things.

Its de facto mayor and last remaining resident, an undernourished-looking Bolian named Kobb, eyes me nervously as he awaits my decision. He looks as if stress has torn away his youth and vigor, leaving only this exhausted, slump-shouldered husk standing before me.

You see, Kobb and his colleagues have been trying to sell this moon for years. The problem is, Yutani IIIa has no resources worth exploiting, and it sits on the edge of the Paulson Nebula, which Federation scientists predict will smother it with lethal radiation in fifty years.

I take one last gander at the pretty little village and nod.

"It's perfect. I'll take it."

His face brightens as he exhales with relief. "Wonderful! How long will it take you to arrange the financing for the purchase?"

"No need. I have the money." I take a padd from my jacket's front pocket, turn it on, and hand it to him. "Press your thumb on the green square, then let the device scan your retina, and the amount we discussed will be transferred to your collective's account."

Kobb blinks in surprise as he processes what I've told him. "Are you serious? You have the kind of wealth that lets you buy an entire moon on just a handshake?"

"I never agreed to shake your hand. But yes, I am that well capitalized." I'm growing impatient with him, so I stare him down. It's not difficult; it's like intimidating a puppy. "My time is valuable, Mister Kobb. Do we have a deal or not?"

"Of course. My apologies, Mister Weizenbaum." He's in such a hurry to get his thumb on the padd that he nearly drops the damned thing. It shakes in his hand as he holds it up to scan his retina. Then it beeps softly, confirming the biometric verification process is complete.

He hands the padd back to me. I put it away as his personal comm device chirps in his pocket. The emaciated blue scientist checks his incoming message with widening eyes. "The credits have already been transferred," he says in a hushed tone of disbelief. "The full sum."

"As promised. This concludes our transaction, yes?"

A giddy nod. "Absolutely." He puts away his personal comm, then reaches out and shakes my hand with fierce gratitude. "Thank you so much, Mister Weizenbaum. I thought we'd never recoup our losses on this rock. You've saved our research program."

I pull my hand free and feign distaste at the fleeting contact. "My pleasure." I tap the communicator on my wristband to hail Shakti on the *Archeus*. "We're all set down here. You can begin." I beckon Kobb away from the village. "You might want to get behind me."

He darts behind me, and only then pauses to wonder at my instruction. "Why?"

I look up.

A dark shape descends from orbit directly above the town, like a spider dropping on a filament of web toward unsuspecting prey. I watch with pride and anticipation; I designed this automated vessel, and I'm eager to see it in action. As it draws near, it casts a shadow over the orderly rows of houses and their immaculate common greensward.

Kobb stares agape at the machine and points upward. "What . . . what is . . . ?"

It answers his question before he finishes asking it. Repulsor beams flash from its belly, pulverizing the storybook houses into kindling and rubble. The picturesque brick town hall is crushed into red gravel seconds later, before a wide-dispersal phaser beam sterilizes the ground from one edge of the town to the other, setting ablaze anything that can burn. A great tower of smoke rises from the ashes and mushrooms beneath the demolition ship's belly. My dark angel of destruction activates a force field a few meters in front of me and my shocked witness, then sweeps the field away from us, scooping up the burning debris like a shovel of golden light. Moments later, the wreckage of the failed science colony is pushed over the edge of the artificial plateau, and it plunges into the jungle, which swallows it up as if it were nothing.

The demolition ship ascends, returning to the outer darkness whence it came.

The Bolian beside me shivers, his face a mask of horror and grief. I have no pity for him. We all learn to live with disappointment eventually.

I once aspired to buy a planet; I had to settle for a moon. Even so, I was forced to liquidate my stake in the resort for less than half what it was worth in order to get off Orion with a fortune in my hands and no price on my head. Regardless, I still had more than enough to make this investment and retain enough capital to finance what comes next.

Transporter beams flare across my empty swath of alpine real estate, and a swarm of small construction robots materializes. These have been deployed from another automated starship in orbit, one programmed to build upon this site my new abode, the most advanced cybernetics laboratory and fabrication center I've ever conceived.

The robots waste no time. As soon as the transporter effects fade, they start excavating granite to create a shielded foundation in which to assemble the fusion reactor that will power my redoubt. Drilling lasers split the air with piercing shrieks, and the disintegrating stone kicks up clouds of acrid gray fog.

Though it will take months to build this sanctuary, I intend to supervise every moment and detail of its construction.

Just one tiny obstruction remains to be dealt with.

I cow Kobb with a look that brooks no debate. "Get off my moon."

MARCH 2378

18

A soul flickers in my hands, its spark of awareness fragile and faltering. What else would you call a naked brain, disembodied but alive? Philosophers have spent millennia trying to define the essence of the soul, and science has had its hat in the ring for a few centuries now. So far, the best explanation I've been able to devise is that the soul is the core of sentience, the seed of knowledge that tells us we're all nothing more than conglomerations of star dust and borrowed energies—and nothing less than unique cells of awareness, expressions of a universe that wants to understand itself and needs intelligent life to act as its agents in time.

To create life, to incept a soul from inert elements and inspiration, is a heady sensation. How can I help but feel the engines of creation are at my command? In the past year, I've willed twenty-nine new sapient minds into existence, nurtured them to stability . . . and killed them.

"Creative destruction" is the euphemism I've heard for endeavors such as mine. A more vulgar translation would be the proverb, "You need to break some eggs if you want to make an omelet." A crude reduction of an underlying truth, but an accurate one. Put simply, to discover the secret of resurrecting dead positronic brains, I must first have dead positronic brains to resurrect. It seems self-evident once it's pointed out, but the reality is a bit more troubling.

Any one of these minds could have thrived if given a chance, but that was never an option. I see no point in constructing bodies for these sacrificial minds. I've also resisted imbuing them with anything more than the most rudimentary programming. Bad enough I need to usher them into existence only to snuff them out; at least this way they're nothing but inchoate, insensate entities without memory or context. They barely have time to know they exist before they vanish into oblivion.

I patch the newest brain into the master console on my workbench in the center of the lab. I need to run a complete set of benchmark tests and diagnostics to make certain this brain is stable before I induce a fatal cascade anomaly. Initially, I had planned to make only one of these and work on it until I learned how to restore it. I even convinced myself that once it was resurrected, I would build a body for it. But there were undetected hardware flaws in the first brain's neural network, and the cascade anomaly not only collapsed its matrix, it melted and fused its synaptic relays. After that, its only value to me was as a paperweight.

All the subsequent brains have endured their cascade failures with better grace. At least, none of them were reduced to smoking slag by the anomalies. That indignity came later, as I documented two dozen ways in which not to try to reactivate a failed positronic matrix. The scorched remnants of my failures populate the shelves of an otherwise empty case along the wall beside the door. Most of the time I turn my back on them, choosing to work while facing walls of transparent steel that look out upon the sea of treetops surrounding my island of folly. Tonight a storm lashes the jungle with gray sheets of rain driven by screaming winds, and majestic forks of blue-white lightning rend the darkness. Had I ever dared to look upon such brilliant violence with human eyes, I'd have been blinded; my cybernetic visual receptors, on the other hand, filter and process the spectacle with ease, allowing me to observe it with wonder.

A crash of thunder is followed by an unexpected voice from behind me.

"Hello, Doctor Soong."

I freeze like a criminal caught in the act. Then I turn, first my head and then my body, to face my unwelcome visitor. His gaunt mask of a face is tilted at an angle that bespeaks curiosity. For someone who's seemingly just come in from the rain, he's perfectly dry. "Tyros."

The android envoy looks around the spacious main laboratory, which is cast in spectral light and crisp shadows by another blaze of lightning. "A most impressive lab."

I'm in no mood to humor him. "How did you get in?"

He folds his hands behind his back and begins a slow stroll around the room's periphery. "Your security systems are quite good." He shoots me a sly look. "They could be better."

I feel exposed as I watch him peruse my pages of handwritten notes that lie scattered about the floor, the numerous holographic displays filled with my incomplete formulas and schematics, and the countertops strewn with half-built components. "What do you want?"

"Had your fill of the casino business?"

"It served its purpose." *Why is he taunting me?* "Answer me. Why are you here?"

He feigns offense. "Just checking in. You left Orion

in quite a hurry. I was worried you might be in danger." He stops, picks up a new type of phase discriminator I've been tinkering with, and examines it for a second before discarding it in an offhand manner. Then he resumes his perambulation of my lab. "Have you reconsidered our invitation, by chance?"

"Not for one moment."

His steep brows climb a few millimeters higher on his broad forehead. "Maybe you should. We have a new member, one I think would intrigue you: Rhea McAdams."

It takes effort not to react when I hear the name of Vaslovik's holotronic android. Tyros is right; I would relish a chance to study her up close, perhaps win her confidence and steal a look at what makes her tick. Heaven knows I've had no luck replicating the holographic matrix Vaslovik and his partners developed on Galor IV. But I refuse to be baited. "You didn't come here to roll out the red carpet. Why don't you get to the point?"

He stops in front of my storage case of ruined positronic brains. My victims. His countenance darkens as he peruses the grim tableau on the shelves. Without asking permission, he opens the cabinet's doors, picks up one of the blackened hemispheres, and studies it with a sorrowful expression. "What happened here?"

"A failed experiment." The best lies are the ones wrapped in bits of truth.

Tyros frowns, then reverently sets the scorched brain back inside the cabinet. "Is this the result of your attempts to reinvent Vaslovik's holotronic android . . . or your blunders in trying to copy his resurrection of your wayward Juliana?"

Damn him. He's known the whole time. "Am I supposed to justify myself to you?"

"I didn't come here to judge, Doctor." He shuts the cabinet's doors. "But I'd like to give you some advice, if you're willing to hear it."

"You've got one minute. Speak quickly."

He walks toward me, his stride casual, his bearing calm. "Ask yourself, Doctor: What's the point in trying to copy someone else's achievements? Is it an act of vanity, the delusion that your genius is so without equal that no one else is allowed to build upon your work? Should knowledge advance only by your hand?" He stops in front of me and lowers his voice. "Or is this about revenge? Do you feel slighted in some way? Maybe by Vaslovik, or Juliana?" A shrug. "It doesn't matter, really. My advice to you is to turn your talents toward making something new. Create something for its own sake, like when you made your sons. Life has to be lived forward, Doctor. You should try looking that way sometime." For half a second, I almost expect him to clap a hand onto my shoulder. Instead, he musters a wan smile and heads for the door.

"The next time you drop by to talk, knock first."

He replies without looking back. "There won't be a next time."

NOVEMBER
2379

19

I stare at words I prayed I'd never read. They circle in an endless loop, dominating every circuit in my neural net. All my safeguards aren't enough to save me from paralysis. Immobilized with grief, I stare at the screen, but I no longer really see it. It's just light and color, shapes and lines, a surreal mosaic signifying nothing. I struggle to process the news, but I can't believe it's real. I never knew I could feel this empty.

Data is dead.

The details hardly matter, but I keep going over them, rereading them again and again, as if I'll uncover some loophole, some simple misunderstanding that'll mean my son isn't gone. Starfleet's official report says my boy sacrificed himself to save his captain and stop some lunatic's doomsday weapon. They're calling him a hero. I wish that made a damned bit of difference, but it doesn't. I never wanted him to be a hero. I never wanted him to join Starfleet. From day one I'd said they'd be the death of him, and now they've proved me right.

I bring my fist down on a half-assembled positronic brain and smash it into dust.

Data's captain wants to honor him with posthumous

awards and fancy words. Who cares? What made Picard so precious that my son had to die for him?

A display screen shatters as I ram my fist through it. I pick up the gutted panel and hurl it across my lab, through a cluster of ion tubes, unleashing a cloud of toxic gas and jets of flame.

On a ship with hundreds of personnel, including security officers whose job it is to defend their ship and captain, why was it Data who had to sacrifice himself in the stupidest manner possible? Firing a phaser into the heart of a doomsday weapon? It took Data—my son, the paragon of nigh-immortal artificial intelligence—to point a phaser, pull a trigger, and blow himself up? Would he even have tried to do something this stupid if Picard hadn't done it first?

Rage overwhelms me, and I tear through my lab, breaking anything I can hit, tearing apart computers and equipment, using the broken chunks of one to pummel the next into twisted wreckage. Each tremor of impact feeds my primal desires as I imagine it's Picard I'm ripping limb from limb. Smoke and dust cloud the air. Steam and gases jet from severed pipes and hoses. I rip an electron chromatograph analyzer from its nook in the wall and hurl it against the glass case full of slain minds, all of which implode into fragments mingled on the flooded floor.

This is Picard's fault. Why did he put himself in danger? Didn't he know what Data would do? Was there no one else he could have sent on a suicide mission?

I pound my fists against one of the transparent steel windows and try to break through it, believing irrationally that my rage will somehow permit me to defy the laws of physics. Damn you, Data! Why did you have to be so noble? Why did you ever think their lives were worth more than yours? Why would you destroy yourself for them? How could you?

My body could go on indefinitely, but my rage falters when confronted by its own futility. Beaten, I crumple onto my hands and knees, overwrought and helpless, sobbing as I paw the debris-littered floor. I should never have tried to cheat death. If only I could have died rather than live to see this day . . . I could have met my end believing that my genius was without equal, that my son was immortal, that my legacy would live on. Instead I've seen my greatest works made obsolete. My sons are dead. My only true love lies in the arms of another. I am forgotten.

Everything I've done has been for nothing.

And it's all my own fault.

I let my delusions of greatness drive Juliana from me. I programmed Data to see the world in such stark and absolute terms. And I was arrogant enough to think no one would ever do as I had done, and build upon my work as I built upon the labors of so many others. I thought I was the sine qua non of neurocybernetics and synthetic biomechanics. Now I see that I was only a link in a chain of progress, part of an ongoing continuity of discovery. I was never meant to be the apex of achievement, just another step on the long upward journey of science.

I could still give myself the gift of ignorance. My memories are both more permanent and more malleable than they were when I was flesh and blood. I could selectively erase all my memories dating back to the moment I finished my transfer into this body, reset myself to the moment where my biological life ended . . . and then induce my own cascade failure. A virtual stroke, of sorts. I could die as the man I was, instead of this wretch I've become. I could meet my long darkness with all my delusions intact. Cold comfort would be better than none, I think.

It's not a bad plan. I could program the entire sequence of events, erasure and cascade anomaly, ahead of time and then let them play out. One moment of courage, and I could have a moment of bliss before oblivion takes me. I wouldn't even know that I'd done it to myself. I would die thinking myself a victim of an error in my neural net, the casualty of an accident. A far more preferable end than my next best solution, which would be to immolate myself by plunging myself into a star with my memories intact.

Shakti's comm tone chirps from an overhead speaker. I try to ignore it, hoping she'll desist and leave me in peace, but she's persistent. It seems she's not willing to take no for an answer this evening. I heave a sigh of surrender and open a channel. "What?"

"I've acquired some new logs from Picard on the Enterprise.*"*

I shake my head. "I don't care."

"They contain newly declassified information. I think you need to see it."

Bitter and angry, I snap at her. "I said I don't care!"

"It's about B-4. To be more precise, about B-4 and Data."

Stunned, I stare at the ceiling speaker for nearly two seconds as the news penetrates my leaden shroud of mourning. Then I scramble up from the floor and sprint for the door, stutter-stepping and dodging around the obstacles I've strewn about in my tempest. I race out of the lab and back to my small living space, taking the most direct path to a working display screen. I stumble to a halt in front of the one mounted on the wall in my main room and activate it. Shakti, ever helpful, has already routed to it the new batch of logs for my review.

I read them all in a matter of seconds, wide-eyed at the madness and the possibilities of the news they contain. Shinzon, the lunatic who lured the *Enterprise* into the battle that claimed Data's life, used my other son, B-4, against them as a Trojan horse. It doesn't say how, when, or where this Shinzon acquired B-4, but that's not important right now. What snares my interest is the note from Picard's log about Data's efforts to help his brother.

Data thought he could "uplift" B-4's consciousness by copying his own memory engrams into B-4's positronic matrix to stimulate the development of new neural pathways. It was a generous impulse on Data's part, but a sadly misguided one. B-4's positronic brain wasn't designed to function at the same level as those I built after it. It wasn't even supposed to stand up to long-term operation. I made it as a proof-of-concept, a simplified test model. His processors, his neural architecture, even his phase discriminator—none of them are capable of running the kinds of programs that I wrote for Data. But that stripped-down prototype is now the storage vessel for all of Data's memories, up until shortly before he died. In essence, all that Data ever experienced, all he saw and knew, is preserved inside of B-4.

Good lord, it's a disaster waiting to happen.

B-4's matrix could never incorporate that information. His memory-access protocols are two generations behind Data's. At best, he might tap into some uncompressed files from Data's memory, but most of that knowledge will be little more than gibberish to him.

Shakti interrupts my worried musings. *"Noonien? You seem upset."*

"I *am* upset."

My confession seems to surprise her. *"Why? I thought this would be good news."*

"Well, it's not. While I'm thrilled that Data had the

foresight to create an offline archive of his memories, it's a shame he chose to store it inside B-4's head."

"Odd. I found the notion rather poetic. All that he was lives on inside his brother."

How little she understands. "All that he was? Hardly, my dear. Data was more than just the sum of his memories. He had programs and subroutines of all kinds to govern the way he thinks, the way he acts, how he processes his perceptions, how he feels emotions. None of that was uploaded into B-4—just the memories of the life he lived. Memories that are quite literally worse than useless to B-4." I'm gripped by a horrifying realization. "We have to help him."

"Noonien, what's the matter? Is B-4 in danger?"

"More than anyone but me realizes." I call up my private archives and decrypt B-4's design schematics. It's been decades since I looked at them or gave them a moment's thought. But now there's no margin for error; I need to know precisely what I'm working with. "B-4's mind wasn't made to hold the kind of information Data uploaded into it, and he was never meant to have the kind of long-term existence that his successors did. His memory storage blocks aren't properly buffered to isolate them from his operating circuits. When he suffers his inevitable cascade anomaly, it won't just take out his neural net—it'll wipe his memories, too. And then every last shred of Data's life will be erased from the universe forever."

"How long does he have?"

"Hang on. I'm searching Picard's logs for facts to fill in some variables." I cobble together what few bits of hard intel are available and make some educated assumptions based on what I knew of B-4's benchmark results when I abandoned him more than thirty years ago. The numbers tell a grim tale. "My best guess? He has about four years until his neural net starts to break down. After that, he'll be living on borrowed time—and so will Data's memories."

I download B-4's schematics from my archive to my own memory—never know when I might need them. Then I close the files on the display and start a new project. "Shakti, have the maintenance 'bots clean my lab right away. I'm sending you a list of new hardware that I need. Order it and have it brought in by an unmanned cargo drone as soon as possible. Then get me an encrypted back channel into Starfleet's comnet. We need to get new alert daemons in place to keep tabs on B-4. I want to know where he is, who he's with, and what he's doing at every moment. We can't afford to lose track of him. Understood?"

"Perfectly."

"Good." I send her my equipment list, and then I call up Data's schematics and begin isolating core systems from one another, so that I can review each independently. Dissecting my earlier work, I'm dismayed by many of my choices; it's a wonder Data remained functional for as long as he did. Even when I was designing the basic emotion chip to correct what I'd considered to be the single greatest omission from his original design, there were thousands of other systems I would have loved to upgrade, if only there had been time. Now, lurking in the shadow of death is the possibility of a new beginning, an opportunity for atonement.

I'm going to save B-4 by building a new body for Data—a better one, the one he should have had. My son will live again.

OCTOBER 2380

20

"A landmark legal decision was handed down today by the Federation Judiciary Council," says the pretty female Kriosian talking head on the Federation News Service vid channel. *"In the matter of* Patek v. Maddox, *the council voted unanimously to recognize the android B-4 as a sentient being and a Federation citizen, with full protection under the law."*

The mention of my son's name is the first thing to distract me from my project since his case first went before the judiciary council nearly six weeks earlier. I turn from my workbench to watch the rest of the report, riveted at the great step forward the Federation has just taken.

"Starfleet officer and respondent Captain Bruce Maddox spoke with members of the press immediately after the decision was announced." The screen switches to an image of Maddox, who looks older and wearier, and maybe even a shade wiser, than when I saw him last. He speaks with his chin held high. *"Today's decision in the Federation's highest court was a victory for all sentient life. Our government reaffirmed its commitment to seek out and respect such life in all its forms, to honor the principle of 'I think, therefore I exist.' It has been my*

privilege to defend B-4's right to self-determination, and to protect him from those who would take advantage of him—whether for personal gain or in the name of science. I won't presume to know what Doctor Noonien Soong might have wanted for his creation, but I can't imagine he gave life to these beings just so that others could take it away. And I am very pleased today to find that the Judiciary Council shares this view."

The image changes to something else as FNS moves on to its next breaking story. I turn my attention back to my work, but I'm distracted as I reflect on this exciting new development. Maddox, of all people, has become a crusader for AI sentient rights. I guess people really *can* change. Perhaps that means there's hope yet for me, as well.

My work on Data's new body is proceeding beautifully. While awaiting the delivery of raw materials and new equipment for my lab, I spent the first six weeks of this project designing an upgraded body that would rival even my own current form. I put to use every bit of knowledge I've gained in the forty-odd years since I designed Data, in disciplines ranging from positronic circuitry to materials science to advances in AI programming. His new body will weigh thirty-four percent less but be four times as durable. All his cosmetic details will appear fully human, and, like my own, will be completely under his control. He will be a far more sophisticated chameleon than I am. I even fixed the quirk in his language database that made him eschew the use of contractions. It's taken longer than I expected, but I think it's been worth it.

There's still a lot to do, of course. I'm building him new eyes, and I'm planning full-spectrum enhancements to all his sensory inputs. He'll be able to see things other beings can't even imagine, hear on frequencies no organic being has ever sensed. His hair and skin will be able to withstand temperatures as cold as liquid nitrogen and as hot as molten lead. He'll be able to bend decimeter-thick duranium rods as if they were saltwater taffy. And don't get me started on his reflexes and motor skills; let it suffice to say he'll be capable of wonders undreamed of.

And his mind? I've only just begun fabricating the core processors, but this is going to be the finest work I've ever done. It might not rival Vaslovik's celebrated holotronic technology, but it will be the fastest, most dynamic, and most stable positronic brain I've ever designed. I admit, I stole a few ideas from Vaslovik and his team on Galor IV. Using a holographic matrix to stabilize the neural net during the initial programming phase is something I can do without altering its core design, and I think they were right: it will prevent cascade anomalies. This might not be how they applied the principle, but I'm certain my interpretation of their idea will be just as effective, even if it's not a permanent feature of the matrix.

There are still some serious obstacles ahead, unfortunately, and they all relate to B-4. As much as I want to give this gift to Data, I don't want to do it at B-4's expense. I've hurt my boys too many times. Never again. I won't sacrifice one for the other; I won't accept the loss of B-4 any more than I'd accept Data's death. The problem is that extracting Data's memory engrams—which also contain complex nested patterns for Lore's and Lal's memories, which Data downloaded into himself after their deaths—could destabilize B-4's primitive neural network. He wasn't designed to serve as a conduit for such complex information any more than he was meant to implement it. It would be like trying to copy the massive AI-driven software of a modern

Starfleet starship into the memory banks of a ship from the start of the previous century. It not only wouldn't work, it would risk inducing a fatal crash in the less-advanced system.

My only chance for salvaging Data's memory engrams without destroying B-4 in the process is to first upgrade B-4's firmware and operating software, so that his neural net can more efficiently manage the use of its positronic circuits and memory storage. I've been studying his schematics and software code for the past eleven months, and I believe I'm close to finishing a patch application that will solve these issues and radically improve B-4's cognitive functions.

Unfortunately, keeping his brain from melting during the transfer is the least of my logistical hurdles. First, I need to think of a clandestine way to reach B-4 and gain access to him for a period of sufficient duration to complete this procedure. That'll be harder than it sounds. While I don't expect him to put up much of a struggle, Starfleet's not about to let me walk in the front door of its Annex at the Daystrom Institute on Galor IV and tinker with my elder son.

Funny thing about surviving a war against a power like the Dominion: it has the effect of making formerly open and trusting societies such as the Federation into security states. They employ biometric security at all their important facilities these days, a paranoid reaction to the threat of infiltration by Gamma Quadrant shape-shifters. That's going to make my task harder.

Another issue is that there's no way for me to engineer this process from a distance. I'll need to put Data's new body beside B-4's, connect them with a hard line through a computer loaded with the necessary applications to govern the memory transfer, and watch over them until it's done. It should take only a matter of minutes, assuming I preload all the core operating systems into Data's new body, but how am I supposed to put my boys in the same room?

It's not like when I summoned Data—and, accidentally, Lore—to me on Terlina III by triggering their recall circuits. B-4 doesn't have a recall circuit—not that I'd trust him to find his way across interstellar space to answer such a signal. I could break into the Annex just long enough to make contact with B-4 and then lead him out; after all, he is self-mobile. Then I remember that he's also painfully slow-witted, and extremely likely to draw attention to us. It'd be easier to make a clean escape while dragging an anchor at the end of a chain.

The alternative is to bring Data's new body to B-4 at the Annex. Sounds simple, doesn't it? Now remember that I need to carry a man-sized body inside a transporter-shielded military facility without being detected or intercepted. Sure, I could try to sneak in and deactivate the transporter scrambler, but doing so will likely set off a whole new slew of alarms. By the time I neutralize the scrambler and beam Data into the Annex, I'd very likely be surrounded by an armed company of Starfleet security personnel. Hardly what I'd call a discreet approach.

Fortunately, there's still time to sort this out. If all goes well, Data's new body and brain will be tested and ready by April. Which means I have exactly that long to concoct a plan.

2381

21

I'm so deep into the delicate process of balancing the signal inputs from the new body's visual receptors that for several seconds I tune out the angry buzzing from the wall panel by the door. This is precision work, with no margin for error; if I get this wrong in the slightest degree, Data will be cursed to see double for the duration of his second life.

That accursed signal threatens to break my focus. An interruption is the last thing I need right now. "Shakti! Turn off that alert!"

It goes silent, and I take a deep breath. My focus restored, I finalize the atomic bonds on the left eye's primary retinal integrator, then set down my tools. Only once I'm a few steps away from the table do I permit myself the satisfaction of an angry sigh. Even from across the room, my own eyes are sharp enough to see that something has tripped the proximity alert by entering the Yutani system on a heading for my moon.

"What now?" I grumble to myself. "More deluded prospectors? Another well-meaning but utterly useless would-be colony manager? Or maybe Tyros reconsidered his—" My grousing is silenced by the image forming on the screen. The long-range sensors have assembled a confirmed profile for the approaching vessel. It's a Borg cube. "No!"

I check my redoubt's shields and cloaking system: all functioning perfectly. Not even the Borg should be able to penetrate my veil of secrecy. They can't know I'm here, can they? What could they possibly want? For a moment I'm afraid Tyros's AI fellowship has struck some dark bargain with these monsters, offering up my location and my secrets in return for . . . what?

Better not to find out. "Shakti, is *Archeus* ready to fly?"

"Yes, Noonien."

I run back to the worktable. "Any second now, I expect the Borg to hail us. Keep them talking long enough for me to bring Data's new body to the ship." I roll up my toolkit, secure it closed with a press of Velcro to fiber, and sling it by its strap over my shoulder. "As soon as I'm aboard, we're out of here." I'm sliding my hands under Data's nearly complete new body when a searing flash of green light overloads my visual receptors. A hash of static gives way to darkness, but my ears still work—and what I hear is a thunder more terrible than any I've ever imagined. The ground rumbles under my feet, and my lab rings with the delicate music of glass and metal objects trembling wildly against one another. "Shakti! What'd you say to them?"

"They never hailed us! They just opened fire!" As the thunder grows deafening, I can barely hear her say, *"Don't move! I have to beam you—"*

Everything erupts into fire and madness. Hand-sized chunks of shattered transparent steel slam against me, driven by a wind of fire. I feel as if I've been swatted by the hand of a god, and as I'm sucked into the raging maelstrom, Data's body is torn from my grasping fingers, my reflexes and my strength unequal to the ferocity of the shock front buffeting me.

The sickening sensation of being hurled like a leaf on the wind gives way to numbness and silence . . . and as consciousness slips from me for the most fleeting instant, my damnably fast android brain has time to wonder if this is the moment of my death.

Then I feel the tug of gravity and the kiss of cool air. My sensory network struggles to reset itself, having been pushed past its limits by the fury of the storm. Then my logic catches up to my sensations, and I realize it was no tempest that carried me away. It was a blast wave. Tactile sensations are the first to return; I feel the cold metal of a starship deck under my bare palms, and the curved edge of a transporter pad.

My hearing returns to normal after a few seconds of tinnitus. I hear the throbbing rhythm of impulse engines, the hum of EPS conduits channeling power throughout my ship. Olfactory sensors detect sickening odors of charred metal, fabric, and polymers, and I realize to my dismay that I'm their source. Even as my visual receptors reinitialize and cycle through their frequencies before a final check of monochrome levels and then the default setting of visible spectrum with minimal false-spectrum overlays, I fear to look at myself. I dread what a self-examination will reveal, but if my hands are any indicator, the rest of me is likely a wreck. Large swaths of my synthetic skin have been melted away, revealing electromyomers and servos and circuitry.

With effort, I stand. My balance is unsteady because one of my feet is barely attached. As I lurch forward toward the open doorway, the pathetic whining and grinding of my battered form echoes in *Archeus*'s close confines. I steady myself with one fire-flensed hand against a bulkhead and limp forward to the cockpit. My reward is a grim but breathtaking spectacle.

Yutani IIIa is ablaze. My once-verdant moon is a black and red ball of molten rock. Its atmosphere has been blasted away, its deep but narrow sea cooked off in a hellstorm. Nothing living remains on its surface.

I ask in a brittle, mechanical-sounding voice, "Where are the Borg?"

"The cube has already left orbit and is departing the system at Warp 9.997."

Hanging onto the back of the pilot's chair to prevent myself from collapsing to the deck, I ease myself into it and pull up Shakti's sensor logs on the master console. I replay the details of the attack. The Borg didn't target my lab directly. In fact, they unloaded their barrage on the closest part of the surface to their original approach vector, then reversed course as soon as the planet was cooked to a radioactive cinder. "This makes no sense."

Shakti sounds as shaken as I feel. *"What makes no sense?"*

"They weren't here for me." I'd heard the recent reports of Borg attacks on planets in this sector and its neighbors, but I thought those incidents were just part of a next-level escalation in their long-simmering conflict with the Federation. But what I'm seeing now on long-range sensors is something else entirely. There are more than seven thousand Borg cubes deploying in a radial pattern across Federation, Klingon, and Romulan space. This is no attack, not merely an invasion. According to panicked reports flooding the comm networks, the Borg are laying waste every populated world in their path, regardless of their affiliation or relationship with the Federation. The Borg are even destroying unpopulated Class-M worlds and moons, such as mine, without warning or mercy. This is beyond total warfare, beyond genocide. It's omnicide.

I steal one more look back at the glowing ember of

Yutani IIIa, and I know better than to ask Shakti about Data's body. It's gone forever, consumed by that holocaust. *Archeus*'s cloak is operational and engaged, which is probably the only reason that cube didn't come back to finish us off. I lay in a course for the only safe destination I can think of, far from the Federation.

As my ship comes about on its new heading, the placid vista of space fills the cockpit windshield, and against that dark curtain of stars I catch my nightmarish reflection. Most of my flesh has been blasted away, leaving only a few scorched patches clinging to my face and torso. My clothes and my tools are gone, and my internal systems have survived but sustained serious damage. I have most of what I need aboard *Archeus* to restore myself, but it will take a great deal of time, especially without the resources of a full lab at my disposal.

Fortunately, I have time to spare. My destination is months away. I accelerate *Archeus* to warp speed, bound for a world with no name . . . because I have nowhere else to go.

22

Four months of high-warp silent running . . . for this.

I stand in the middle of Vaslovik's and Juliana's villa, their home overlooking their new Eden of a world . . . and I am surrounded by ashes. Only a few blackened timbers remain upright, orphaned amid the collapsed charcoal debris of the house. The bitter stench of the fire lingers, though everything is long since cold. This place was abandoned and left to burn months ago, or perhaps even earlier. My only solace is that there are no bodies here.

I had come hoping to beg Juliana's forgiveness and Vaslovik's help. If anyone possessed the knowledge and resources to help me save my sons now that the Borg have robbed me of hope and fortune, it would be them. Pride be damned; I would gladly have prostrated myself, confessed my sins, and pleaded without shame for absolution and aid.

But the lovers are nowhere to be found.

I've spent days picking through every handful of carbonized dust, desperate to unearth some clue to where they might have gone. Any cryptic note would suffice, would give me a direction in which to turn my restless flight. It's no use, though. They've left me nothing to follow, no evidence to analyze, no riddles to parse. Just the gutted ruin of a house hundreds of light-years from anything resembling civilization.

As for me, I'm a wreck, in more ways than one. I've made the best repairs I can to my systems, but without a proper lab, some of my more advanced capabilities will be impossible to restore, including my chameleon-like alterations of my hair and skin, and my ability to copy retinal patterns. For the foreseeable future, I will have to be content with myself as I am.

I turn in a slow circle, taking in the animal cries of the rainforest behind the burnt lot where the villa once stood, and the rush of wind over the valley below. The sun is setting in the distance, and I recall watching Vaslovik and Juliana admire its purpling majesty. At a loss for a new destination, I sit down, cross-legged, and face the sunset.

Paralysis sets in as darkness falls. Not a physical infirmity, mind you, but a psychological one. Try as I might, I can't conceive any reason to get up. *Archeus* is only a short walk away, through the forest, but I have no desire to go back. What's left for me in the Federation? Perhaps nothing at all, unless by some outrageous miracle Starfleet stopped the Borg. Why should I go back to a quadrant littered with burning worlds? And if it survived, how widespread is its damage? How incalculable were its losses, both military and civilian?

Even if the situation is far less dire than I fear, what can I do now? I'd invested all I had in that lab on Yutani IIIa. All the raw materials I needed, the equipment, the generators . . . it cost me everything. It was to be my magnum opus, and it's gone up in smoke. I've made myself a persona non grata on Orion these days, and I can't think the Ferengi would be very happy to see me on their metaphorical doorstep. I admit, for several seconds I was tempted to risk falling prey to the whims of Starfleet and the Federation government by revealing myself to them in the hope that they might give me a lab and the resources I need to start over; with a team of assistants, I might be able to reproduce my work in three months instead of twelve.

Then I remember what has happened to nearly every new technology developed under the allegedly benign auspices of Starfleet. The horror stories of the inception of the Genesis Device, the conspiracies surrounding the phasing cloak on the *Pegasus,* the numerous abuses of sentient AI rights, their officially sanctioned crimes against the Bak'u . . . the list goes on and on, I assure you. I have no desire to add my name and inventions to that shameful litany.

I disengage my temporal reconciliation circuits and surrender myself to the vagaries of time and space. My thoughts run in circles as part of my brain ticks its way through picoseconds, and my body lingers, immobile and exposed to the elements, as days bleed together. The sun rises at my back, throwing my shadow down across the valley. It sets before me, its apparent arc shifting infinitesimally as the new Eden makes its elliptical journey around its star. Rain slashes down from black-bellied clouds, and lightning rends the landscape; mist shrouds the valley in the minutes preceding the dawn; great flocks of avian reptiles wheel and turn in beautiful, complex formations, their passage across the sky nothing less than poetry come alive.

Days become weeks, and I remain amid the ashes, which even now are washed away with every passing squall, blended into the surrounding soil or carried off by the wind. Nature makes its slow but inexorable advance to reclaim the lot around the villa, and I bear witness, an observer of infinite patience. In the not-so-distant future, creeping vines, spreading grasses, and opportunistic mosses and fungi will make short work of the burnt wood. A decade from now, there will be hardly anything left to suggest a house ever stood here.

Maybe, if I am lucky, this planet's aggressive flora will consume me, as well.

Despair has made a statue of me. It holds me here, mute and motionless, anchored to the ground by my guilt. I've failed my sons yet again. I know B-4 can't have much longer, a few years at most, and that I'm squandering precious time, but I no longer have any idea how to help him. I had the perfect plan, one that could save him and Data both, but it's been taken from me, and I have nothing else. Just like when Lore stole Data's emotion chip, I've failed to plan for the worst, for the unthinkable. I forgot to have a backup plan, and it's my sons who will pay for it.

Then a thought occurs to me. I remember that for all of Vaslovik's tendencies toward reclusive behavior, he has always lingered along the periphery of civilization because he needs it. That hasn't changed. I've lost all my resources to the Borg's invasion . . . and so has he. All the ancient wealth he once accessed at will, all the great interstellar corporations that provided him with technology and raw materials, the Byzantine web of lies he'd spun decades in advance to enable himself to move undetected through civilization—those things have also very likely been destroyed, or at least badly compromised, by the Borg's rampage through Federation space. I've been forced to rebuild my secret life in seclusion, and it's not just possible but highly probable Vaslovik has been compelled to do the same. This might be the only time his defenses will be down for the next century; I'll never have a better chance to find him.

After lingering motionless in the ashes for fourteen weeks, two days, six hours, thirty-three minutes, and nineteen seconds, I blink. Then I stand, turn, and walk back to *Archeus*.

It's time to go home.

OCTOBER
2383

23

The last breaths of winter twist unseen between the buildings of New Glasgow on Galor IV. A cool breeze wafts over the dermal sensors of my left forearm, prickling the skin with gooseflesh. I barely register the sensation as cold, but my body is made to mimic natural human reactions. Around me, a few other patrons seated at some of this café's other sidewalk tables shiver and adjust their scarves or hunch their shoulders forward against the thermal shift. I pick up my demitasse of *raktajino* with a twist of Kaferian lemon zest, take a long sip, and pretend to lose myself in the day's headlines on my personal padd.

Hidden behind a well-padded visage with brown and mild eyes, I project an air of almost beatific calm. In fact, I do such a fine job of impersonating a normal person that no one can see I'm panicked, desperate, and running out of time and ideas.

It took me more than four months to make the journey back to Federation space after I left Vaslovik's abandoned paradise. When I returned, I was at first relieved to find that the Borg's insane jihad had been stopped, and that the Federation still existed. Then I learned, little by little, of the true scope of the damage and casualties this region of space had suffered. Almost every Class-M world or moon within a hundred light-years of the Azure Nebula had suffered some form of assault by the Borg. Many, like my own moon, had been sterilized without putting up the least resistance. Others made futile efforts at self-defense. Only a few were fortunate enough to be spared the full brunt of the Borg's assault. When the crisis was ended, more than sixty-three billion sentient beings had been slain, on neutral worlds as well as on planets of the Federation, the Klingon Empire, and the Romulan Star Empire.

Those that survived counted themselves lucky . . . until the shortages began. Hundreds of billions of people had been turned into refugees, and with nearly forty percent of Starfleet's ships destroyed, the Federation's ability to maintain order was stretched to its limits. The greedy and the cruel wasted no time in capitalizing on the misfortunes of the displaced. For the first time since the twenty-second century, the peoples of Earth and its closest allies knew the sting of want, the harsh realities of an economics of scarcity rather than surplus. Hard lessons to face so soon after a tragedy of this scope, but that's the way life is: arbitrary and uncaring.

Still, I have to give credit where it's due. Even with sharply limited resources and widespread troubles, Starfleet has done a fine job of maintaining order and facilitating the rebuilding efforts on several worlds, and the current Federation government has risen to the challenges of the day with more finesse and keener acumen than I would have expected. With each day, the Federation recovers a bit more and the spectre of a grim future retreats.

If only my recent efforts had been so fruitful.

I've spent more than two years looking for any trace of Vaslovik. I'd thought it would be easy to reacquire his trail. Many of my news daemons and Trojan horse programs remain in place at various financial institutions, and I've only recently encountered some difficulties circumventing Starfleet's new security features on its communications network. I expected to find ample evidence of Vaslovik acting through his many personas to shore up his holdings and ensconce himself and Juliana in a new redoubt. Instead, I find all his previous channels have gone silent. Most of his alter egos and fictional heirs have been declared dead, as their residences of record were on worlds annihilated by the Borg invasion. Those that might reasonably have been expected to escape, however, have also vanished and been declared legally dead. His assets have been reclaimed by planetary governments and the Federation for humanitarian purposes.

It never occurred to me until now that an epic catastrophe such as this might have been a boon to Vaslovik. He's proved repeatedly to be smarter, better prepared, and more forward-thinking than anyone expects. Perhaps he foresaw the possibility of a disaster such as this and made preparations to use it as cover for his final exit from the interstellar stage. It sounds outrageous, but it's the only explanation I can think of that makes sense. I don't believe for a moment that he and Juliana fell prey to the Borg, or to anyone else. They must be somewhere. Just not any of the myriad places I've looked for them, unfortunately.

I tried haunting the financial centers of Bolarus IX, even though I was embarrassingly conspicuous among the cerulean throngs of Bolian financiers in their white suits. Thinking that Vaslovik and Juliana might stick to the edges of Federation territory rather than venture too deeply into its space, I visited all the border worlds on which Vaslovik or his other personas maintained business fronts: Syrma, Rhaandar, Ascella, Cebelrai, Nusakan. On each world I was met with the same story: missing chief executives and owners, confusion, whispers of state receivership, and then, like a self-fulfilling prophecy, the seizure of assets by local authorities.

Everywhere I looked, the financial empire of Vaslovik turned to vapor. On Penthara, a fleet of his cargo ships and automated construction vessels was commandeered by Starfleet; on Zibal, mines he owned under several aliases were reclaimed under the doctrine of eminent domain; and on Kostolain, his continent of automated factories was repurposed for the creation of terraforming technology, by order of the Federation's Department of the Interior.

Before the Borg invasion, I could have proved not only that Vaslovik had existed under many other identities, I could have documented what he owned and where. Now, I would be hard-pressed to prove that Vaslovik himself ever existed at all. This might well be the greatest sleight-of-hand deception I've ever seen, written on a nearly galactic scale.

I can't pretend any longer to be his pursuer. He has long since slipped from my grasp. Whatever I'm going to do now about B-4 and Data, I'll have to do it without his and Juliana's help. There's no more time to waste; B-4's neural net could start to degrade at any time. I have to devise some means of getting to him inside the Annex here on Galor IV. Unfortunately, since the Borg invasion and the rise of a new rival—an alliance of interstellar powers known as the Typhon Pact—the Federation in general and Starfleet in particular have become justifiably security-conscious. Breaking into the Starfleet Annex before the invasion would have been difficult; now it verges on the impossible. Several key defense systems have been upgraded, I suspect there have been changes to its interior layout, and the entire building is now rigorously shielded against sensors of all kinds.

If not for the fact that I don't trust Starfleet any more than I'd trust the Romulans or the Klingons, I could just walk up to the front door and knock. But I fear that would end badly for me, and possibly far worse for my son. Still, I should be grateful to Starfleet for one thing if for nothing else: thanks to Maddox's impassioned legal argument in defense of B-4, my sole surviving son, my three original prototypes, and the remaining components of Lore's body have all been transferred from the *Enterprise* to Maddox's care here at the Annex, at B-4's request. All my extant work has been gathered in one place: a state-of-the-art neurocybernetics research laboratory. For the first time in ages, it feels as if Fortune herself smiles upon me.

Let's hope the feeling lasts long enough for me to save my boy.

JANUARY
2384

24

There's an old saying on Earth—and I'm paraphrasing here—that if you give a million monkeys a million word processors and let them type randomly for some arbitrary but ultimately ridiculous span of time, those apparently immortal primates will reproduce the complete works of William Shakespeare. I've never had occasion to test this assertion, but after three months of laboring in vain to penetrate the new firewalls at the Annex, I'm wishing I had a few million of those monkeys to throw at the problem.

That's not to say I've been wasting my time on Calor IV. I've established numerous aliases and safe houses, installed dozens of backdoor codes for rapid site-to-site beaming using remote commands to the planet's transporter network, and passed my downtime inventing something new to help me achieve my goal of reaching B-4 undetected: nanite spy-flies.

My flies are marvels of nano-engineering. Too small for organic beings to see and silent to biological ears, they are also phase-shifted by .002 millicochranes when deployed—just enough that, coupled with their nanoscopic size, they are practically undetectable to most security scanners. I've created several dozen of these remote-programmable tiny drones to go where I currently cannot: inside Maddox's lab at the Daystrom Institute Annex.

Now I pass my days and nights inside a rented apartment on the edge of Talburgh, the closest town to the Annex. Each day a few of my flies escape the Annex, and I send in a few more to take their place. I dispatch them in rotating squadrons of twelve, but I don't expect all of them to reach their intended destination. A strong wind can knock them off course for days, which has made my collection of actionable intelligence a rather hit-and-miss affair.

What can I tell you? No plan is perfect.

It was also necessary to sacrifice a bit of resolution in order to ensure my flies wouldn't be detected and inadvertently lead Starfleet—or anyone else—back here to me. Consequently, my flies record only basic vids with low-quality audio. Complex sensor data was too much to ask. They could have transmitted real-time updates from inside the Annex if not for the facility's high-powered scattering field. Intended to block unauthorized transporter beams, the field is also quite useful for obstructing unauthorized signal traffic. In order to transmit their recordings back to me, my flies have to first get out of the Annex and move clear of the interference. Maddox is a bit of a recluse, so the front door—the only way in or out—doesn't open very often. As a result, the news I gather from my flies is sometimes days old by the time I'm able to download it and perform my analysis. It is, to put it mildly, a less than ideal situation.

Sequestered behind locked doors and drawn curtains, I sit and wait for the soft beep of my control console, which I use to program the flies with their orders and retrieve the vids they send back. The long hours in between I fill with mental labors, writing software patches for my own mind, updating my own programming, and preparing an upgrade for B-4.

A soft tone rises from the console. I swivel my chair and confirm that Fly 47 has cleared the field. I download its vids and put it into standby mode. It has made another thorough reconnoiter of the Annex's interior, and it's the first of my flies to successfully carry out my instructions to follow Maddox himself into his private laboratory. Unlike the austere empty spaces of the Annex's ground floor, Maddox's lab is stocked with new computers and tools. He is with B-4, who sits beside him like a child told to stay out of the way while grown-ups work. An optronic cable links B-4's brain to a long bank of high-power computers.

Working with slow precision, Maddox carefully dismantles the positronic brains of my first three failed prototypes. The display screens behind him are jammed with code I recognize from my early days on Omicron Theta. After all these decades, Maddox is finally unlocking the secrets of my operating system for positronic brains. Good for him. It's about time.

It doesn't surprise me that Maddox has no use for Lore's remains, since they no longer have a positronic brain for him to study. But I do find it interesting that while he seems to have spent a great deal of time and effort taking apart my failed prototypes, he seems to have made no attempt to dismantle the one other android in his lab that was ever completely operational: Lal.

What's staying his hand? Is it sentimentality? Some old pledge to Data that I was unaware of? Or could it be that B-4, despite his tragically limited capacity for understanding the world around him, simply refused Maddox permission to touch her? I suppose it's possible that Maddox is just being thorough, trying to make certain he's learned all he can from the earlier prototypes before he moves on to a more advanced model based on Data's own matrix, but part of me would like to believe that this man who argued so adamantly for B-4's rights might have a shred of decency in him, after all. I wish there was some way to know for certain what's in his heart, but I don't know how to program a nanite fly to tell me that.

The screens of code that surround him and the real-time status readings from B-4's brain, on the other hand, I understand all too well. My son's neural net is becoming unstable, and the degradation is already accelerating. Maddox is doing everything he can think of, but I know the dead ends he's driving himself into, the false starts that will look so promising until he meets their fatal flaws. If I don't reach B-4 soon, it will be too late. For a moment I consider going to the Annex, turning myself over to Maddox, and entrusting myself to his conscience. But then I remember that he still wears a Starfleet uniform and is bound by an oath of duty. Who knows what he would do if confronted with my existence? But does that really matter now, when so much is at stake? Wouldn't that be a risk worth taking?

I'm still weighing that question as I review the vid file. Maddox turns to a smaller terminal beside his workbench and opens a comm channel. *"Maddox to Annex Ops."*

I hear a man's voice reply; it sounds hollow and distant. *"Ops. Go ahead, Captain."*

"Send a priority signal to Captain Picard and Commander La Forge on the Enterprise. *Request they proceed here at maximum warp, and tell them it's an emergency."*

"Can you explain the nature of the emergency, sir?"

"It's classified. You have your orders. Send that message right now.*"*

That's persuasion enough for the junior officer. *"Transmitting now, Captain. Ops out."*

The channel goes quiet, and Maddox slumps into his chair with the grave countenance of a beaten man. B-4, as ever, is oblivious of his worsening peril. I know the kind of pride that drives Maddox; it's the fire I used to see in myself, before the universe punished me for my hubris. If he's calling La Forge for help, B-4's condition must be critical. I need to get in there before anyone else arrives and complicates an already delicate situation.

I activate my wrist comm to *Archeus*. "Shakti, call up our latest intel on Starfleet's deployments. How soon can *Enterprise* get here if it travels at its maximum warp factor?"

She answers without delay. *"Approximately forty-six hours and nineteen minutes."*

"Start a countdown. I have that long to get inside the Annex and bring B-4 out. Then start monitoring all comms into and out of the Annex. We might not be able to decode them, but a sudden spike in traffic might give us some warning if we trip an alert."

I get out of my chair and project a holographic scale replica of the Annex's interior, in a cutaway view that removes its west wall so I can study the interior. Starfleet did an excellent job of reinforcing its structure when they rebuilt it after the attack ten years ago. The only spot where I can even contemplate breaching its security is its main entrance. Precision demolitions could do the job, but I can't help but hesitate when I see how exposed I'd be while making the attempt. Using a weapon capable of blasting through the entrance from a distance would be no better, as it would kick up an unholy ruckus and negate my own element of surprise. If it were possible for me to attack all of the door's systems at once, I might be able to get through before tripping any number of sensors, but even though my brain can perform eighty quadrillion operations per second, I still have only two hands. I'm fast, but even I have limitations.

If only I had more time—and a huge reserve of materials, industrial equipment, precision tools, and a lab designed for high-end applied subquantum physics—I could engineer some kind of portable energy dampener. If I had one of those, I could walk right up to the door, negate all its security systems and backup force fields with the push of a button, phaser my way in, and reach B-4 in less than a minute. And if I had a horse's body and a horn on my forehead, I'd be a goddamned unicorn. Think, you old fool, think! There must be some way to bypass the—

"Noonien?"

I snap back, "What?"

Shakti, bless her, is unfazed by my temper. *"When I initiated the signal intercepts on the Starfleet channels serving Maddox's lab and office inside the Annex, I detected a phased echo in the subharmonics of the data subcarrier frequencies. I thought you should know."*

Like Maddox, I slump back into my chair a broken man.

We're not the only ones spying on the Annex. Someone else has tapped into Starfleet's communications and is watching Maddox.

Or maybe someone is watching *me*. If I've stumbled onto a counterintelligence operation, I might have just undone all my months of preparation with one careless blunder.

I refuse to sit and wait to be captured. "Shakti, beam over my isolation suit."

"Why? What are you going to do with it?"

I stare at the holographic map of the Annex. "I'm gonna find a way inside that lab."

25

From where I'm standing, it's 27.2 meters to the Annex's main entrance. I can cover that distance in just over two seconds. I estimate that I can place the jury-rigged demolition charges I'm carrying inside my isolation suit in less than forty seconds. Allowing another three seconds to move clear of the blast effects, and a fraction of a second to trigger the detonator, I can breach the front door in forty-five seconds.

I'm confident I can reach Maddox's lab in the sublevel in thirty seconds if I use the emergency stairwell. But then I'll still need to get through the lab's secure entry, and that's where my timetable falls apart. I've been unable to hack Starfleet's new security codes, so I'll have no choice but to force my way inside. It would take me nearly two minutes to cut through with a plasma torch. I could blast through in half the time, but not without having to retreat into the stairwell to avoid becoming collateral damage of my own explosion.

The problem is that neither method is viable, because the Starfleet garrison that defends the Annex will reach me in forty-five seconds, and I can't hold them off and set the charges at the same time. But even if, by some miracle, I accomplish that feat, I would still need to gain entry to the vault inside the lab, where Maddox has been storing all the androids for their own protection. In the time it will take me to reach the door and try every permutation of its possible access codes, I will almost certainly be reduced to free radicals by a barrage of phaser fire.

I've been rooted in place like an invisible statue for the past nine hours, since early afternoon. Watching this place in every spectrum I can perceive has been fascinating but not very helpful. I see the glow of motion sensors embedded in an irregular fashion beneath the ground for twenty meters around the Annex, waiting to detect the pressure of footsteps, the radiant heat of a living body, or the unauthorized transmission of a signal. Energy shines as it moves to and from the various sensors that dot the Annex's walls. Roving guards pulse with body heat and are surrounded by unique bioelectrical auras produced by their brains and nervous systems.

Darkness has long since fallen, and I still don't know how to reach my son without getting myself killed before I can help him. I keep hoping Maddox will leave the Annex for some reason, and in that moment of enhanced vulnerability, I can dash over the ground sensors and force my way through the open door, saving myself nearly forty-five seconds. That would be enough to get me inside the lab, and maybe even into the Vault, but I'd need several minutes more. Locking myself in the vault with B-4 isn't an option, because I need Maddox's computers to do this. Inside the vault we'd be cut off from them—not to mention trapped.

Enterprise will be here at any moment, but I just can't seem to reason this out.

I hear footsteps in the woods behind me, on my right. I turn my head slowly and look back. Three figures garbed in snug-fitting black fatigues and masks crouch just beyond the tree line. They huddle around a small portable comm device of some sort; I haven't seen one like it before; only its compact subspace transceiver assembly betrays its function. One of them enters commands on its interface while the others watch the Annex. I assess their physiques, body mass distributions, and centers of gravity, and conclude that all three are male humanoids in prime physical condition. Each of them carries two long cylinders on his back. Studying them in several spectra, I see signs of concealed equipment and fully charged beam weapons.

The leader gives the signal to advance, and they sprint forward, as quiet as phantoms. As they pass me, I get a good look at the cylinders on their backs. They're carrying transporter pattern enhancers. Fools! Even those can't help a transporter penetrate the scattering field.

I watch them, expecting to hear the alarms sound at any moment when they race across the field of ground sensors . . . and then I see that several of the sensors have been deactivated, clearing a direct path to the main entrance. I glance upward at the surveillance devices on the wall facing this direction. They, too, have gone dark. Whoever these people are, they have been expertly trained, superbly equipped, and well briefed. In a word, they're professionals.

Working as a team, they breach the front door in just under thirty seconds and with barely a sound from their corrosive demolition package. If I had to guess, I'd say they've perfected a form of programmable parasitic plasma. Quite brilliant and tremendously exotic. They slip inside the Annex, moving on the same path I'd have taken, directly toward the emergency stairs.

And no alarms have sounded. There is no sign of

response from the Starfleet barracks. Somehow, these elite thieves have done what I could not: they hacked Starfleet's newest security system with almost comical ease. If their tactics on the sublevel are as efficient and well-rehearsed as those that got them inside, they'll breach Maddox's lab any minute now. And once inside, they'll have access to the vault—and the hard-wired controls for the scattering field.

Suddenly, those pattern enhancers they were carrying make a lot more sense.

I can't risk letting them get offworld with the androids, but I'm not qualified to confront three armed professionals on my own. I need to summon help—and to do that, I need to figure out why the alarms haven't sounded.

Then I realize they've left their comm unit outside. I run to it and try to make sense of its controls. Its interface is a mishmash of alien symbols I've never encountered before, and my built-in universal translator doesn't have much luck parsing this gibberish, either. I consider smashing it with my hands, but for all I know that might gain me nothing. I try accessing some random functions, but any processes already engaged are locked out.

This is interesting, though: the alien interface is superimposed over a Starfleet command screen. Apparently, the intruders exploited some kind of remote-access back door that enables them to take control of the Annex's security system, spoof its sensor feeds, and deactivate targeted systems with great specificity. Well, it stands to reason that if it can deactivate systems, it can activate them just as easily. I can't bring back any of the systems the intruders have already nullified—those are locked out from further changes—but I can do some new tampering of my own. I make a quick review of my options and settle on the most promising one:

The Daystrom Institute's general alert. With a tap, I fill the night air with the sweet music of whooping alarms. Several seconds later my little symphony expands to include the rumble of running feet, as armed Starfleet security personnel pour out of the barracks.

From inside the Annex comes the muffled shriek of energy weapons—several blasts in quick succession. I see a shimmer in the air as the Annex's scattering field stutters out. Starfleet troops flood into the building through its blasted-open door, but I know they'll never reach the sublevel in time. I pry open a panel on the side of the comm terminal and dump in my last packet of nanite flies. Then I close the panel—half a second before the unit dematerializes in the sparkling flare of a transporter beam. Just as I expected, the thieves had someone waiting to extract them—and clean up the evidence they left behind.

With the scattering field down, I receive signals from my nanite flies inside the Annex. I command them all to transmit their last six minutes of recorded surveillance. In a burst of raw information, I see the entire sequence of events inside the building, culminating in the thieves' successful escape via transporter with all the androids from the vault, followed by an explosion that destroys all of Maddox's research and archives.

If Starfleet is true to form, they'll shut this planet down in less than an hour. And if the *Enterprise* is as close as I think it is, the thieves can forget about making a break for orbit. No, they'll have to lie low and try to find another way off this planet—which means I might have time to track them down before they do. If I can get close enough to them—within two hundred kilometers, give or take—I should be able to detect the nanites I put in their comm terminal and then program my flies to spy on their command systems and communications.

Since they must be using a ship of some kind, there are only so many places they can hide. They can't land it in the wilderness—*Enterprise*'s sensors would notice them in minutes. Their best chance at evading detection is to hide in plain sight, inside one of Galor IV's sixteen surface starports. All air traffic is likely to be suspended within the hour, so I'll have to travel between cities by maglev train. It'll take longer than flying, but it's not as if my quarry will be any more mobile than I am. Even if they don't stay with their ship, they're likely to leave the androids and their equipment aboard rather than risk being seen with them.

I have no idea what I'll do after I find their ship. To be honest, I'm improvising.

Weighing on my thoughts is the fact that even after I recover B-4, I can no longer use Maddox's lab. Once again, I'm without the resources I desperately need. But that problem will have to wait its turn. I have more pressing crises to address.

Right now, I am certain of only one thing in all the universe.

No matter what it takes, I will save my son.

Harsh winds whip dust across the plateau beneath *Archeus*. The four black-clad officers from the *Enterprise* regard me with incredulous stares. I expected resistance from Worf, but I'm surprised to find La Forge has grown so cynical. He's not at all the man I came to know through Data's years of personal logs as my son's closest friend. Was it a mistake to reveal myself to them?

Worf scowls at me. "Your story is . . . hard to believe."

"Trust me, I've barely told you the half of it."

The female officer with the raven hair and dark eyes still holds her Orion blaster ready at her side, as if daring me to give her a reason to use it. "From what you've told us, it sounds like you don't have much love for Starfleet. So why step out of the shadows now?"

I'd forgotten how slow-witted the average person is. "Isn't it obvious?" I tilt my head toward the massive factory that fills the valley below our mountainside aerie. "I've seen the enemy, thanks to the nanites I smuggled into their agents' portable comm terminal. We're up against an elite unit of the Breen military. Judging from the scale of that factory, I'd say they're well entrenched and likely outnumber us by a large margin. Hardly a fight I want to face alone."

The fourth member of the Starfleet team, a Troyian man whose emerald green face is framed by close-cut coppery hair, is the only one still aiming his sidearm at me. "In other words, you want to use us as cannon fodder. Not exactly the beginning of a beautiful friendship."

Clearly, I'll need to work harder to earn their trust and obtain their help. If they were just random Starfleet personnel from any other ship, I wouldn't take this risk. But this might be my last chance to save my son; like it or not, I need them. La Forge and Worf were Data's friends, as were many of their shipmates and their captain. My son called these people his family; he trusted them without question, and he gave his life for them. If I'm to ask them to walk into fire with me, I owe them nothing less than the truth. And if I learned nothing else from running a casino, it was that sometimes you simply have to roll the dice and let Fortune have its way.

"Listen, we're on the same side here. I'm presuming you know that B-4 was one of the androids the Breen took from the Annex, and that he's on the verge of a major cascade failure. I can help him, but first I need to find him. I'm asking for your help, and offering you mine."

My proposition is not well received. Their brows crease with distrust and indecision, and they volley wary glances from one to another. Through it all, the Troyian's weapon remains aimed and steady. After a few seconds, he, La Forge, and the woman all look at Worf. Clearly, the Klingon is the ranking officer of this group. He clenches his jaw, exhales angrily, and directs his fearsome stare at me. "Why should we trust you?"

I almost laugh. "I let you follow me this far, didn't I?"

That catches him by surprise. He sounds offended as he replies, "Are you suggesting you led us here on purpose?"

"Worf, my ship has a cloaking device and can outrun yours by two-tenths of a warp factor. If I hadn't wanted you to follow me here, I'd have left you in the dark a week ago." Finally, the Troyian lowers his blaster a few degrees. I take that as my cue to turn away and start walking down the trail to the mountain pass, which leads to the valley. This is a calculated risk; I hope that trigger-happy Troyian doesn't shoot me in the back.

Two seconds later, I still haven't been gunned down. I smile and call back over my shoulder to them. "Come on, already! Let's get this show on the road."

PART THREE
ELEGY

26

Secluded in his ready room, Picard had spent the past several hours immersed in three reports he had requested as preparation for the current operation. Before leaving on the away mission, La Forge had submitted a detailed history of the work of Doctor Noonien Soong and the verified capabilities of the many androids he was known to have created during his lifetime. Lieutenant Chen had compiled an exhaustive update and analysis of the latest Starfleet Intelligence reports about the Breen, their culture, and the various species that had been discovered to exist behind its masks of conformity. Last but not least, Lieutenant Šmrhová had prepared a tactical summary to refresh Picard's familiarity with Breen starships and space-combat maneuvers.

He had started with the tactical briefing because it was the shortest of the three. Next he had delved into the report of Doctor Soong, a reclusive and eccentric figure whose reputation had always intrigued him. Three cups of hot Earl Grey tea later, he'd finished absorbing that slice of history, and found himself daunted by Chen's massive thesis on the Breen. Now, hours later, he was thoroughly engrossed by its fascinating insights into their collective psychology and Chen's astute analysis of several competing theories regarding the origins of their social model. Far from some dry historical extract, it read like a secret history, a work of literary archeology.

Recalling how awkward Chen's interactions with him and the rest of the crew had been when she first came aboard more than three years earlier, and comparing it to how vital she had become to the ship's operations, he smiled. She never ceased to impress him.

He set his padd down on his desk, rubbed his eyes, and contemplated procuring a fresh cup of Earl Grey from the replicator. Then came Šmrhová's voice from the overhead comm.

"Captain Picard to the bridge."

Banishing his fatigue, he pushed back his chair and moved quickly toward the door, which swished open ahead of him. The muted chorus of computer feedback tones and the ambient hum of the ship's power and ventilation systems washed over him as he stepped out onto the bridge. The dark-haired tactical officer—who was serving as the ship's acting first officer while Worf, La Forge, and Choudhury were planetside—got up from the center seat and stepped forward to intercept him. They met in the center of the bridge. "Report," he said.

"Dygan's picked up several signals on long-range sensors." She nodded at the Cardassian operations officer, who relayed the information to the main viewscreen. "Based on the energy profile, I'd say we have a cloaked Breen starship following a patrol route through the system."

"How long until we're inside their sensor range?"

Šmrhová looked at Dygan, who checked his console, then swiveled around to face her and Picard. "Less than four minutes," he said.

Picard cursed their luck. The away team was scheduled to check in on the encrypted subspace frequency in half an hour. He folded his arms and fixed Šmrhová with a grim look. "Thoughts, Lieutenant?"

"If we leave the system to avoid being detected by the Breen patrol ship, we'll be out of range to receive the away team's signal and send the response code." She glanced at the viewscreen and frowned. "Unfortunately, the alternative—engaging the Breen ship in combat and risking an alert being sent to every Breen vessel in the sector—is no better."

A three-minute countdown appeared on the viewscreen, posted by Glinn Dygan, who again turned his chair toward the captain and Šmrhová. "Sirs, I have an idea."

"By all means, Glinn. Speak freely."

"Thank you, Captain." He entered a command on the ops console, reverting the image on the viewscreen to the gas giant the *Enterprise* was orbiting. "This planet has a very powerful magnetic field and high concentrations of metallic hydrogen in its atmosphere. We can conceal ourselves inside the upper atmosphere and evade detection by the Breen patrol. It might be easier to resume the mission if we don't have to chart a new course back into the system."

Šmrhová acted out her resistance to Dygan's proposal with a raised palm. "Hang on, Glinn. If we do that, we'll be all but blind down there. We'll have no way of knowing when the patrol ship has cleared the system." She looked at Picard. "We'll also be cut off from the away team. There's so much interference inside the atmosphere that we'll never get a signal in or out."

Faur looked up from the helm console to join the discussion. "There's another risk, Captain. Storm conditions are brutal down there, and shields won't work. Hit the wrong patch, and we could take critical damage in a matter of minutes. Piloting a starship in that environment is *extremely* dangerous. Case in point: remember what happened to the *da Vinci* at Galvan VI."

Picard didn't need to be reminded. The catastrophic damage suffered by the *Sabre*-class starship assigned to the Corps of Engineers had been the leading story on the news for a week after its salvage of the *U.S.S. Orion* had gone wrong, resulting in the loss of more than half of the *da Vinci*'s crew, including its second officer, chief engineer, and all but one member of its security force. The prospect of the *Enterprise* sharing such a tragic fate was one he dared not contemplate. He looked at the continuing countdown on the screen, then at his acting first officer. "Lieutenant, we have approximately two minutes before the Breen are on top of us. If you have an alternative to Glinn Dygan's proposal, now would be the time to suggest it."

Her frustration was evident. "I'm sorry to say that I don't have one, sir."

"Then the discussion's closed." Picard returned to his chair and sat down. Šmrhová followed him and settled into the XO's seat on his right. He lifted his chin and raised his voice. "Dygan, route auxiliary power to the structural integrity field. Helm, take us into the atmosphere, one-tenth impulse." As the officers at the forward stations executed his orders, he thumbed open an intraship PA channel from his chair's armrest. "Attention, all decks. This is the captain. Evacuate the outer sections, seal emergency bulkheads in those areas, and brace for impact." For a moment he was mesmerized by the swirling violence of the gas giant's liquid-metal atmosphere as it filled the viewscreen. Then he composed himself and finished his announcement with the grim reminder, "This is not a drill."

The tactical officer's mechanically scrambled voice cut through the hush on the bridge of the Breen cruiser *Mlotek,* and its automatic translation intoned flatly inside first officer Pazur's snout-shaped helmet. "Sir? We've picked up something interesting on long-range sensors."

The last thing Pazur wanted her day to be was *interesting.* Anything other than boring tended to lead to only two possible outcomes: a violent altercation ending in some degree of death and destruction, or a calamitous mishap that had the potential to land her and any number of her overworked crew members in a brig, a work camp, or an executioner's lineup. She crossed the bridge and looked over the tactical officer's shoulder at his screen. "What is it, Zadlo?"

He called up a screen of readings that, to Pazur, resembled little more than a jumbled mess. "I registered a momentary sensor contact, in orbit of the fifth planet." He pointed at a detail in the flurry of symbols and static. "It was just a flicker, and I thought it might have been interference from the planet's magnetic field, so I ran it through some filters to clean it up. I know this isn't much, but we might want to check it out."

"I'm not ordering a course change for that, Zadlo." She waved her gloved hand at his screen. "That could be anything. A meteor hitting the atmosphere. A weather phenomenon."

Zadlo turned and looked up at her. "I disagree, sir. Look at the disturbance in the planet's upper layers. Heavy ionization, coupled with unusual distortions in its regular convection pattern. I think a starship disrupted that planet's upper atmosphere."

It was a presumptuous interpretation of the sensor data, in Pazur's opinion, but not an impossible one. Still, she was reluctant to deviate from the commander's orders without a very good reason. Other first officers had been replaced for similar errors of judgment. "All right, Zadlo, tell me this. If those anomalies were caused by a starship, where is that vessel now?"

The tactical officer hunched over his console, striking a less confident pose. "I don't know, sir. I've been unable to find it, even though I'm sure it was there." He looked up and added, "I think it might have been a cloaked vessel."

Was he just hedging his bet? Pazur couldn't let this go unchallenged. "Based on what?"

"A surge of high-energy particles emanating from the planet's upper atmosphere. It's an effect consistent with a close pass by a cloaked Klingon starship, maybe one that's trying to use the planet's magnetic field as an additional defense against our sensors."

To her dismay, the longer Zadlo talked, the more sense he made. Still, it was her job to be the voice of reason and restraint. "Such a surge could be generated by any number of natural phenomena or artificial technologies."

The tactical officer sounded mildly annoyed. "True, but what's more likely, sir? That a reverse-spin quark strangelet slipped through a random fluctuation in the M-lattice and initiated a self-annihilating chain reaction inside the planet's atmosphere? Or that a cloaked Klingon warship has learned we're conducting operations on the third planet and is spying on us?"

Pazur salvaged her pride by declining to reply to Zadlo's snide sarcasm, and she turned away to issue orders. "Helm, new course. Take us into polar orbit of the fifth planet, then coordinate with tactical on a full sensor sweep by descending latitude."

"Yes, sir," answered the pilot, a new recruit named Tren.

The gas giant slowly expanded on the main viewscreen until, a few minutes later, its banded atmosphere filled the screen from edge to edge. Tren confirmed the *Mlotek* was in a polar orbit, its dorsal hull rolled toward the planet's surface, and Zadlo began his tedious sensor sweep.

Observing her crew's efficient teamwork with quiet pride, Pazur almost didn't mind that this would likely be a complete waste of time. If nothing else, the search exercise would be good practice for a real crisis.

Heavy footfalls echoed in the corridor behind her, a thudding step whose cadence she knew well. She turned and saluted her commanding officer, Thot Raas, as he strode onto the bridge. Before she could get a word out, he snapped, "Why have we deviated from our route?"

Pazur lowered her salute. "Zadlo detected readings consistent with the presence of a cloaked starship in orbit of the fifth planet. None of our vessels are supposed to be in this system except us, so I ordered a full sensor sweep, starting from polar orbit."

Raas had a reputation as a harsh taskmaster, one who rarely rewarded competence but was swift to punish errors of judgment. He stepped past Pazur and loomed over Zadlo. "Show me the sensor readings and explain your analysis." Pazur listened from a discreet distance, fearing the worst, but Zadlo stayed calm as he presented to the commander all the data he'd shown Pazur, and the tactical officer wisely explicated his conclusions with concision and humility. After he'd finished, Raas nodded once. "Very well. Good work. Continue the search." He turned to Pazur. "What other steps have you taken to find this cloaked vessel?"

"So far, the sensor sweep is our only action."

"Not good enough. If that ship has moved away from the planet, we might be wasting our time here while it runs circles around us." The commander turned his back on Pazur and marched over to the communications officer. "Vess, send a priority signal to the other ships in our battle group. I want them back here immediately, to set up a tachyon detection net. If there's a cloaked enemy vessel in this system, I want it hunted down with prejudice." Vess acknowledged the order with a tiny nod and set to work transmitting the summons. Then the commander turned back toward Pazur. "In exactly seventeen minutes, run a battle drill."

"Yes, sir." The order turned a few heads subtly toward her and the commander, but the bridge crew continued working and pretended they hadn't overheard Raas's order.

Raas left the bridge in a hurry, no doubt to check in with his own superiors from the privacy of his quarters. As soon as he vanished down the shadowy corridor, Pazur felt her tension abate; the bridge was hers again.

Seven minutes later, as she watched the prismatic beauty of the gas giant's atmosphere glide past on the viewscreen, she decided with mischievous amusement to call the battle drill early. *Why should the commander get to have all the fun?*

27

Where the mountain's slope ended, the factory began. The sprawl of dark metal and crimson light had been hidden from view during the away team's descent inside the narrow pass, so when the four Starfleet officers and their peculiar new acquaintance cleared the final jog in the trail, they found themselves staring up at a towering industrial behemoth. As much as La Forge wanted to imitate Worf's stoic demeanor, he couldn't stop his jaw from dropping. He had never seen anything quite like it, and he was at once impressed and terrified.

"Hold up," Worf said. He pulled back the cuff of his sleeve and checked his chrono. "Time to check in." He tapped twice the transceiver hidden in his collar, priming it for a voice channel. "Secure frequency Three-Delta-Green: Worf to *Enterprise*."

He waited several seconds, then repeated the hail. After half a minute without a response, he looked at Choudhury. "Are we still outside the scattering field?"

She checked her tricorder. "Affirmative. Fifty meters to disruption point."

Worf scowled, while La Forge masked his concern. That had been the first unsuccessful scheduled check-in.

Two more in succession would mean the mission was scrubbed and the away team was abandoned. He shook off his worries as Worf motioned the group onward.

Choudhury led them toward the black labyrinth of steel and smoke, then halted just short of clearing the chest-high rock formations at its edge. The security chief signaled everyone to halt and get down. La Forge took a knee beside Velex, who kept a watchful eye on the android Soong. Tense silence hung over them while Choudhury scanned the path ahead with her civilian tricorder, using a simple echolocation setting that wasn't affected by the scattering field. Then she shut it off and waved everyone back into motion, and inside the complex.

The factory's internal passageways were massive—wide enough for thirty people to walk abreast with elbow room to spare, and over fifty meters tall. Overhead, the dense lattice of pipes, cabling, and power conduits admitted only the tiniest hints of the sky. Ragged clouds of gray vapor drifted between the machines, which shook the ground with a deep and ominous rumbling. Several minutes passed without conversation as the team forged ahead into the deserted maze, and the path behind them vanished beyond a shroud of ozone haze.

Increasing the magnification of his cybernetic eyes, La Forge peered into the workings of the factory. He still had no idea what its purpose might be, but he began to recognize a number of troubling details in its technology: hints of biomechanically inspired systems, an idiosyncratic asymmetry, and a great deal of distributed redundancy. Restoring his field of vision to its default setting, he viewed the yawning sprawl of titanic machines with new apprehension.

"This is Borg technology," he said.

Worf and Choudhury stopped and turned back to face him. Then the first officer looked up and around, as if expecting Borg drones to drop out of the machine, even though the Borg had ceased to exist nearly three years earlier, after being benignly assimilated by their ultra-advanced progenitors, the Caeliar. The Klingon shot a stern glare at La Forge. "Are you sure?"

"Positive. The entire layout of this place is modeled on the architecture inside a Borg cube. Same distributed systems, redundant backups, the works."

Soong ran his hand across the exterior of a broad, circular structure with a domed top. "Not all of it. Some of these big machines are based on Federation designs. You might not recognize them because they're older, but Brock-Cepak was mass-producing generators like this one about sixty years ago. We had one for the colony on Omicron Theta."

Velex cast a confused look at their surroundings. "Who would use Federation tech and Borg tech in the same operation?"

"The Borg, for one," Choudhury said. "They never reinvented something they could assimilate from someone else. If a Brock-Cepak generator was the best solution for this"—she glanced up and around—"whatever this is, then they'd steal one or copy one. If the Borg built this, we'll probably see bits of tech from lots of different cultures."

"I'm looking at some of it right now," La Forge said. He pointed at an ungainly cluster of components that in any other context would look like the result of an accidental collision. "That mishmash up there has Romulan plasma regulators, Klingon-style heat sinks, and something that looks like a crude copy of Starfleet's bioneural gel packs."

Worf checked his tricorder, then he pointed forward,

toward a break in the long wall of machines, just over fifty meters ahead on their right. "I've found an access port to the factory's core. We should continue." He resumed walking, and the team fell in—Choudhury at his side, Soong in the middle of the group, and Velex and La Forge in the rear, keeping an eye on Soong.

As they turned the corner and continued down the narrower side passage, Velex asked La Forge in an anxious whisper, "What do you think the Breen are doing with leftover Borg tech?"

"I'm pretty sure I don't want to know. But I think we're about to find out."

The passage ended at a locked hatch. Choudhury and Worf stepped back from it and beckoned La Forge, who joined them at the portal. Worf nodded at the hatch. "Can you open it?"

La Forge eyed the door's hardened security features. "Maybe. It could take a while."

From behind him, Soong interjected, "Let me take a shot." Without waiting for anyone to respond, much less give him permission, Soong shouldered past La Forge and set to work looking for weaknesses in the door. After a few seconds of mumbling "mm-hm" and "aha" under his breath, the eccentric old scientist in a youthful android body glanced back at La Forge and extended an open hand. "Tell me you have a pair of gravitic calipers."

"Never leave home without 'em." La Forge opened a flap on the torso of his suit; the inside of the flap was lined with easily concealed tools of various kinds. He plucked out the miniaturized calipers and passed them to Soong.

A soft but high-pitched oscillating whine issued from the device as Soong adjusted its setting and directed its effects upon the hatch's lock mechanism.

Then a loud clack reverberated inside the door and echoed through the oppressive lattice surrounding the away team. Soong handed the tool back to La Forge, then grabbed the hatch's lever and opened it with a theatrical flourish that reminded La Forge unfavorably of Data's late but unlamented brother Lore.

Worf stepped through the hatchway first, followed by Choudhury. Soong tried to usher Velex through ahead of him, but the Troyian motioned Soong forward with a wave of his blaster. La Forge let Velex stay directly behind Soong, and ended up the last one through the portal.

He stepped inside the ten-kilometer-long enclosed space and froze. The away team stood beside a massive, automated assembly line. Millions of robotic arms and hands worked with surgical precision, combining mass-produced components into fully integrated finished products.

No matter where La Forge looked, he saw Data's face.

It was a factory for mass-producing Soong-type androids.

Choudhury stared in wide-eyed horror at the legions of androids packed into pods that lined the walls like honeycomb. Worf's features hardened with rage. Velex looked stunned. Soong seemed perversely intrigued. In a strange way, La Forge understood how each of them felt, even though he was at a loss to put a name to his own stew of emotions.

Turning in a slow circle, Choudhury asked, "How many do you think there are?"

La Forge was reaching for his tricorder when Soong answered. "Approximately twenty-one million, four hundred ninety-three thousand, assuming the filled pods I see are all packed to capacity." Soong looked around at the legions of empty pods. "I'd estimate this facility has the capacity to store as many as fifty million." He cracked a twisted smile. "Say hello to my family."

Unearthly groans and peals of thunder from the gas giant's atmosphere resounded through the hull of the *Enterprise* and reminded Picard of ancient tales of Earth's storm-tossed mariners. He tried to push the harrowing din from his thoughts by focusing on reports from the ship's lower decks. Doctor Crusher had her hands full in sickbay; despite his warning to evacuate the ship's outer sections, several dozen personnel who'd had to remain behind at critical posts until their backup stations came on line suffered mild radiation poisoning. That threat continued to plague the *Enterprise*'s crew even now. The shields were unable to function in the hypercharged atmosphere, leaving the *Sovereign*-class starship exposed to its scourge of lightning and the unpredictable caprice of its four-hundred-kilometer-per-hour winds.

A jolt rocked the ship hard to starboard, and Picard's hand clenched the armrest by reflex. Determined to deny the storm the privilege of his attention, he skipped ahead to the latest update from Glinn Dygan and assistant chief engineer Lieutenant Taurik. The pair had established a complete internal force field that mirrored the shape of the *Enterprise*'s hull by reprogramming the structural integrity field's emitter network to operate in a dual-frequency mode. It was an ingenious solution to their current predicament; it kept more of the ship's internal volume available for service than closing off large areas with broader force fields, and it avoided the risks associated with inverting the geometry of the ship's external shield emitters, which were unreliable in conditions such as these. He made a mental note to add commendations for both of them when he recorded his daily log.

Lightning tore across the main viewer, which blanched with static. A thunderclap hammered the ship, dimming the overhead lights for half a second. Picard realized his breath had caught in his chest, and he forced himself to exhale. *That was close.* He wondered how long the *Enterprise*'s luck would hold in this nightmarish environment. Then he winced as another fork of electricity ripped through the swirling violet gases ahead of the ship. *This is ridiculous. Being down here is almost as risky as being attacked by the Breen.*

He got up and stepped over to the security station, where Šmrhová was filling in for Choudhury. She looked up as he approached, and straightened her posture. "Sir."

"As you were." He waited until she relaxed, then he continued. "We can't stay down here forever. There must be some way to know when the Breen have moved off."

Šmrhová shook her head. "I've tried to filter out the interference from the atmosphere. It's too erratic and too powerful for passive sensors to pick up anything except noise. I might be able to boost the active sensors by routing them through the main dish assembly, but—"

"But that would be the same as sending up a flare to the Breen," Picard said, finishing her thought. He frowned. "What we need is a periscope."

She reacted to his offhand remark with a quizzical wrinkling of her brow. "A what?"

"An ancient form of optical scope, made with mirrors," Picard explained. "On Earth in the early twentieth century, submersible aquatic vessels used them to observe activity above the water's surface while the ship remained submerged. What we need is the modern equivalent of a periscope—something to let us gather intelligence from above without revealing ourselves."

Glinn Dygan swiveled his chair around from the ops console to join the discussion. "What about sending out one of our shuttles as a scout?"

Šmrhová looked doubtful. "I considered it. But the winds and electrical phenomena in the atmosphere are too severe. Even on autopilot, there's an eighty-five percent chance any small craft we send out there will be destroyed in under ten minutes."

Picard stroked his upper lip as he pondered their options. "What if we use a runabout? They have enough power to navigate inside the Badlands. They should be able to handle this."

"Maybe," Šmrhová said. She entered commands into her console, then brushed a few strands of her black hair from her eyes as she looked up at Picard. "We have one runabout left on board, the *Cumberland*. And it might be up to the flight. But I don't think it's our best option."

"Explain."

She stepped aside so Picard could stand next to her. As he stepped around the security console, Dygan got up and walked back to look over the top of the panel. Šmrhová started calling up new screens of information with light taps on the interactive panel. "A runabout would only be able to give us intel from a limited arc of visibility outside the atmosphere. If the Breen ship were on the far side of the planet, the runabout might not see it until it was too late. There's also the risk that the Breen might detect the runabout's engines before it sees them."

Picard nodded. "I see your point. Can you suggest another alternative?"

She finished inputting commands, and a schematic

took shape, dominating the console's display area. "A web of passive sensor probes, deployed at regular intervals of longitude and latitude as we cruise inside the atmosphere. They can ascend to shallow depth, just inside the cloud cover, gather data from orbit, and relay it back down to us."

Certain he saw a flaw in her plan, Picard asked, "How are they supposed to send us that data through all this interference?"

Šmrhová grimaced. "I haven't figured that part out."

"I have an idea," Dygan said. "Taurik and I can modify some sensor probes to transmit short data pulses on a super-low-frequency subspace channel, like the kind used by cloaked Klingon ships. In theory, an SLF channel should be immune to most of the interference."

Nodding, Šmrhová said, "That might work."

It sounded good to Picard, but even if it proved unsuccessful, it would keep the crew occupied and focused on something productive. "How long?"

"Three hours to refit the probes," Dygan said.

Šmrhová added, "Another ninety minutes for deployment."

"You have four hours. Make it so."

Executing a search pattern was an intricate bit of tedium, but Pazur was committed to seeing it done well. The first officer circuited the bridge of the *Mlotek,* sneaking peeks at the consoles of her subordinates and assembling the glimpses into a mental snapshot of their progress.

The ship was circling its way south from the planet's northern magnetic pole, its orbit lasting longer with each circumnavigation as it approached the gas giant's equator. High-energy tachyon sweeps so far had found no evidence to support Zadlo's suspicion of a cloaked vessel, but it was too soon to declare the search's outcome negative. It was possible they were herding a cloaked intruder toward the antarctic pole—and inevitable discovery.

Communications officer Vess turned toward Pazur. "Sir. The cruisers *Gwiazda* and *Obranca* have confirmed they are en route at maximum warp. ETA, just over one hour."

That was good news; reinforcements would speed the search. "What about the *Zemsta*?"

"It'll arrive in approximately two and a half hours."

Zadlo turned from the tactical station and nodded at Pazur to indicate he had news. The first officer told Vess, "Forward those reports to the commander," then stepped away to confer with Zadlo. She sidled up to him to keep their discussion private. "Report."

"No signs of cloaking device interference in the atmosphere, but I found something else." He called up a screen of data showing what looked like a scratch across the planet's cloudy surface. "It's an ion trail. It's faint, but we picked it up with the new contrast imaging scanners."

Pazur knew not to draw hasty conclusions. "What could cause that?"

"A trail that size? Either a small comet composed of highly radioactive elements, or a starship maneuvering on impulse power." He switched to a screen of navigational scans. "I checked. There were no asteroids or comets on collision trajectories with the planet."

"What would a cloaked vessel gain by descending into the atmosphere?"

"Nothing," Zadlo said. "The charged particles and electromagnetic interference would disrupt its cloak and shields, leaving it completely vulnerable. I can imagine two scenarios consistent with this evidence.

First, a cloaked vessel lost its ability to cloak for some reason, and chose to use the planet's atmosphere for cover. Or, second, our intruder had no cloaking device."

She reached past Zadlo and called up a chart of the star system around them. "If there is a ship inside the gas giant, the fact that it's hiding suggests its commander would prefer to avoid a confrontation—but then why didn't it simply retreat when we left our patrol route?"

The question lingered between them for a few moments until Zadlo replied, "There's something here they want or need."

"Or something they're not willing to leave behind. Continue searching for that ship." She turned and moved back to the bridge's central command position. "Vess, hail the *Obranca* and *Gwiazda*. Have them do a full sensor sweep of the system on their approach. Then signal our garrison on the third planet and tell them to start looking for intruders."

Huddled with Soong and the away team around a dormant android they'd pulled from a storage pod, La Forge watched with morbid fascination as the renowned scientist dismembered and disemboweled the mass-produced copy of his work. Gifted with superhuman dexterity and visual acuity by his new android form, Soong operated with the speed and brutal precision of a cybernetic Jack the Ripper, arranging excised synthetic organs around the artificial corpse.

"Just as I thought." Soong plucked a tiny component from his patient's brain and held it up for everyone to see. "A Type-L phase discriminating amplifier." The detail's importance seemed lost on the others, but it gave La Forge a chill of dark remembrance. Soong nodded at him. "Open its left temporal panel. I want to get a look at its positronic matrix."

La Forge coaxed open the panel on the side of the android's head. The sight of a face identical to Data's beneath his hands summoned melancholy memories of his friend. He recalled helping Data repair and install his emotion chip after recovering it from Lore's damaged brain, and the time he let Data shock himself half to death to trigger his dreaming subroutine. *This thing isn't Data,* he reminded himself. *None of them are.* Looking around at the legions of inactive androids, the word that kept creeping unbidden into his thoughts was *abomination.*

Soong poked at the dissected android's inert brain circuitry. "Very interesting," he mumbled. "All the pieces are here. The lights are on. But nobody's home." He shifted an internal circuit panel and tapped a tiny circular chip with his fingertip. "There you are. Exactly where you shouldn't be, and right where I expected." He touched a tiny metallic instrument of inscrutable purpose to the chip. "Hmmph. Blank. Thank heaven for small mercies."

"Enough," Worf said, his patience clearly on the wane. "What have you found?"

The scientist deflected the query with a knowing look at La Forge. "Ask him. He knows." Then he glanced at Worf with the gleam of an inveterate troublemaker. "And so do you, I'd bet."

His accusation turned Worf's attention toward La Forge, who sighed and gestured at the body. "This is a copy of Lore." He frowned. "More precisely, it's a copy of him as we last knew him, when he'd teamed up with those rogue Borg."

Worf bristled at the news. "How can you tell?"

"The Type-L phase discriminating amplifier, for

starters. Data's body used a Type-R." La Forge turned the inanimate head to call attention to the open panel. "But this is the giveaway. See that little round bit? That was the original configuration of Data's emotion chip—the one Lore stole from him on Terlina III—before I helped him fix it. Which means this body is based on a scan of Lore that included the chip. And judging from the technology in here . . ."

A rare look of alarm crossed Worf's face. "These bodies were made for the Borg."

Choudhury leaned forward, her serenity transformed to intensity. "What are you two talking about? Why would the Borg mass-produce Soong-type androids?"

"It was a renegade faction," La Forge explained. "A few months earlier, we'd 'infected' them with the concept of individual identity. The drones in the infected cube split off from the Collective and ended up lost and unable to function. That was when Lore found them."

Worf continued the narrative. "He made himself their leader and turned them into crazed killers. Then he used tricks and lies to take control of Data."

"I know this story, from Data's logs," Soong cut in. "Lore promised the Borg he'd free them from the imperfections of flesh and lead them to a fully synthetic existence. There was just one problem: he didn't know how to transfer organic consciousness into a positronic brain."

Anger welled from a place inside La Forge that he'd hoped never to face again. "To solve that problem, Lore made Data experiment on a living subject." The memory of the torments he'd endured at Data's hands made him wince. "They started with me."

His revelation made Choudhury stifle a small gasp of horror, and Velex averted his gaze rather than bear witness to the pain that still burned in La Forge's eyes.

Soong looked around at the vast workings of the

factory. "That explains why none of their matrixes are initialized. If they were made as vessels for the Borg to transfer into, they'd have been left blank on purpose. So, the good news is, there's no chance of them waking up and storming us like some kind of cybernetic zombie mob."

With obvious reluctance, Worf asked, "What is the bad news?"

"The only thing stopping them from *becoming* an army is a bit of programming."

La Forge nodded grimly. "And the Breen plan to provide it."

"Not if we stop it," Worf said. "It would not make sense to program each android separately. There must be a control center that can program them all at once."

"That must be why they wanted the earlier Soong prototypes," Choudhury said. "If we find the control center, we'll probably find the stolen androids."

Worf looked at Soong. "If we find it, can you stop these androids from being activated?"

Soong flashed a trickster's evil smile. "Are you kidding? I could melt their brains and burn this whole place down."

"Good." Worf stood tall, looking ready to take on the world. "Let's go."

28

In the three years that Lieutenant Aneta Šmrhová had served aboard the *Enterprise*, she'd had few opportunities to really impress Captain Picard. By reputation, he was a fair and patient man who took an interest in promoting the refinement of his officers—but he was also known for expecting the best of his people in even the most trying of circumstances, and on a ship such as the *Enterprise*, which was crewed by some of the most accomplished officers and noncoms in Starfleet, it was difficult to be seen as exceptional.

She knew the satisfaction of her ego was the least of her concerns at that moment; if her plan proved successful, it might earn her a moment of longed-for recognition from the captain, but what really mattered was whether it served the ship and the mission. The captain needed reliable information from orbit, and it was her duty to provide it to him. Whether her work was acknowledged was unimportant in the grand scheme of things.

But it's important to me. She clamped down hard on her feelings. *Stop that.* An update from Dygan appeared on her console and renewed her focus on the mission. After making a quick review of his report, she turned toward Picard. "'Operation Periscope' is ready, Captain."

"Launch the probes," Picard said with a dramatic thrust of his arm.

Several gingerly taps on her console fired clusters of modified probes into the maelstrom of the gas giant's atmosphere. Though they vanished from sight on the main viewer almost instantly, the SLF pulse transmitters Dygan had installed inside them sent back clear readings. "All probes are away and proceeding to their assigned coordinates."

Picard leaned forward, his manner pensive. "Glinn Dygan, how are the probes faring against the wind currents? Are we sure they'll be able to hold their positions?"

Dygan checked the probes' telemetry on the ops console. "The probes are experiencing minor course deviations from turbulence en route to their final positions, but so far the effects from the atmosphere are within expected parameters. As the probes gain altitude, they'll encounter less resistance. They should be able to maintain formation for up to a day."

"Very well. Continue to monitor their flight performance."

"Aye, sir."

The next hour passed with little conversation to break the monotony of the rumbling tempest outside the ship and the ambience of feedback tones inside the bridge. Šmrhová reviewed the ship's security status while Dygan managed the deployment of the probes. She was relieved to see the radiation-exposure issue had been addressed for the time being. As long as the *Enterprise* didn't linger more than a day inside the supercharged soup of the gas giant, it would likely emerge with only minor maintenance needs in its outer sections. All the personnel who had been affected by radiation exposure had been treated in sickbay and cleared for duty by Doctor Crusher or one of the senior physicians on her medical staff. Regardless, just to err on the side of caution, Šmrhová adjusted the security division's duty schedule to give its radiation-exposed personnel an extra twenty-four hours each to recover before returning to service.

She finished making her final changes to the roster as Dygan declared, "All probes are in position, Captain. We can begin gathering sensor data."

"Proceed," Picard said.

Garbled, intermittent spurts of information stuttered across the security console. Šmrhová applied a host of filters and signal boosters until the data on her screen resembled something useful. Even then, she was dismayed by its poor resolution and sharply limited range.

Picard threw an expectant look at her. "Lieutenant? Report."

"We're receiving data from the probes, but the planet's weather patterns are causing serious interference, even on the SLF channel. Our 'periscope' also has numerous glitches and blind spots, and I suspect we might experience occasional blackouts."

The captain's expression betrayed no reaction. If her news disappointed him, he hid it well. "What is our effective range and angle of observation?"

"Range: sixty-five thousand kilometers from the edge of the atmosphere, and we have a near-total field of vision—excepting the blind spots I mentioned." She relayed a relevant item of tactical information to the command terminal beside his chair. "There's a Breen heavy cruiser in high orbit, executing what appears to be a search pattern around the low equatorial latitudes."

Picard studied the intel about the Breen ship, then he glanced at the main viewscreen before looking back at Šmrhová. "The away team's next check-in is less than two hours away. Can we use the probes to make contact with them?"

"No, sir. The probes' comm systems are limited to the SLF channel. They can't receive or transmit on the secure frequency we selected for the away team."

"*Merde.*" He got up and smoothed the front of his jacket with a quick tug. "We need to get rid of that ship and make contact with the away team, Lieutenant. Keep working on it."

Šmrhová nodded. "Aye, sir."

"I'll be in my ready room." Picard crossed the bridge and exited to his private office. Šmrhová beckoned a relief officer to take her place at the security console as she moved to the center seat, keenly aware she had failed yet again to impress the captain.

Three years and counting.

"That's the control facility down there," La Forge whispered to his shipmates.

He lay prone to the right of Choudhury atop the factory's cold metal roof, peering over the edge at the ugly gray outbuilding several dozen meters below. The structure looked as if it had been cobbled together from thousands of chunks of mismatched scrap, but La Forge was certain it was the factory's control center. The away team had found it by scaling a ladder to the factory's roof, following the spaghetti junctions of its information system, and tracking its dwindling relays here. Unassuming as the building might appear, its importance was revealed by the fact that every system in the entire facility was hard-wired into it. Through a doorway that slid open to let some soldiers exit, La Forge spied several individuals wearing Breen masks with nonmilitary clothing. *Probably scientists or technicians,* he figured.

Just beyond the outbuilding was a landing pad of more recent construction. A Breen cargo transport was parked there. Sickly green light spilled down its aft ramp from its main hold. La Forge increased the magnification of his cybernetic eyes as a squad of Breen troops guided a large antigrav frame inside the ship. Suspended like suits from the frame's top lattice, arranged in ranks and files, were forty dormant androids from the factory. Deeper inside the ship's hold, he saw the bottom edge of another such antigrav frame that had already been loaded and secured. He made a mental calculation of the interior volume of the ship's hold, and concluded it could easily be hiding a third frame full of androids. *That's more than a hundred of those things, packed up and ready to go. And who knows how many the Breen have already shipped out?*

Worf was stretched out on the rooftop to Choudhury's left, his trained eyes studying the movements and positions of several dozen Breen personnel below. The troops were being split into teams of three or four. Some were sent inside the factory, some around its perimeter, and others into the adjacent mountain pass.

"They are on alert," he said as softly as he was able. "Those are search deployments." He crawled backward on his knees and elbows, and La Forge and Choudhury followed him. When they were far enough from the edge to avoid being observed by the Breen on the ground, they pushed themselves up to low crouching stances and fell back to regroup in a space beneath some pipes and between two enormous fan housings, where Velex and Soong were waiting. Worf shot a hard look at Choudhury. "They have been alerted to our presence."

The security chief looked concerned. "Maybe a Breen ship spotted the *Enterprise*. The troops scrambling down here could be just a precaution."

Her interpretation didn't seem to convince Worf. Then his eyes narrowed, and La Forge recognized the look of his friend forming a plan. "We can turn this to our advantage." He pointed at the pass. "Choudhury and I will head into the mountains and harass the Breen with guerrilla tactics. This will draw their forces to us—leaving the control center with few defenders." He nodded at Velex. "You will escort Doctor Soong and Commander La Forge to the control center and neutralize any threats they encounter." Velex accepted the mission with a curt nod.

Soong's face was a mask of wide-eyed disbelief. "Are you kidding? That's your plan? Doesn't that seem just a tad *simplistic* against an enemy like the Breen?"

"Sometimes the simplest plan is best," Worf said.

La Forge shrugged at Soong. "I'm with Worf. The more moving parts a plan has, the more ways it can go wrong. Just stay under cover unless Velex or I tell you otherwise. We'll get you inside the control center. After that, the rest is up to you."

The scientist let out a derisive huff. "You have no idea what you're doing, do you?"

Worf drew his blaster. "We will see soon enough. Move out."

It never ceased to amaze Choudhury that someone as large and bulky as Worf could move with such agility and stealth. They were half sliding, half climbing down a cluster of vertical pipes on the factory's exterior. There was no time to be slow or careful. The timing of the Breen patrols was as regular as clockwork, which meant Worf and Choudhury needed to take cover before the next trio of armed troops turned the corner thirty meters to her left.

She reached the ground first and sprinted a dozen meters toward a large, cube-shaped heat exchanger that was linked to the facility by a wide aboveground conduit. Worf jumped down from the wall a few seconds behind her and followed her across the perilous stretch of open ground. A perfectly timed somersault enabled her to roll to cover against the side of the heat exchanger, in a squat with her blaster in her hand. Worf breezed past her into the shadows barely a step ahead of the Breen patrol, which appeared precisely on time.

Huddled in the darkness, she and Worf slowed their breathing and became still. Choudhury imagined herself as a natural extension of the rocky ground, a part of the night, a soul at one with the wind. She purged her conscious thoughts and dwelled in the moment. At her back, Worf was the bedrock, unseen and unyielding. Crunching steps drew near, the gritty sound of boots on rocky soil. Then the Breen stepped into Worf and Choudhury's field of view. Two of the Breen carried compact battle rifles; the third wore a sidearm and carried a neural truncheon, the trademark melee weapon of the Breen military. The two Starfleet officers tracked the Breen with only their eyes rather than risk moving their heads, then they relied upon their ears. Finally, the receding steps faded away, until only the wind remained.

Worf tapped her shoulder. They holstered their weapons and slipped away, up a narrow trail into the myriad hiding places of the mountain range, whose bizarre towers of rock made her think of granite blades. As they sidestepped between an enormous thrust of gray stone and the mountainside, the thunderous roar of fusion engines filled the valley and echoed off the rocky slopes. Choudhury looked back and saw the Breen transport lifting off and heading for orbit.

She said nothing, and neither did Worf, but they both knew that letting the Breen ship escape with its cargo of more than a hundred Soong-type androids, even dormant ones without active positronic brains or functional programming, was a grave tactical error. But it was one they would have to address later, after the mission.

Can't obsess over what's done, she reminded herself. *For all we know, they've made off with thousands of those things. We need to focus on where we are and what we're doing. Our primary objective for now is to recover the stolen androids and destroy this factory.*

Worf halted and directed her attention at the trail ahead. It forked, with its branches heading in opposite directions across the mountainside for a ways before doubling back at a higher altitude, where each intersected another path leading toward the peaks lining the pass. He indicated with a gesture that he would head right. She acknowledged with a confirmation that she was going left. Then they split up and stole away, each to a different vantage point from which to snipe the Breen and raise havoc as a distraction for Velex, La Forge, and Soong.

Several minutes later, she stopped at the corner of her trail's switchback, surveyed the landscape below and above her position, and nestled herself deep into a crag in the rock wall, behind a large boulder. She drew her blaster, set it for maximum power, and waited.

After a short while, her transceiver vibrated gently against her throat. She tapped it twice and heard Worf's voice, low and steady. *"Worf to Choudhury. Confirm status."*

Because of the scattering field, there was no way

to contact La Forge and Velex to ask if they remained ready. *We'll just have to hope they're in position and good to go.* She hoped this didn't turn out to be another tactical error. "Ready."

Worf's voice was deathly calm. *"Fire on my mark."*

Arm braced atop the boulder, Choudhury selected her first target and took a deep, calming breath to steady her aim. Then he gave the order, and her readiness became action.

"Fire."

Hostile screeches of blaster fire echoed off the mountainside and re-echoed within the metal maze of the factory around La Forge. Now he understood why Worf and Choudhury had taken the risk of moving to higher vantage points before opening fire: the acoustics between the mountains and the industrial complex amplified and multiplied the sonic barrage of their weapons. Though there were only two of them harassing the Breen with fire from above, it sounded as if an entire platoon was waging an assault on the valley.

Velex, La Forge, and Soong stayed low to the ground, sheltered behind a long cluster of broad pipes. Their left shoulders were pressed against one of the factory's towering walls of machinery, just inside the exit closest to the control center. La Forge lay in the middle of the group, monitoring the movements of the Breen patrol outside with his tricorder. Limited to a primitive echo-location mode that relied on ultrasonic pulses, it wasn't as accurate or as detailed as a Starfleet device, but it was more than capable of tracking basic movements at short range. Of the nearly dozen personnel it detected in and around the control center, all but a handful of them scrambled into action when the shooting started.

"Look sharp," he whispered to Velex. "They're taking the bait."

The Troyian adjusted his grip on his blaster. "Just tell me when."

La Forge looked back at Soong. "I'll cover Velex while he moves ahead to the control center. You stay here until I signal you to move up and join us."

"Got it," Soong said. "Good luck."

When the last of the enemy troops had cleared the area, La Forge slapped Velex's foot, cueing him to advance. The Troyian sprang to his feet and dashed around the corner, blaster in hand. La Forge tracked his progress with the tricorder. In a matter of seconds, Velex had reached the next point of limited cover, just a few meters shy of the entrance to the control center. La Forge put away his tricorder, crawled forward to the corner, and peeked around it. From across the empty stretch of gravel road, Velex beckoned him to move up.

His heart racing, La Forge got to his feet and sprinted away from the factory, toward Velex. He was halfway there when something unseen slammed into his face, and something else swept his legs out from under him. The engineer landed on his back, dazed and blinded with pain. He reached reflexively for his nose, which throbbed with deep pain and coated his hand with fresh blood. Blinking to clear the red haze from his vision, he saw Velex break cover and move toward him. Then several humanoid shapes shimmered into view between them.

Velex tried to aim his blaster, only to be cut down in a savage flurry of disruptor fire. His charred corpse crumpled in a twisted heap as the shapes between him and La Forge solidified. They were Breen soldiers—the snoutlike masks were unmistakable—but they wore a type of armor La Forge had never seen before. It was black and silver, with a scaly texture, and it featured what he surmised was a compact power cell on its back. The one detail he did recognize was the metallic gold stripe down the center of each soldier's helmet, starting just above their long, narrow visors. That was the mark of the Spetzkar, the Breen military's elite special forces.

The Spetzkar trooper who'd toppled La Forge pointed his rifle at the engineer's face. A harsh crackle of machine noise issued from his mask's vocoder and was instantly parsed into English by some unseen universal translator on his uniform: "Drop your weapon."

La Forge tossed away his blaster and lay very still, his open hands raised in surrender. The Breen commando backed up but kept his weapon trained on him. Then two of his comrades seized La Forge by his arms and hauled him to his feet. They held him while the first commando searched La Forge, relieved him of his tools and other equipment, and tossed the contraband on the ground. Another trooper approached them, and this one's helmet had thin red stripes on either side of its gold band. *Probably a noncom,* La Forge reasoned. *Or maybe the commander.*

Some untranslated conversation passed between Red Stripes and the other Spetzkar. Dangling in their iron grip, La Forge mustered his best poker face.

Please don't let them find—

His silent plea was denied as two more Spetzkar ushered Soong out of the factory at riflepoint. Another round of machine noise was volleyed between Soong's captors and Red Stripes, who barked some terse commands and pointed at the control center. His men let go of La Forge, then one of them poked him hard in the back with his weapon's muzzle, prodding him toward the ramshackle outbuilding. Nodding and wiping blood from his face, La Forge started walking, and Soong fell in beside him as they neared the entrance.

He hoped Worf or Choudhury had seen what just happened to him, Soong, and Velex. Because if they hadn't, their guerrilla campaign was about to take a sharp turn for the worse.

"They simply appeared," Choudhury said, struggling to keep her voice down. "Until I saw them through the holoscope, I thought they were Jem'Hadar." She ducked a centimeter lower behind a rock formation, paranoid there could be shrouded Breen commandos anywhere, even right next to her. Until that moment, she had never envied Worf's keener olfactory senses and hearing. "Their markings were unmistakable, Worf. They were Spetzkar, a whole platoon of them."

"Stay calm," he counseled her. *"Remember your blind-fighting instruction. Stay under cover as long as possible. Meet me at Soong's ship."*

"Acknowledged." She tapped her concealed transceiver once, closing the channel. After a long, calming breath, she studied the mountainside and mapped its moonlit terrain in her mind's eye. Visualizing her path from one area of cover to the next, she plotted a route back to the pass, one that would let out close to the trail that led to Soong's ship.

Before doubt could paralyze her, she willed herself into motion. On each leg of the hike up the mountainside, she was exposed and vulnerable for only a few seconds at a time. *As long as no one's looking in my direction with UV or thermal imaging, I'll be fine.* She crawled on knees and elbows between two points of relative safety, eager to stay as far out of sight as possible. Along the way, she found herself questioning the wisdom of whoever decided this mission should have no reinforcements and no extraction plan.

Tucking herself under a low overhang of rock, she

paused to assess the relative risk of the next hop in her trek up the mountainside. Sweat trickled down her forehead and pooled above her eyebrows, and strands of her black hair felt as if they'd been plastered to her forehead. A film of dust had formed on her teeth, filling her mouth with the unpleasant flavor of dry earth, and she struggled to muster enough spit to expel the taste.

She estimated it would take her another twenty minutes to reach the mountain pass, and another ten after that to reach Soong's ship. A quick check of her chrono placed her ETA at the rendezvous right around the time of the away team's next scheduled check-in with *Enterprise.* She hoped she and Worf both reached the rendezvous point alive—and that the *Enterprise* was still out there somewhere, waiting to bring them home.

The interior of the control center was just as much a hodgepodge of mismatched technology as its exterior, and that didn't surprise La Forge in the least. What left him slackjawed in shock and horror was the sight of Soong's first three prototype androids all but reduced to scrap atop portable worktables in the center of the room. The body of Lore lay in a discarded heap in the corner, and a small shape that he assumed was Lal's body lay inside an open body bag atop another worktable, apparently awaiting its turn for a brute-force dissection.

B-4's limp form lay on a worktable beside a bank of computers. An optronic cable linked his still-functioning positronic brain to the control center's master systems board. La Forge wondered how long the poor android had until his neural net suffered a fatal collapse.

The four Breen in the room who wore civilian-looking garb made a point of ignoring the entrance of the Spetzkar and their prisoners. They seemed more like indentured servants than valued experts, based on La Forge's reading of the interpersonal dynamics at work in the room.

One of the Spetzkar studied La Forge and Soong with a Breen military-grade scanner. The commando spat a storm of crackling gibberish at Red Stripes, who looked at his prisoners. "You are humans," came the briefly delayed translation of his own static-scratch noise.

La Forge gave free rein to his sarcasm. "What gave it away?"

"Identify yourselves."

Feigning labored concentration, La Forge replied, "I can't recall. Must have amnesia." For once, Soong had the good sense to keep his mouth shut. La Forge tried to change the subject. "Nice trick you've got there—the shrouding. Did you learn that from the Jem'Hadar?"

"We didn't ally ourselves with the Dominion because we believed in its cause." Red Stripes conferred with one of his subordinates for a moment, then turned back toward La Forge, drew his sidearm, and pointed it at the engineer's head. "Identify yourself and claim protection as a prisoner of war, or I will kill you."

"Since when do the Breen respect laws regarding prisoners of war?"

"We have accepted certain legal limitations as prerequisites for membership in the Typhon Pact." Red Stripes charged his weapon, filling the room with a whine whose pitch rose swiftly beyond the range of human hearing. "But we reserve the right to execute spies."

Soong blurted out, "Don't shoot him! I can help you, but I need him to do it."

Red Stripes shifted his aim from La Forge to Soong. "In what way can you help us?"

"I know how to program the androids in your factory." All the Breen in the room stopped what they were doing and turned toward Soong, who played dumb. "That is what you're trying to do, right? Figure out how to program their positronic brains? I mean, they're not much use without working brains. Just big, stupid paperweights."

The commander edged closer, all but touching the tip of his mask's snout to Soong's nose. "And you believe you can program these androids to their full potential?"

"I'm reasonably sure I can, yes." Soong nodded at La Forge. "But not without him."

"What is he to you?"

"My assistant," Soong lied. "The first decent one I've had, actually." He smiled. "Give us two hours, and we'll show you how to make those androids do anything you want."

Red Stripes contemplated the proposition. He and the other Breen looked at one another—an affectation La Forge found odd, considering they couldn't see one another's faces. He wondered if perhaps their understanding of other nonverbal cues, such as the subtle nuances of body language, were so well developed that they could silently express ideas with something as simple as a shift in stance or a fleeting microgesture. Then the commander spat a flurry of noise at his subordinates. Most of them left the room; a few others moved to assist the civilian Breen in bringing more of the control center's workstations on line.

Red Stripes motioned La Forge and Soong to adjacent terminals with a wave of his disruptor. "Bring the androids on line in one hour, or I'll kill your assistant. Do you understand?"

"Perfectly," Soong said. He cracked his knuckles, then set to work writing code in a blur on the terminal's holographic interface. He glanced at La Forge and with a quick tilt of his head directed him toward B-4. "Start a level-one diagnostic on the working prototype. I want to make sure its matrix remains stable before we do anything else."

La Forge saw the method in Soong's madness, and didn't know whether to admire the man or hate him. But he knew there were lives that needed to be saved—starting with B-4's. He sat down and accessed the android's neural link. "Whatever you say, Doctor. You're in charge."

Vess hadn't yet finished routing the report from the Spetzkar commander to Pazur's station when Thot Raas stomped onto the *Mlotek*'s bridge and confronted the first officer. "I'm told you sounded an intruder alert on the planet, and that prisoners have been taken."

It would be impolitic, Pazur knew, to ask the commander how he'd learned these things before she'd had the opportunity to inform him. He was under no obligation to tell her, and she had no way of proving whether he had a direct line to some source of intelligence on the planet's surface or had somehow coerced Vess into bypassing the chain of command. All she could do was cope with the situation as she encountered it. "Yes, sir. Two prisoners are in custody. A male Troyian accomplice was killed while resisting capture. The Spetzkar commander reports there are more accomplices who have not yet been apprehended."

"Have the two in custody been identified?"

Pazur called up the report on her screen and motioned for Raas to inspect it. "Not yet. They've refused to give their names, though they've bartered for their lives by offering to help program the androids we found in the factory."

"So, we just happened to catch a pair of expert cyberneticists?"

The first officer hedged her bet. "Unknown, sir. They claim to have such expertise, but it will be some time before their claims can be verified."

The commander leaned closer to Pazur's console, then cocked his head at a pensive angle. "Did the garrison commander send up biometric scans of the prisoners?"

"Yes, sir, as per standard procedure." Anticipating his next order, she asked, "Shall I compare them to known persons of interest in our databanks?"

Raas straightened. "At once."

She fed the prisoners' scans—which included facial-feature mapping, genetic markers, and other subtle details of their physiology—into the *Mlotek*'s main computer. She expected the process to be time-consuming enough that she might beg a shift alone to analyze the results. Instead, the computer returned two matches almost immediately. Pazur opened the dossiers and read off their key details for the commander. "Two humans. The first has been positively identified as Geordi La Forge. Rank, commander. Billet, chief engineer, *U.S.S. Enterprise*. In addition to his expertise in starship propulsion, he also holds advanced ratings in cybernetics and computer programming, with a concentration in artificial intelligence. The second prisoner's identity is unknown, but based on his age and other factors, there is a 98.4-percent probability that he is a direct descendant of noted Federation cyberneticist Noonien Soong."

The commander sounded pleased. "Maybe his claims of being a cybernetics expert aren't so far-fetched, after all." He thought a moment. "An officer of La Forge's stature wouldn't be here on his own. Inform the rest of our battle group we've identified our prey as the *Enterprise*."

29

None of the dozens of tasks and adjustments Soong asked of La Forge were enough to help him forget they were under the constant scrutiny of a Breen special forces commando. The Spetzkar trooper lingered only a few meters away, near the sole exit, his rifle cradled with its muzzle aimed at the floor but ready to draw down on them at the slightest provocation.

The four scientists hovering over Soong's and La Forge's shoulders, on the other hand, were a constant source of distraction. They observed every task La Forge executed, and every line of code Soong wrote or tweaked, with a steady buzz of vocoder noise that none of them saw fit to translate for his or Soong's benefit. He had no doubt, however, that they were capable of understanding every word that passed between him and Soong.

He finished his latest diagnostic series and was about to pass the results to Soong when he had an idea. When the Breen scientists all were watching Soong for a moment, he accessed the controls of his Federation-style user console and activated a secondary function, an interface mode that presented information in a UV wavelength invisible to eyes and devices attuned to the visible spectrum. It was a feature incorporated into Federation systems to make them more accessible to such species as the Choblik and the Pak'shree. Adjusting his left cybernetic eye to see UV wavelengths, he perceived the second screen superimposed over the original. Then, working in the ultraviolet mode, he composed a brief message:

B-4's matrix is starting to fail. I'm not sure how long he has before cascade failure. We need to get him out of here and back to the Enterprise.

As the Breen civilians resumed their observation of his work, La Forge embedded his message with a self-launching program to activate the UV mode on Soong's terminal, then relayed it to Soong with his latest batch of data. "Here's the latest diagnostic report," La Forge said. "Let me know what you think we should do."

Soong opened the report, and La Forge turned back toward his console and waited to see if the cyberneticist would pick up on his subterfuge. *I know his eyes can see in the UV spectrum. The question is, will he notice that his terminal autolaunched its UV mode and see the message?*

More mechanical chatter filled the moments while Soong stared at his console. Then the disguised android started keying in commands. "This is good work, but we're not done yet. Let me send you the next test series." He shot back a reply with a brush of his hand over the screen.

La Forge watched both the diagnostic panel and his UV interface update in tandem. On the former was a new set of tests and stopgap measures to slow the breakdown of B-4's matrix. On the latter was a short reply to his message:

We don't have time to get him to Enterprise. *I can fix him here, but not with an audience. We need to get rid of the guard. After that, the rest should be easy.*

Fearing that one of the Breen's visors might be equipped with a UV-sensitive filter, La Forge quickly banished the message from his screen, then waited to confirm that there was no suspicious reaction from the scientists haunting his every move. The snout-masked quartet seemed oblivious of the surreptitious communication between Soong and La Forge. Most of their attention remained focused on Soong's labors, which they observed while polluting the room with their vocoder noise. Reassured they were not privy to the UV screens, he fired off another urgent hidden message to Soong: *How are we supposed to get rid of the guard?*

The answer came seconds later, but it wasn't what he'd hoped for:

No idea. I'm making this up as I go.

It took all of Choudhury's willpower to slink carefully up the trail to Soong's ship when what she wanted to do was run there. Darting from one piece of rocky shelter to another, she put Worf's advice to use, and let herself rely on senses other than sight. She opened her mind to the sound of the wind between the rocks, the slightest disturbance in the pebble-strewn sands, and the smell and taste of the dry dusty air. Shallow breaths and light steps minimized her own presence on the pitch-dark trail from the pass, and the profusion of vertical rocks jutting up from the ground ahead gave her cover as she emerged onto the moonlit plateau.

She scouted ahead with a peek around one of the rocks. Under the ship, against one of its three landing pylons, she noted a shape she hoped was Worf. A single tap on her transceiver, followed by a pause, then another single tap: that pattern sent a silent hail to Worf. If he had observed her arrival on the plateau, he would respond by silent code, as well.

Her transceiver vibrated silently against her jugular, three times in quick sequence, and she exhaled softly with relief, then emerged from cover. Worf had stepped out from behind the ship's landing gear, and he walked toward her in long strides. They met in a near-embrace, both of them too professional to let their private relationship show too openly while on duty, even when no one was around to see it. He asked, "Are you all right?"

"I'm fine." She touched his torn collar. "You?"

"I am unhurt." He turned his intense stare toward the factory complex in the valley below. "Now that we know the Breen have shrouding armor, we will need new tactics."

They moved to the plateau's edge. Choudhury considered their options and realized only one was prudent. "We should switch to a defensive posture." She eyed the trails along the mountainside and around the complex. "We can't risk an assault against an opponent we can't see. Our best bet is to set traps on the routes they'd use to track us up here."

Worf crouched as he surveyed the local terrain. "That seems wise. However, we have limited armament, and the Breen seem to have neither a weapons cache nor a munitions dump."

"There are other ways to set traps." She got down on one knee beside him and pointed toward the pass. "There are some loose boulders above that elbow in the trail. We could set a tricorder to generate a resonant frequency inside the rocks. Voilà—instant rockslide."

He looked diabolically amused. "The Capellan Snare. A very old trick." He pointed at the factory. "There may be industrial chemicals or equipment in there that we could use to make explosives. The main assembly area is also large enough to provide places to hide."

"That'll buy us some time. But sooner or later, we'll have to make a run at the control center, and they know it." She let out a small, cynical chortle. "I bet you're wishing now we'd brought more firepower." She hooked a thumb over her shoulder at Soong's ship. "Did we check inside the good doctor's ride? Maybe he has a few bits of illegal ordnance we could use."

Her suggestion drew a frown from Worf. "I tried to get inside before you arrived. I was unable to find an entrance."

"Probably for the best," she chided him. "Knowing you, we'd have hijacked it and made some kind of kamikaze attack on the factory by now."

"The thought did cross my mind."

She shook her head. "Well, here's another thought for you: we should try to get our hands on a couple of those Breen shroud-suits. If we can do that, we might be able to reach the Breen's scattering field generator. Once we neutralize it, Soong's ship can beam us all out with the stolen androids before the Breen know what hit them." With a teasing smile she added, "And then you can thank me for coming up with a viable exit strategy."

"I will take that under consideration." He pointed in cautious gestures at various spots in the landscape. "We should arrange our traps in a way that suggests we have fortified a position somewhere other than here. By concentrating the deadliest traps closest to our decoy base, we can draw more of the Breen out of position while we search for the scattering field generator."

Choudhury gave an approving nod. "It's risky, but I like it. It has momentum." She checked her chrono. It was almost time for the next scheduled check-in with the *Enterprise*. Was it possible Worf had overlooked that because of the recent brush with the Spetzkar? She decided to remind him. "By the way, we have less than an hour till—"

He shushed her with a raised hand. Their eyes met, and in his she saw the fierce light of a hunter who knows he has become the hunted.

His other hand moved with slow grace toward the blaster holstered on his hip . . .

Behind them, a translated voice hissed over a buzz of noise, "Don't move."

Another vocoder-filtered voice snapped, "Disarm yourselves." Moving with exaggerated caution, Worf and Choudhury each drew their blasters using only two fingers on the grips. As soon as the muzzles had cleared the holsters, the voice said, "Toss them over the edge." The two sidearms cracked and clattered as they smashed against the rocks far below.

Gloved hands seized Choudhury's collar, yanked her backward, then hurled her down onto her back. Worf landed hard a couple of meters away, and she saw a Breen step on his chest as another did the same to her. Her arms were pulled taut with violent precision, and magnetic manacles snapped shut around her wrists, hard and icy cold. A half dozen more Spetzkar deactivated their shrouds as their comrades cuffed Worf, and the newly visible troopers helped their comrades haul Worf and Choudhury back to their feet. Machine-speak orders and acknowledgments flew back and forth, then she and Worf were shoved forward, down the trail to the pass, surrounded by half a platoon of Breen.

So much for momentum.

The door behind La Forge opened with a soft hiss, which was followed by the heavy clomps of marching feet. He looked up from his work in the control center's main room to see a squad of Spetzkar commandos escort Worf and Choudhury into the room. The two officers had their hands bound in front of them, but they appeared unharmed.

The Spetzkar commander entered behind the group, circled around them, and faced La Forge and Soong. "Have you completed the updates to the androids' programming?"

La Forge looked at Soong, who swiveled around with insolent sloth. The scientist regarded the Breen officer with naked disdain. "It's a rather complicated process. Just because you want it done in an hour doesn't mean it's possible."

"The programming for the androids was already ninety-eight percent complete. If you are the expert you claim to be, it should not take you this long just to activate their brains."

Behind the commander, another Breen trooper scanned Choudhury and Worf with a handheld device, then tapped in some commands and waited while Soong continued to argue. "If you know the androids' programming that well, you shouldn't need me to fix it."

"We don't. But why expend time and effort when a simpler, faster solution is available?" He drew his sidearm and held it casually at his side—an action La Forge found far more menacing than seeing it melodramatically waved about. The commander turned and asked his subordinate with the scanner, "Has the *Mlotek*'s computer identified the new prisoners?"

The trooper checked his device. "The Klingon is Worf, son of Mogh. Rank, commander. Billet, first officer, *U.S.S. Enterprise*." He paused and tapped at the device. "The human female matches no records in our database, but we calculate a ninety-one percent likelihood that she is Lieutenant Jasminder Choudhury, chief of security, *U.S.S. Enterprise.*" He looked at La Forge. "Also, according to our intelligence files, this one is actually Commander Geordi La Forge, chief engineer, *U.S.S. Enterprise.*"

The commander edged closer to Soong. "Interesting. Assuming the one we killed earlier was also from the *Enterprise,* that would be four Starfleet officers out of uniform, trespassing and engaged in hostile activities against us. I believe that qualifies as espionage." He pointed his disruptor pistol at La Forge, but kept his attention on Soong. "I know the names of your companions, but not yours. Tell me who you are, or La Forge dies."

"My name is Tejinder Soong. Noonien Soong was my father." He raised one eyebrow. "As long as we're making introductions, who the hell are you?"

The commander lowered his weapon. "I am Thot Kren."

"Nice factory you have here, Kren. Win it from the Borg in a card game?"

Soong's sarcasm didn't seem to faze Kren. "It was exploration, not a game of chance, that led us here, Mister Soong. But finding the factory certainly counts as good fortune. We would never have had the resources or expertise to build something like this on our own."

"I didn't know the Confederacy had a need for fifty million android citizens."

"Not citizens. Soldiers. Expendable ones."

La Forge watched anger redden Soong's face and harden his visage. "Those aren't mere robots in there," the scientist snapped. "Those are sentient beings!"

"Not without programming they aren't. And we don't plan on making them self-aware."

Soong started to rise from his chair, but reversed himself as the guard by the door raised his rifle. Easing himself back down, he glared at Kren. "So. You plan to churn out an army of slaves. And do what with them? Become the big dog in the Typhon Pact? Bring the Federation and the Klingon Empire to their knees? Conquer the galaxy?"

"Precisely." Kren turned and extended his empty hand to one of his men, who handed him a display tablet. Kren turned it toward Soong. "This is your ship we've captured?"

"Maybe." As Kren's sidearm started to rise, Soong quickly added, "Yes."

Kren handed the tablet back to his subordinate. "When you're done here, you'll need to open it for inspection. But first . . . stop stalling and bring those androids on line. Now."

Soong looked surprised. "I told you, I can't. It'll take several more hours at least to—"

"I don't believe you. If you fail to comply, I will kill one of your companions."

"Please," Soong begged, "I'm not making this up, I—"

Kren aimed his pistol at La Forge.

"All right, wait!" Soong turned toward his console and started working. "I can get them on line in just a few more minutes, if you'll let me work."

Worf lunged forward, then was jerked back by the trooper holding his collar. The Klingon bellowed, "Soong! Do *not* cooperate with them!"

His outburst didn't slow Soong's furious tapping at the console—but Thot Kren pivoted with great slowness until he faced Worf. Then, moving with deliberate steps, he confronted him. "That's exactly the sort of defiance I've come to expect of a Klingon. It's the sentiment of a true warrior to be so cavalier with his own life." He raised his disruptor and fired.

Jasminder Choudhury disintegrated in a crimson flurry. After her dying scream and the screech of Kren's weapon had faded away, Worf's savage roar continued to shake the room.

La Forge slumped in his chair, stunned silent, his rage and sorrow captive to his abject terror. An arm's reach away, Soong sat paralyzed and gaped in horror at Kren.

Worf's bitter howls ceased as a trio of Breen slammed their neural truncheons into his torso, shocking him half-conscious and dropping him to his knees.

Thot Kren looked at Soong and La Forge. "Keep working. You have thirty minutes to activate my androids"—he waved his disruptor lazily at Worf—"or this one dies next."

As La Forge and Soong resumed work, a knowing look passed between them: there was no more time for perfect plans. There would be no more waiting for a perfect moment. The Breen commander had crossed the line from threats to open warfare.

It was a decision La Forge planned to make him regret.

30

Palpable anticipation stirred beneath the tense undercurrent of activity on the bridge of the *Enterprise*. It surrounded Picard, who felt it like an undertow. He noticed Šmrhová and Dygan sharing glimpses of mutual excitement, and he knew before the tactical officer spoke that good news was at hand. The raven-haired young woman wore a proud countenance as she met Picard's expectant gaze. "Captain, your periscope is ready."

"Well done." He rose from his chair and strode forward. "On-screen, Lieutenant."

The image of churning vapors slashed by strokes of lightning was replaced by a split screen. On the left was a tactical display showing the *Enterprise*'s position relative to the four Breen ships within the star system; on the right was a rotating series of images, each showing one of the four Breen ships accompanied by its relevant technical specifications. As Picard studied the situation report, Šmrhová handed over the security console to a relief officer and joined Picard in the center of the bridge. He frowned and confided, "A rather grim picture."

"The ship in orbit is following an aggressive search

pattern, using tachyon-based sensors to probe the atmosphere. The other three ships are all on direct headings to join the search. We can evade the one ship currently in orbit, but once all four start overlapping their scans, they'll pinpoint our location in a matter of minutes."

He decided to test the young lieutenant. "What do their tactics suggest to you?"

She studied the information on the main viewer. "They're not acting on a hunch. The fact that they've retasked four starships to the search indicates they're aware they're tracking a high-value target and not something small, like a scout or a bird-of-prey." Another moment of thought, and her brow creased with concern. "If they've captured or killed the away team, they might have identified them—in which case it's likely they know they're hunting us."

"Unfortunately, for now we need to assume that's true. Which means we need to make a decision in the next few minutes: whether to withdraw, attempt a rescue of the away team, or engage the Breen ships in combat." He turned a worried look at the screen. "Because once those ships make orbit above us, we'll be trapped." He noted Šmrhová's steely resolve. "What's your recommendation, Number One?"

Now that he'd put her on the spot, several other officers around the bridge stole sidelong looks to see how she handled herself. After only a few seconds of consideration, she said, "The prudent choice would be to withdraw now and avoid direct engagement." She looked at Picard. "But I suggest we hold position for another two minutes before leaving the atmosphere."

Dygan turned from the ops console looking perturbed. "Captain, that would be a grave mistake. The incoming Breen vessels will make orbit in just under three minutes. Any delay on our part could result in our being trapped inside the atmosphere. With all respect to Lieutenant Šmrhová, I advise immediate retreat."

"Thank you, Glinn," Picard said. "Your points are well taken—though I don't recall asking for them." He turned back toward Šmrhová. "I concur with your timetable, Lieutenant. Make the ship ready for orbit."

"Aye, sir," Šmrhová said. Picard returned to his chair as the acting XO started snapping out orders. "Tactical, arm all weapons and charge shield generators—we'll need them as soon as we clear the atmosphere. Helm, take us to the planet's southern magnetic pole and prepare to make orbit inside its nexus. Ops, stand by to reroute power from the SIF to shields and phasers, and start a two-minute silent countdown, on-screen." She turned aft, toward the master systems display. "Chen, as soon as we clear the atmosphere, hail the away team and monitor their frequency for a response." With an upward glance, she added, "All decks, Red Alert. All hands to battle stations."

Confirmations of Šmrhová's orders came back in quick succession, and she made a fast tour of the bridge stations to verify that all was set as she'd commanded. Watching her work, Picard admired her air of confidence and her attention to detail, though he suspected both might be the product of some suppressed insecurity. *As long as she does her job well,* he reminded himself, *it's best not to question the hows or whys. Take it at face value.*

On the main viewer, the countdown dwindled to its final seconds. The tactical readout showed the lone Breen ship in orbit making a sweep of the planet's opposite pole, and its three reinforcements still just outside weapons range but closing at flank speed. This would be close.

"Helm," Šmrhová said in a strong voice, "take us up!"

The bridge crew acted in concert, everyone playing their part expertly, as the *Enterprise* ascended from the thundering depths of the atmosphere back into the familiar comfort of vacuum. Dygan switched the main screen to its standard forward view with a semitransparent tactical schematic superimposed over its left third.

Picard watched the ship's chrono display on the command panel beside his chair. As it changed over to 0200, he heard the feedback tone of an incoming signal being received at the master systems display. Lieutenant Chen verified its authenticity, then declared, "It's Worf!"

"On speakers," Picard ordered.

Everyone paused to listen as the Klingon's baritone resounded across the bridge. "Enterprise, *this is a prerecorded message. We have found a Borg-created factory that is mass-producing Soong-type androids. It is under Breen military control. Velex and La Forge have been captured, along with our mysterious 'good Samaritan.' Choudhury and I will attempt to rescue them and recover the stolen androids, but our odds of success are poor. I recommend the* Enterprise *destroy this facility by torpedo strike immediately, and at any cost. Worf out.*"

The brief message cast a dark spell over Picard's mood.

Dygan reacted to an alert on his console. "The Breen ships have traced Worf's comm signal to us. All four vessels are moving to intercept with shields raised and weapons charging."

So much for a clean escape. "Helm, set course for the third planet, full impulse. Engage."

Gloved fingers seized Worf by the back of his collar and yanked his head up from the floor, jerking him back to consciousness. Thot Kren stood over him, holding Worf with one fist and punching the Klingon's face with the other. "You left a transmission device in the mountains!"

Worf snarled but said nothing. Kren hit him again and broke his nose.

"My men detected its signal! Who did it contact? What message did you send?"

All the Breen commander got from Worf was a bloodied smile. If the Breen had detected the signal, that meant Worf's transceiver—which he'd torn out of his uniform collar and hidden under a landing strut of Soong's ship on the plateau after he made contact with Choudhury—had received the check-in signal and verification code. It also meant the *Enterprise* was still here and likely already en route to reduce this valley and everything in it to superheated vapor.

Mission accomplished, he gloated.

Thot Kren threw Worf back to the floor and pivoted toward Soong, drawing his disruptor as he turned. "Your time is up. Can you bring the androids on line or not?"

Soong swiveled his chair to face Kren. "I brought them on line four minutes ago."

The Breen raged through his vocoder, "Why didn't you inform me *then*?"

From outside the control center came a sudden and sustained shrieking of disruptor fire, followed by berserker roars so loud they trembled the ground and shook the walls.

The cyberneticist flashed a diabolical smirk. "I was waiting for that."

Thirty seconds earlier . . .

Standing guard outside the entrance to the control center, Spetzkar trooper Feid heard a low rustling from inside the factory. He beckoned his partner, Nolik, warned him with a gesture of the disturbance inside the massive industrial complex, and signaled they should shroud.

He activated the camouflage circuit on his own suit, and together the two commandos faded from the visible world into their realm of monochromatic gray twilight. They acknowledged each other, then Feid braced his rifle against his shoulder as he moved toward the factory's nearest access point, a broad gap in its towering wall of pipes and scrap metal.

Nolik stayed close on Feid's right flank, checking high and low, and occasionally making a quick pivot and backpedaling while watching behind them for trouble.

The two of them reached the wall and put their backs against it. Feid remained on point, and he edged toward the corner and stepped carefully around it to scout the path ahead.

Shuffling toward him was a wall of identical humanoids, their faces blank, eyes aglow, arms limp at their sides. It was a mob that filled the entire width of the passageway, twenty meters across, and it stretched back as far as he could see, into the smoky haze of the factory. There had to be hundreds of thousands of them, and their front rank was less than twenty meters from the exit and advancing in halting steps . . . until one of them looked directly at him. Then its face contorted with rage. It let out a roar and sprinted toward him.

All the other androids beside and behind it, a quarter million of them at the very least, painted the night with battle cries and joined its pell-mell charge.

"Fall back!" Feid cried as he opened fire at the oncoming flood-crush of androids, still not sure how they'd seen past his shroud.

He sidestepped to let Nolik join him on their two-man skirmish line, both of them firing a steady barrage of disruptor fire into the rioting throng. Androids fell by the dozens, collapsing in smoking heaps of melted metal and sparking circuits, but others hurdled over their fallen brethren and pressed forward, rapidly closing the distance to the exit.

More troopers charged to join him and Nolik, adding their own firepower to the mix. One of them started calling for reinforcements even as another sounded a call for retreat.

Then one of the androids got hold of Nolik, who blasted it at point-blank range—but not before it tore off one of Nolik's arms. He and his attacker collapsed to the ground, both of them equally incapacitated. The situation on the battlefield degenerated into mayhem. Androids poured out of the factory and swarmed the platoon of Spetzkar defending the control center. Panicked cries crowded Feid's comm channels as he fired at damn near anything that moved while watching the rest of his platoon vanish, one after another, into the teeming mass of mechanical rage. Then his backward stumbling ended as his back struck a wall, and the last thing he saw was a pale golden face twisted in murderous fury.

Shouts of panic, screams of pain, and cries of terror crackled from the comms of Thot Kren and his two

Spetzkar commandos. They and the four Breen technicians seemed at once frantic and paralyzed, pivoting and fidgeting with indecision as the situation outside turned calamitous.

Worf kneeled on the floor and listened with sadistic glee to the rising pandemonium.

Heavy impacts resounded on the control center's locked outer door, accompanied by the groaning of overstressed metal and the snap-crack of splintering polycarbon panels.

Kren pointed at the anteroom that separated the main laboratory from the entrance and barked a long string of untranslated vocoder noise at his men, who hefted their rifles and scrambled out of the lab. Working together in the anteroom, they pushed heavy furniture against the door, then braced themselves to hold the line against a tidal wave of mindless violence.

An argument raged between the Breen technicians, two of whom ran toward a jury-rigged console in the corner, a piece of Breen technology. Kren turned and shouted at them, "Stop!"

The two Breen at the console yelled back, "We have to drop the scattering field! There's no way out without a transporter!" They turned their backs on him and resumed working.

The commander fired and disintegrated the pair of them.

Their two colleagues spat a storm of noise as they lurched at Kren, who turned again and fired off a snap shot, vaporizing the remaining Breen scientists.

In the fraction of a second it took Kren to turn his back on Soong and pull a trigger, the android scientist crossed the room in a blur and was all but on top of him. Kren was very fast—faster than Worf would have expected—and he nearly brought his disruptor around in time to add Soong to his list of kills. Instead, Soong swatted the weapon from Kren's hand with such speed and ferocity that the Breen actually recoiled by the tiniest degree, caught by surprise.

As the disruptor clattered across the floor toward La Forge, Worf sprang from the floor and got his manacled hands over Kren's head and closed his right arm around the Breen's throat.

In the anteroom, the two Spetzkar turned to see what was happening behind them.

La Forge lunged from his chair, grabbed the disruptor pistol as he rolled, and landed prone and shooting. His deadly barrage slammed into the two Spetzkar and vaporized them.

Kren staggered under the burden of Worf's dead weight on his back and the crushing pressure of the Klingon's lock on his throat. The Breen threw himself backward against a wall, perhaps hoping to break Worf's grip and knock him free—an outcome made exceedingly unlikely by the magnetic manacles that bound Worf's wrists and made his choke hold all but impossible to force open. Kren tried to stretch his arm to reach a fearsome stiletto sheathed on the side of his boot, but Worf refused to let him bend forward.

The Breen threw desperate backward jabs with his elbows. A few even connected well enough to crack some of Worf's ribs. His chest ached and his breathing became a fight of its own. *This has gone on long enough.* With a feral roar and a twist of his upper body, he broke Kren's neck. Vertebrae shattered with a wet crunch, and Kren sagged in Worf's arms, a sack of flesh and bone. Worf let the body fall, and it struck the floor with a dull slap.

Standing over his vanquished enemy, Worf felt . . . nothing. There was no honor, no satisfaction, no catharsis of revenge. It simply *was,* and Worf felt secretly alarmed to find himself so numb in the aftermath of mortal hand-to-hand combat.

La Forge dusted himself off and glared at Soong. "What the hell happened out there?"

"He asked for an army." Soong looked up from his console to nod at Kren's corpse. "I gave him one: mine." He kept talking as he walked to the portable table on which B-4 lay. "I programmed them to attack anything that looks like a Breen. Don't worry, now that we've got the control center, I sent them a command to leave us be." He retrieved some cables from the shelf underneath B-4. "Now we can start the real work."

Worf checked his chrono. "My message went to the *Enterprise* at 0200. If they responded immediately to my request for a torpedo strike, it will take them fifteen minutes to reach firing range, which means we have six minutes to get off this planet."

La Forge hurried to the console the Breen technicians had accessed moments earlier. "This unit controls the scattering field. If we can shut it down, Soong's ship can beam us out of here with time to spare." The engineer paused before touching its interface. "There's just one problem: this is Breen technology. I have no idea how to use this thing."

"Let me try," Worf said. "I saw the Breen use systems like this when I was a prisoner during the Dominion War. I might be able to shut down the field."

Soong called out, "Let him work, La Forge. I need you over here. Now."

"For what?" La Forge asked as he joined Soong next to B-4.

"To help me save my son," Soong said, "before it's too damned late."

31

The *Enterprise* lurched and rocked as disruptor blasts and near-miss torpedo detonations hammered its faltering shields. Picard could barely hear his own shouted orders over the bone-rattling concussions. "Transfer power from forward shields! Continue suppressing fire!"

On the main viewscreen, the image of the third planet, which Lieutenant Choudhury had named Mangala, was still a small disk but growing slowly larger as the ship sped toward it at full impulse. Another brutal impact against the *Enterprise*'s shields left the holographic image projected over the forward bulkhead distorted and pixelated for half a second.

If we could go to warp, this would be over by now. Picard resisted the urge to curse the docelerite that kept his ship mired at impulse, and which made it impractical to fire photon torpedoes and shift to evasive maneuvers. Without precision navigation at warp speed, a task the docelerite made impossible, there was no way to guarantee the torpedoes would strike their intended target from this range. There was also the possibility that torpedoes limited to impulse flight could be picked off by sharp-eyed Breen gunners on the ships pursuing the *Enterprise*.

Around the bridge, consoles stuttered and lights flickered as another salvo from the Breen attack group pummeled the *Enterprise*'s aft shields. Picard's fingers seized white-knuckle tight on the armrests of his chair to keep himself from being thrown forward to the deck.

"Firing aft torpedoes," Šmrhová said above the clamor, "dispersal pattern Echo Blue!"

Picard checked his command display and monitored the salvo's effect on the Breen ships. The inverted-V of detonations forced the four cruisers to veer wildly to port and starboard. They would adjust their headings momentarily, but Šmrhová had just bought the *Enterprise* crew a few more seconds in which to regroup. He gave her an approving nod. "Well done."

She acknowledged his praise with a shy smile, and without missing a beat. "Firing aft phasers. Four hits. No damage, but it's keeping them off balance."

"Keep it up, Lieutenant. Time to firing range on the planet?"

Šmrhová replied, "Five minutes."

For a moment, Picard was sure the planet on the viewscreen looked significantly closer. Then another barrage thundered against the *Enterprise*'s shields, and he realized that for the next five minutes his destination would remain painfully far away.

"Plug the cable into the fourth jack," Soong said, directing La Forge while lying on the worktable he'd parked next to B-4's. "We have to use the computer as a buffer."

Uncertain what Soong was setting up to do, La Forge hesitated. "Is this really necessary? I thought we could reprogram B-4 without—"

"Just do it! We're wasting time!"

La Forge recoiled from Soong's outburst, then did as he'd instructed. "It's in."

"So you *can* follow instructions. Good, that'll be helpful." Soong tore his shirt and reached under his left armpit. His hand emerged holding an isolinear chip, which he held out to La Forge. "Been saving this for a special occasion. Insert it into the main bus. Hurry!"

Holding up the chip, La Forge remained at a loss. "What are we doing?"

Soong's temper grew shorter with each delay. "Would you pay attention? Put it into the main bus, then follow the prompts on your display. It's a self-running program. I just need you to keep it safe from power surges and shut it down when it's done."

Following orders had never been a problem for La Forge, as long as he understood why those orders were given. He refused to be bullied into action without knowing the details. "I'm not doing a thing until you tell me what's going on." Hoping for the best, he made an educated guess. "Are we transferring Data's memories into one of the factory androids?"

The question drew an appalled glare from Soong. "Are you out of your mind? Put a full consciousness into a matrix whose hardware is based on Lore's flawed design? I wouldn't risk that even if it *was* an option."

"Why isn't it?"

Soong breathed an exasperated sigh and rolled his eyes, as if he were answering the stupidest question ever asked. "Because none of those androids have operational software. Just copying over Data's memories won't be enough. Memories without sentience, knowledge without self-awareness, is utterly useless! To make him live, he needs the spark of life. That ineffable *something* that makes us all more than the sum of our parts. He needs a *soul*."

La Forge was sure that lurking behind Soong's lofty rhetoric there was something unsaid, something terrible that gave the engineer a sick sense of foreboding. "What're you saying? You're gonna overwrite B-4's mind to save Data's?"

"No!" Soong sat up, aghast and enraged. "Do you really think I'd murder one of my sons to save the other? Good God, La Forge, what kind of monster do you think I am?"

Worf halted his so-far futile efforts to access the controls for the scattering field, and shouted at La Forge, "We do not have time for this! Do as he says!"

"Not till I know what I'm *really* being asked to do!"

Soong seethed behind a sullen glare. "All right, La Forge, listen closely. I'm telling you this because you need to know. More importantly, because *I* need you to know. Before I can fix B-4, I need to remove Data's engrams from his positronic matrix. We're going to copy Data's memories into *my* matrix, while mine are buffered in the computer. Once that's done, the program on that chip you're holding will upgrade B-4's firmware and software, so that he can go on living indefinitely without risk of a cascade failure. Then it'll dump my memories back into my neural archive, and reactivate Data in his new body. Got it?"

La Forge stared at Soong, certain he'd misheard some detail. "*His* new body? Don't you mean . . . in *your* body?"

Soong cracked a bittersweet smile. "Po-tay-to, potah-to."

"What'll happen to you?"

"What should have happened a long time ago." He pointed at the computer's exposed main bus. "Now get on with it. We don't have all day, you know." Confident his point had been made, Soong lay back down on the table and waited.

The chip was cold in La Forge's fingers, and as

he held it in front of the open slot on the computer's main bus, his hand trembled. Then he guided the chip into its slot. On the display, a prompt confirmed the program's launch, and all it required of him now was a single touch on the interface to start its work. With one tap, he would end the life of Noonien Soong in the hope of saving two others. It was a cold-blooded exercise in moral calculus.

From the table, Soong whispered, "This is our last chance, Geordi."

La Forge knew there was no more time to think, only time to act.

He started the program.

32

Soong was alone in a sea of white light, a disembodied consciousness manifesting itself in the form of his preferred self-image: young and fit, with a wide, cocksure smile. He was clothed in his favorite outfit—a pair of loose beige trousers, well-worn dark brown leather sandals, and a white linen shirt with the sleeves rolled up loosely above his elbows.

He was neither warm nor cold, neither awake nor asleep, neither alive nor dead. Drifting through the void, he felt himself drawn in by a strange attractor, as if he were being pulled forward by invisible chains. It was gravity, he decided; not the kind that bends spacetime but the kind that binds souls to one another, the kind that compels strangers to cross crowded rooms.

A pair of blurry forms emerged in the distance, their details slow to resolve, as if they were surfacing from some unfathomable depth. Soong was patient; hours or even days could elapse in this cybernetic limbo while only seconds passed in the physical realm. Soong walked toward them, despite the absence of solid ground beneath his imaginary feet. It was like running in a dream, his mind struggling to bridge the chasm of nothingness in a few great strides but feeling trapped as if in amber. He forced himself to stop fighting; what was to be would be, in its own time and not before, and it would not be resisted when its moment came.

Soon enough, his companions in the ether became clear. His two sons were identical to each other, yet different from him, in whose image they'd been made. They wore their hair slicked tight against their skulls, while his was loose and free. B-4 wore a drab tan coverall, just as he did on the worktable where he lay beside Soong. And the projection of Data, who lay sleeping at the feet of his older, simpler brother, was attired in his Starfleet uniform.

B-4 cocked his head at Soong's approach. "Are you also my brother?"

Soong felt love and pity for B-4. "No. I'm your father. I'm here to help you, and Data. But to do that, I need you to do something for me."

"What can I do?"

He patted B-4's cheek. "Go to sleep, son. You'll feel better when you wake up." Without argument, B-4 sat down on the non-ground, stretched out, and slipped into a dreamless slumber. Soong kneeled beside Data and gently shook his shoulder. "Data? Wake up." Data's eyes moved beneath his closed eyelids, as if he were dreaming. *Maybe he is,* Soong mused. He nudged him again. "Son, this is your father. It's time to get up."

Golden eyelids fluttered weakly until they were half open, and Soong looked into the pale eyes of his youngest son. Data squinted up at him, and he sounded groggy. "Father . . . ?"

"Yes, son. It's me. Wake up. We need to talk."

Soong helped Data sit up and watched him blink as he looked around in confusion. "I do not understand." He glanced at B-4, then cast an imploring look at Soong. "Where am I?"

"Where do you think you are, Data?"

Data's brow furrowed as he concentrated. It felt cruel to Soong to make Data jump through hoops this way, but he needed to be sure his son's memories were intact. After almost two seconds of effortful thought, Data's face snapped into an expression of epiphany. "The last thing I remember is uploading a copy of my memories into B-4's positronic matrix. . . . I thought it might help him develop new neural pathways. Was I successful?"

"I'm afraid not. But it wasn't your fault, Data. You couldn't have known he wasn't made for that. The good news is, I'm making some upgrades that'll improve his cognitive functions over the next few months. He'll never be what you are . . . but then, no one ever could."

"That is very kind of you to say. Thank you." Data looked down at B-4, then at his own hands. He seemed puzzled. "Why am I unable to recall any events after my memory upload?"

Soong sighed. He'd known this part of their conversation would be inevitable. He hoped that Data, whose matrix was now fully infused with human-style emotions, would be able to cope with it. "Because less than a day after you uploaded your memories into B-4 . . . you died."

Shock and surprise, a wince of denial . . . then Data shuddered before composing himself. His voice was hushed, and he averted his gaze from Soong. "How?"

"You sacrificed yourself to save your captain from a madman named Shinzon." As much as he wanted to rail about the stupidity of that decision, Soong knew this was a delicate moment, the kind that called for a benevolent falsehood. "What you did was very brave, and noble. I . . . was proud of you, son." Then a grain of truth slipped out. "But I just couldn't accept losing you that way. And when I heard your memories had been preserved in B-4's mind, I knew I had to find a way to save you. I had to bring you back."

Data looked up at Soong, his features vacillating between hope and fear. "Have you found a way?" His eyes widened as Soong nodded. "How?"

"The short answer? After you left me on Terlina III, I transferred my consciousness into an android body, the finest one I've ever built." He remembered his advanced prototype that was destroyed by the Borg, and he frowned. "Well, the finest still in existence, anyway. But you need this body more than I do, Data. So I'm giving it to you."

Powerful emotions left Data searching for words. "But . . . Father . . . *no*."

"Yes, Data." He clasped his son's shoulders. "I know this is confusing, that you have questions, probably more than you know how to ask right now. But when you wake up, you'll have access to more answers than you've ever imagined."

"I do not understand."

Soong smiled. "You will. Remember how your mother and I imbued you with memories from the four hundred eleven colonists on Omicron Theta?" Data nodded. "That was one of Juliana's finer ideas. I've decided to do her one better: I've given you *my* memories, Data. And not just selected ones, like those I put on the emotion chip. All of them. My whole lifetime of experience, all my knowledge. It's yours now." He patted Data's golden cheek. "All that I know, all that I'm capable of, all that I am, my son . . . I give to you."

"Father, please do not do this."

"It's already done, Data. When you wake up, you'll see the future through my eyes and shape it with my hands. You'll inherit my life, body and soul."

Tears welled in Data's eyes, and his jaw trembled.

"But . . . if I inherit all that you are . . . what will happen to you?"

"I'll live on through you, Data, as all fathers hope to live on through their sons. Your resurrection is my immortality." White light enveloped them, softening the details of their features as their shared limbo began to decay. "Time to live, Data."

Data thrashed like a wild animal in Soong's grip. "No! Not like this!"

Soong shook him. "Data! Stop it!" His son froze and stared at him. He did his best to adopt a soothing tone. "Listen to me. I need you to do one last thing for me." Data nodded, and the innocence of his tear-streaked face made Soong wish he could live his life over and get it right this time. "Remember me, son—not as I was . . . but as I tried to be." The light was so bright now that he could no longer see his son's face, only the apparition of his silhouette. Noonien Soong used his final moment of consciousness wisely and well:

"I love you, Data."

Data opened his eyes and bolted up to a sitting position atop the worktable. "Father . . . ?" The face and visage of Noonien Soong lingered in his memory even as he acclimated to his new circumstances. With all of his father's knowledge integrated into his own, he knew where he was, what was happening, and how little time there was to do what needed to be done.

Beside him, B-4 sat upright and turned his head to look at him. "Hello, Data."

"Hello, brother." Data disconnected the optronic cable from his own brain, then he detached the one linking B-4 to the computer. As he got up from the table, he found himself face-to-face with Geordi La Forge. "Hello, Geordi. It is good to see you."

La Forge stared at him with wonderment. "Data? Is it really you?"

"Yes." He looked at B-4 and pointed at Lal. "Pick her up and hold her, then stand here." B-4 obeyed his instructions while Data hurried past La Forge to Worf's side and gestured at the Breen console. "May I, Commander?"

Worf nodded and stepped aside. As Data decoded the Breen interface, using information his father's nanite spies had gathered while hidden inside the Breen ship that brought the stolen androids to this world, his old Klingon compatriot watched with quiet admiration. Then Worf stepped away, picked up the slain Breen commander, and hefted the body over his shoulder.

A final flurry of taps on the control panel shut down the Breen's scattering field. Using the transceiver inside his head, he opened a channel to the *Archeus.*

As soon as contact was made, Shakti responded with a panicked warning: *A ship in orbit is targeting your coordinates! Transporter standing by!*

For the benefit of his friends, he spoke his commands rather than transmit them as raw data. "Shakti! Launch the ship and lock onto our signal!"

Locked!

Data joined his friends in the center of the room. "Energize!"

The prismatic shimmer, mellisonant hum, and invisible embrace of a transporter beam enfolded Data and his friends—then it was overpowered by the roar of destruction as a wave of fire turned the world white.

One minute earlier . . .

A pall of smoke lingered over the bridge of the *Enterprise,* a gray haze tinged with the noxious odor of melted circuits and burning polymers. Consoles went dark on the port side of the bridge as a rapid series of impacts hammered the ship, and searing-hot phosphors rained from the overhead as a plasma relay overloaded with a deafening report.

Picard brushed half a dozen burning motes from his sleeves and shoulders with stoic aplomb. "Steady," he said, projecting calm to his crew. He ignored the torrent of damage and casualty reports on his command panel, focusing instead on the main viewer's tactical display. Mangala dominated the forward view, and the android factory's coordinates switched from stand-by yellow to in-range red. "Lieutenant Šmrhová, arm torpedoes and lock on target."

Another jarring hit rattled the ship. Dygan called out, "Aft shields collapsing!"

"Torpedoes locked," Šmrhová answered from the security console.

"Fire at will," Picard said. When his order wasn't immediately confirmed, he looked at Šmrhová and saw in her pained expression a mix of desperation and regret. "Lieutenant?"

Her hand trembled above her console. "Sir, the away team . . ."

He understood her reluctance. Worf, La Forge, and Choudhury all were like family to him, but the demands of the uniform had to come first. Worf had recommended this action knowing full well the risk to himself and the away team, and Picard trusted his first officer's judgment without question. He hardened his heart for what had to be done. "You have your orders, Lieutenant. Fire torpedoes, full spread, and suppressing fire aft."

"Aye, sir." Šmrhová's hand fell like the blade of a guillotine onto her console and launched the torpedoes. The cluster of missiles streaked away from the *Enter-*

prise, blazed through the atmosphere at one-eighth the speed of light, and descended on their target. As they struck the planet's surface like fire and brimstone, Šmrhová unleashed a fresh salvo of torpedoes and phaser fire at the four Breen ships that continued to harass the *Enterprise.*

An intense flash of white light erupted at the target, and when it faded a second later it was replaced by a ring of fire that expanded at supersonic speed from the blast point. Within five seconds a massive plume of black ash, smoke, and dust obscured the detonation site. "Target destroyed, Captain," Šmrhová said, her tone flat and dispassionate.

The persistent, irregular concussions of attacks by the Breen ships ceased. Dygan checked his readings twice, then looked back at Picard with a surprised expression. "The Breen ships have broken off and engaged their cloaking devices, Captain."

"Thank you, Glinn." Picard understood the grim pragmatism of the Breen's actions. Now that the factory was gone, they apparently saw nothing left there worth fighting for and chose to cut their losses. This wasn't a victory that anyone would hold up as an example of textbook tactics at Starfleet Academy, but Picard was happy to be spared the bloody attrition of a fight to the death after the damage his ship had just suffered. "All decks, cancel Red Alert. Send updated damage and casualty reports to the XO. Bridge out." He hid his bitter regrets and misgivings over the loss of the away team as he said to his team on the bridge, "Well done, everyone."

Grateful nods of acknowledgment were followed by relieved sighs, and the tensions of battle abated as the crew set themselves to the less exhilarating but equally important tasks of restoring the ship to its normal operating status. Then an alert on Dygan's console made the Cardassian sit up. "Captain, sensors have detected a ship ascending from the planet's surface." He looked back at Picard. "It's the ship we followed here, sir."

Šmrhová silenced a warbling tone at her station. "They're hailing us—audio only."

Daring to hope for good news, Picard stood. "On speakers." A nod from Šmrhová confirmed the channel was open. "This is Captain Jean-Luc Picard of the *Starship Enterprise*."

"Captain, this is Worf, requesting permission to land."

The sound of the Klingon's voice dispelled Picard's somber mood. "Granted, Number One. And might I add, it's good to hear your voice. Did you recover the stolen androids?"

"Only two of them—Lal and B-4. I've also captured new Breen military technology requiring immediate analysis."

"Very good. Is the rest of your team with you?"

The long delay in Worf's response alerted Picard that something was gravely amiss.

"Captain . . . you and Doctor Crusher need to meet us . . . alone."

33

Picard stepped out of the turbolift to find Doctor Crusher holding her surgical kit in one hand, waiting for him outside the door to the main hangar bay, at the far aft end of the ship's main hull. "It's still pressurizing," she said. "Any idea what's going on? Is one of them hurt?"

"I'm afraid you know as much as I do right now." He checked the safety gauge beside the door's security panel. "I'm sure Worf will fill us in."

The pressure gauge shifted from yellow to green, and the automatic lock on the door released. Acting out of habit, Picard tugged his uniform jacket smooth as the door slid open with a soft hiss. Crusher followed him into the hangar.

Ahead of them, standing alone in the center of the landing deck, was an elegant civilian transport ship of a type Picard had never seen before. The fluid curves of its silvery exterior reflected distorted funhouse-mirror images of the hangar, himself, and Crusher. Its shape was sleek and swept back, like a raptor diving toward prey, and it had what he assumed was a spacious command deck beneath a long black canopy on the dorsal side of its tapered bow. Sleek, low-profile warp nacelles were tucked discreetly beneath its downward-sloping wings.

The ship barely fit inside the hangar. Its bow, high above Picard's and Crusher's heads, was mere meters from the compartment's forward bulkhead, and its stern was lucky it hadn't been scraped when the hangar's scalloped doors had closed behind it.

A low hum drew Picard's attention upward. The outline of a broad hatch appeared on the ship's otherwise seamless exterior, and then the portal was pulled inward and aside. A wide ramp of the same unblemished silver extended from the doorway to the hangar's deck. Picard and Crusher moved to the end of the ramp and waited.

Worf was the first to appear in the hatchway and descend the ramp. La Forge followed a few paces behind him. Anticipating their bad news, Picard masked his dismay for the sake of morale and decorum. He greeted his two most-senior officers at the bottom of the ramp, his mood subdued. "Welcome back, gentlemen." Neither man looked him in the eye. As much as he hated to do so, duty compelled him to ask questions to which he'd already intuited the answers. "Velex? Choudhury?"

The query made Worf clench his jaw and stare at the deck. La Forge seemed to search for words, but in the end all he could do was look at Picard and give a sad shake of his head.

"Mister Worf, you mentioned you'd captured some Breen technology."

La Forge gestured up the ramp. "It's in the hold, sir. We should have a team from security take it for analysis." He looked at Crusher. "We also have a Breen fatality, if you want to add a new anatomical study to the Starfleet Medical database."

Crusher muffled her surprise. “All right.”

Footsteps at the top of the ramp attracted everyone’s attention. B-4, still wearing the same ugly tan coveralls as when the crew had last seen him, descended the ramp carrying the inert form of Data’s late daughter, Lal. Cradled in her uncle’s arms, she seemed as if she might be only sleeping, because she looked exactly as she had when she was alive, eighteen years earlier.

B-4 walked past Picard without a word of greeting, and came to a stop a few meters away. Then he turned and looked back, toward the top of the ramp. Picard pivoted and followed B-4’s gaze to see the figure standing alone in the hatchway. It was the same person he and his crew had seen on Galor IV—a perfect likeness of Noonien Soong in his late twenties, with gently tousled brown hair, a fair complexion, and bluish-gray eyes. The man wore dark shoes and trousers, a white shirt, and an antique-style brown leather vest with rawhide ties. He walked quickly down the ramp. Face-to-face with the four *Enterprise* officers, he wore a beatific smile.

Then he spoke.

“Hello, Captain.”

The unique inflection of his voice had been unmistakable. Picard stared in wonder at the man before him and replied in a shocked hush, “Data . . . ?”

“Yes, sir. It is good to be back.”

Overcome with elation, Picard grinned like a fool. He had a thousand questions to ask and a thousand things he wanted to say, but all he could manage to utter was, “How?”

Data shared a curious look with Geordi, then he chuckled softly. “It is a long story.”

Tearful with joy, Crusher threw her arms around Data and wrapped him in a smothering hug. “My God, it’s good to see you, Data! Welcome home!”

"Thank you, Doctor."

He pulled back a bit, and Crusher let him, though she kept hold of his arms. "We'll have to contact Will and Deanna on the *Titan,* as soon as possible."

"I would like that."

To Picard's surprise, Data had tears in his eyes. "Data, are you all right?"

"Yes, sir. But I am still unaccustomed to this new body my father gave me. It was made to feel a full range of human emotions, and I am finding them . . . a bit overwhelming."

The captain smiled at Data's abashed reaction to his own feelings. "No more simply turning them off, eh, Mister Data?"

He seemed to appreciate the irony of his predicament. "Unfortunately, no."

Picard heard the doors sigh open behind him. He turned in time to see Worf leaving the hangar deck. Until that moment, he hadn't realized the man had slipped away.

Data seemed puzzled by Worf's abrupt and wordless departure, and he looked to his friends for an explanation. "Did I say something to offend Worf?"

La Forge placed a reassuring hand on Data's shoulder. "No, Data. That's not about you." Seeing that Data still lacked the necessary context, he added, "Choudhury."

A sharp intake of breath signaled Data's sudden understanding. "Ah."

"He's glad to see you, Data," La Forge said. "He just needs some time right now, is all."

Everyone stood silent for a moment, out of respect for Worf's loss and in remembrance of the slain security chief who had been their trusted friend and colleague for over three years. Despite the profound sadness

Picard felt for her loss, he couldn't help but continue to marvel at the presence of Data, who more than four years earlier had died for him aboard the Reman warship *Scimitar,* and who now stood before him not only resurrected but more human than ever before. Unable—no, *unwilling*—to conceal his jubilance, he stepped forward and embraced his friend. "Welcome home, Data." As they parted, he added, "I'd thought you were gone forever."

Data's eyes glistened with tears. "If not for my father's sacrifice, I would have been."

34

Everywhere that Worf went aboard the *Enterprise,* he saw reminders of Jasminder Choudhury. He recalled discussions they'd had in one corridor or another, moments they'd shared in the Riding Club, the hours they'd spent together in her quarters or his, and countless shifts together on the bridge. Plagued by his memories, he lived now under a permanent shadow.

Padd in hand, he stopped outside the door to Picard's ready room and pressed the signal. A moment later, he heard the captain's reply from the companel beside the door. *"Come."*

The door slid open with a faint pneumatic gasp, and Worf walked inside to find Picard seated behind his desk, reviewing information on his desktop terminal. The older man looked up and took note of the padd Worf held. "Is that Data's visual memory download of the factory?"

"Yes, sir." He handed the padd to the captain. "We also downloaded detailed memory files from B-4. The Breen who brought him to the planet did not think him a threat. His records of the Breen cruiser's engineering systems were very detailed."

Picard nodded as he perused the information on the padd. "Well done, Number One."

"Have you read my after-action report?"

The captain set down the padd and turned a cautious eye toward Worf. "I've made a cursory review of your report and La Forge's. Why do you ask?"

"I do not think we should tell Data about the Breen transport we saw leave the planet."

A frown deepened the worry lines on Picard's face. "The one filled with androids."

"Yes, sir. We have deprived the Breen of the ability to mass-produce Soong-type androids, but there is no telling how many unprogrammed prototypes they shipped offworld."

Picard tapped his index finger on the desktop. "That is a troubling detail, and I share your concern—both for the tactical significance of this discovery, and for how it might affect Data. But the fact is, we can't share *any* information with Data—not this, or anything else."

The injunction took Worf by surprise. "I do not understand."

"This version of him is not the same being we served with for fifteen years, Mister Worf. The Data we've just welcomed home technically isn't a Starfleet officer."

"I thought you offered to reactivate his commission."

Disappointment and confusion led Picard to heave a tired sigh. "I did. He said he would 'consider the offer' and get back to me. . . . This new incarnation of Data seems different from the man I remember. Something is driving him—something he doesn't want to talk about." The captain fixed Worf with a piercing stare. "Not unlike another officer of my acquaintance."

Bristling at the veiled accusation, Worf buried his

fury and his grief beneath a stony façade. "You will have to be more specific, Captain."

"You don't need to pretend that the death of Lieutenant Choudhury is just another casualty in the line of duty. Your relationship with her was no secret."

Worf looked away, out a viewport at the warp-streaked stars drifting past. "It was also no one's business but ours." Fighting not to show his temper, he met the captain's look. "There is no need for us to discuss this further."

"If that's your wish, I'll respect it. But I have to insist you make time to talk about it with a member of the counseling staff."

Anger started to get the better of Worf. "That will *not* be necessary."

"I'm making it an order, Number One."

Seething, Worf grumbled through gritted teeth, "Aye, sir."

Without waiting to be dismissed, he turned and walked toward the door. He halted as the captain snapped, "Worf!" His face burning with shame for the emotions he could not master, he looked back at Picard, who continued in a more forgiving tone. "Please accept my personal condolences for your loss. She was a fine officer, a trusted friend, and a truly remarkable woman. My report will note that she died bravely—as a hero."

"That would be a lie." Bitter rage and bottomless grief left Worf feeling hollow. He had lived too long, seen too much, and grown too cynical and jaded to take comfort in such empty platitudes. The truth was far uglier and offered not a whit of solace. "She was murdered because of an order I gave. Cut down in cold blood. Her life was wasted, taken in vain, just as Tasha Yar's was. There was no honor in her death. No glory. Only cruelty . . . and evil."

Worf had nothing else to say. Judging from the beaten look in Picard's eyes, neither did he. Unable to draw another breath in the stifling confines of the ready room, Worf turned and left to continue mourning a life he could never replace, and a death he could never avenge.

35

La Forge entered the aft hangar deck to find Data alone beneath the open dorsal hatch of his inherited starship, the *Archeus,* directing the activities of numerous automated machines that were loading equipment and refueling the vessel. Data himself was dressed in loose, casual attire similar to what he'd been wearing when he'd first come aboard several days earlier. He greeted La Forge with an easy smile and a friendly nod. "Come to see me off?"

"Looks that way." He forded the flurry of busy machines scurrying around the deck and joined Data beneath the ship.

"Geordi, I want to thank you for letting me use the science labs to restore my new body to its fully operational status." Data looked himself over, inspecting his own handiwork, then he favored La Forge with a warm smile. "It would not have been possible without your help."

"My pleasure. I just wish you weren't leaving so soon. Seems like you just got here."

A sympathetic nod. "I understand. But there is much I need to do." He looked around at the autoloaders. Without a single spoken command from Data, they converged under the open hatchway, grouped themselves into an efficient close formation, and were gently lifted upward by a pale yellow tractor beam. The two men watched the cluster of machines vanish inside the ship's main hold. "Captain Picard tells me B-4 has asked to be returned to Galor IV. It seems my brother has come to consider Captain Maddox a friend."

"With good reason. Bruce took quite a stand for B-4." La Forge was amused by the irony of Data's former nemesis becoming his brother's staunchest advocate. "How times change, eh?"

"Indeed." A melancholy silence filled the space between them, and unlike in years past, Data seemed to take immediate notice of it. "Are you troubled about something, Geordi?"

Torn between his misgivings and his desire to respect Data's privacy, La Forge was slow to respond. "I heard that Captain Picard offered to reactivate your commission. And that you refused." Confronted with that fact, Data looked away, as if he were ashamed. "Why, Data?"

Data's mien grew solemn. "I have known for some time that my father did not approve of my decision to join Starfleet. But until I acquired all his memories, I did not understand how deeply my choice had offended him. Out of respect for the sacrifice he made to bring me back, I think I owe it to him to consider alternatives rather than try to resume a life that ran its course."

His choice of words made La Forge uneasy. "Ran its course? Data, what are you talking about? Your life's not over."

"No, the one I am living now has just begun. But the android you knew as Data, the one whose body and mind experienced nearly forty years of continuous consciousness . . . he is gone, Geordi. I possess his memories. I recall the life he lived, as well as others—Lore's, Lal's, my father's—but I am not him." He pointed at his head. "My brain, my body, and my programming are all far more advanced than his. Now that I have finished repairing myself, I have come to realize how different I am from the person whose life I am meant to continue."

Incredulity wrinkled La Forge's brow. "What're you saying? You're not the *real* Data?"

"I am not sure." Overhead, the cargo doors on *Archeus*'s ventral hull closed with a low thrumming that resounded off the hangar's walls and deck. "The fact is, I am a copy of his essential information, like the contents of an old computer transferred to a new one. Whether that makes me a new model of Data, or an upgraded copy of the old one, I cannot say."

La Forge found Data's reasoning disheartening. "I'll admit you look different, and you have some new abilities, but are you really so different from the Data I knew?"

Data cocked his head and arched his eyebrows. "My new positronic matrix is so different from my last one that, if I wished, I could use contractions with ease."

"Then why don't you?"

He shrugged. "It is difficult to explain. I think the most truthful answer is that I am accustomed to expressing myself this way. It is part of who I am."

"Sounds to me like you're the same man adjusting to new circumstances."

The youthful android grimaced and shook his head. "I understand why you would take comfort in that idea, but I cannot share your confidence that I am, as you say, 'the *real* Data.'"

Offering his hand, La Forge asked, "Are you still my friend?"

Data shook La Forge's hand. "Always."

"Then you *are* the real Data. Case closed."

He smiled and released La Forge's hand. "Thank you, Geordi." Then he reached into his pants pocket, took out a metallic device shaped like a cylinder the size of a finger, and handed it to him. "I want you to have this. It is a comm device you can use to reach me in an emergency."

Holding up the gadget, La Forge asked, "How does it work?"

"Quantum particle entanglement." He took an identical device from his pocket. "Short audio messages can be recorded and sent instantly from one device to the other. Press here to record, and there to send. If that green light is on, it has recorded an incoming message."

La Forge had never seen anything like it. "Data, this is incredible! Where'd you get it?"

"It is something I threw together based on one of my father's old designs."

"Something you *threw together*?" La Forge chuckled to mask his envy. "Wow." He shook his head and pocketed the transmitter. "Thanks. I'll try to save it for a special occasion."

"I shall do likewise."

Data strolled toward the port-side ramp, and La Forge walked alongside him. "What about Lal? Are you taking her with you?"

"No," Data said. "That would be too great a risk. On my behalf, Captain Picard asked Starfleet Command to keep her body safe in the secure vaults beneath its headquarters in San Francisco. When I am ready, I will come back for her."

"Ready? To do what?"

They stopped at the bottom of the ramp, and Data faced La Forge with an expression of intense focus. "Do you remember our last mission to Galor IV, Geordi?" La Forge nodded, and Data continued. "After that mission ended, the body of my mother, Juliana Tainer, was stolen from its stasis pod in my lab. I have long suspected that Emil Vaslovik took her because he hoped to one day reanimate her positronic matrix."

"But, Data . . . that's *impossible.*"

Data's eyes narrowed. "No, it is not." His countenance became steadily more grave as he went on. "There were many times I considered going in search of Vaslovik, but I could never be certain his efforts to revive my mother would succeed, and in any case I had a duty to Starfleet. But now I have all of my father's memories. He *saw* her, Geordi. She was alive, rejuvenated, and she was with Vaslovik in 2375, less than a year after her body was taken from the *Enterprise.* That means Vaslovik—or Flint, or Akharin, or whatever name he now travels under—knows how to revive a positronic matrix after a total cascade failure." He took La Forge by the shoulders. "That man knows the secrets of life and death. No matter what it takes, Geordi, I *will* find him.

"And when I do . . . my daughter will live again."

COLD EQUATIONS

CONTINUES IN BOOK II

SILENT WEAPONS

ACKNOWLEDGMENTS

I have a tendency to let my acknowledgments run on too long, so this time I will try to be brief.

I'd like to thank my wife, Kara, for her patience and encouragement.

My sincere gratitude goes out to author Jeffrey Lang, whose *Star Trek: The Next Generation* novel *Immortal Coil* (2002) served as the direct inspiration for this trilogy. I also wish to pay special respect to the work of Rick Berman, who wrote the TNG episode "Brothers," from which I adapted a key moment in the first scene of Part Two.

Thanks are also owed to my *Star Trek* brain trust, which consists of fellow authors Scott Pearson, Dayton Ward, Kevin Dilmore, William Leisner, David R. George III, Keith R.A. DeCandido, and Christopher L. Bennett. Their sage advice was a true godsend on this project.

Finally, I wish to extend thanks to you, my readers, for making this effort worth all the trouble.

ABOUT THE AUTHOR

David Mack remains a mystery to science.
Learn more at his website:
www.davidmack.pro